LANA FERGUSON [...] r shy from spice or sass. A fa[...] [...] [...] [...] into her hands at fifteen, and she's never been the same since. When she isn't writing, you can find her randomly singing show tunes, arguing over which Batman is superior, and subjecting her friends to the extended editions of *The Lord of the Rings*. Lana lives mostly in her own head but can sometimes be found chasing her corgi through the coppice of the great American outdoors.

VISIT LANA FERGUSON ONLINE

LanaFerguson.com

Lana-Ferguson-104378392171803

LanaFergusonWrites

LanaFergusonWrites

Also by Lana Ferguson

The Nanny
The Fake Mate

The Fake Mate

LANA FERGUSON

PIATKUS

PIATKUS

First published in the US in 2023 by Berkley Romance,
An imprint of Penguin Random House LLC
Published in Great Britain in 2023 by Piatkus

1 3 5 7 9 10 8 6 4 2

A CIP catalogue record for this book
is available from the British Library.

ISBN 978-0-349-43965-5

Printed and bound in Great Britain by Clays Ltd, Elcograf S.p.A.

Papers used by Piatkus are from well-managed forests
and other responsible sources.

Piatkus
An imprint of
Little, Brown Book Group
Carmelite House
50 Victoria Embankment
London EC4Y 0DZ

An Hachette UK Company
www.hachette.co.uk

www.littlebrown.co.uk

To my oldest friend, who at the time of publication of this book most likely still hasn't finished it because of the "weird wolfy shit." I love you, asshole. You don't know what you're missing.

The Fake Mate

1

Mackenzie

"I'M SEEING SOMEONE."

In retrospect, the lie comes much easier than I thought it would. It feels icky, lying to the woman who's raised me since I was twelve, but in the face of my seventh bad date (or has it been eight now? I've honestly lost count) in three months—it also feels necessary.

My grandmother, Moira, has a reaction as immediate as it is expected. *"What?* Who? Someone from work? Is it someone I know?"

I know if I don't shut down this line of questioning quickly, it will spiral into a full-blown interrogation.

"No," I say quickly. "You don't know him."

I think that this part at least isn't so much of a lie, since I don't know him either. Since he doesn't exist.

My grandmother means well, she does, but her taste in men—be they human *or* shifter—is downright terrible. I have caught movies with shifter model train experts who wanted to scent me on the first date, I have gotten coffee with human data analysts who asked if I could somehow keep my tail in human form (I don't even want to explore the thought process there); every bad date has only solidified the idea that I am better off focusing on my job rather than my grandmother's wishful thinking that I will find a nice man to settle down with and give her a litter of grandchildren. As if I don't have enough to deal with. Sometimes I think Gran is no better than the dates she sends me off with when it comes to my omega status.

It's rare, what I am—but it doesn't make me all *that* different from any other shifter. Maybe once it did, back when shifters were still living in secret underground hierarchy systems unbeknownst to everyone else—but now it just means that I have an annoying stigma following me around that I'm somehow better in bed than other shifters. I swear, anyone I've ever told has expected me to spontaneously go into heat at a whim. Hence, I mostly keep it to myself nowadays.

"How long have you been seeing him? How old is he? Is he a shifter? I know how busy you are, dear, but I'm not getting any younger, and it would be so nice to hear the pitter-patter of—"

"Gran, it is *way* too soon to be thinking that far ahead." I shudder at the thought of crying babies. "It hasn't been that long. It's still new. Like, very new. Practically still has the plastic wrap on it."

"Oh, Mackenzie, why didn't you tell me? Are you trying to break my heart?"

"You know work has been insane. We've had four bar fights in the last month—not to mention the pileups from all the black ice we've been getting . . . It's been an utter nightmare in the ER. I think I'm getting carpal tunnel from all the stitches I've given lately."

"You work too hard, dear, couldn't they transfer you somewhere not so . . . fast-paced?"

It's a question she asks often, but she knows my answer already. I love working in the ER. Even on the most harrowing of days, I still go to bed at night knowing that I'm saving lives.

"Gran . . ."

"Right, right. So tell me about your mystery man. At least give me a species, dear."

I know the most obvious choice to keep her appeased.

"He's a shifter," I say, still feeling icky for lying. "You'd love him." I make a quick decision based solely on knowing that Gran will see right through me if I try to say I met my mystery man anywhere else, since I don't really *go* anywhere else. "I met him at work."

I can practically hear her clicking her heels together. She's probably doing a little dance in her kitchen as we speak, thinking that her granddaughter is finally going to settle down with a nice wolf who will give her and my grandpa grandchildren. It makes me feel that much more guilty. Thinking about the model trains date strengthens my resolve though.

"I have to meet him. When can I meet him? You could bring him to dinner . . . You haven't been to visit in too long, honey. It would be so nice to see you and your new friend."

"No, no," I say quickly. "I told you, it's new. We're taking things slow. I don't want to jinx it, you know? It could . . . make things awkward at work."

"At least give me a name, will you?"

I panic, unable to think of a single name. There are dozens of eligible fake boyfriends working on my floor at this exact moment, and I can't recall any of them. Is this punishment for lying to Gran? Is the universe cursing me for being a bad granddaughter? I can feel my hippocampus practically melting into a puddle of goo in my head, blanking on even one syllable that might wrap up my poorly planned lie in a neat little bow.

"Oh, well . . ." I can feel my mouth going dry as I scramble for something, *anything*. "His name? His name is—"

Now, I can count on one hand the number of hospital staff at Denver General who I don't vibe with. One of the benefits of being, at twenty-nine, one of the youngest ER doctors is that everyone treats you like the baby on staff, and while it *can* get annoying sometimes, it means that I have made very few enemies while working here the last year. In fact, I would even go so far as to say that most people I've come to meet while working here *like* me. But that doesn't mean there aren't exceptions. I mean, I'm likable, I think. As long as the other party in question isn't trying to sniff my neck.

However, that isn't to say that every one of my work relationships is all sunshine and roses. And of course it's with this thought that the break room door opens, revealing thick, midnight hair that nearly scrapes across the top of the doorframe, attached to the massive frame of one of the few physicians who fall into the "don't vibe with" category. His permanent frown set in a wide pink mouth turns my way, settled below piercing blue eyes that regard me in the same way they always have in the time I've known him—a stern look that says he's unhappy to have another living, breathing person in the same room he's entered. And of course because the universe seems to be punishing me for my white lies before I can even finish getting them out—it is *his* name, unfortunately, that is the first one that my brain seems to be able to formulate.

"Noah," I tell Gran in a hushed tone, so that he can't hear me. "His name is Noah Taylor."

Gran is gushing, her voice fading as I watch the surliest shifter I've ever met give me his back to crowd the coffeepot, gears of the worst kind turning in my head. It's not the *dumbest* idea I've ever had, I think. I mean, it's certainly not the best, but there are worse options. Probably. And besides, it's not like he would actually have to meet her or anything. Maybe he snaps a picture with me and cracks a smile for the first time in his entire life. That could give me at least a few weeks' reprieve, right? What could be the harm in an innocent little picture? Surely even Noah Taylor takes selfies.

Actually, I wouldn't put money on that, now that I think about it.

"Gran, I need to get back to work," I say, cutting off her incessant line of questioning that I can't hear anymore. "I'll call you tomorrow, okay?"

"All right, but I want more details when you do. Don't think this is the last of this conversation."

"Right," I tell her, absolutely knowing it isn't. "Sure thing."

I'm still staring at Noah's back as he pours coffee into his mug, watching his massive shoulders rise and fall with a sigh after what must have been a long night. Noah is an interventional cardiologist on staff at the hospital, not to mention the head of his department, and he comes in pretty high demand. Anyone who walks through our doors with a bad ticker gets an instant referral, and from what I can tell, the guy might actually sleep here. I'm not convinced he hasn't made a den of some sort in the basement. He's been working here far longer than I have, years even—but it took me only one meeting to recognize how much of an ass he is. Especially since in our first meeting he said that I "barely looked old enough to tie a suture." Let's just say he's not one to rub elbows with his fellow shifters for camaraderie's sake alone.

He catches me staring when he finally turns to take a sip from his cup, one perfect brow raising in question as he notices me. "Can I help you?"

"Maybe," I say honestly. "What sort of night have you had?"

He looks uncertain as to why I would ask the question, or why

I would even care in the first place, pausing for a moment before he huffs out a breath.

"Horrible, if you must know," he tells me. "Two heart attacks back to back. I've placed seven stents in the last five hours. And if that isn't enough, now I have to deal with the damn board and their ignorant—" He narrows his eyes, seeming to realize he's actually holding a conversation with a fellow employee that doesn't involve glowering. "Why do you ask?"

"Oh, because . . . professional courtesy? You looked . . . tired. Sounds like you had one hell of a night."

Noah looks unimpressed by my attempt at friendly conversation. I think idly it's probably the first time anyone has ever attempted it with him. "Exactly. So forgive me if I'm not up to chat."

I roll my eyes. "As if that's anything new."

"Right," he says flatly, holding up his mug. "I think I'll take this in my office."

"No, wait!"

Noah turns, that perplexed expression still etched into his features as he's probably realizing that this is the longest conversation he and I have had in at least the last six months; I can't actually remember the last time he returned my polite *hello* when I pass him in the corridor, now that I think about it. Not that anyone would blame me. I think the last time we spoke, he told me my shoe was untied without even slowing his pace. I'm not sure that even counts as conversation.

He's looking at me with annoyance now, like I'm wasting his precious time. "Yes?"

I can't believe I'm considering asking the Abominable Ass of Colorado to help me. It might be the worst idea I've ever had, but I'm in it now.

"I was wondering"—I know I'm going to regret this—"if you would take a picture with me."

Noah looks utterly confused. "Pardon?"

"A picture. Maybe you could smile in it too? I'm willing to pay. In better coffee, or snacks—" He looks like he doesn't know the definition of the word, and honestly, that tracks. "Okay, so no snacks. Whatever you want. I just need a picture."

"Explain to me a situation where taking a picture with me helps you somehow."

"Well, you see, that's complicated." Noah blinks at me for about three seconds before he turns to leave, seemingly done with the conversation, and I call after him again. "Okay, okay," I sigh. "Look. I know this is going to sound ridiculous, but I need to use you."

His eyebrows nearly shoot into his hair. "Excuse me?"

"It's not a big deal, it's just, I needed someone from work, and I kind of blanked when she asked, and your name sort of spilled out since you were *right there*, and all I need is a picture, really. I think that would buy me some time at least to—"

"What on earth are you *talking* about?"

I take a deep breath, regretting this already. "I need you to be my fake boyfriend."

He lingers in the doorway for a good number of seconds, ones where I can feel my stomach churn in embarrassment. I *know* that I should have given Gran a random name. I *know* that I could have told her I was fucking a random colleague on the side and properly silenced her with a blush—but I didn't do any of those things, and if I can't buy myself some time, I'm looking at a fun-filled Friday night with some egghead explaining cryptocurrency to me. (Did I mention that I have been on some *really* bad dates?)

Noah takes a sip from his mug, swallows it, then closes the

break room door. He crosses the space to pass the other little wooden tables that fill the room, his considerable bulk settling into one of the padded chairs on the opposite side of the one I'm occupying. For a moment he says nothing, studying me with a mercurial look as the old wall clock to my right ticks the seconds away, but then he takes another sip from his mug, swallowing it with a bob of his Adam's apple before he sets it down on the table.

"Explain."

~

"SO." NOAH'S CUP is almost empty, his expression hardly any different than it had been ten minutes ago when I began to explain my horrible dating history and my aversion to experiencing even one more bad date—all leading up to my lie. "You want me to pretend to be your boyfriend . . . so that you don't have to get a boyfriend?"

"You don't even have to do anything."

"I fail to see the need for me at all then."

I'm pretty sure I've never been this close to Noah. At least not for this long a time. I can sense a sharp tinge of suppressants rolling off him, which I find odd; most male shifters choose to forgo them, too hung up on their ego to miss out on clouding a room with their scent in the hopes that a female shifter will come running. Maybe it's a professional decision? His scent might not be pleasant. Although, I think I can discredit that theory, given that, strangely, I can faintly make it out even under the chemical tang of his suppressants, making me think he needs a stronger dose. Not that I'm complaining, since I think it might be a nice scent. It's woodsy. Like pine needles and crisp air. It reminds me of running in the snow on all fours.

But this isn't what I should be focusing on.

"Well, a picture, maybe. So I can prove you're real. That will hold her off for a few weeks, at least, with my schedule. Surely you know how to smile, right? You can think of something you enjoy, like glaring at small children or criticizing baristas at Starbucks."

"I don't do either of those things," he snorts. "Thank you very much."

I shrug. "It was a guess. Come on, it will cost you nothing, and you'd be helping me out."

"Helping you out." Noah looks pensive as he stares down into his mug, raising it to his mouth to drink the last of his coffee down. "And tell me again why I would do that?"

I scowl. It's honestly so annoying that he might be one of the most good-looking men I've ever come into contact with—shifter or otherwise. His features are angular, and his blue eyes are sharp in contrast with his smooth, fair skin, as if he sees more than you want him to, and I won't pretend that his aquiline nose doesn't rustle up ideas about what he might be able to do with it . . . If only his personality weren't so sour.

"Intraspecies camaraderie?" Noah looks unmoved, and I groan. "Seriously, would it kill you to do something nice for once? This is based on the assumption that you recognize what doing something nice looks like and know how to properly execute the task."

Noah is studying me again, eyes moving over my sandy blond hair and my amber eyes and even my mouth that is currently pressed into a pout, almost like he's considering. *What*, I can't be sure. I can't tell if he's thinking about helping me out, or if he's trying to find the most satisfying way to tell me I'm screwed.

"I have never been much for intraspecies camaraderie," he says finally, and I feel my stomach sink, knowing this was the worst idea I've ever had. "But . . ."

I perk up. "But?"

"I think we can reach an agreement that is more mutually beneficial."

Now it's my turn to look confused. I can't think of a single thing that Noah Taylor would need from me, or anyone else for that matter, given that I've never seen him speak to anyone for even a fraction of the time he's been speaking to me without barking orders at some point.

"And what could I possibly do for you?"

Honestly, I'm preparing for the worst. He's probably going to ask me to pass the buck on his consults to one of the other cardiologists, which would be a total pain in the ass, given that he knows he's the most highly requested one. Maybe he'll ask me to clean his office for the pure enjoyment of watching me do it. That feels like the sadistic torture Noah might be into. I can't even imagine what his office looks like. I bet it doesn't even need cleaning. He probably has plastic covers on all the chairs and surfaces. I could offer to put in admission orders for him for some agreed-on span of time. That would be annoying, but doable, at least. Definitely worth staving off a few more horrible dates, since I am apparently too spineless to simply say *no* to my Gran's puppy-dog eyes.

Oh God. What if he asks me for sex? I've pegged him as some celibate sourpuss who gets by with angry masturbation on the weekends, but what if Noah is like every other horndog I've come across? That is absolutely the one thing that is completely off the table, and I will kick him in his stupidly large shins if he is dumb enough to suggest it. It's not like he knows I'm an omega—there's no way he could—so surely it isn't going to be anything kinky he's after.

I tense when Noah leans forward in his chair, his fingers lacing

together as his hands rest on the table, and his piercing eyes meet
mine with that blazing intensity that they never seem to lose when
I am unlucky enough to cross paths with him. They don't look like
the eyes of someone who is about to ask me for sex, at least. Or
maybe they do, given the context. I don't know. It's hard to think
with him staring at me like he is. But as it turns out, Noah has no
intention of asking me for any kind of sordid favors. What Noah
proposes is much worse, and the craziest part is the way his expression absolutely doesn't change, not even a *tiny* bit, when he says:

"I need a mate."

Now it's my turn to blink at him. Stupidly, if I had to guess.
"You need . . . a mate?"

Noah nods, like it's a perfectly reasonable thing he's said. Like
he didn't just propose the shifter equivalent of marriage and the *last*
thing I'm interested in to a veritable stranger who I don't think he
even likes (I'm not taking it personally or anything, he doesn't seem
to like anyone) over bad hospital-lounge coffee.

"And fast," he adds.

Out of the fire, into the frying pan, I guess.

2

Noah

THIS IS A terrible idea.

Even as I suggest it, I am expecting to regret it, but given that the proverbial answer to my problems has miraculously fallen into my lap, I am inclined to take the lifeline being offered. I'm aware of Dr. Carter—young, opinionated, a little too chatty for my tastes—not my first pick for a pretend mate, but with a disciplinary meeting with the board happening in barely an hour over some choice omissions on my part, I see few other options.

"You need . . . a mate?"

I can see the confusion etched in the set of her soft-looking mouth and her delicate brow, furrowed in thought above her bright amber eyes. I'm aware it's not a simple request, what I'm asking her, but I am desperate and perhaps crazy enough to ask it, anyway. Especially given that there seems to be something in it for her as well.

"And fast," I tell her, and am met with more puzzlement.

Dr. Carter places her hands on the edge of the break room table, her slim fingers tapping along the edge while I give her a second to try and compute what I'm saying. Time is not something I have the luxury of, but I've been told (repeatedly) throughout my life that you catch more flies with honey than vinegar, and if there was ever a time to test that theory, it would be now.

"Mate is . . . a pretty big upgrade from me asking you for a selfie."

I nod. "Yes, but . . . think about it. A picture buys you, what? A week? Two, at most? My cooperation could buy you much longer than that. Months, even, if it suits you."

"But I'm trying to snag a fake boyfriend to *avoid* mating," she says with distaste. "Not exactly looking to saddle myself with the real-life personification of Oscar the Grouch to avoid more bad dates." She has the good grace to look slightly apologetic. "Sorry. No offense."

"None taken," I tell her truthfully. "Trust me, I'm not interested in biting you."

Her nose wrinkles as if she's offended, which seems to contradict her earlier objection, or perhaps it is some general offense. I can't be sure. "Well, me either," she huffs. "From you or anyone else."

"Then I think we stand to benefit each other well," I tell her. "I don't need to bite you to pull this off." She still looks unsure, and I scrub a hand down my face, sighing. "There is . . . something about me that I have put a great deal of effort into keeping hidden. Something that would threaten my position here, and I find myself suddenly . . . exposed."

"What, did you maul a hiker or something in a rut?"

I press my lips together in a frown. "Hardly. I am the picture of control."

"Clearly," she deadpans.

I think she might be poking fun at my expense, but I overlook it, given that her refusal could cost me my job. "There are . . . hindrances, for people like me. Ridiculous archaic notions that might have kept me from advancing to the position I hold now, and because of that . . . I might have failed to inform the board of my status when I was hired on."

"What status? A shifter? There are plenty of shifters working here, me included."

My nostrils flare, the idea of my carefully guarded secret crumbling to pieces making me all the more irritated. "Not like me."

"I don't follow."

"I'm . . . an alpha."

She narrows her eyes at me as if I might be teasing her, but then I see the suspicion fade as she seems to study me, no doubt looking for signs of the fabled Big Bad Wolf behavior that is so often associated with my designation. Alphas are rare, to be sure, and perhaps that is why there are so many outlandish notions associated with the status. In another time, it would mean that I was destined to lead a pack, to carry on a clan . . . but in our more modernized society, it simply means that I am a little stronger, a little faster, a little . . . *more* than the average shifter.

Which might be why there are so many stigmas tied to the label.

She's still regarding me carefully, but she doesn't look at all put off by the idea of what I am. There is even something in her expression almost . . . curious? It's very different from how I expected her to react. In the past I have been met with wariness and sidelong glances when people discovered what I am, which is why I decided in college it would serve me to do my very best to keep anyone from finding out. And yet here I am, spilling my guts to a coworker I barely know in hopes that she might be the answer I'm looking for.

"You don't . . . Hm." Her nose wrinkles again—it seems to be a habit of hers—like she's thinking. "Actually, you know what? I could see that. Now that you mention it. It explains your sparkling personality."

I narrow my eyes. "Most of the rumors surrounding alphas are grossly overexaggerated."

"I heard you made a CNA cry once."

"Also grossly overexaggerated."

"I don't know, my friend Priya in Anesthesiology swears people saw the poor girl running out of the room with—"

"Listen, I'm actually pressed for time. The point is, I have managed to successfully do my job here for years now without going into any fits of uncontrollable rage or without biting orderlies or whatever other stories people tell one another to keep people like me from entering high-pressure professions—and a damned *anonymous tip* shouldn't be the thing that takes it all away from me."

Her eyes widen. "Someone turned you in?"

"It would appear so."

I still have the slight urge to rip something in half when I think about it, but I assume that wouldn't help my case in the slightest.

"So what does having a mate have to do with it?"

"It is a widely accepted theory that mated alpha shifters are considerably more . . . docile than those that are unmated. Ridiculously, it's believed to be a free pass in our line of work. An unmated alpha might only be destined to be someone's hired security or prized fighting champion—but a *mated* one isn't looked at twice."

"I wonder why."

"Some silly notion about fated pairs and filling what the other lacks, or something like that."

"So biting me is supposed to be your Xanax, basically."

"For lack of better verbiage, yes."

"Yuck," she says, looking genuinely put off by the idea. "Sounds like the board has been talking to my gran."

"I can't tell if you're leaning any particular way on this, Dr. Carter."

She crosses her arms then, leaning back in her chair and giving me a sly smile that tells me she's likely about to be intolerable. "So, the Big Bad Wolf of Cardiology needs my help." She nods idly to herself, looking away from me as if considering it. "This is kind of cool, actually. Have you ever asked anyone for help before? Am I robbing you of your rigid virtues right now?"

I frown. "Hysterical."

"I'm sorry," she laughs. "It's not funny, I know. You're totally right that you shouldn't even be worrying about this in the first place, given that you're, like, amazing at your job—" I feel my eyebrows raise at the compliment, as well as her agreement about how ignorant this entire situation is, but she holds out a hand to keep me from commenting. "Don't get excited, you're still kind of a dick, mostly. No offense."

My lips press into a line. I guess I should have anticipated that. "None taken, I guess."

"But still. It's a bullshit stigma." Her expression softens. "I get why you're so upset. Are they threatening to let you go over it?"

I'm not sure that she can actually grasp how upsetting this is, but I can appreciate her commiseration. I raise my shoulders high enough to be called a shrug, grinding my teeth. "I'm not sure. I was only told that I would need to meet with the board to discuss my status as an unmated alpha. The tone of the memo did not instill confidence. It's not something I'm willing to leave to chance, given all the time I've put in here."

"Hm."

The seconds tick by on the nearby wall clock, and I know each one brings me closer to the meeting that could rob me of everything I've worked for, and now it seems by some strange twist of fate—everything boils down to this tiny blond physician who might actually be enjoying my suffering. I'm not sure what to even make of it.

"So," she says finally. "Tell me what this would look like. How do we convince people that we're *mated*"—she makes a face as she says the word, like it's hard for her to get out—"when we never speak to each other, and you smell like cheap suppressants?"

I rear back in surprise. "Excuse me? Cheap?"

"My bad," she says in apology. "I wasn't trying to be a jerk, I just meant, since I can still smell you . . . ?"

This takes me by surprise. "You can?"

"Yeah? Am I not supposed to? I figured you needed a stronger dose. I assumed you were taking them so none of the nurses tried to ask you out or something."

"I'm . . ." It's been quite a while since something has stunned me, but the idea that Dr. Carter can scent me, even now, definitely does it. There shouldn't be a nose on this Earth that should be able to smell anything on me but the medical tang of my suppressants. I pay good money every month to make sure of that. "I am on the highest dose deemed safe for my weight of the best suppressants money can buy," I tell her dazedly. "There is absolutely no way you can still scent me."

She shrugs. "Smells a bit like pine needles." She must notice my mouth gaping open, because she adds, "It doesn't smell bad or anything? Anyway, so how would we pull this off?"

I think some part of me hadn't expected her to actually consider this; I mean, it's ludicrous after all, so that could be why I am thrown for a moment as to how to answer her question. I simply hadn't thought this far ahead when the preposterous idea popped into my head after hearing her plight.

"Right. Convince them. Yes." I cross my arms, staring at the table as I think it over. "We could . . . tell them we've been keeping our relationship a secret."

"And why would we be doing that?"

"You're a new physician here," I say, still thinking. "You've been here, what, six months?"

Her eyes narrow. "Over a year now."

"Right. Sorry. Regardless, it would be a perfectly reasonable line of thought that you might not want to be romantically associated with someone with my position and level of seniority starting out; I assume you wouldn't want to gain some perceived advantage based on the achievements of your mate. Surely you would want to carve your own way without being tied to a big name. This would be a more than adequate reason to keep our pairing quiet."

She looks a bit thrown by my assessment of her character, but doesn't comment.

"And the suppressants? I mean, in theory . . . how would we have been having sex all this time if you're dosed up?"

I can't help but frown at her again. "I assure you that the suppressants don't hinder me in that way at all."

"Wow, really? Didn't strike you as the dating type."

"I'm not."

"You *definitely* don't strike me as the 'hit it and quit it' kind of—"

"I don't think this line of questioning is prudent."

"Fine, fine." She's nodding at the air again, her nose doing that thing once more that *definitely* must be a habit. I can't decide if it is annoying or endearing. "So, this whole thing still seems more to your benefit than mine. I mean, I want to get a break from the dating scene, not land a whole-ass fake mate."

"My scent would keep every shifter within a ten-mile radius from even *considering* approaching you romantically."

I watch her eyes widen, the soft pink of her mouth parting in quiet surprise at the certainty in my tone. "How can you be sure?"

"Because no one who scented me on you would dare touch you."

She looks surprised again, that same part to her mouth, but there's something else there now. Something that blends with her surprise and looks oddly like curiosity again. I think I can safely assume I am the first alpha she's ever come across. Not a far-fetched idea, given that I only know one other than myself. I watch the slim line of her throat bob with a swallow, her lips pressing together as she averts her eyes.

"Interesting," she counters quietly.

I can see the thoughts practically racing in her head, her expression calculating as she appears to consider every possible angle of what I'm offering, or rather, requesting.

"So, what, we just . . . spend our lives in mutually beneficial fake love?"

Now it's my turn to wrinkle my nose. "Hardly. I just need to buy myself some time to figure things out."

"Makes sense," she answers offhandedly, still appearing deep in thought. "So, like, a couple of weeks? A month?"

"I'm not sure," I tell her honestly. I still don't know if it's a good idea to be laying all my cards out for this woman I've hardly ever spoken to before today, but at this point, I'm in it now. "I have a job offer in Albuquerque that I am considering. They've been headhunting me for a while, and they've offered me a chief of staff position. Their opinions on my alpha status are not as dated as those of the board here, and given my perfect record here . . ."

"But if they found out you've been lying—"

"I wouldn't call it a lie," I argue.

"—that you've been purposely *omitting* your alpha status the entire time you've been working here . . ."

I nod solemnly, not ashamed of my omission, since it's a ridiculous stigma to begin with, finding it a necessary evil. It's not as if they specifically *ask* for this clarification during an interview, given that doing so could potentially draw in accusations of discrimination, and it's this minor detail that has helped ease any guilt I might have had for not mentioning it. "It could potentially paint an unflattering picture of me. Also something I'd rather not leave to chance."

"So we're mates till this blows over, and then you disappear, and we fake break up?" She looks contemplative. "Can mated pairs even break up?"

"With difficulty," I inform her. "It's an option, to be sure. Or you can continue to use my name to get you out of dates, if you prefer. It doesn't matter to me. You can spin whatever story you like when I'm gone."

"How romantic," she laughs.

"I assure you, this is a business transaction, Dr. Carter. Romance won't be a part of it."

She smiles wide then, all perfect white teeth and little dimples in her cheeks that my eyes linger on for a second too long, seeming to be finding this entire conversation mildly amusing. "Right," she says. "That sounds perfect."

I feel the knot in my stomach begin to unwind, but only slightly. "It does?"

"I mean, I get to be free of the dating scene *and* have a leg up on the Boogeyman of Denver General?"

"Excuse me?"

"Don't worry, they don't actually call you that." At my frown, she adds, "Well, *most* of them don't."

"Does this mean . . ." I can actually feel nerves fluttering in my chest, the possibility of all my hard work slipping through my fingertips because of something as silly as my genetic makeup being utterly unacceptable. "Does this mean that you'll do it?"

"Hm." She taps her chin with her finger, looking more pleased with herself than I'd like. "I mean, it *does* sound kind of fun."

"Dr. Carter, we don't have time for—"

"It's Mack," she interrupts. "Everyone calls me Mack. I think we're past 'Dr. Carter,' given that you're asking me to allow everyone to think I let you sleep with me on a regular basis."

I feel my throat go dry, her crassness doing something entirely different than what it should. Something hot flares in my chest at the brief flash of images that crop up from her crude joke that I absolutely don't have time or need for, and I quickly shove them down as I keep my expression blank.

"Mack? Your name is Mack?"

"Eh . . . I mean, technically it's Mackenzie, but no one calls me that except my gran."

"I think I prefer Mackenzie."

"Somehow this doesn't surprise me," she chuckles. "Fine. Whatever. I don't care what you call me."

"So . . . is that a yes?"

"You have to meet my gran at some point. If I do this, you're going to really sell it on my end. I'm talking about family dinner, anecdotes—the whole nine yards. I don't want my gran pulling out her little black book for a *good* while."

I'm sure my displeasure toward the idea is written all over my face, but I see little other choice. "Fine. I can . . . do dinner."

I wait as she stares back at me, every second settling heavily on my skin like a weighted blanket. Finally, she takes in one long breath before she blows it out, her expression telling me that she might be as surprised by her answer as I am.

"Yeah," she says, sounding only half-sure. "I'll do it."

I hadn't even realized I'd been holding my breath until the air rushes past my lips in relief. I nod slowly, checking the time on the wall as I prepare to lay down my plan that can hardly be called anything other than "on the fly," and praying that it will be enough to buy me the time I need to sort out this mess. Maybe even find the bastard who sold me out and make them regret it. I think to myself that I might have misjudged Dr. Cart—or rather, *Mackenzie*—finding her to be far more reasonable than I had previously thought. This could even be a fairly pain-free process.

"So," she says with more amusement than I think is necessary. "What's the plan, hubby?"

I have to stifle a groan.

On second thought . . .

3

Mackenzie

"WHY DON'T YOU explain this to me like I'm five," Parker says, dumbfounded.

I pause from unwrapping my candy bar, unsure of how I can elaborate any more than I already have. "What part aren't you getting?"

My best friend of sixteen years sits in his little cubicle in the IT room down in the basement level, looking at me as if I'm barking at him rather than speaking. It's actually funny, since he's seen me shift dozens of times over the course of our friendship. Not that Parker is laughing. In fact, his usual pale cheeks are colored with a tinge of scarlet that I'm well aware comes from anxiety. It makes his freckles stand out more, which I am also well aware annoys him.

"I don't know," he says exasperatedly, running his fingers through his bright red hair. "Maybe the part where you told the hospital board that *Noah fucking Taylor* is your secret *mate*?"

Ah, right. That part.

I mean, to be fair, I'm still having a hard time believing I actually went through with it. When Noah explained his predicament to me, it sounded like the plot of a K-drama or something. I'm pretty sure I read this entire scenario in a synopsis while scrolling through Netflix a few weeks ago. If I weren't almost one hundred percent sure that Noah has never told a joke in his entire life, I might have even bet that the entire thing was a prank. And yet, here I am, unwrapping a Twix while perched on Parker's desk, having gained myself one very surly mate, at least as far as the hospital administration is concerned.

"Keep your voice down," I hiss. "Someone could walk by."

"Oh, and then I'd be an accomplice, would I?"

I roll my eyes. "Don't be so dramatic."

"How exactly did you manage to convince the board that this whole thing isn't total bullshit? Which it is, by the way. You know that, right?"

I'm still having trouble with that part myself. I was only about thirty percent confident that Noah would be able to pull this little stunt off, half agreeing just so I could get a good seat for the show . . . but damn. The guy knows how to command a room. Must be an alpha thing.

I pull one of the chocolate bars from the wrapper, shrugging. "Turns out, when Noah talks, people listen. Who knew."

"Are we playing some sort of game I'm unaware of where you give me as little details as humanly possible until I spontaneously combust?"

I reach out and boop his nose. "Are you pouting? You're so cute when you're flustered."

"I'm gonna need more details, Mack. You're killing me."

I wave him off. "He had this whole spiel about how we'd been keeping our relationship a secret so I could bolster my reputation based on my own merit or something. Honestly, it was pretty convincing. He even had them *apologizing* for invading our privacy by the end of it. It was honestly amazing."

"And they actually bought that?"

Another shrug. "I guess so, since we signed a disclosure."

"Jesus, Mack. Have you even thought about what your—can you please stop?"

I pull the candy bar from my mouth. "What?"

"Stop scraping the toppings off with your teeth." He grimaces. "It's disgusting."

"But the cookie is my favorite part. You know that."

"It doesn't make it any more of a pretty process to watch. Plus, I don't want your icky chocolate fingers all over my desk."

"Did you just say 'icky'?"

"I swear to all that's holy, I will boot you out of my cube."

"Yeah, yeah." I return to what I was doing. "They should sell the cookies by themselves then."

"Whatever. What about Moira? You think your gran is going to buy that you're suddenly mated?"

"Just dating," I clarify.

"What?"

"We're mated here, but dating with Gran."

It's a subtle distinction, but an important one.

Parker snorts. "Oh, so now you've got multifaceted deceptions going on? Whipping ourselves up a tomfoolery tiramisu, are we?"

"You're ridiculous. It's going to be fine," I assure him. "Just think. A nice long stretch of not having to pretend to give a damn about some guy's fantasy football league."

"I would say that's a victory—except now you have to spend time with Noah fucking Taylor."

"I don't think that's his actual middle name."

"Are you sure?" Parker throws up his hands. "How would you know? You lumped yourself in with his little conspiracy plot without knowing a thing about him!"

"I didn't have a lot of options."

"Why didn't you ask me?"

"Because we've been friends since middle school?"

"Haven't you ever read friends to lovers?"

"Have *you* read friends to lovers?"

"I am not going to justify my literature choices to you."

"Literotica, you mean."

"It's romance, you jock. It's nice."

"Why are you reading romance? Things with Hot Yoga Guy not working out?"

"Hot Yoga Guy is just fine, thank you very much. We're having dinner this weekend."

"Mm. I wonder what he looks like out of spandex."

Parker huffs. "Stop changing the subject."

"Technically, it's very relevant to the subject. I don't think Gran would suddenly believe you're into women. I mean, she did catch you making out with Trey at prom."

He looks offended that I would bring it up. "I still can't believe you let her chaperone."

"I didn't exactly have a lot of say in the matter."

"Ugh." He rubs at his temples. "This is making my brain hurt. You know this ends badly, right? There's no way this ends pretty."

I lick away the caramel from my teeth as I study the bare cookie that's left, considering. He's probably right, honestly. I have no idea how we're going to pull off this charade in the long run, but it also feels like Noah has a lot more to lose than I do, so maybe that's why I'm feeling so calm about the entire thing.

"I'm thinking of it like kismet."

Parker slinks down in his office chair, running his hands over his face. "Have you even thought about how difficult this is going to be? I mean, he's not your average shifter. He's an *alpha*, Mackenzie. Have you not heard the stories? Plus, you're an omega! What if he tries to lay some wolfy claim on you?"

"Oh jeez," I snort. "Hardly. I've worked with him for a year, and he hasn't fallen in weird, cosmic love with me yet. We're fine."

"But he's been on suppressants, right? I know I'm just a regular ole human, but I would think that would make a difference. Plus, it's not like you've been hanging out with the guy on a regular basis. I don't think passing each other in the hall counts as interaction. Does he even know what you are?"

"Huh," I say bemusedly. "You know, I didn't even mention it. I completely forgot. I don't think it matters. I think the whole alpha/omega thing is just some old wives' tale. It's not like there's many of us around to be making accurate assumptions of how we affect each other. It's fine."

"So, are you going to tell him?"

I tilt my head back and forth, considering. While I'm *pretty* sure that the chances of Noah suddenly wanting to sink his teeth into my mating gland if I tell him what I am are slim—I suppose there is always a possibility. Still. I can always just cut ties if that happens. Getting an *actual* mate is not something on my to-do list. Maybe not ever, really.

I wave Parker off. "And risk him going all Jacob Black on me?"

"What?"

"When you see her*, suddenly it's not the earth holding you here anymore. She does."*

"Is this a *Twilight* reference?"

"*Eclipse*, actually, and don't look so judgy. I'm not going to jus-tify my obsession with the series to you again."

"Jesus." He rubs his eyes. "And if you . . . you know."

I arch an eyebrow. "Know what?"

"You *know*," he stresses, looking uncomfortable. "What if you go into—Well, *you know*."

I might laugh at him if I weren't one hundred percent sure it would make him more annoyed. "Are you asking me about my heat cycle?"

"Have you even considered it?"

"Of course I have." Sort of. Briefly. For like a second. "I'm not due for another one for months. So no worries there. *Relax*, Parker. No one is carrying me back to their den anytime soon."

"I just know that's how your mom and dad ended up—"

I cut him a look. "Don't."

"Sorry." He winces. "I know you don't like talking about them. But that is what happened."

"I'm not them," I mumble. "I'm not falling in love with Noah at first sight and begging him to *actually* mate me the first time my hormones go out of whack."

"Fine," Parker concedes with a sigh. "So this is *really* about your gran's little black book of horrors?"

"Model *trains*, Parker," I stress. "Do you know who owned the first model train set?"

Parker lifts one eyebrow. "No?"

"Well, that makes one of us. One of Napoleon's great-nephews, apparently."

"Do you think it was because he was short too?"

I snap my fingers. "That's what I said! It went over well with my date."

"I'm sure." Parker gives me a *look*, the same one he is always giving me when he wants to tell me I'm being stupid. "So why *did* you agree to this?"

"I told you. I'm tired of Gran always—"

"Try again."

I narrow my eyes, taking a bite of my naked Twix cookie (it really is the best part, and it is my life's mission to find this cookie out in the wild with no toppings) and chewing it slowly. "I don't know," I admit finally. "I did sort of step in this myself. After all, I'm the one who approached him first, remember? The whole scenting bit sounds like a necessary evil too. I mean, apparently, one little cuddle with Noah, and all the other shifters will steer clear!"

Parker rolls his eyes. "Because that's not going to be awkward."

"Whatever. It's no big deal. And I don't know. If I'm being completely honest? The guy seemed pretty desperate. He might be an asshole, but he's a good doctor. It's bullshit that they would try to take his job when he's never given them a real reason to."

"Aren't we the white knight? Since when do we care about helping out Noah Taylor? He's not just an asshole, Mack. He might be a demon. Did you hear about the time he tripped that CNA and broke her nose?"

"I haven't actually heard that version, but I'm told that the whole thing was 'grossly overexaggerated.'"

"That's what he *wants* us to think," Parker mutters.

"It's going to be fine." I take another bite, nodding to the air. "Totally fine."

Parker scoffs. "I'll take Famous Last Words for two hundred, Alex."

I lick my fingers, still nodding idly as I begin to pick at the second candy bar, assuring myself that this *will* be fine. I mean, it's just a few lies and a fake relationship. Nothing bad ever came from that.

~

ANOTHER THING THAT I can count on one hand is the number of times I have naturally run into Noah Taylor at work—this afternoon's meeting of our new supersecret power-couple duo included—so I am surprised to see him twice in a day, especially at the end of a twelve-hour shift when people are beginning to get out for the morning. He looks surprised, pausing from blowing warmth into his hands under the awning as I step through the automatic glass doors while still shrugging into my coat. The wind ruffles his dark hair so that it whips around his face, and the lamplight casting down on him from the doors makes his eyes seem darker than they are as they regard me. I notice again how *big* Noah is. Has he always been this tall? Have I simply not noticed because I always avert my eyes when I pass him in the hall? He has to be at least eight inches taller than me, and I'm not exactly short at five foot seven.

"Dr. Carter?"

I stop gawking at him, my mouth quirking. "Is that any way to address your mate?"

"Oh." He makes a face. "Right. Good call . . . Mackenzie."

I laugh as I start to wind my scarf around my neck. "You're going to have a real tough time with this, aren't you?"

"I am admittedly not used to having to be so . . . aware of another person."

"Wow." I know he isn't trying to be funny, the concept of all this is surely alien to him, but damn if he isn't striking me as amusing with how utterly sincere he seems to be. "This is going to be a disaster."

"It'll be fine," he says stoically. "Although, we should set a meeting soon. If we're going to pull this off, we're going to have to learn to be more familiar with each other."

I pretend to be aghast. "You could at least buy me dinner first before you jump right into: *learning to be familiar with each other.*"

Noah sighs, his breath coming out in a cloud in the cold September air as he shakes his head, looking exhausted. "I am happy that you are finding this so amusing, but right now I need a shower and a bed, and then I need to forget this day. We can regroup tomorrow. I can make lunch reservations, if you're free?"

"Let me think." I pinch the bridge of my nose, mentally going over my schedule. "I have work through Friday. What about Saturday? I have yoga at eleven, but we can catch a late lunch?"

"Yoga?"

"Yes. It's a great stress reliever. Maybe you should try it sometime. I hear it's hard to perform open-heart surgery on yourself."

"I'll pass," he answers. "Saturday is fine. I have surgery that afternoon, but it isn't until four, so I'm free before that." He checks his watch. "So, I suppose we should exchange numbers, and then we can . . . go from there?"

"I do hear that the first test you have to pass is 'What number would you call in a crisis?' on *The Newlywed Game.*"

I didn't intend to tease him this much, but he makes it so easy. He's like a garden statue, only more . . . rigid. Taller too. "Anyway, here's my number," he tells me, fishing out his wallet to pull an actual *business* card from it. I would laugh if I weren't so sure that Noah is most likely nearing a pulmonary embolism after the day he's had, taking the card graciously to read the neat typeset there. "Cool," I note. "Maybe I should get business cards."

"I can recommend an excellent print shop, if you're in the market."

I don't even have the heart to tell him I'm joking at this point. "Oh yeah. Sure. So, I guess . . . I'll text you later?"

"Yes, we can check in after some sleep." He lingers there for a moment, fidgeting as if he's chewing on something he can't quite get out—looking from me to the ground to me again with a pinched expression. "I suppose I should . . . thank you. For today. You saved me back there."

"I take my Hippocratic oath very seriously," I deadpan. "Saving lives, and all that."

"Right." His mouth does something strange, quirking a bit like it wants to smile but has forgotten how to. "Oh, and . . . I suppose I should . . ." He looks around at the nearly empty parking lot, his brow furrowing as he presses up on his toes to make sure there is no one around before he suddenly walks toward me, corralling me toward the large row of bushes that are planted on either side of the rear entrance. "I guess . . . I should . . ." His expression looks pained. "There's no polite way to do this, so I'll just . . . ?"

Now, I'm very tired—a twelve-hour shift will do that to you on its own even without all the plotting and the life-altering decisions— so maybe that's why I am slow on the uptake to whatever Noah is having so much trouble with. His hands make my upper arms feel like little twigs when his thick fingers close around them, poking his head up once more to make sure no one is watching.

"Noah, what are you . . . ?"

I admit it has been . . . *a while* since I've been at all intimate in any form or fashion with a man—be they human or not—so I'm sure that's another reason that contributes to my cluelessness when Noah begins to crowd me.

"Sorry," he says quietly, still looking pained. "It won't be very potent right now, not until I stop suppressants"—he already looks annoyed at the thought of having to stop taking them, but I assume the question will arise as to why he would still need them now that we're *public*—"but for now, it will have to do."

It dawns on me then, his intention, and I am suddenly a lot more awake than I was when I came outside. "Oh, you don't have to—"

I don't get to finish what I was saying, given that Noah is in total business mode right now, already leaning to pull me to his large frame for a very strange and awkward hug that crushes me to his front. I immediately notice that same sharp tang of his suppressants that clings to his clothes as it creeps into my nostrils, but underneath, from this close . . . I can just make out that faint scent of pine and fresh winter that is crisp and cool and actually pretty pleasant once you single it out. The whole thing throws me so off guard that I don't even have time to react at first, the wool of Noah's coat nearly cutting off my air supply as he hugs me like it's the first time he's ever done this to anyone. He could sever my spine like this, if he tried harder. I know we had talked about the benefits of his scent in regards to his end of the bargain, but I hadn't expected him to be so "straight to business" about it. I guess that was my first mistake.

This is Noah Taylor, after all.

I know what scenting is, because I'm almost thirty and have had relationships that lasted more than a few months at a time, but it's usually something I've experienced by accident during sex. Definitely not something I've purposely done in the bushes outside of my workplace. Besides the fact that we can literally turn into wolves outside of city limits (they passed that law in 1987 after some guy barreled through a storefront after getting too drunk), being a shifter means that our bodies work a little differently than your average human. Scents affect us, mark us, even *drive* us sometimes—and therefore they inadvertently take up a big role in our lives. Especially since a shifter has three times as many scent glands as a normal human, each one sensitive to the touch and the largest being right at the base of the throat, just waiting for some shifter partner to come along and meld his open scent with it. It's practically like making out until you're dizzy, and you smell like your boyfriend's cologne, except the cologne doesn't wash off for days at a time, depending on the potency.

"Noah," I mumble into his clothes. "This isn't—"

"Oh. Right. This won't last long. Let me—"

I actually squeak when he curls his body against me so that he can press his neck to mine, feeling the chill of his bare skin as he nuzzles there gently, the prickle of his five-o'clock shadow, sharp and tingling on my skin as my body tenses in response. My lips part as my breath catches, my knees suddenly taking on the physical property of off-brand Jell-O as Noah stiffens. The gland at my neck feels warm when he touches me, a prickling heat there that creeps deeper inside until it spreads through my limbs. He makes some sound in his throat as if he's trying to clear it but fails, his breath warm against my neck for one brief moment before he pulls away.

He looks confused, less awkward than before but no less out of sorts, frowning at me with his lips pressed together tightly. I watch his eyes dip from my face to my throat before finally capturing mine, his lips parting only to close as he finally remembers himself.

"That should . . ." He blinks, eyes dipping to my throat again. "That should do it."

My voice is strangely quiet, but I still manage, "Ten-mile radius, right?"

"Give or take," he assures me, looking serious.

We're going to have to work on recognizing a joke at that . . . lunch date. First thing. For sure. After this. Why does he look a fraction more good-looking than he did a minute ago?

"I'll uh, hold you to that," I say, feeling awkward myself now when I realize that Noah is still firmly gripping me by the arms. "We should, um, move away from the bushes."

Noah releases me immediately, and the look on his face tells me he hadn't realized he was still touching me either, finally managing to actually clear his throat as he steps away. "I'll see you tomorrow, Dr. Car—I mean, Mackenzie."

"Sure." I cross my arms across my chest even if only to steady myself. My damn knees are actually weak. What the hell is up with that? Is it an alpha thing? "See you tomorrow, Noah."

His gaze lingers for a moment before he shakes his head as if clearing a thought and nods curtly to give me his back. A back that makes it hard not to notice how broad it is. And that's not something I usually notice. I don't care how *broad* a guy is. So why is my subconscious doing a creepy mental eyebrow waggle at Noah's width?

I keep close to the bushes as I watch him retreat to his shiny black Mercedes in the nearby lot, letting him put ample distance between us before I finally allow myself to take an actual breath. The cold air in my lungs on the inhale clears my head, but it doesn't clear away Noah's scent that's still clinging to me. Even with the medicinal quality of his suppressants, it feels strong now that I've experienced it up close, and I don't even pretend to resist the urge to press my nose to my shoulder to breathe in more of it. Something about it makes my skin feel tight, like it's too small to hold me—that same sensation of running through the snow on all fours pulsing inside for the briefest of moments. It's pleasant in a way like it was patented and made solely for my benefit—and just thinking this makes me cringe.

Knock it off, Mackenzie. We don't believe in that uber-compatibility nonsense.

Still, I press my nose to my shoulder for a deeper draw of Noah's lingering scent.

Yeah, I think. *If I were a male I wouldn't want to be within ten miles of that either.*

I blow out a breath, tapping one foot on the ground and then the other to remind my damn knees who's boss before I head toward my car.

4

Noah

AS TIRED AS I was when I left work this morning—I don't sleep very well. I constantly toss and turn throughout the day, my blackout curtains doing nothing for my restlessness. It's . . . strange, what touching Mackenzie elicited in me, a reaction unlike anything I can remember experiencing before. But then again, I have spent a good part of my adult life avoiding people to the best of my ability to circumvent situations like the one I've found myself in.

I rationalize that it's because it's been years since I've touched someone so familiarly; that's why my body had reacted the way it had when I embraced her. That's all. I can't pretend that it hasn't been . . . a long while now since I've been intimate with anyone, and even when I had been I have always been careful to avoid scenting them. I know what the potency of my scent might do to someone, and I have done my best to avoid the possibility of a partner beginning to cling to me after experiencing it. Which is probably *why* it's been so long since I've touched anyone like I touched Mackenzie. It's just not worth the trouble, given how hard I've worked at keeping my status private.

Yes, I think. *That's definitely why I felt so dazed yesterday.* The light airiness of her honeysuckle-like scent had simply been a shock to my system, nothing more.

Although none of this explains why I can't fucking sleep.

By nightfall, my phone ringing at my bedside is the nail in the coffin of my attempts at getting anything close to sleep, and I reach for it blindly as I roll over on my pillow. "Hello?"

"Noah," a familiar voice says from the other end. "How are you?"

"Paul," I mumble wearily.

Paul Ackard is about thirty years my senior and, oddly enough, the closest thing I can call to a friend. We still keep in touch fairly often, given the mentor-like relationship we developed during my time working up to the position I hold now. Hell, Paul is the one who put me up for the head of department position when he retired.

I roll my neck, attempting to sit up in bed. "Exhausted, currently."

"Rough night?"

I laugh dryly. "You don't know the half of it."

"I might," Paul answers. "I know someone turned you in."

My mouth falls open. "How did you hear about that?"

"I worked at that hospital for twenty-five years, Noah," Paul chuckles. "I have quite a few friends there."

I blow out a breath. "You didn't say anything, did you?"

"Of course not," he scoffs, sounding mildly offended. "I recommended you for the position regardless of knowing about your designation. Why would I turn around and blab to the board?"

"Right," I say with a shake of my head. "I'm sorry. I know you wouldn't do that. It's just been such a crazy week."

"I can imagine," he says kindly. "Which is why I wanted to see how you were dealing with it."

"Oh, I . . ." I frown, wondering if it's safe to tell Paul about

Mackenzie and our . . . arrangement. I trust Paul, I do, but with everything that's happened in the last twenty-four hours, I find myself wary of a lot of things. "I'm managing. They're not going to fire me, at least."

"That's good," Paul sighs. "I didn't get the whole story. I was worried. Do you have any ideas who might have done this?"

I swing my legs over the bed, stretching. "Not really. There are so few people that know. I can't fathom who might have figured it out, with the dosage of suppressants I've been on."

"That's true," he agrees. "I'm glad that you're handling it . . . but, still. I worry about it being out there. You know the fuss Dennis put up when you were promoted over him. He'd love to have something like this over you." He makes a disgruntled sound. "You don't think he has something to do with the board finding out, do you?"

I shake my head. "I don't see how he could. We've never spoken outside of work, and he has no connection to any of the people in my life that know. Which is an extremely small circle, mind you."

"True." Paul is quiet for a moment, considering. "Still. Be careful."

There's a guilt pang in my chest over keeping quiet about Mackenzie, but if nothing else, I tell myself it's for her safety. That helps, but only a little.

"I will," I assure him. "It's going to be fine."

I hope, at least.

"Well, keep me updated," he urges. "I'm happy to help in any way that I can."

"I appreciate that," I say honestly.

"Try not to stress about this. They'd be stupid to let you go regardless of your status. You're the most brilliant interventional cardiologist that hospital has ever seen. Outside of myself, that is."

This makes me laugh. "Of course."

"Talk soon, Noah."

"All right," I tell him. "Talk soon."

I sit at the edge of my bed for a moment after hanging up, blinking wearily out the window near my bed at the setting sun that has nearly disappeared past the horizon. I can officially say that sleep is not going to happen.

———

IT'S WELL AFTER dark when I decide that a day like today deserves a strong drink, nursing a glass of scotch by the hearth of the woodstove in my living room as I lounge in my favorite chair. It's been about five minutes since I got a text from Mackenzie, and I've spent the entirety of that time reading it more than once as I try to decide what to send back. I'm also trying to remember the last time I sent anyone a text that wasn't work-related or to my mother.

> **MACKENZIE:** Hey, hope you slept well! This is
> Mack aka Mackenzie aka Dr. Carter. I'll
> probably be busy the next couple of days if
> things keep going like they have been. But
> you can definitely text me if anything
> mate-related comes up and you need me.
> I'm totally down for any espionage-related
> matters. I forgot to tell you that my yoga
> session usually runs till noon on Saturdays,
> but there's a cafe that I love close to the
> studio if you want to meet there this
> weekend. Here's the address. Let me know if

that works. Totally ready for our first
scheming session.

I think for the dozenth time since somehow miraculously pulling off this whole charade that I could not have picked a worse
partner in crime, getting the feeling that Mackenzie Carter is absolutely going to make this entire experience an insufferable one. She's
having entirely too much fun with it, that's for sure. When I see her
again, I should stress once more how detrimental this could be to
my career if it goes south.

When I see her again.

I take a slow sip from my scotch glass, letting my phone drop to
my lap as I watch the flames dance behind the closed door of the
woodstove. I can't yet rustle up any ideas as to who might have
found me out, or why they would report it to the board; I'm not
even sure what someone would have to gain from my being let go,
but I have been thinking about it. It's clear to me that it must be a
personal matter, of that I am at least sure, which doesn't narrow
things down, given that the general consensus of me in the hospital
is that I am intolerable outside of my work.

I take another sip from my glass, silently cursing my luck. Six
years. Six *whole* years of managing to keep my secret while employed at the hospital, only to see it all dissipate with one email.
More than that, if you count the years of residency and med school
where I started really cracking down on keeping it under wraps.
Utterly ridiculous.

I sigh as I pick my phone up, knowing that this is my bed now,
and I have no choice but to lie in it—a thought that strangely brings
me back to Mackenzie Carter. I read her text again, for the seventh

time now, downing the rest of my glass before I set it on the side table.

> **ME:** I know the place. Does 12:30 work? Does
> that give you enough time to finish up?

It takes her far less time to answer than it did for me to.

> **MACKENZIE:** That works. How are you
> doing? Freaking out yet?

This takes me by surprise. Mostly because, like my texting habits, I can't remember a time when anyone has worried about me in a way that wasn't related to work or my mother.

> **ME:** I'm fine. You?

> **MACKENZIE:** Oh, you know. It isn't like this is
> the first time I've had a fake mate boyfriend
> conspirator. No big deal. I'm an old pro.

My lips twitch.

> **ME:** Right. I suppose it is a good thing that I
> am in such good hands for my first
> prevarication then.

> **MACKENZIE:** I know I'm a doctor, but I'm still
> going to have to insist you use less words
> that I have to stop and Google.

ME: Noted. I'll text you tomorrow to
check in.

MACKENZIE: I'll be waiting by the phone,
lover.

I shake my head as I let my phone drop to my lap, covering my mouth for absolutely no reason, given that I am alone in my house. It's not as if Mackenzie is here to catch me smiling.

THE FEELING IN my chest is a new one, that's for sure. Or at the very least, one I can't remember the last time I've experienced. It's an odd fluttering, like nerves, but for what I can't pin down. Am I nervous about the agreement I've entered into, what it will mean if we can't pull it off? Or am I nervous to see Mackenzie again, knowing how much of my career rests in her hands?

Either way, I'm watching the door as I hold a table at the little café. I check the clock again, noticing the time, frowning when I realize it's five minutes past our agreed meeting time. Has she changed her mind? I know I could text her, but part of me worries she actually has, and then where will I be?

I haven't seen her again in the days since I scented her outside of the hospital—an experience I'll not soon forget. In fact, I've been mostly uncomfortable since the incident, seeing as I stopped taking my suppressants that very night, feeling antsy in a way I don't ever remember feeling. I've been placating myself with the knowledge that it's most likely unease that comes from our strange partnership.

Her texts have helped, at least. Each one has assured me that she hasn't changed her mind. At least not yet.

I'm saved from my growing worry when the glass door swings open at the entrance of the café, the little bell dinging above it to signal her arrival as she walks through the front door. Oddly enough, I *smell* her before I fully recognize her, her scent still clinging to me as much as I'd meant for mine to cling to her. It hasn't left me since that morning in the bushes, if I'm being honest, and now that she's nearby, it's considerably more potent.

I'm not yet sure if that is a good or bad thing.

She wiggles her fingers in a wave when she notices me sitting at a table in the back corner, and I return it as she moves through the crowd toward me. Her thick tresses are piled on top of her head in a messy bun, her face slightly flushed red as if she'd only just finished her workout. She unwraps herself from her heavy coat before she settles across the table from me, revealing neon fabric that covers her from wrist to neck to ankle but the tightness of it still leaves little to the imagination.

"Sorry," she tells me as she sits. "Session started late. Instructor got stuck in traffic." She pushes one honeyed tendril from her forehead, tucking it behind her ear. "I should have texted you to let you know."

"It's fine," I tell her, pointedly not looking at her outfit. It's very tight. Is this standard yoga wear? "I haven't been here long."

It's a lie, but she doesn't have to know that.

"So . . ." She leans on her elbows. "How are you? Still freaking out?"

"I haven't freaked out."

Her lips twitch. "Literally all of your texts have felt like you were checking to make sure I hadn't changed my mind."

"Well . . . I can't say that I haven't worried that you might."

She waves me off. "Stop your fretting. I'm not going to ditch you, promise." She leans in closer then, looking serious. "So, what's our plan?"

It takes me a second to register the question, since her leaning in only worsens the potency of her scent, which clouds between us. Why have I never noticed it before all of this?

"Our plan," I answer distractedly. "Right."

She smells a bit like me as well, I think idly. *But I guess that's the point.*

She presses a hand to her stomach then as she cranes her neck, sniffing the air. "Shit. I'm hungry. Do you mind if I grab something first?"

"Oh, that's fine. I . . . let me. I'll get it."

She looks at me strangely. "You don't have to."

"It's the least I can do," I insist. "Since we're supposed to be on a date."

Her cheeks flush, but barely, her eyes widening. "Oh yeah. I guess that's true." Her expression returns to normal, and she leans back in her seat with a smile. "Never thought I'd be on a lunch date with scary old Noah Taylor. Can't pass up the opportunity."

I frown. "Old?"

"It's an expression. Don't get all pissy." Her nose wrinkles. "How old are you, anyway?"

"Thirty-six."

"Oh, that's not so bad. I guess that kills my plan of settling down with a drastically older man for money," she says flippantly.

I shake my head. "Are the jokes part of the deal, or do you intend to let up on them at some point?"

"To be determined. You kind of make it easy."

Not sure what she means by that, but okay.

"What do you want to eat?"

"Get me the soup of the day."

"Don't you want to know what it is?"

She shakes her head. "Nope. It's soup. I'll like it."

"Okay?" I slide out of my chair, pulling my gaze away from the length of her throat when she lifts her arms above her head in a stretch. "Anything else?"

"They have a good copycat pink drink here. Can you get me one of those too?"

I make a face. "Pink drink?"

"Just ask. They'll know what it is."

I nod. "All right then."

Ordering her soup is easy enough, but the look the waitress gives me when I ask for Mackenzie's "copycat pink drink"—that I could have done without. I bring it all back to the table and set it in front of Mackenzie, who looks delighted until she notices I haven't gotten anything for myself.

"You're not going to eat?"

I shake my head. "I ate at home."

"I think you're behind on the concept of a date."

"That's an understatement," I tell her truthfully.

She smiles around the straw of her drink. "Oh, right. I forgot who I'm talking to."

"I'm sorry," I say, not sure why, really. "This is new for me."

"Yeah, yeah. It's fine. All my dates in the last good while have been unwanted, so I'm not that much better off. Don't worry about it."

"Have they really been so bad that you would agree to

something like this?" She looks at me with one raised brow as she opens the lid of her soup container, so I add, "Not that I'm complaining."

"Awful," she says. "I'm talking real bottom of the barrel stuff here. My last date? He asked me if it was true that shifters had a *halfway* form."

"I don't follow."

"Like"—she grimaces, remembering—"he wanted to know if I could keep the ears and tail if we were to . . . you know . . ."

It only takes me a second. "Gross."

She laughs, taking a careful slurp from her spoon before humming in content. "Beef and barley. Yum."

I'm still curious as to what her story might be, but I get the sense she doesn't want to elaborate, since . . . Well, she doesn't.

"So," she says instead. "What do I need to know about you? Give me your top five most important Noah facts."

"Top five?"

"I'm sure you have at least five."

I frown at the table. "I've been an interventional cardiologist for the last three years."

"No kidding?" She gasps softly, but even I can tell she's being facetious. "Not doctor stuff, dummy. Give me some actual facts. Stuff a mate would know."

I have to think about that. Are there actually any noteworthy facts that one might deem *intimate*? "Um . . . I completed my specialization residency here. Under the former department head, Dr. Ackard. He's the one who recommended me to take his place. We're still friends, actually."

"This is still doctor stuff, Noah," she laughs. "Although, you having an actual friend is definitely top secret information."

I give her a helpless look. She must sense my struggle, because she tosses me a bone.

"What about your parents?" She licks a bit of broth from her spoon, and my eyes catch the movement of her tongue, distracting me for a second. "They live here?"

I nod dumbly. "Yes. They live uptown."

"Fancy," she notes. "Are they as grumpy as you? Or are you some sort of anomaly?"

"They're . . . normal. I guess. Quiet. They like golf and brunch. Not much to tell there. Yours?"

"Don't have them," she says casually. "My gran and grandpa raised me. Since I was about twelve."

"Why?"

Her brow knits. "It's not going to come up on a test or anything."

"I'm curious."

And I am, strangely.

She looks wary of telling me, but after a minute and another bite of her soup, she shrugs, relenting. "My mom died when I was little. Car accident. My dad was never okay after that. They were mates, you know? Like, one of those fairy-tale romances. The whole nine yards." She looks away from me then, her eyes distant. "When she was gone . . . he just sort of fell apart."

"Did something happen to him?"

She pauses, her spoon resting against her bowl as her lips tug down. "I think I reminded him of her. I think it got too hard to look at me. Probably why he took off."

I'm not sure how to process this, feeling a sharp tug of sympathy in my chest but not knowing what to do with it or how to even begin to express it. "I'm . . . very sorry."

"Don't be." She waves me off, returning her attention to her food. "It's ancient history."

"Still. It had to have been a hard thing to experience as a kid."

Mackenzie shrugs. "I barely remember them now. Just goes to show you that mating is overrated. I'll stick to being an aficionado of all things pretend mate."

"You did say you were an old pro," I remind her flatly.

"Exactly," she says with a grin. She waves her spoon at me again. "Seriously. It's not a big thing. My grandparents are great. Well, except for the whole blind date nonsense. But that's all Gran. She thinks I need to 'settle down' to be happy or something." She cleans her spoon again with her mouth, eyes studying my face, and again I can't pretend to miss the motion of her tongue against the plastic. "She's going to be over the moon about you."

"Sounds like a lot of pressure," I mutter.

"Nah. You're a doctor. You're a shifter. She's already planning our wedding, and she's never even met you."

"Again, a lot of pressure."

"Don't worry," she laughs. "When you run off to Albuquerque, I'll make sure to talk proper shit about you."

"Fair."

She polishes off her soup, making a satisfied sound before she drops the plastic spoon into the bowl and pushes it away. "That was great. Thanks."

"Soup seems like a pretty cheap payment for the favor you're doing me."

"It's a down payment," she says seriously. "Expect much bigger requests going forward."

My mouth quirks. "Of course."

"Oh my God, did you almost smile just now?"

"Absolutely not."

"Oh, good. I was afraid you might hurt yourself."

"Is your coat the same color as your hair?"

Mackenzie looks as surprised by the question as I am to have suddenly asked it. I'm not even sure why I did, it's just that I've been curious ever since she walked in here.

She blinks. "What?"

"Sorry. I just . . . that's something I would know, right?"

"Oh. Yeah. I guess." She nods airily. "It is. Same color. Was that your way of asking if this is my natural hair color?"

"I . . . No? I was just curious. It's a nice color."

It is, really. With the sun streaming in from the wide windows of the café, the wheat-like shade of her hair seems to catch the light in a way that makes it appear almost golden. Even as I think these things, I find myself wondering where the train of thought is coming from.

She pulls out her phone, distracting me from this line of thought, concentrating on the screen as she ignores me to tap something out there. "Sorry," she says. "I wanted to make a note of your first compliment. Who knows when you'll give me another?"

"You're determined not to make this easy, aren't you?"

She shrugs, smiling as she puts her phone away. "Where would the fun in that be?"

"Mhm."

"So you didn't finish telling me your five facts."

"I'm still trying to think of them, to be honest."

"What's your favorite food?"

I have to think about it. "Steak?"

"How do you eat it?"

"Medium rare."

Another nose wrinkle for my trouble. "Ew. Do you have to go so wolfy with it?"

"It tastes better." I cross my arms against my chest. "What's yours?"

"Soup," she informs me without any hesitation.

"Any particular one?"

"Nope." She shrugs. "If it's in soup form, I'll eat it."

"That's . . . interesting."

She looks at me curiously. "Is *your* coat the same color as your hair?"

"I . . . maybe a little darker? It's been a while since I shifted. The suppressants stave off the need to."

"That's how you end up mauling a hiker," she tuts.

I roll my eyes. "Hardly. When was the last time *you* shifted?"

Her nose wrinkles, drawing my eye. "Mm. Not since my last heat cycle. I went to one of those heat spas outside of town. They have a lot of woods around the place."

It hadn't occurred to me, the implications of my question— because of course she shifted during her heat. The hormone spikes make it incredibly uncomfortable not to. I wish this had come to mind *before* I opened my mouth. Now I'm unwittingly thinking about Mackenzie's heat cycle. Which is not at *all* appropriate.

"Did you stop taking your suppressants, by the way?"

"I did." It's not something I'm particularly happy about either. "For the last couple of days now."

"How long do you think it will take for them to fully get out of your system?"

I don't tell her that they're already making a good go of it, if the potency of her scent is any indication. "I don't know exactly, to be honest. I haven't been off of them since my teen years. Why?"

Her expression is unreadable, but her nostrils flare ever so slightly in an inhale. "Just curious."

"Cat will be out of the bag then," I grouse. "Everyone at the hospital will know."

Mackenzie's mouth splits into a grin. "They're going to be even more afraid of you than they were before."

"I'm glad you find the idea so amusing."

"I'm trying to decide what rumors I can start about you. Would you prefer people thinking you once played bass in an all-shifter heavy metal band or that you belong to a secret alpha biker gang?"

"Is there a third option that involves me being an interventional cardiologist and nothing else?"

She blows a raspberry. "You're no fun."

"Are we actually going to be able to pull this off?"

She must notice my uncertainty then, her amusement dissipating as she gives me a more serious expression. "I won't screw things up, I promise."

I think back to our conversation after we spoke to the board; she had promised something similar then, despite how remarkably easy the board had accepted our ruse. Almost as if they had just been desperate to not have to be put in the position to deal with the alternative. Her promises are unnecessary, I think, given that she could have told me to fuck off instead of agreeing to help me in the first place, but I can't lie and say her dedication doesn't put me at ease.

"Okay," I say, taking her at her word. "When will I be expected to perform for your grandmother?"

"She wants me to bring you to dinner soon," Mackenzie says with a grimace. "She's wasting absolutely no time. I think I can hold her off for another week or so, at least. Hopefully that will give us a bit more time to prepare."

I don't tell her that I'm fairly certain that all the time in the world would not be enough to prepare us for this ridiculous situation, assuming it would be unhelpful.

"Do you work tomorrow?"

She nods. "Day shift. You?"

"I have two consultations in the morning and then a bypass at three."

She bites her lip. "How long do you think it will take for the rest of the staff to hear about us?"

She doesn't necessarily look worried when she asks, but I can tell that underneath her jokes and her quips, Mackenzie is at least considering what our lie will mean for our lives at the hospital. I can already imagine the rumor mill, an ER physician barely out of her residency being the secret mate of the biggest ass of Denver General (yes, I'm aware of my reputation), the hottest gossip ever to circulate. It's going to make for an interesting workday, that's for sure. I can already feel my quiet existence slipping right through my fingers.

I chuff out a laugh, albeit a dry one, shaking my head. "Trust me," I tell her. "They already know."

5

Mackenzie

I HAVE TO admit, there had been a part of me that had actually believed that it wouldn't be a big deal, this thing between Noah and me. My last few shifts have been so busy that I hadn't taken the proper time to lift my head up and notice my coworkers being dodgy. Sure, I assumed the news would get out, but I don't think I'd actually prepared myself for how interesting literally *everyone* would find it. I guess I underestimated how rarely this place gets fed good gossip. Our story might as well be blood in the water.

I can see it now in the furtive glances when I walk down the hall, hear it in the whispers that seem to stop as soon as I enter a room; hell, an RN I've never met before approached me in the break room only an hour after my shift had started to ask me if I was *actually* seeing Noah Taylor. I couldn't exactly tell if she was envious of me or worried I was in a hostage situation. To be fair, either scenario is entirely within the realm of possibility. I mean, Noah might be surly, but he is arguably also very hot.

By lunchtime, I'm half considering taking my food into a bathroom stall to get a break from it all, but I reason that the best way to disperse the curiosity quickly is to face it head-on as if nothing is amiss. Parker sidestepped my invitation to eat with me in the hospital cafeteria, claiming he had a server issue he needed to work on, but I suspect he is punishing me for what he feels is a bad judgment call. He likes to pretend he's my mother sometimes.

I find out quickly I hadn't needed to look for a lunch date at all, having underestimated the number of people who would want to grill me about my new relationship status. Gossip, it seems, is an ample incentive for social interactions. I've barely had time to unwrap my plastic spoon and open my apple juice when a familiar face plops down into the seat across from the table.

"You have to tell me everything."

I take a sip of my juice to give myself a moment to form an answer, noticing how excited my friend Priya looks and taking it as a bad sign. I have to remind myself that I cannot tell anyone else the truth, even if the other person is someone I like. Noah would be pissy as it is if he knew I told Parker.

I feign ignorance. "Sorry?"

"Don't you dare." Priya rolls her eyes, flicking her long, inky hair over one shoulder. "How could you not tell me?"

"I . . ." I shift in my seat. I'm not the best liar in the world. I should have taken that into account before I jumped into this agreement so readily. "You see, Noah and I decided before I started that we wouldn't—"

"I mean, I get it," Priya huffs. "I heard from Jessica in Radiology"—I have never met Jessica from Radiology, and I'm already wondering what makes her the authority on my fake relationship—"that you didn't want to, like, color your reputation with his or something. Totally respect that and all, but I can't believe I've missed out on a year's worth of gossip. What's it like?"

My brow arches. "What's what like?"

"Don't even," Priya tuts. "What's it like being with an *alpha*?"

"Oh." Right. That's supposed to be a unique experience. I guess it would make sense that other shifters would be curious about it. I try for a casual response. "It's honestly not any different than any other shifter guy. Mechanics are all the same."

"Bullshit," she scoffs. "It's so rare for an omega and an alpha to hook up. It has to be mind-blowing, right?"

Oh. Right.

Suddenly I'm second-guessing my decision to tell Priya what I am.

"Well, I . . ." I try to think of something that might sate her curiosity. "It's definitely the best I've ever had."

Honestly, it's almost unfair that I have to lie about this without ever having gotten the chance to try it out for myself.

"But I mean—" Priya looks around before she lowers her voice, like she's afraid of being overheard. "Is it true they have . . . You know. Right? Do they?"

She's absolutely lost me. "What do you mean?"

"You know . . ." Another furtive glance around us, and then she leans in closer. "A *knot*."

Oh. *Oh.* Wow. That's not something I've actively considered yet. The mechanics of Noah's . . . private parts. Knotting had been at the very bottom of my list of things I wanted to ask Noah about during our lunch date yesterday.

"Oh, um." I can feel heat at the tips of my ears and in my cheeks. "That's . . . Well."

"Oh my God, you're blushing. You have to tell me what it feels like. Does it hurt? Do you have to get used to it? How long does it usually last after it happens? Are you, like, stuck together for an hour or something?"

I was not prepared for the knotting section of the fake mate quiz.

"Oh, it's . . . great," I tell her, figuring the least I can do is substantiate her fantasy. "Life-changing, really. Once you go knot you'll . . . want for . . . not."

Priya bursts out laughing, gaining us attention from an elderly gynecologist sitting nearby who I recognize from my rounds. I mentally urge him to turn back to his tuna salad, knowing even someone in his field is most likely as unprepared for this conversation as I am.

"*Shh.*" I lean in conspiratorially. "I'm totally kidding. It's not that big of a deal."

"Says you," Priya snorts. "God. It must be so nice to have someone to spend your heat with." She looks almost wistful. "Those heat hookup apps are a fucking nightmare."

I can't tell her that I wouldn't know on either front. No way would I ever let anyone's incisors near me when I was on my heat.

"I can't even imagine what it's like being with Noah," she barrels on, blessedly changing the subject. "Does he frown during sex?"

Now it's my turn to laugh, because I could actually picture it, strangely. "It's a sexy frown."

I feel like I shouldn't be thinking about sex with Noah, because that feels like crossing some imaginary line, but I can't help it. A girl can only discuss knots for so long before unwarranted mental pictures start to pop up. I mean, Noah is . . . not bad-looking. Big too. If he smiled once in a while, I bet he would do all right for himself in that department.

It's perfectly natural to imagine it, I think. Especially since I'm sitting here having to talk about my supposed *experience* with it; I'm not sure how it hasn't occurred to me yet, the supposed compatibility between an alpha and an omega. I know from medical school that an alpha can't even properly knot with anyone *but* an omega—which has me wondering if Noah has experienced it himself. This entire line of thought has me pressing my thighs together a little tighter, beyond my control, a strange tingling between my legs as my heart rate picks up a few beats.

"But he must not be so bad," Priya points out, dragging my mind out of the gutter. "Not if you mated him. Right?"

I consider that, if for no other reason than to save myself from the train of thought that's working me up. I definitely don't need to be getting horny in a hospital cafeteria over a man I'm *pretending* to date. A week ago, her question would have been easy to answer, but now that I've spent a little time with Noah, I'm not so sure. I'd built up a perception of him in my head, just like everyone else who's ever come across him, I'm sure, but now I'm wondering if a lot of the things I've heard about Noah have been *grossly overexaggerated*, as he would say.

"He's not as bad as he wants you to think he is," I tell her, believing it, weirdly. "He's just intense."

"Understatement of the year," Priya scoffs. "I'm dying to know how you guys met."

Uh-oh. That's not something we went over. Why is that not something we went over? It's the first thing people ask. We really are terrible at this dating thing.

"Ah. Well. It's a funny story actually." It could be a *hilarious* story, given that I'm not even sure what I'm about to say. "What happened was—You see—"

Priya's cell phone begins to ring, and she gives me an apologetic look. "Hold that thought."

I listen to her tone go from expectant to urgent, telling someone on the other line that she will "be right there" after less than a minute of speaking. My whirring brain says a silent prayer of thanks.

"Sorry," she groans. "They need me on the third floor." She pauses before leaving, looking at me expectantly. "You two are coming to Betty's retirement party this weekend, right?"

"Two?"

"You and Noah!"

"Oh." I can already envision Noah's look of distaste. "Actually, I haven't run it by him. Totally slipped my mind."

"Well, hurry and go ask him. You *have* to bring your scowly hubby. I have a bet with my tech that he turns into a bat at night."

I roll my eyes. "I'll be sure to check his schedule."

"Perfect," she says. She points at me with narrowed eyes as another thought seems to cross her mind. "But I still want that story next time I see you."

"Sure," I tell her. "You got it."

She blows a kiss in my direction. "See you later!"

I stream a puff of air between my lips when she's gone, grateful for the bullet I just dodged. How in the hell did Noah and I fail to come up with a "how we met" story? It's practically the foundation of every relationship.

Then again, I'm trying to imagine a scenario where Noah and I would have met organically outside of work and then also fell in love organically to the point where I would let him bite me and spend the rest of my life with him—and I'm drawing a blank. So it makes sense that we forgot that little detail.

Although, thanks to Priya, I'm definitely not having too hard of a time imagining how we might have met outside of work and fallen into bed together. Again, not a safe line of thought.

I shake my head as I'm finally able to give my soup (broccoli and cheddar this time) proper attention, making a mental note to add a "meet cute" to the list of things Noah and I need to fabricate.

If that's even possible.

~

NEAR THE END of my shift, after enduring a few more hours of whispers and stares and direct interrogations from people I've hardly even talked to before today, I decide to seek out my cocon-spirator and see how his day has fared. I need to know how dark his mood is before I hit him with a party invite this soon in the game.

I haven't been to Noah's office since the very first time I met him, doing my best to avoid it before all this, but it's easy enough to find on his floor. His nameplate outside the door is shiny and neat and professional-looking, reminding me of the man himself. I raise my fist to knock lightly against the wood, hearing his low voice beckon me inside as I turn the knob to push the door open.

Noah is sitting at his desk when I open the door, leaning back in his chair with a frown on his face and his fingers laced across his stomach. He seems surprised to see me, his expression changing minutely when I enter, giving him an awkward smile as I start to open the door fully and step inside.

"Hey. It's me, you're so-called—"

I close my mouth as the door swings wider to reveal that Noah is not alone, an older male shifter who I recognize but whose name I can't recall standing on the other side of his desk. I know he works on this floor with Noah, at least. His hair has already begun to gray around his ears, giving me the impression he must be at least a decade older than me and maybe even Noah, his skin an unnatural tan shade that someone like him could only get by spending a lot of his spare time in a tanning bed, given where we live. It makes him look . . . leathery, to be honest. I guess I've never noticed since this is the first time I've seen him up close. I mentally curse myself for nearly blowing our cover.

"Oh," I say awkwardly when I collect myself while shooting Noah a wary glance. "Sorry. I didn't know you were in a meeting."

The older man smiles, waving away my apology. "It's all right. I just stopped by to chat with your mate about a patient I'm having some trouble with. Congratulations, by the way. The whole department is beside themselves that our resident genius has apparently been off the market for over a year. Don't know how he kept it a secret all this time."

"Oh yeah." I laugh nervously, shifting my weight from one foot to the other as my eyes dart from Noah, who looks stern, back to the man whose smile seems off somehow. "Well, you know Noah . . . he's a stoic one."

"Right," the man chuckles. He steps closer to offer his hand. "I'm Dennis, by the way. Dennis Martin. I don't think we've officially met."

"Oh, right. You're a cardiologist, too, aren't you?"

"That's right," Dennis says with that same smile that is starting to creep me out. It feels forced. "Not nearly as important as your mate here. Just one of the worker bees."

I'm not sure what to say to that, glancing at Noah to catch him rolling his eyes out of Dennis's line of sight.

"You must be so proud to be with a department head," Dennis goes on. "I can completely understand why you wanted to keep it a secret though. Wanting to make a name for yourself outside his shadow is very admirable."

"Yeah, well . . ." I shrug noncommittally. "Gave it our best shot, at least. You know how gossip goes."

Dennis's eyes crinkle as his smile widens, nodding. "Right." He gives Noah his attention then, seeming to be done with our conversation. "I'll check with you later about that patient file. See what you think."

"Sounds great," Noah says flatly. "I'll shoot you an email after I've gone over it."

"Perfect." Dennis smiles at me again. "Good to meet you, Dr. Carter."

"Mack is fine," I answer out of habit.

"Mack," he echoes. "Have a good day."

I watch as Dennis walks past me to leave us, waiting until he's closed the door behind him before raising one eyebrow in Noah's direction. "He seems like buckets of fun."

"He's a pain in my ass," Noah grumbles. "He still thinks he should have been given the department head title because of his seniority, but he's too much of a kiss-ass to be outright uncivil with me. So instead, I have to put up with his fake niceties even though he spends most of his time bad-mouthing me to anyone who will listen."

"Yikes." I stick out my tongue. "Sounds like a bitter bitch to me."

Noah's mouth twitches, the closest he's come to smiling since we started our little arrangement. "He is that." He cocks his head. "Did you need something?"

"Yeah." I cross the room to drop down into the chair opposite his desk, tucking one leg under my thigh as I get comfortable. "But I also wanted to see if your day was as wild as mine."

Noah's brow furrows. "Wild?"

"I have seriously had at least ten people ask about you. Half of them I've barely even spoken to before. You didn't get any of that?"

Noah looks surprised. "Not really. It was business as usual."

"Ugh." I shake my head. "Probably because they're too scared to ask you. I guess I'll be the one to bear the brunt of the gossip."

Noah looks apologetic. "Sorry about that."

"It's fine," I tell him. "So far, it's mostly been funny. I'm pretty sure at least three of the people I talked to today insinuated you had some kind of alpha mind-control powers and worried I might be in a captive scenario."

"I guess as far as reasons why you would saddle yourself with me go, that one isn't completely far-fetched."

"Hey, don't be all mopey. There were at least four others who I'm almost positive were jealous. Just saying, you've got options out there when we fake break up."

He frowns. "I'll pass, thank you."

"Suit yourself."

"I'm sorry," he offers again, looking genuinely concerned. "That you're having to deal with it."

I wave him off. "It's okay. I'm a big girl. It's annoying, but it's entertaining at least." I grin at him slyly. "You'll deal with worse when you meet my grandmother. I assure you she will be ten times more insufferable than anyone working at this hospital could ever hope to be. I'll make that your penance."

"Something to look forward to," Noah says dryly.

"I'm sure it will be sooner rather than later," I grumble. "Gran isn't going to sleep until she's fed you and confirmed that you're real."

"Is it really such a novelty that you would find your own significant other?"

My brow quirks. "Are you trying to make a jab at me?"

"No, no." He looks genuinely contrite. "I just meant . . ." He rubs at his neck, and there is a wafting of his scent that comes with it that feels stronger than it had been only days ago. I guess his body is clear of any lingering effects from the suppressants. "I just find it surprising that you would even need your grandmother's help in that department in the first place."

Oh. Is Noah Taylor actually saying I'm attractive? That wasn't on my fake mate bingo card.

"It's just not on my list of priorities," I tell him honestly. "Men are complicated. Shifter men even more so."

Noah gives me a commiserating nod, almost like he's silently apologizing for his gender. I *don't* say that he doesn't know the half of it; my omega status means that dating is a headache even *without* Gran's "help." Seriously. The minute they find out what I am it's nothing but breeding and baby talk. It's funny, people tend to *avoid* alphas like Noah, but seek out people like me due to some nonsense stereotype about us being hypersexual or something. I guess in a way we both have our downsides to what we are. Which, coincidentally, reminds me I have yet to tell *Noah* about my designation. He hardly seems the type to start howling at the moon on my behalf, so maybe it's weird to continue to not mention it.

Although, I can't say I'm not curious now. After seeing Priya at lunch, it's been hard not to consider the, ah, finer details of Noah's alpha anatomy. I can't just ask, right? That's not cool. I wonder how many days you have to be fake dating before it's okay to ask about the structure of your pretend boyfriend's dick? More importantly, why does the thought of said pretend boyfriend's dick make me feel tingly inside?

"How was your day otherwise?"

His question distracts me, and that's probably a good thing. "My day?"

"Yes, I . . . I guess I'm asking how you're doing in general? I would hate to think of you struggling for my sake."

Now he's worrying about me. Another unexpected square for my bingo card.

"Oh. Well. Yeah? It was fine. I had to set a broken arm for a woman with a pain tolerance of about a negative seven, so that was fun. Even with anesthetics, she acted like I was killing her. I'm surprised you didn't hear her wailing from all the way up here."

The corner of Noah's mouth tilts, so subtly I might almost miss it. "That sounds like loads of fun."

"You better be careful," I tell him seriously. "People catch you smiling like that, it will hurt the whole 'brooding scowl monster' vibe you've worked so hard on."

He rolls his eyes. "Duly noted."

"Anyway. So I was wondering. What's your schedule like this weekend?"

"This weekend?"

"Yeah . . . See, I was actually coming by to ask you about Betty's retirement party Friday night."

He cocks his head. "Betty?"

"One of the nurses in obstetrics," I tell him. "She's retiring. She's been here forever. She delivered Tim Allen."

"Tim Allen?"

"He was born here."

"Really?"

"Dude. We have like *one* famous person. Well, unless you count Dog the Bounty Hunter. Which I do. How did you not know this?"

"I guess Denver trivia isn't my forte."

"A resident genius, but doesn't know about Tim Allen," I tut. "It'll be the first story Betty tells you."

"I'm not sure I've actually met Betty."

"Well, at least we know she's not one of the nurses who you've maimed."

He rolls his eyes. "Hilarious."

"I know it's probably not your thing, but you know, since we're all 'mated' now . . . I thought it might be weird if we didn't go together."

"And you're set on going, I take it."

"I do tend to make a habit of socializing," I tell him seriously. "I know. It's a horrible habit."

To my surprise, Noah smiles again. Well, sort of. It's more of a slight tilt of his lips, but I'm learning that's about as good as I can expect.

"Horrible," he echoes.

"I don't want to force you, though, if it's going to be a complete nightmare for you. I can totally make something up about you being busy or something."

"No, I . . ." He frowns, thinking. "I can go."

My eyebrows shoot up. "Really?"

"Did you not want me to?"

"No, no." I shake my head. "I guess I'd just assumed there's no way you would want to."

"Like you said," he reasons, "I'm sure people will expect it."

"Right." I can't say why, but for some reason, his answer makes me feel some distant cousin of irritation, but it's gone as quickly as it comes. "I guess it's a date then."

He's the one to look surprised now.

"Just kidding," I quickly correct.

He nods slowly. "Right."

"To be clear, though, literally everyone is going to be grilling us."

"You think so?"

"Oh, we are hot gossip number one. My friend Priya is practically foaming at the mouth."

He grimaces. "Should I be worried?"

"I think we can handle it," I assure him. "We just have to pretend like we're a deliriously happy couple, right?"

"Right," he confirms.

"Oh. Also, we need to be thinking of a story about how we met."

"How we met?"

He's still frowning at me like he's trying to figure something out. Or maybe that's just his face. Actually, that's plausible.

"Apparently, it's a hot topic that keeps coming up. I managed to dodge the question today, but Priya is not one to let things go."

"Does it need to be overly sensational?"

"That depends," I say seriously. "How opposed are you to the idea that you wrote me highly emotional poetry?"

His expression isn't the least bit amused.

"Fine, fine," I laugh. "It can be simple. I mean, we can stick mostly to the facts, really. We met at work. We could even stick to the simple truth to begin with. That we met when I came to your office for a consult question. Then we start adding the murky bits about hitting it off and falling in love and whatnot."

"I'm surprised you remember how we met," he says.

"You asked me why a resident was bringing you a consult."

"I did?"

"You don't forget someone saying you look 'barely old enough to tie a suture,'" I answer, surprising myself by laughing.

"Wow." He shakes his head. "I really am an asshole, aren't I?"

"I used to think so, but . . ." Weirdly, I'm still smiling. "I'm starting to think it's just part of your charm."

"Charm," he echoes.

"I'm surprised too," I tease.

His grin is still slight, like most of the time he graces me with a smile, but it really is starting to grow on me. Honestly, it sort of works for him. I like how every smile or laugh from Noah feels earned. I wonder absently if there is a possibility that I'm the first person he works with to ever see him smile. It's a mildly satisfying idea.

"Anyway, I don't want to keep you. I just wanted to check in and see what you thought about the party."

"I'll try my best not to embarrass you," he deadpans.

I laugh again, knowing that he's most likely only half joking. "Cool. So I guess I'll let you—"

"My scent has faded," he says suddenly.

I go still, one hand on the arm of the chair as I freeze in a position between standing and sitting. "What?"

He blinks, looking as surprised by his sudden outburst as I am. "Sorry. I just . . . I can't smell it as much anymore. Hardly at all."

"Oh." Is this what he's been brooding over? I press my nose to my coat, inhaling. "I guess you're right. I hadn't even noticed."

"I should . . . I mean, it wouldn't make sense for it to fade if we were supposedly living together and sharing a bed."

Now, why does *that* make me flush? He didn't say anything about sex, just sharing a mattress. There's no reason to get flustered.

I blame Priya and all her talk about knots. Since my brain apparently now goes straight from Noah to bed to knots when given the opportunity.

"That . . . makes sense."

Noah scratches at the back of his neck, looking out of sorts, finally clearing his throat as he rises from his desk chair. "Okay. So I'll just . . ."

I don't remember going to a complete standing position, and I notice my pulse has picked up a few dozen beats in anticipation. I reason that it is nothing more than a biological response, some hormonal nonsense that I have no control over. I have to remind myself that this is business, just a necessary thing that we have to do to keep up our ruse.

"Yeah," I say quietly. "Yeah, you can."

I sidestep the desk to try and meet him halfway, wanting to get this over with.

It's a damned hug, I think. *Stop acting like a schoolgirl.*

I can see Noah struggling with it, the awkwardness of it all, and I try to ease the tension by holding my arms out and giving him what I hope is an encouraging smile. "Lay it on me, I guess."

"Right." Yeah, he still looks entirely too serious for my liking. It makes this weirder. "I'll just—"

He reaches out like he's approaching a baby deer, hands cautious of where they are touching as his large frame invades my personal space. I feel his fingers at my waist first, his thumbs skimming across the front pocket of my scrubs as his palms apply a light pressure on either side of me, and the sensation of his hands curling around to find the small of my back makes my breath catch. I hope he didn't hear it.

"Sorry," he whispers again. "I'll be quick."

I think I nod, but he's too close for comfort now, his scent clouding my senses as he pulls me to him. I close my eyes when my cheek presses against his chest, the button of his doctor's coat biting there slightly as I feel his face press into my hair. At first, I think I'm imagining the way one of his hands seems to climb higher on my spine, but when it presses between my shoulder blades as if trying to bring me closer, I have to reevaluate that assessment.

I realize I'm waiting for it, suspended in a state of wanting to hold my breath and breathe in deep as I wait for his skin to touch mine and leave behind a piece of himself. I feel it in a brush of his nose first, the faint sound of him inhaling as the tip of it skims along my throat, and I swallow thickly as my fingers unconsciously curl into the fabric of his coat to steady myself. Which is necessary since my knees are doing that stupid Jell-O thing again.

He's shaved since the last time he did this, his cheek smooth when it presses warm against my neck, and I could be imagining the way he trembles ever so slightly, but I don't think so. There's a sound in his chest like a groan but softer when his throat slides across mine, and again there is that all-over tingle that prickles over my skin in response. It's both pleasant and uncomfortable, like an itch that needs to be scratched, but I can't reach.

It's just your hormones, I tell myself. *It doesn't mean anything.*

So why am I breathing so hard when he pulls away? And what's more, why is *he*?

It doesn't help that his scent seems stronger now, and I have to assume this has something to do with him stopping suppressants— but the potency of it almost makes the room spin as I cling to him. There's a warmth in my stomach and my chest that seems to pulse, and when I try to swallow, I find my throat dry. I close my eyes, thinking this might help me get a grip, but all it does is make all my *other* senses light up that much more. There is an impulse that is fleeting but strong, one that has me fantasizing about turning up my face and kissing him. Which I know is ridiculous. Not to mention ill-advised.

So why am I wondering what he tastes like all of a sudden?

"Sorry," he says again. His sudden distance when he pulls away is almost a shock to my system, and I notice his eyes are a darker blue than they were a moment ago. "I didn't mean to—" His lips press together as he clears his throat. "Sorry."

I swallow, but it's still difficult. "You keep saying that." My voice sounds all wrong. "It's just part of it, right?"

"Right," he answers quietly, jaw tensing like he might be grinding his teeth. "Just part of it."

I turn my face only so I don't have to look at him anymore, pressing my nose to my shoulder. "I think . . . that'll do."

"Yeah." I can see him nodding from the corner of my eye, slowly, like he's in a daze. "That should, um, do it."

I'm not sure when we realize that his hands are still resting gently against my hips, where they settled after he pulled away from me. He draws them back quickly like he's embarrassed, averting his eyes. Oddly, I almost feel disappointed when he stops touching me.

"Right. Well. I guess I'll be thinking about that story."

"Oh." Our fake origin story is strangely the last thing on my mind at the moment. "Yeah. I'll be sure to text you later."

Another tight nod. "Sure."

Does his scent have to be so nice? It makes it hard to think. It has to be his alpha genes. No wonder he was so religious with his suppressants. If he went around smelling like this, other shifters would either be terrified of him or throwing themselves at him.

I sidestep away from him, putting a bit of well-needed distance between us. "I better hurry up and get out of here," I say with a nervous laugh. "People catch me smelling this much like you, they'll think we've been making out in your office."

Noah makes a strange face that makes me regret the joke, but it's gone as quickly as it comes.

"Have a good night, Mackenzie," he tells me, his voice sounding thicker than it did a minute ago.

"You too." I try for a smile. "See you tomorrow."

I escape before I have the chance to do anything stupid, a good number of hormone-driven suggestions flitting through my brain that are not only ludicrous but also completely unwarranted. The air outside Noah's office is considerably less . . . *Noah*, and breathing it in offers a tiny bit of clarity from the urges his scent brings, ones that I know have nothing to do with us and everything to do with biology.

It's just your hormones.

I repeat this to myself at least a dozen times on the way to my car, but that doesn't make me think about it any less.

6

Noah

I WON'T SAY that I have been *stressing* about tonight, but I definitely haven't been anything remotely close to excited for it. Mackenzie has informed me since coming to my office earlier this week that this get-together we're going to is at a *bar*, something I haven't stepped foot inside since my twenties. I might not have been so willing to tag along had I known.

I check my watch as I glance toward the double doors that lead out of the main lobby of the hospital; Mackenzie texted me ten minutes ago that she was changing and that she would be right down after—and like some sort of massive idiot, I'm currently leaning against my car in the parking lot waiting for her like we're about to go to prom or something. I know that if I told her this was my first actual date in almost a year, she would probably have all sorts of teasing things to say.

Not that this is a date, I mentally correct.

Although, I can't pretend that the idea of a date with Mackenzie, fake or not, has definitely had a small part to play in my nerves this week. Especially after that strange moment in my office the last time I saw her.

I don't know what possessed me to assert the need to scent her again; I remember her talking as if she'd been about to leave, but the entire time her lips had been moving, all I could seem to focus on was the sweetness of her scent and how little of mine had been left to mingle with it. For a brief moment, the idea of sending her back out into the world without marking her again had made me deeply uncomfortable. Which in turn makes me deeply uncomfortable for a myriad of other reasons.

It's been many years since I have gone without suppressants, so long that the strange urges and emotions that come with the lack of them feel alien. It's only been a handful of days since I stopped taking them, and that fact alone is enough to make me worried as to how much worse these behavioral side effects might affect me as more time passes without my daily dose. Something about touching Mackenzie had only brought about the urge to touch her *more*, and I have racked my brain since then for a single time in my adult life when I had wanted to touch a woman so much, even if the urge had been fleeting. It's probably best that we've both been too busy this week to talk outside of texting—even if there *has* been a part of me that has been slightly antsy about the distance. I assume this is some strange alpha instinct I've never had to deal with before.

One thing is for certain, I am going to have to get a better handle on things if we are to continue this arrangement.

I pull my jacket tighter as a gust of cold air whips by, checking the time on my phone again. What is she changing into, anyway? Could it actually be a prom dress? I should have just waited in the car like a normal person. It's probably stupid to think this is somehow more chivalrous.

I'm just about to say fuck it when I notice the glass doors sliding open from across the parking lot, spotting a familiar tousle of sandy blond hair as Mackenzie pushes up on her toes to look for my car. She doesn't immediately notice me even though I am fairly close by, and this means that I have a good thirty seconds or so to grapple with the odd pause she gives me with what she *has* changed into.

Her skintight black jeans hug every part of her down to the leather boots that stop just below her knees, and her equally fitted red sweater under her black peacoat clings to her in a similar fashion, one that makes it very difficult for a person to look anywhere but her. Or at least, that's exactly the effect it's having on *me* right now.

She smiles when she finally catches sight of me, waving her hand as she starts my way. The closer she gets, the more I am able to assess the exact depth of the vee in her sweater—as well as the dangling black chain fastened around her neck that disappears down between her breasts, where I refuse to let my eyes go.

"Hey," she says as she approaches, looking me up and down. She *ooh*s over my dark jeans and my blue button-down under my jacket, even reaching out to pick at the lapel, looking impressed. "Look at you! You clean up nice, Dr. Taylor."

I have a tight noose around my thoughts, forcing my gaze to remain safely on her face as I clear my throat. "So do you."

"Why, thank you," she says with a playful bat of her eyelashes. "Are you ready to go?"

"As ready as I'll ever be," I mumble back, turning to open the door for her.

I don't close it until she's safely tucked inside, circling the car to climb into the driver's seat. She's just finished buckling herself in as I start to do the same, and when I'm finished I notice the gleeful smile on her face, raising my eyebrow at her in question.

"So, on a scale of one to ten," she says, "how much are you going to hate this party?"

I hmph under my breath as I start the car, shaking my head as I put it into reverse so that I can back out of the parking lot. "Solid eleven," I grunt.

Her giggling doesn't end until we've pulled out onto the street.

I'M NOT SURE what's stranger, me in a bar or me in a bar with my coworkers. There is a brief but noticeable silence that settles among them when Mackenzie and I walk through the aged wooden door, the back corner of the bar where everyone is gathered going crickets for at least five seconds before chatter resumes. Mackenzie immediately waves to someone I don't recognize, a pretty woman with dark hair and a bright smile who looks, well . . . delighted, actually.

"Mack! Over here!"

She turns to me before moving on, squeezing my hand in encouragement. "Hopelessly in love, right?"

"Right," I answer, hyperfocused on the warmth of her fingers. "Deliriously happy."

Mackenzie grins before she pulls me through the crowd of bargoers toward the group near the back, and the same woman, who I assume must be a friend of hers, immediately makes a space for us at the round booth where she and a few others have taken up residence.

"Go on," the woman urges the others sitting around the table. "Scooch over." She gives her attention back to Mackenzie as we slide into the booth seating. "Thank God you came. Conner is here."

Mackenzie wrinkles her nose. "Ew. Is he still trying to get your number?"

"Literally every time he calls me up to Orthopedics. Do you know how many elderly patients there are in Denver who need hip replacements? Because I fucking do."

"Yikes." Mackenzie's nose is still wrinkled in distaste. It is only at this very second that I realize I am still watching her do it. Thankfully, she seems to remember me then, snapping me out of it. "Oh. Sorry. Priya, this—"

"Oh, I know who he is," the woman, or *Priya*, says. "We've worked together a lot."

I feel panic setting in. "We have?"

"Priya Mehta," she laughs. "I'm the on-call anesthesiologist. I'm always the one knocking out your patients."

"Oh." The panic turns to slight embarrassment. "Sorry, sometimes I—"

Priya waves me off. "Honestly, it would shatter my entire illusion of you if you had recognized me."

I have no idea what to make of that, but she's smiling, so that has to be a good sign.

Priya points to the rest of the table, introducing them one by one. "This is Matías Hernandez"—she gestures to the broad man with tawny skin to her left—"an endocrinologist. And that's his wife, Jamie"—the petite woman with auburn hair and freckles next to Matías gives me a small smile with a matching wave—"one of my radiology techs. Oh, and that old man over there is—"

"Paul?"

"Noah," Paul says, his graying mustache tilting with his smile. "Never thought I'd see you at one of these things."

"I'm . . ." I feel Mackenzie's arm loop through mine suddenly, and when I look down at her, she gives me an encouraging smile. I remind myself the touching is necessary, just part of the ruse. "Well." I paste on a smile of my own, remembering myself. "There have been, ah, a few developments since you left."

Paul chuckles. "You're telling me. Whole table has been chittering about it ever since I sat down."

I glance at the other members of the table, finding them all looking elsewhere all of a sudden. Pretty much confirming what Paul has just said.

Mackenzie leans to nudge Priya with her shoulder. "Rude."

"Well!" Priya throws up her hands. "You guys dropped, like, the biggest bomb the hospital has ever heard. Our Mackenzie? With Cardiology's version of a Nosferatu?"

"Thank you," I deadpan.

Priya looks apologetic at least. "Sorry."

"She's had a few already," Jamie, the one she mentioned was her tech, chimes in. "You'll have to forgive her."

"Think I'm gonna need a few more," her husband, Matías, snorts.

"I don't think we, ah . . . thought it would make this many waves," I offer.

"I guess we didn't account for how *nosy*"—Mackenzie gives Priya a look of what I think is faux irritation—"our coworkers were."

"She hasn't even told me how you guys got together," Priya pouts. "Isn't that mean, Noah? We're supposed to be friends."

"You're the one who ran out on me at lunch," Mackenzie argues.

"*And* I told you I wanted that story next time I saw you," Priya accuses. "Come on! Tell us. Noah? Was it love at first sight?"

"I—" I look to Mackenzie for help, and I can see by her expression that she can tell I'm struggling. We had agreed to keep it simple, but all of a sudden I find myself terrified I'm going to fuck things up. "Well, I—"

"We met at work," Mackenzie blurts out, saving me. "Obviously."

"Right," I add, nodding in agreement as I collect myself. "Mackenzie had . . . come by my office to consult on a patient having an acute MI."

Jamie's eyebrows furrow. "MI?"

"Myocardial infarction," everyone else at the table says at once.

Jamie rolls her eyes, muttering something like, "*Doctors.*"

"So *anyway*," Mackenzie presses on, helping me out, "I had heard all the stories about Noah Taylor, as you can imagine."

This isn't something we discussed. "What stories?"

"Oh my God. You name it." She points at Priya. "What was the one about Noah ordering everyone out of an elevator because he wanted to ride it alone?"

"It had been having *mechanical* issues," I huff. "I just urged them to take the stairs."

Priya clicks her tongue. "But you rode it?"

"Wait," Mackenzie laughs. "I'm willing to bet he was trying to be punctual for something."

I make a face. "I had a ten o'clock meeting."

"I knew it." Mackenzie laughs harder, and I notice the arm still looped through mine tightens its hold. I can't say I dislike it. "Only you would risk plummeting to your death to make a meeting on time."

"I'm not even sure I want to know about the other yarns that have been spun about me," I grumble.

"There's always that nurse you made cry," Jamie says.

I sigh. "That was—"

"—*grossly* overexaggerated," Mackenzie finishes with a chuckle.

I feel my lips twitch at her glee even when I'm trying my best to look stern, shaking my head at her.

"Wow," Matías chuffs. "I was thinking you guys being a couple seemed a little sus, but you two are definitely in love."

Mackenzie's laugh falters for only a second, and I tense against her when I scent a burst of her honeysuckle-like fragrance tickling my nostrils. I swallow thickly when she seems to collect herself moments later, her scent dissipating as she leans her head on my shoulder.

"Hopelessly in love," she half sings.

I'm still looking at her as I mutter, "Deliriously happy."

"Okay," Priya groans, sticking her tongue out. "Never mind. I've decided I am too single and definitely still too sober to be assaulted by you two and your bliss. I'll just assume you immediately fell in love and lived happily ever after post–myocardial infarction."

"As one does," Mackenzie says seriously. She nudges Priya again. "There's always Conner."

Priya points at her with narrowed eyes. "That's it. You're on re-fill duty. Let's go."

"Fine, fine," Mackenzie laughs. "I need a drink, anyway."

I scoot out of the booth to let them out, lingering when Matías and Jamie follow after them.

"I'm making him dance with me," Jamie explains as they pass.

Mackenzie hangs back while the others head toward the bar, her hand grabbing mine as she looks up at me with concern. "You okay to hang by yourself for a little bit?"

"I'm fine," I assure her. I can tell that she's still worried about leaving me on my own, so I add, "Go have fun."

She flashes me a smile, giving my fingers a squeeze as a similar sensation ensues in my chest. I watch her for longer than is necessary, for some reason wanting to make sure she makes it through the crowd okay, only able to relax when I catch sight of her and Priya laughing about something at the large wooden counter while they try to flag down a bartender.

"So," Paul says as I settle back into the booth. "Mated, huh?"

I reach to rub at the back of my neck. "Yeah, it's . . . been interesting."

"Funny how you never mentioned it to me," he says with a hint of amusement in his voice, creases forming in the warm brown skin around his eyes. "Considering I am probably the only person from work you keep regular contact with."

"Sorry," I offer. "We didn't . . . It's complicated."

"It wouldn't have anything to do with your alpha status being outed, would it?"

"That's . . ." I struggle for anything remotely close to a good excuse, coming up short. "Is it obvious?"

"Not to the average bystander," Paul chuckles. "But I know you."

"It's been a fucking mess, Paul," I sigh.

"I imagine," he offers. "So what is Dr. Carter's role in all this?"

"She's . . ." I turn my head, my lips pressing together as I watch her head tilt back with mirth at something Priya has just said. "She's helping me out."

"From what Priya tells me," Paul notes, "Dr. Carter is something of a saint."

"She is," I mutter back, still looking at my pretend mate as she laughs.

Paul reaches for the glass in front of him, and when I finally tear my attention away from Mackenzie, I notice he's smiling into it as he takes a drink, his dark eyes glittering. "You two are very convincing. Watching you two together, no one would suspect that you aren't an item."

"Oh, we're just . . ." I frown down at the table. "Honestly, I'm surprised she even agreed. It makes no sense from anyone's point of view why she would."

That part is definitely true, and something that is constantly on my mind. Even with her reasoning that I'm keeping her from another string of bad dates—it's a lot to take on, this thing we're doing, and it feels as if I have much more to benefit from it.

"Well, you did say she's a saint," Paul says.

I nod. "I did."

I notice he's smiling again, almost like he has a secret, and with a subtle shake of his head, he gives his attention back to his glass. "I look forward to seeing how this plays out."

"Hopefully in something other than disaster," I huff.

"Just be careful," Paul warns again. "You're too bright to let this ruin you. It would be a waste all around."

"I will," I tell him. "If nothing else . . . I wouldn't want to jeopardize Mackenzie's career. I couldn't live with myself if I dragged her down with me." I catch Paul looking at me with that strange smile again, and raise an eyebrow at him. "What?"

"Nothing, nothing," he laughs. "Like I said, I look forward to seeing how this plays out."

I'm not really sure what he means by that, and decide that asking will most likely just get me more sly glances.

"Noah!"

My head whips to the side at the sound of Mackenzie's voice, catching her pushing through the crowd again. I notice her cheeks are slightly more flushed than they were when she left. She offers a quiet apology to Paul before she leans in to whisper in my ear, and there is an imperceptible (or at least, I hope it is) shiver that passes over me when I feel her breath wash against the shell.

"Dennis is here," she whispers. "He was asking somebody at the bar if they'd seen us." I can smell the fruity drink she must have downed before she came back. "Just follow my lead." Before I even have time to be confused, she reaches for my hand, tugging me from where I'm sitting. "Come dance with me!" I must make a face, because Mackenzie barks out a laugh. "Oh, come on. Dance with me, sourpuss."

I'm momentarily distracted by the warmth of her palm, even more so by the inviting quality of her smile. Like she *really* wants to dance with me. It makes it hard to say anything other than "Okay." I slide the rest of the way out of the booth, casting Paul an apologetic glance. "Sorry."

"Go, go," he urges. "Dance with your mate."

His smile is as sly as it's been for the last five minutes, but I don't have time to be uneasy about it with Mackenzie pulling me across the floor like she is. She pulls me closer when we're encased in the swarm of people there, taking my hands and placing them on her hips before she hooks hers behind my head.

"I figured he wouldn't bother you if you were dancing with me," she explains.

"Oh." I nod, turning to scan the crowd to see if I can catch sight of him. "Good call."

"Two birds," she hums.

I arch an eyebrow. "What is the other bird?"

"When will I ever get to say again that I danced with *Noah fucking Taylor*?"

"That's an interesting takeaway," I chortle.

"My friend Parker calls you that," she admits. *"Noah fucking Taylor.* You really are a weird kind of celebrity at work."

"I never meant to be," I tell her.

Strangely, her smile widens. "I'm starting to get that. Just part of your charm."

There it is again. I still can't get used to anything in relation to me being referred to as *charm*.

"How much did you have to drink?"

She wrinkles her nose. I have definitely decided it's endearing. "Just a cosmo." She notices my hesitance to believe her, rolling her eyes. "And a couple of shots."

"We should make sure you pace yourself for the rest of the night," I laugh. "Don't want you to get sick."

She winks at me. "It's fine. I have my alpha here, right?"

That same shiver slides along my spine. It's just a sentence, a simple one at that . . . So why do I feel so tense all of a sudden? It doesn't help at all that her scent is a little thicker now; I'm assuming we can blame the alcohol for that.

"Right," I murmur back, trying to keep my expression even.

We continue to sway to the slow song that's playing over the speakers, and at some point, her head lolls a bit so that her cheek presses against my chest. "You smell good," she sighs. "Did you know?"

Dangerous, I think. I should probably end this dance.

"I can't say that I did," I manage.

She presses her nose to my shirt again, breathing in. "Well, you do."

"Thank you," I answer, my voice tighter than it was a moment ago. "Um . . . So do you."

She tilts up her chin to give me a dreamy sort of smile. "I do?"

I swallow thickly. This feels *very* dangerous. Especially given the fact that I am suddenly getting strong and outrageous ideas about what her mouth might feel like. I can't even pinpoint where the thoughts are coming from. Then again, I can't really process much outside of her smile right now. It feels impossible, how much she increasingly affects me. More than anyone ever has. That's for sure. Is it *really* just because I haven't ever gone off my suppressants for so long?

"Yes," I grind out, forcing my gaze up and over her head just so I can clear my thoughts. "Where did you see Dennis?"

"Oh." She turns her head, craning her neck. "He was over there with Betty."

"I still don't know who Betty is."

Mackenzie giggles. "It's so funny how everyone knows you, but you don't know anyone."

"I . . . don't make it a habit to make friends."

"Clearly," she teases. "But . . . we're friends. Right?"

"I . . ." I can't help it. I peek back down at her, and from this angle I have a clear view of the plunging vee of her sweater where the soft swells of her breasts rise and fall with every breath. I have to will myself not to look, feeling like some sort of teenage animal. "Yes. We're friends."

That same smile that makes my chest feel tight. "What an honor."

The song fades away then, and its absence seems to knock some sense into me. I clear my throat as I let go of her waist (even as my fingers feel like they might scream with protest), making a show of peering out over the crowd as a more upbeat tune starts to play. "Do you want another drink? I'll definitely need one or five to dance to this kind of music."

"I'll wait a bit," she says. "That last shot got to me, I think."

"Probably a good idea," I muse. "I'll meet you back at the table."

She looks at me curiously then, studying my expression with a discerning one of her own—but for the life of me, I have no clue what she's thinking. She gives her head a little shake as if to clear her own thoughts away, pasting on a smile that feels more practiced than the one she'd given me during our dance. "Sure. If Dennis bothers you, just holler. I'll be sure to beat him up."

"Perfect," I laugh. "I feel much safer now."

She tosses me a wave over her shoulder as she meanders back in the direction of our table, and I take a deep breath of air that is less clouded with her scent after her retreat. It makes it a little easier to think.

I really do need a drink.

~

A LOT OF things happen over the next hour.

I do get that drink, and polishing it off does wonders for my nerves and the tension that comes from being in such a crowded place. At some point, Priya loudly announces that she has decided I am good enough for Mackenzie—something that makes the entire table burst into laughter. I meet Betty, and she *does* tell me that she delivered Tim Allen. She also tells me I'd better not break Mackenzie's heart, and for a seventy-something-year-old woman, she comes off as pretty intimidating. Paul says good night and heads home after giving me another sly smile and knowing look, and I can't pretend I'm not a little jealous of his departure. Although, I have to admit—I've had a relatively good time tonight. Mackenzie has made sure of that.

My faux mate in question has been considerably less touchy-feely than she'd been on the dance floor, and I can only assume this is due to her sobering up a little bit more after her round of shots. She's still touching me familiarly, her arm still looped with mine whenever she isn't using it to sip her drink or expressively tell a story—but I haven't seen that sweet smile or that dreamy look since that song ended. She definitely hasn't sunk into my embrace again. Which I suppose a more rational me would be relieved over. Drink or no, it's not a good idea for us to be too familiar with each other outside of what's expected of us.

Even if every inhale brings on more of her sweet scent that threatens to drive me crazy.

Tonight is the closest thing I've had to a date in I can't remember how long, and even if it's completely false and only for show, it's honestly sort of . . . nice. Spending time with other people. I've spent so long sequestering myself off from others to keep my secret that I had forgotten how pleasant an experience socializing can be when given the proper chance.

But it could very well be the company I'm keeping.

"You doing okay?"

I glance down at Mackenzie, who is leaning into me conspiratorially, her voice low so that only I can hear it while Priya tells a terrible joke to an ophthalmologist she brought back to the table.

"I'm fine," I tell her. "I'm having a fairly decent time."

"Wow," Mackenzie laughs softly. "Noah Taylor having a *fairly decent time.* Someone alert the media."

"Cute." I press my lips together. "I suppose socializing isn't as horrible as I first pegged it to be."

She lets out a mock gasp. "Oh my God. Next week I'm going to have to drag you out of a rave or something."

"I wouldn't bet on that," I say, cringing.

She smiles up at me, not the inviting one from earlier that had made my stomach twist, but still a soft and sweet number that says she's genuinely happy to hear this. "I'm glad you're having a good time. It's not good for someone to keep all cooped up to themselves like you do."

"Is that your professional diagnosis?"

Her face splits into a full-on grin, flashing me her teeth. The stomach knots are back. "It is. No need to seek a second opinion."

"You guys are grossing me out," Priya groans from across the table, breaking apart our quiet conversation. "I liked you better when you were grumpy," she adds, pointing at me in accusation. "At least then I wasn't so jealous."

I chuckle under my breath. "Trust me. No need to be jealous. Well." I peek over at Mackenzie. "Not of Mackenzie, at least. Maybe of me."

Mackenzie's lips part at the compliment, but Priya makes an *ack* sound. "*Couples.*"

But of course, because nothing about this situation has been easy—the night simply can't end on a good note. I notice him approaching out of the corner of my eye, my body immediately tensing as my smile dissipates. I've never really fully scented Dennis before; blessedly, I have had the good fortune of missing out on it while being dosed on suppressants, but catching a whiff of it now makes *my* nose wrinkle, assaulted by the smell of what feels like cheap cologne.

"Noah!" His voice is loud, carrying over the chatter of the people around us, and everyone at the table turns to look at him as he approaches. "I can't believe you actually came. I didn't think this was your kind of thing."

"Yeah, well." I keep my expression passive. "Now that our secret is out, it didn't feel right to let my mate go alone."

"Of course," Dennis says with a smile that feels disingenuous. "Mackenzie. Good to see you again." He eyes her up and down. "You look fantastic."

My fists clench under the table as he eyes her, and it is only a moment before I feel the gentle slide of Mackenzie's hand over mine, calming me. "Thanks," she says blandly.

"It really is so nice to see you guys out together," he gushes. "I know everyone was worried when the rumor started flying about Noah. It's lucky that he had you up his sleeve, isn't it?"

I can't say why I am on the verge of vibrating with anger—something about Dennis has always gotten under my skin—but without the safety net of my suppressants, I can feel the urge to deck him a lot more strongly than I have in the past. Thankfully, Mackenzie's hand gives mine a squeeze, and something about her touch keeps me from tipping over the edge.

"We're both really lucky," she says, keeping her eyes locked with his. "It seemed silly to worry about what people might think of me when my mate's job was on the line."

"Right," Dennis says, still smiling with that same slimy smile. "So fortunate. We would have hated to lose our best cardiologist."

The table is silent then, the rest of our party looking uncomfortable as I quietly seethe, and it isn't until Mackenzie clears her throat that any of us move.

"Yeah, well." Mackenzie never lets go of my hand. "We should probably get going. Right, Noah? You have an early shift tomorrow."

I briefly wonder how she knows that, but am too distracted with *not* wiping that smile off Dennis's face to dwell on it.

"Right," I agree tightly. "Early shift."

"Oh, of course," Dennis says. "Don't want to keep you. I know how important work is to you." Another gross smile. "You guys have a good night."

No one speaks until Dennis is out of earshot, and then there is a loud burst of air as Priya blows out a breath. "Wow. That guy is a dick."

Mackenzie whips her head around. "You caught that?"

"Oh yeah," she answers. "He does *not* like Noah."

"We probably should get out of here," Mackenzie tells me. "Before you break something."

I unclench my fists, unaware that I was even doing it, blinking a few times as I come back to my senses. "Sorry, I—" I press my lips together. "I just . . . He gets under my skin."

"Jessica from Radiology told me he offered her a ride home from work once and that he made a point to let her know what kind of car he drives," Priya says.

"Fucking Jessica," Mackenzie mutters before giving me her attention again. "Seriously. We can go, if you want."

I shrug. "If you're sure you're ready to go."

"Yeah, I'm good." She turns to Priya as she starts to gently push me out of the booth. "Don't let Conner take you home. I am not going to be in *that* wedding party."

"No problems there," Priya assures her.

Even when we're standing, I notice Mackenzie hasn't let go of my hand. In fact, she keeps a grip on it as she says her good-byes, while Priya gives me one last friendly threat in regard to Mackenzie's well-being, and even the entire time she pulls me through the crowd toward the bar exit. I reason that she's still worried about my earlier edginess. Hell, she can probably scent it on me, I'd wager, and I *could* tell her I'm okay now, that she doesn't have to continue clinging to me.

I let her hold my hand all the way out to the parking lot instead.

～

THE RIDE BACK to her place is a relatively quiet one, at least at first. Mackenzie lets the first several blocks pass in silence, and I can't seem to think of anything to say to cut through it. She stopped touching me when we got into the car, because there was no valid reason for her to do it anymore, and for some reason without it I find myself uneasy. She doesn't open her mouth until we're nearly halfway to her apartment building, and by then, I'm uncomfortable, like I might come out of my skin.

"So . . . all in all, I'd say that wasn't the worst fake date I've ever had."

This draws a quiet laugh out of me, easing some of the tension inside. "You've had more than one?"

"Oh, loads," she says seriously. "I told you I was a pro."

My lips are still curled. "How could I forget?"

"Are you feeling okay? I could tell Dennis was really getting to you."

I shake my head. "I don't know what it is about that guy. It never used to bother me as much as it has been lately. Probably a side effect of going off my suppressants."

"Yeah. It's weird. It's like I could scent it on you the moment he walked up. Almost like I could tell your mood changed. It was sharper somehow. I've never really been able to pick up on things like that as much as I could tonight."

"That's . . . interesting," I note, meaning it. "I wonder why that is."

She's quiet for a second before tossing me a flippant "Must be an alpha thing."

"Must be."

It's quiet again, and with it comes that same uneasiness. It's completely unlike me; normally I am happy to be left to the quiet. Right now, though . . . I really hate it.

Mackenzie saves me again. "Was it super uncomfortable for you? Scenting all those people? I know you aren't used to it since you've been on suppressants for so long."

"No, I . . ." Her question takes me by surprise, but mostly because of my answer. It's something that hadn't occurred to me until she asked. "Honestly, I could only scent . . . you, for the most part."

She turns her head to look at me, and when I glance to my right I catch surprise on her face. Her mouth parts only to close again, like she's thinking, and it's that same contemplative look she'd given me back on the dance floor, like she's trying to figure something out. "That's . . . Huh. I wonder why?"

"I'm not sure." I peek at her again. "Must be another alpha thing."

"Right." She nods idly, but I can tell she's still thinking. "Sure."

Why is this so *awkward*? Maybe it was a bad idea to come with her. It feels like I've wandered into uncharted territory.

There's a question that eats at me, a surprising one that would have never done so before all this. I consider not even asking, but ultimately, it seems that my brain refuses to let me do that. "Did you . . . have fun?"

"I did," she says after a beat. She laughs then. "You make a great fake date, turns out."

"That's definitely a surprise."

"Probably because you've gotten so good at the whole 'scary Dr. Taylor' thing."

I consider that. I *have* done my absolute best to avoid any connection outside of work for as long as I've been here. Honestly, Paul is probably the closest thing I have to a friend, and he found out about me completely by accident.

"I've been so focused on keeping my secret . . . I don't know. I can see how I might have come across."

"Well, maybe it'll end up being a good thing someone turned you in."

"What do you mean?"

"I just mean that it must be nice to not have to pretend anymore, right?"

I frown, thinking. "I guess it is a bit of a relief."

"And when you get to Albuquerque, you can take all the cool things I'm teaching you and use them to make real friends. I think by then we'll have the scowling down to a minimum, surely."

The reminder that I'm leaving is sobering, and I can't really discern why. Nothing has changed since last week, so hearing about the plans that I've had from the beginning shouldn't make me feel so strange.

"Right," I say airily. "I have absolute faith in your abilities."

"I'm right up here," she says, pointing to the building ahead. "Take this next right."

I slow the car so I can turn in, coming to a stop outside the door to her building and parking the car. She unbuckles slowly, lingering in her seat for a moment.

"About earlier . . ." She fidgets a little. "When we were dancing. I hope I didn't make you uncomfortable. I probably shouldn't have had that second shot."

Oh. *Oh.* Has she been worrying about this the entire time?

"No, no," I assure her. "You didn't. It's fine."

"I hope you don't think I was, like, coming on to you. I don't want you worrying about me crossing a line or something."

"No, I—" It would probably be a terrible idea to let her know I've been struggling myself, right? Obviously, she is uncomfortable by the idea of it all. "It's really okay. Blame it on the alcohol."

"The alcohol," she parrots, nodding. "Right. Yeah. So we're okay?"

"We're fine," I urge. "I'm sure it won't be the last time things get awkward. It's a strange arrangement we're in. There are no real guidelines here."

"Okay. Whew." She playfully wipes the back of her hand across her brow, peeking up a little. "Glad that's settled. I guess I'll see you tomorrow then, yeah?"

"Sure." That reminds me. "How did you know I work tomorrow?"

"Oh. My friend Parker is the IT guy. I got him to print me a copy of your schedule." She looks panicked for a second. "Is that weird? I just thought that if someone asked me if you were working or something I should probably know. Now I'm thinking it might be creepy. Shit."

"No, it's fine. Really. I was just surprised that you knew. That totally makes sense." I can tell she still feels weird about it, so I add, "You should probably get me a copy of yours too. Just in case."

"Okay." She nods fervently, looking relieved. "Yeah. I will." She finally gives me another smile, and I'm starting to think that my body is developing some sort of instinctual reaction to it. "I'll see you tomorrow. Have a good night, okay?"

"You too," I murmur, watching her open her door to leave.

She gives me a little wave before she steps inside the building, and I don't leave until she's out of sight. Her worried expression at the thought of having crossed a line sticks with me—for reasons I can't explain. It should be a good thing that she's worrying about it, and it should be a *relief* that she wanted to make sure I knew it wasn't her intentionally coming on to me. So why do I feel so shitty right now?

During the entire drive home, I never came up with a good answer.

7

Mackenzie

THE WEEKEND ENDS up being a disastrous time at work, and after the night at the bar, I don't see Noah for three days. I can't pretend the space isn't a *little* welcome after that awkward moment at the party.

I think I'd expected it to be less easy. Being on a date with Noah. *A* pretend *date,* I remind myself. I've had to remind myself of that a lot this weekend. Maybe it's because I got so weird after my tipsy moment on the dance floor. It's just that he really had smelled *so* good, and with the liquid courage that had been sloshing around in my belly, it was easier than it should have been to forget that it was all fake.

I blame my misstep on my lack of any good *real* dates lately. That had to be what it is. At least Noah had been gracious about it. Although . . . I can't pretend some part of me hadn't been a little miffed over him brushing it off. I blame that on hormones. Maybe if Gran wasn't always trying to set me up with Mr. Hell No, I might have been able to find someone *actually* suitable to bring back to my place and bang all this confusion out of me.

Speaking of Gran.

I know it's her before I even check the caller ID, rolling my eyes as I pull my phone out of my scrub pocket to answer it. This is the eighth phone call from her in three days, and every single one of them has amounted to the same thing, which is:

"So when are you bringing him for dinner?"

I close my eyes as I continue down the hall from the cafeteria, repressing the urge to sigh. "Noah's schedule is crazier than mine, Gran. It's not like either of us gets a lot of free nights."

"Oh, surely you could sneak away for an evening to have dinner with your poor grandmother," she pouts. "You haven't been to see me in ages."

The hallway is blessedly empty right now, and I'm grateful that no one is around to listen in. "I was just there last week."

"And now you're dating someone, and you didn't even tell me."

"I told you, it's new. It isn't my fault that—"

"Besides, it's important for couples to make time for each other outside of work," Gran stresses. "You can't *only* see each other at the hospital. I know how you are."

"We do make time outside of work," I protest. "We went to a bar on Friday."

"A bar," Gran huffs. "You can't have quality time at a bar."

There is a spark of memory that involves Noah's body pressed to mine while his scent made me dizzy—and I think to myself I could make a valid argument against that. I keep quiet since it would most likely just have her picking out flower arrangements and venues though. Also, it still makes me feel a little funny when I remember touching Noah as casually as I did.

"I just don't have a lot of years left, you know?" She sighs. Dramatically, I might add. "I always hoped to see you settled and happy before I kick the bucket."

"We both know you're likely to outlive me."

"Not if my granddaughter keeps breaking my heart."

"Fine!" I shake my head, watching the floor numbers change from three to two and willing the elevator to move faster. "Okay. I'll ask him when he's free."

"Oh, wonderful. I'll make my pot roast. Or is chicken better? Maybe I could—"

"I don't think it matters what you cook," I assure her, tapping my foot. "You don't have to do anything special."

This is going to be a disaster. I had hoped to ease Noah into all that is Moira Carter, but it looks like that's not an option, since she's apparently going to hound me right up to the altar. I'm starting to wonder if this is better than all the blind dates.

I have an errant thought about model trains, and that quickly puts the matter to bed.

"Of course I do! This could be my future grandson-in-law—"

"Gran."

"—and first impressions are incredibly important."

I round a corner, hardly paying attention to where I'm going now. "I'm sure Noah is going to think you're perfectly wonderful as long as you don't insist on acting batshit craz—"

I forget what I was saying as a familiar body comes into view—and I'm thrown by the person standing in the hall outside the ER.

"Noah?"

He looks frazzled, his arms crossed and his mouth taut as he looks up at me from the floor, his brow furrowed.

I can hear Gran's voice distantly, my body having a weird reaction to seeing him after so many days. It's like I forgot how to move all of a sudden. Did he smell this nice three days ago, or is it only because it's been so long since I've been this close to him that's making his scent seem more delectable?

"I have to go, Gran," I tell her absently. "Lots to do. I'll let you know soon."

I'm not even sure she hears me hang up, still muttering about a menu for a dinner that hasn't been set in stone yet.

I'm still just standing there. "What are you doing down here?"

"I was . . ." He looks me up and down, his eyes darting toward the way I've just come. "Were you having lunch?"

"Yeah. Over in the cafeteria."

"Oh."

"Were you looking for me?"

"I . . ." He shifts his weight from one foot to the other, almost like he's uncomfortable. "Yes. I probably should have texted first."

"No, that's okay. I mean, I would have saved you the trip if you had and come to you, but it's totally fine."

"Right." He nods down at the floor, still frowning. "Good. Okay."

The expression on his face is still one of almost worry, and I push away the distraction of his scent as I reach out to press my fingers to his arm in concern. "Are you okay?"

His eyebrow quirks as he looks back up at me. "Okay?"

"Yeah, I mean . . . You don't usually come down to my floor. Plus, you look super stressed. Did something happen? Because I can—"

"No, Mackenzie," he interjects. He scrubs a hand down his face, his eyes darting down the hall. "It isn't anything that—"

"Shit." I follow his gaze, noticing an RN who's turning the corner while perusing a clipboard. "Right. We shouldn't talk about it here."

"Mackenzie, I don't think—"

I'm already scoping the area for a place we can talk since, unfortunately, I am not yet high enough on the ladder to have my own office. "Let me just—" I spot a utility closet down the hall, grabbing his arm a little tighter and dragging him with me. "Come here."

He's still half protesting as I pull him the extra ten feet and shove him inside the cramped space, reaching to flick on the light and peeking back down the hall to make sure no one noticed us before I shut the door.

"Okay," I say, turning to regard him. "My bad. You probably didn't want to be overheard."

"No . . . There's nothing really to—Shit." He blows out a breath, looking more stressed than he did even a minute ago. "I really should have texted you."

"What's wrong? Just tell me."

"Nothing's . . . wrong," he manages, not really looking at me now. "I just . . ." He sighs, seeming almost embarrassed. "I just haven't seen you in a few days."

I tilt my head, not quite understanding. "Okay?"

"I just . . ." I swear, if this weren't Noah Taylor I was talking to, I might think he was blushing. "I haven't scented you in three days." He says the words very quietly, like it's difficult. "I was starting to worry people might notice."

"Oh."

At first, there's a tiny part of me that preens at this information. Some faraway omega hormone that does a little somersault as it parades through my bloodstream. Then I remember what we are, and I feel silly.

"That makes sense," I say almost too quickly. "I'm sorry. It's been so busy. I didn't even think about people getting suspicious."

"Suspicious," he echoes woodenly, eyes fixed on my face now. "Right. Don't apologize. It's been busy upstairs too."

"Still." I shuffle my feet, feeling odd about the whole thing. Which doesn't make any sense. Surely I can't be *disappointed* that he only came to find me to do some maintenance work on our charade. That's the whole reason we're even talking right now, after all. "Wow," I laugh. "Probably weird that I pulled you into the closet then."

"It's fine," he assures me. "I suppose . . ." He looks around at the cluttered shelves on either side of us. "I suppose this is as good a place as any."

My heart rate picks up a couple more beats. Have I started anticipating this? That's normal, right? Given the situation?

Fucking hormones.

"I haven't been in a closet with a guy since freshman year of undergrad," I say with a nervous chuckle.

I notice a slight flare to Noah's nostrils, a flash of hardness in his eyes, but it's gone as quickly as it comes. "I'll be quick," he tells me quietly.

"Okay," I half whisper back.

I've begun to get used to this part, in the sense that I never *really* get used to it at all—holding my breath as Noah closes the distance between us until my back is pressed against the closet door. His hand comes to rest somewhere near my head, like he's steadying himself, and then the other settles at my hip to do the same thing, I suppose. I've closed my eyes at this point, so I can't be sure.

"You don't smell like me at all," he says with a quiet inhale, his tone almost annoyed.

Is he worrying about what people might say had he not come when he had?

"Sorry," I breathe again.

I hear another deep inhale. "Don't be."

I tense with anticipation as I feel his skin slide against mine, that first press of his cheek somewhere under my jaw making me shiver. It's hard to explain what it feels like when he does this—it's like being touched everywhere at once, when his scent blends with mine. There's definitely a reason you normally do this with someone you're *actually* sleeping with.

My fingers reaching out to grip the lapel of his white coat is an instinct; I don't even realize I've done it until the fabric is wadded in my fist. I even *tilt* my head to allow him better access, sighing quietly when his throat glides against mine. My toes curl in my shoes, and I idly think to myself that these little episodes seem to get more and more dizzying the longer we keep them up.

I'm hardly breathing when he starts to pull away. There is even that same small part of me that is silently protesting, wanting me to pull him closer—but it isn't until he turns his head ever so slightly, his lips barely brushing a sensitive place on my neck in what I think is an accident, that my knees buckle a little.

Noah catches me, his arms beneath mine to hold me upright, and when his eyes meet mine—there's a wildness to them that feels unlike him.

"I'm sorry," he manages raggedly. "I didn't mean—" He swallows, drawing my eyes to the motion of his throat. It seems a little difficult for him. "I—"

I'm not sure what he's trying to say, and I'm honestly not even sure if *he* knows. His eyes have drifted down to my mouth, staring at my lips like they're a puzzle he's trying to figure out. I can't really make sense of what I'm feeling at this moment; do I want Noah to kiss me, or is that, too, the result of some ridiculous hormone-driven causation?

To be fair, his mouth does look . . . incredibly soft right now.

I think I'm about to do something very stupid, and I am pretty damned certain that Noah is about to let me, given the way he's started to lean in a little, and the entire room smells like him, and it's hard to think, and I just—

We jolt apart when the door suddenly opens behind us, and I can't imagine what sort of sight we must make to the elderly janitor who frequents the halls here. The bright light of the fluorescents floods the closet as the door opens all the way, and both Noah and I seem to be struggling to come up with a good reason as to why we are shut away in a utility closet that probably smells like we were sucking face in it—if not worse.

"Kevin," I sputter, doing my best to straighten my body even though my knees are a little shaky still. "This isn't what it looks like."

Kevin's wrinkled cheeks dimple further with his sly smile, raising his hands and looking away. "I didn't see nothing."

"No, wait," I try again. "We're not—"

Kevin closes the door to leave us where he found us, and I feel my cheeks heat with embarrassment like I'm some horny teenager who's just been caught at school. I groan as I lean back against one of the shelves, throwing an arm over my face.

"It had to be Kevin," I huff. "He's a gossipy old bastard."

Noah still looks stunned when I sneak a peek at him, his mouth parted in shock as he struggles to make words. "I'm so sorry," he tries. "I never meant—"

I wave him off. "It's fine, it's fine." I ignore the way my heart is still racing. "I mean, rumors only strengthen our story, I guess."

Noah is quiet for a second, blinking at me like he's still processing.

"Right," he finally agrees. "Sure."

"I'll bring him doughnuts tomorrow," I say with a sigh. "That should buy a little of his discretion."

"Okay," Noah says in that same wooden tone.

He looks concerned. Is he thinking about how we almost overstepped just now? Is he regretting it?

Hell. Am *I*?

I try to laugh it off. "This whole scent thing is a real doozy, isn't it?"

"Increasingly so," he says matter-of-factly, still staring at me a little too intensely for comfort.

"At least I smell like you again," I offer.

He surprises me when he steps closer, my body stiffening as he leans in to inhale against my throat. "Yes," he murmurs. "You do now."

"You'd better—" I swallow thickly, my throat feeling suddenly dry. "You'd better go out first," I tell him. "Make sure the coast is clear."

"Okay," he answers softly. "I'll see you later?"

I nod, my lips pressed together as I resist the urge to breathe him in again for fear of what it might do to me. "Yeah. I'll see you."

I don't move as he carefully leaves me alone in the closet, never daring to take a breath until I hear the door quietly latch behind him. The thick aroma of his scent clings to the air, and even a full minute after he's gone, it still makes my knees do the cursed wobbly thing.

It takes me at least three minutes to collect myself and leave the closet, and five more for me to remember that I didn't even ask him about dinner with Gran. However, it only takes me one to decide that I will absolutely not be going to find him again. That feels dangerous to my health right now.

I'll settle for texting him later.

GETTING THROUGH THE rest of my shift proves difficult. Not only because I had to pop an elderly woman's hip back in place after she tripped over her cat (I have never heard a woman curse a feline as much as I did this afternoon), but also because ever since Noah and I left that closet—I can't seem to calm down. My skin is perpetually tingly, and my head feels almost cloudy, like it would rather be somewhere else. It's made it incredibly hard to stay focused. By the last hour of my shift, while I'm carefully tying sutures for the sleeping man who apparently faints at the sight of blood, it is made painfully aware to me that my erratic behavior this afternoon hasn't gone unnoticed.

Liam has been staring at me for the last fifteen minutes while he has assisted me; Liam Avery is something of a friend to me in the ER—having been a big help during my first few months here. I'd been a mess of nerves, having been right out of my residency and in a new place, and he'd always been there to help me get the swing of things. We've always sort of clicked since then. It helps that he's one of the most competent RNs I work with.

"You seem weird," he says finally as he hands me a bit of gauze.

I try to look aloof, but even the feel of the expression on my face feels pained. "I do?"

"Yeah." He adjusts the overhead light so I can see better. "Ever since you came back from lunch."

"Probably just ate something weird," I mutter as I avert my eyes. "Felt a little off."

"Oh."

He's quiet for a moment, and when I peek back up at him, I notice his dark brow is wrinkled in thought, like he's wrestling with something.

I tie off the suture, sighing. "Just spit it out, Li. I can tell you want to say something."

"It's just . . ." He looks sheepish now, running a hand through his dark blond hair. "You came back smelling like Noah."

This takes me by surprise. "What?"

"I mean, I assume that's who it is. I don't actually see Noah enough to know for sure—but it's definitely strong enough to be an alpha."

"Oh, I—" It hadn't even occurred to me how others might be affected by my and Noah's increasingly frequent nuzzlefests. Is it that strong for all the other shifters too? "Yeah, I saw him before I came back from lunch."

"I just worried maybe you had a fight."

I wrinkle my nose. "Why would you think that?"

"I don't know." He shrugs aimlessly. "I mean, we've all heard the stories about Dr. Taylor. It was kind of a shock to find out you two were, you know . . . mated."

I can't pinpoint why, but the obvious incredulity on Liam's face pricks something inside me. It's not full-on annoyance, but it's something incredibly close to it. "We didn't fight," I say tersely. "Pretty much the opposite of that, actually."

I notice Liam's eyebrows shoot up. "Oh. Shit. I'm sorry. I wasn't trying to be a dick. I just . . ." He scratches at the back of his neck. "It's still weird. Getting used to it."

I guess that's fair. As far as my friends here are concerned, the story *is* that I lied to them for a year. I guess it's reasonable to think they would be having a hard time coming to terms with that. Although, Priya hasn't been too weird about it. Then again, I do talk to Liam nearly every day, so maybe that's why he's seemed off this week. Maybe he's feeling awkward that I kept it from him for so long.

"Yeah, about that . . ." I stop what I'm doing, crossing my arms. "I'm sorry I never said anything. I know it's gotta be super weird finding out like everyone did."

"I get it," he offers. "I guess it's just . . . It's hard to picture you with Noah."

I cock my head. "It is?"

"He's just so . . . serious."

Noah's barely-there smile and his quiet laugh crop up then, and despite everything, I find my lips curling slightly. "He's actually not as serious as he likes to pretend. People just aren't his forte."

"So, you're, like, *really* mated?"

I laugh at that. "What is that supposed to mean?"

"I don't know." He throws up his hands. "Jessica from Radiology was telling us in the break room the other day that you might be in some sort of hostage situation."

Fucking *Jessica*.

I roll my eyes. "I am not in a hostage situation. It's all perfectly consensual, I promise."

I can't be sure, but something about the expression on Liam's face looks almost wistful. Is he truly that worried about me?

"I promise," I add, wanting to assure him. "I'm really okay. Great, even. Living the dream, and all that, you know."

"Right," he says with a smile that doesn't reach his eyes. "Well, I'm glad to hear that, at least."

"Seriously, don't worry about me," I say, playfully shoving his arm. "I can take care of myself."

"Yeah." He nods at me, looking a little more himself now. "Yeah, you're right. Sorry. Just worried, you know."

"It's fine." I wave him off, wiping the lingering bit of blood from my now-neat line of stitches. "You can pay me back by taking Mrs. Kowalski's vitals. She's in room 408."

He groans. "She's not here again."

"Absolutely again," I laugh. "She has a 'cough' she's worried about."

"We need to prescribe that woman a friend so she can treat her hypochondria."

"You know," I say seriously, "I think she keeps coming back because she likes you."

"You might be evil incarnate," he huffs.

I make a fist save for my pinkie, bringing the fingernail there to the corner of my mouth and arching my brow. "Dr. *Evil*."

"Nerd," Liam chuffs. "Fine, fine. I'll take care of it."

My smile falters as he gathers up the used gauze to throw away on his way out, chewing at the inside of my lip as I consider the conversation we just had. I surreptitiously press my nose to my shoulder, and sure enough, there is a wave of Noah mixed up with me that washes over my senses, making me dizzy all over again.

"Hey, Li," I call after him.

He turns, eyeing me curiously. "Yeah?"

"Is it really that noticeable? That I was with Noah?"

He frowns. "Pretty sure any shifter would be able to smell you from a mile away."

I'm still thinking about it long after he's left me; I was obviously *aware* that it would be noticeable, what we've been doing—I mean, that's the whole *point*, after all—I just don't think I had actually given it proper thought before now. I feel my cheeks heat as it occurs to me that *everyone* I work with has probably been discussing my supposed sex life with Noah Taylor, and I honestly can't decide what is making me blush harder: the idea of people discussing it or just the actual *idea* of it.

This train of thought can't be good for my health; just the brief fantasy of what Noah might sound like in my bed has me feeling too warm—and I actually reach to give both my cheeks a light slap to snap myself out of it. That's *definitely* a dangerous line of thought. One to be tucked away, I think. I sigh as I get back to work, willing my thoughts to stay in relatively safe territory.

I'm still completely aware I have to ask Noah to dinner. Dinner with my gran. Dinner with my gran who will be smelling Noah all over me and most likely coming to the same conclusions as all my coworkers. Conclusions that involve me spending a considerable amount of time underneath the big, hunky alpha who is probably the hottest person I've ever dated—fake or no.

Fuck.

8

Noah

A WEEK AGO, dinner with Mackenzie's grandmother had been little more than a potential headache. Just something I assumed I would have to get through.

Now the idea of it is fucking terrifying.

I've been trying to pick apart what happened in that supply closet for the last forty-eight hours, something that hasn't gotten any clearer in the time leading up to me picking Mackenzie up for dinner. I am not certain of much about the incident, but of one thing I am absolutely sure.

I almost kissed Mackenzie.

It's unreasonable, and definitely ill-advised, but for one singular moment, there had been no other thoughts in my head outside of the glaring need to feel her mouth on mine. Something about her scent affects me like a drug; not only do I crave more and more of it after each exposure, but I seem to lose all reason when I breathe her in.

I had thought that the distance we've had between the strange moment in my office and now would be enough time to collect myself, but being trapped like this in such a small space with her sweet aroma clouding around me brings back the same foreign urges that had struck me when I'd scented her the day before.

Is it really just because I've forgone suppressants? I mean, since I am altogether *not* as mated as we've led the hospital to believe, it would make sense for me to be distracted by many clashing scents in the hospital, given that there are a good number of female shifters working on my floor, not to mention the building as a whole.

So why is it only Mackenzie who seems to bother me like this?

"—are you even listening to me?"

I blink, remembering where I am, gripping the steering wheel a little tighter and flicking my eyes to the passenger seat, where Mackenzie is looking at me strangely. She's wearing her hair down, the thick mass falling against one shoulder as she cocks her head at me. She's wearing a long-sleeved dress that is slightly formfitting but blessedly nowhere near as much as her yoga clothes—not that it's stopped me from wanting to look. I have definitely tried to make sure to keep my eyes on only the road since she got into the car.

"Sorry," I mutter. "Just nervous."

"Seriously, you don't have to be," she laughs. "I can't even begin to explain to you what a jackpot you are in the eyes of Moira Carter. You actually *could* belong to some secret underground alpha biker gang, and she would tell you she thinks it's absolutely delightful."

"It seems like your grandmother is more concerned with you settling down in general rather than having any real preferences as to who you might do it with."

Mackenzie is still smiling despite my concern. "It's not like that, exactly. I think she worries about leaving me on my own. I was kind of a mess when I came to them—I mean, just your average preteen hormonal depression that made me into a bit of a mute for a few months, but . . . I don't know. Even now that I'm an adult, she never stops worrying about me."

"She wants to make sure you're taken care of," I muse.

"Mhm." Mackenzie makes an amused sound. "Hasn't quite come around to the novel idea that I can take care of myself."

"If anyone could," I murmur to no one.

I don't see her smile, but I can feel it, I think.

"Good thing I'm bringing home a nice alpha to make sure my den is good and protected so that I can give him pretty babies while he gathers food."

"Your gran's ideal ending, I presume."

"Yeah. Whatever. I know she means well."

"I'll be sure to convince her that you will have a very nice den. Only the finest chicken carcasses for my mate."

Mackenzie barks out a laugh. "Oh my God. You made a joke! Was that your first one? Are you hurt in any way?"

"Always a delight, you are."

"Sorry, sorry. It's just kind of fun."

I perk up as I make the next turn. "What is?"

"Seeing this side of Dr. Taylor."

"Oh." There's an odd prickling in my chest, but that could just be her scent, which is still threatening to suffocate me. "Well. I've been practicing how not to be so, um . . ."

"Tense? Scary?"

"Sure," I concur with a roll of my eyes. "For your grandmother."

Mackenzie sits up in her seat, peering out the window as she gestures to the next house. "Well, let's hope it paid off. That's the place."

I slow the car so I don't miss the driveway, taking in the perfectly normal-looking ranch-style house in red brick. It probably shouldn't be as formidable as it feels.

"Oh shit," Mackenzie says.

Her mouth turns down into a frown, and there's an uneasiness to her now as she regards me carefully. I catch her pressing her nose to her shoulder, and then her eyes meet mine with concern. "It's faded."

I can't even pretend not to immediately catch her meaning. I noticed when she first climbed into the car, after all. I swallow heavily. "I know."

I can tell she's remembering the last time I scented her; her lips roll together and her lashes flutter, and even this is enough to make breathing a little harder.

"You should probably do the thing," she says airily.

"The thing," I parrot.

"You know . . ." Her nose wrinkles as she reaches to unbuckle her seat belt. "The *thing*."

Something flushes under my collar, some prickling heat creeping into my chest as my throat tightens. It's becoming a familiar sensation, this odd warmth that plagues me whenever I scent her— becoming more and more of a problem the longer I'm off suppressants. I can't remember a single time in my life when it was this uncomfortable to be around a woman of my species.

"Right," I manage tightly. "The thing." I swallow, eyes glancing to the driveway. "Should I just . . . ?"

"I can—" She moves awkwardly in the passenger seat, bringing her legs up and under her so she can lean over the console. "Like this?"

Like this only brings her closer, my tongue feeling too thick with the way the sweet fragrance of her invades my senses. "Right. That should—" I reach to unbuckle myself. "Just . . . be still."

I'm not sure if I'm telling her this for her benefit or mine, honestly.

I cup my hand around the back of her neck, noting again how soft her hair is. It slides over my knuckles silkily as my palm settles just below her hairline, pulling her closer. I have to close my eyes for this part, silently chanting a mantra about how this is just a means to an end—none of it actually helping the way my skin tingles when I tuck my face against her neck.

It's a necessary thing—my cheek pressing against the soft skin of her throat—but her answering shudder has me squeezing my eyes tighter, clenching my jaw a little more. I turn my face to graze her throat with mine, mingling our scents into a burgeoning aroma that clouds the small space of the car. I can hear her breath quicken and feel her body stiffen everywhere she's touching me, and for the briefest of moments there is a bizarre urge to pull her to me as tightly as I can and bury myself in the smell and taste of her.

Which is utterly insane, and it is this realization that has me hastily pulling away from her.

"That should—" Can she hear how loud my heart is beating? "That should do it, I think."

Her cheeks are flushed as she nods slowly, turning away from me to breathe in against her shoulder again. There is a part of me that protests when she pulls away to settle back into her side of the car, and I shove it down as she nods more confidently.

"That will definitely work," she says, her voice huskier than it was a moment ago.

"Remind me . . ." Honestly, I just need to get my mind somewhere else. "Remind me what the parameters are."

Her eyes are heavy-lidded, almost like she's sated. It shouldn't be enticing. "Parameters?"

"What does your grandmother know about us?"

"Oh." She nods dazedly. "Right. Yeah. Our star-crossed romance?"

"Yes," I answer. "That."

"We've only been dating for a month," she tells me, sobering a little. "You asked me out for coffee in the break room, because you were captivated by my beauty and feminine charms." She notices my eyebrow quirking. "I have an assload of feminine charm, thank you very much."

"Clearly," I answer with only a hint of amusement.

Humor is good. Humor makes me feel less like I want to kiss her.

"We've been on a few dates a week since then," she goes on, ignoring me. "I haven't met your parents yet, but you think I am the bee's knees."

"Excuse me?"

"The tits?"

I frown at her, and she laughs, diffusing the tension even more, thankfully.

"You think I'm great," she clarifies. "I hung the moon. We are deliriously happy. You've never seen a model train in your life."

"What does that have to do with anything?"

She shakes her head. "Never mind. Are you ready for this?"

"I . . ." I take another glance at the very innocent-looking home we're parked in front of. Nothing about it suggests that I have anything to worry about when going inside. "As ready as I'll ever be."

"Good." She gives me an encouraging nod. "Just remember—whatever you do . . . You *absolutely* do not want to see the wedding book."

"The what?"

"Just trust me on this."

She's already getting out of the car before I can press for more details on *that* strange warning, and I realize when her door closes that she's expecting me to follow.

It's just a normal house with normal people, I remind myself. *There's nothing to worry about.*

Even with all my assurances, for some reason I still find myself terrified to go inside.

MOIRA CARTER IS a delightful nightmare. It's really the only way I can describe her.

She's loud, opinionated, caring, funny, and most of all, she is completely obsessed with Mackenzie's well-being. Not that I can label this a flaw, by any means. I doubt anyone would argue that caring too much is a point against a person. I've survived a fierce hug and a warm welcome from this small, graying woman who laughs too loud and talks too much, everything about her the exact opposite of the family gatherings I'm used to. I can't really decide what to make of it, honestly, but I wouldn't say I dislike it.

"So," Moira is saying from across the table as she hands me a bowl of peas. "How long did you have your eye on my Mackenzie?"

I busy myself with scooping more peas than I've ever eaten in one sitting onto my plate, if only to give myself a moment to think. "Oh, I . . . Well. You know. Mackenzie is . . . hard to ignore."

Moira smiles. "Because she's so beautiful, right?"

"Gran," Mackenzie chides. "Can you not?"

"Shush," Moira clucks. "Do you know how long it's been since you brought someone home to meet us?" She pats her husband on the arm, looking put out. "What's it been, Phil? A year? Maybe more?"

Moira's quieter counterpart and Mackenzie's grandfather—an average-sized man in his midseventies who seems content to let his wife do most of the talking—nods absently as he tucks a bite of pot roast into his mouth.

"Been a while," Phil answers gruffly.

"See?" Moira tuts. "You can't just bring someone like Noah home and not expect me to gush. I mean, my goodness. I've never even met an alpha. Have you, Phil?"

Phil shrugs, pushing his mashed potatoes around. "Knew a guy at the auto shop once. Big fella. Could take a tire off in twenty seconds. It was the damnedest thing."

"But Noah is a *doctor*," Moira gushes. "What a match you two make!"

I can almost feel myself blushing, Moira having been praising me for just being . . . *me* since we sat down for dinner.

"Oh, well . . ." I push my fork through my peas distractedly. "It's . . . very nice being with someone so familiar with the field."

From the corner of my eye, I notice Mackenzie smiling. Something tells me that part of her is enjoying my discomfort. I can sense an entire heap of teasing building up in her that she'll be subjecting me to later.

"Not to mention how fortunate it is for you two to find each other," Moira goes on, cutting her roast. "I mean, what are the chances?"

My brow furrows, pausing midbite. "What do you mean?"

"Oh!" Mackenzie's outburst is sudden. "By the way, Gran. I forgot to tell you—Parker is seeing someone new."

"That boy," Moira huffs. "He never tells me anything. Someone from work?"

"No, no," Mackenzie says. "Someone he met at hot yoga."

Moira looks taken aback. "What in the world is that?"

"It's just . . . yoga, but hot. They crank up the heat so you sweat more."

"Is that what you're doing?"

Mackenzie nods, taking a large bite of potatoes. "Mhm." She works down the massive bite. "You sweat like a whore in church, but it's a good workout."

"*Language*, Mackenzie," Moira chides.

Weirdly, I barely even notice her words, too deep in a train of thought that involves a contorted, sweating Mackenzie on a yoga mat.

What on earth is wrong *with me?*

"Well, either way," Moira barrels on. "Good for him. He's such a good boy, Parker."

"Gran, he's creeping up on thirty. I don't know if you can keep referring to him as a 'good boy.'"

"Oh, hush."

I shake away any lingering thought of Mackenzie in her too-tight yoga clothes sweating in a studio somewhere, chalking it up to proximity and the invasive urge that's possessed me lately to kiss her every time she's within three feet of me.

"So Mackenzie tells me the hospital has been making a fuss about your designation?"

I press my lips together, not entirely comfortable with too many people knowing this particular fact, but I suppose I can't fault Mackenzie for sharing it with someone so close to her. She is, after all, *saving my ass*, as she would say.

"Just a bit," I tell her, downplaying it. "I'm hoping it will be resolved soon."

"Bunch of nonsense, if you ask me," Moira huffs. "I mean, my goodness. For us to be judging people based on their identity in this day and age! It isn't as if you can help the way you're born. I mean, it's never been a problem for Mackenzie. You don't see them breathing down her neck about being an omega."

I go still, nearly dropping my fork. Something about the word that seems to ring in the air long after Moira has said it makes every muscle in my body go rigid. I turn my head to meet Mackenzie's gaze, finding an apology in her eyes. I realize this is most likely something I should have already known—so I quickly mask my surprise even with the chant of *omega omega omega* ringing in my hindbrain like some sort of caveman shout that is as irritating as it is unavoidable.

"Of course," I manage tightly, hoping I sound calmer than I feel. "Less stigmas, I guess. You've never heard horror stories about omegas mauling hikers."

But there are plenty of other stories, some carnal part of my brain whispers, a voice that I know doesn't belong to reason but instead to the more basic part of me.

"It's almost like fate that you stumbled across each other," Moira says gleefully. "No other way to explain something so rare!"

"Right," I say with a wooden smile. "Fate."

I feel the brush of Mackenzie's fingers at my knee beneath the table, and can see the concern in her eyes when they meet mine, almost like she's afraid I'm angry. Which I'm not, oddly. Sure, it would have been nice to know before sitting across from my fake girlfriend's grandmother that said fake girlfriend is the biological counterpart to all that I am; maybe I might have switched to a less potent suppressant rather than staving off them entirely if I'd known that being around Mackenzie unsuppressed might slowly drive me crazy. At least the strange things I've been experiencing have a valid explanation, at the very least.

Mostly, I'm finding it hard to be angry about any of this when the alpha in me is already weaving daydreams about impossible, crude things that would most likely have Mackenzie throwing a punch. Hell, I'm considering throwing myself one just to knock some sense back into me.

I keep my expression even for the remainder of dinner—smiling when needed and answering as calmly as I can—all the while feeling a simmering *something* building in my belly that begs to be addressed.

Strangely, Mackenzie's fingers remain lightly against my knee for the remainder of dinner.

———

"NOW, YOU TWO make room for dessert," Moira calls from the kitchen. "After pie, I can show you my book!"

Mackenzie groans as she leads my still-tense figure from the kitchen to the living room and out the patio doors that open to a wooden deck connecting to the backyard—dragging me into the dark space that is only lit by the moonlight that spills over the grass and down the steps leading away from the deck.

"Listen," she starts. "Don't be mad."

"Mad," I echo.

"I know I should have said something before," she says in a rush. "It's not like I was *hiding* it from you, exactly, it's just . . ."

I'm genuinely curious as to her reasoning for keeping something so important from me, so I only continue to look at her expectantly in lieu of answering.

Mackenzie sighs. "Look, I know all the dumb stories about alphas and omegas and *fated pairs* and all that bullshit—and I just didn't want you to go all crazy on me if you found out. We have a good thing going here. I don't want to change that."

"You realize that by not telling me, you were putting us both at risk for some sort of misstep we can't take back."

"Don't tell me you believe in all that garbage about us affecting each other more," she scoffs. "It's all a bunch of nonsense."

"Is it?" I swallow thickly. "It's been quite a while since I was off my suppressants, but I can never remember being this . . . affected by someone's nearness."

This takes her by surprise. Almost as much as it does me for saying it. "You're . . . affected by me?"

"I only mean that it's . . . difficult. Scenting you. More than it was before. Knowing what I do now, I have to assume it will only get worse as time goes on."

"Oh."

"You really haven't noticed?"

Her nose wrinkles. I've decided it isn't annoying.

"I mean . . ." She reaches to rub at her neck. It makes her scent bloom in the air. It's extremely distracting. "I thought it was . . . I don't know. You're already a lot, Noah. I guess I just assumed that was all you."

"I'm a lot," I repeat dumbly, not quite sure of her meaning.

"I just mean . . . you already smelled good *before* you stopped your suppressants. I just thought you were . . . a lot."

She says the phrase again like it makes total sense, but I'm still not sure it does.

"So what do we do about this?"

She is quiet for a long moment, her eyes calculating as she considers. It's reminiscent of that look she gave me on the dance floor at the bar—like she's trying to figure out some puzzle in her head. I can see when she comes to a decision, throwing me for a loop when she actually *smiles*.

"Why do we have to do anything about it?"

"What?" I make an exasperated sound. "Mackenzie. I can't continue to be close to you without being on some form of suppressants."

"Why not?"

"You *know* why," I huff. "Eventually, being around each other is going to drive us crazy. We won't be able to interact at all without feeling the need to—" I catch the way her eyes widen, and I clear my throat. "It's a terrible idea." I reach to pinch the bridge of my nose, sighing. "Maybe this entire thing was."

"What?" Her tone turns desperate. "It's seriously not as big of a deal as you're making it, Noah."

"You're being reckless," I accuse. "I'm thinking of you here. I wouldn't ever want to put you in a position that you might regret."

"I'm a big girl, Noah," she grumbles, crossing her arms as she looks at the ground. "I know what I can handle."

I feel my frustration building, her flippancy only making it worse. "I don't think *I* can handle it, Mackenzie."

She peeks up at me with a confused expression, moonlight painting one side of her face and making the amber in her eyes seem to glow. "What?"

"It's getting . . . *very* difficult," I admit quietly. "To scent you. To not be affected by it."

Her mouth parts, then slowly closes again. "Oh."

"Which is why I don't think it's a good idea to—"

"Mackenzie? Noah?" Moira's voice rings out from inside the house, startling us both. "I got the book out. I'd love to show Noah some of my ideas."

"Oh my God," Mackenzie groans. "Not the fucking wedding book."

"What *is* it about this book?"

"She's coming outside," Mackenzie says with a panicked voice. "Jesus. She's got this damned book where she's planned out my *entire* wedding, Noah."

"You're kidding."

"Mackenzie?" Moira's voice is getting nearer. I can tell through the slight crack in the patio door that she's entered the living room. "Are you out there?"

"You have to kiss me," Mackenzie says suddenly.

This throws me off. "What?"

"Kiss me," she repeats. "Right now. It'll make her leave us alone."

"I don't think it's a good idea for me to—"

"If you don't kiss me, she's going to have us combing through that book *all* night."

My eyes dart to the patio door, where a very Moira-like shadow is nearing the glass. "I don't want you to have to—"

"Just shut up and *kiss* me."

I feel her hands at my collar just before she tugs me down to her mouth—her lips colliding with mine only moments before I hear the creaking sound of the glass door sliding in the track behind me. I hear a distant *oh* followed by a soft chuckle, but even when the door quietly slides closed it feels like a faraway thing, because suddenly . . . all I can seem to focus on is Mackenzie's mouth.

I'm fully aware of the biological happenings that come with being so intimate with a female shifter—but Mackenzie's lips on mine feel much less textbook than I'd believed it could be up until this point. The soft shape of them melds against me as her fingers fist the collar of my shirt, and beyond all reason, I can feel the barely-there slide of her tongue over my lower lip, which makes me groan in a way that feels far from pretend.

I can't fathom what drives me to open my mouth any more than I can guess at why her tongue tangles with mine, but as her flavor explodes there, making me dizzy, I can't really contemplate anything more than the way my hand fits against her spine when it finds a place to rest there. Does she even realize what she's doing?

Fuck, do *I*?

Something in the back of my head tells me I should put a stop to this, that I should pull away from her before things get complicated—but that voice is viscerally silenced by the soft sound that emits from Mackenzie's throat, one that I all but swallow down as my fingers find their way into her hair. I am a mess of scent and touch and sensation as her body presses closer to mine, and I am fully aware of the way I'm getting hard against her stomach—I just can't seem to do anything about it.

I can't say how many seconds it takes to break away from her—to untangle myself from her soft body and her softer mouth—but when I'm finally able to, I find her breath as ragged as mine, and her lips as red and as swollen as my own must surely be.

Her lashes flutter dazedly as the tip of her tongue swipes at her lower lip, and I feel a carnal need to pull that same tongue back into my mouth, to kiss her until the sun comes up, maybe. I'm not sure.

I'm very careful, as I peel myself away—trying to steady my breathing even as all of my senses scream at me to get closer to her.

"This is—" I have to clear my throat, my voice sounding all wrong. "This is what I mean," I warn roughly. "We won't be able to control things like this. If we keep this up."

Mackenzie is still looking at me, her eyes moving over my face in a lazy but calculated way, as if she's considering the pieces of a puzzle. I watch her tongue trace her lip again, and I'm pretty sure if she does it one more time, I will go insane.

"Say something," I urge. "Help me figure this out. I could get back on my suppressants, or maybe . . . Maybe we should call the whole thing—"

"What if we just . . . do it?"

I freeze, staring at her. Surely she said something different than what I heard. "What?"

"We could just . . . try it out," she goes on. "See what all the fuss is about."

"You can't be serious," I say incredulously.

"Why not?" Her eyes look less glazed now, sharper, like she's really thinking about this. "I mean, it's not like it has to be a big thing," she reasons. "We're already pretending to date. Why not enjoy it a little?"

"I can think of a dozen reasons as to why that's a bad idea."

"I can think of one reason why it's a very good idea," she counters, nodding at my still-tented pants. "I mean, it doesn't seem like you're *too* opposed to it."

I press my palm against the stiff front of my dark jeans, immediately regretting my actions when it makes my traitorous cock throb. I hiss through my teeth, closing my eyes. "Mackenzie . . ."

"Seriously, what's the harm? It sounds like neither of us have had much luck in the dating department lately. I mean, if we had, we wouldn't be in this situation in the first place. Plus, you're leaving soon! It seems like a win-win to me."

"It sounds like a very good way to make things complicated."

"I'm not going to go all dickmatized on you," she snorts, barreling on before I even have a chance to process that phrase. "It's just sex. No need to make a big thing of it."

I stare at her openmouthed, this turn of events nothing like what I could have ever expected when she got into my car a few hours ago. I can honestly say I've never been propositioned for sex like some sort of business deal. The entire thing is . . . bizarre.

But not enough to make it easy to turn down.

I meant it when I said there were a dozen reasons why it's a bad idea—so why in the world have I not definitively said no yet? Why am I standing here considering what she's saying, trying to make it seem reasonable in my head? Is it just hormones, or is it . . . something else?

"Dessert is ready," I hear Moira call from the other side of the patio door, making me jolt as I'm realizing I'm still hard on Mackenzie's grandmother's deck. I hear another soft giggle. "Whenever you two are done."

I close my eyes in embarrassment. I don't think I acted this way even when I was a teenager. I take a deep breath to steady myself, and when I open my eyes again, I'm startled by the sight of Mackenzie right next to me, her hand reaching to gently press at my shoulder as she peers up at me in the half dark.

"We'll talk about it after," she says, her voice low and her eyes full of promise. Her fingers slide down my bicep to trace one of the lines in my sleeve, and the sudden burst of her scent threatens to knock me on my ass. "Just . . . think it over. Okay?"

I have to remain outside for several more seconds before I can will the most traitorous part of me to calm down—Mackenzie's wild proposition bouncing around in my head in tandem with all the reasons why I should turn her down.

And I will. Turn her down. I absolutely will. It's a terrible idea. Horrible, really. There are a million things that could go wrong. I *will* turn her down.

At least . . . that's what I'm telling myself.

9

Mackenzie

NOAH HASN'T SAID a word since we left Gran's, and I can't tell if it's because he's embarrassed by my proposition or because he's actually considering it. In my head, it had seemed like a perfectly reasonable and logical thing to propose—or at least, it had seemed that way in the afterglow of that kiss. Because it was . . . a *hell* of a kiss.

I'm not stupid. I know a lot of what I felt out there on Gran's deck was just hormones and biology and compatibility—but that doesn't change the fact that it felt *really* good. Noah's kiss had been rough and messy and a little bit desperate (but that might have been me, who can say), but not once in my life have I been so turned on by just a kiss, and it makes me wonder how good everything *else* might feel with Noah Taylor. Plus, I'm honestly getting a little tired of being revved up in offices and closets and having to brush it off for no real reason.

I mean, when will we ever get a chance like this again? If biology is going to dictate how compatible we might be in bed to-gether, why not enjoy the benefits? We're medical professionals, after all. It can be like . . . an experiment of sorts. Plus, it's not like

I've had a lot of luck in the phallic department, since every date I've been on in months has been an utter disaster.

He's still quiet when we pull up to my apartment building, and I linger in the passenger seat for a second too long as I try to think of what I should do here. I've never had to *convince* anyone to sleep with me before, and I'm not even sure if I should. Is this somehow beneath me? Or am I *more* empowered by trying to take the bull by the horns, as it were. Honestly, I'm too horny to care.

"Do you want to come up for a drink?"

There. Simple. Easy. Only slightly suggestive.

Noah frowns. It really is a sexy frown, I've decided. "Are you asking me for a drink, or something else?"

"Both? Maybe?"

"Mackenzie . . ." He pulls his hands from the steering wheel to pinch the bridge of his nose. "I'm really not sure that's a good idea."

"Why not?"

"Because we have an arrangement, and sex was not part of the deal. It could make things very complicated."

"Think of it as a perk." I snap my fingers. "Oh! An addendum! Contracts have those all the time."

"I'm not sure any contract has ever had a sex addendum."

"Ours could," I venture.

He looks at me with an odd expression then, his brow furrowing. "I'm still confused as to why you would *want* to."

"What do you mean?"

"I mean, well. You're . . . And I'm . . ." He sighs. "I just feel like you could easily find another partner who would be a lot less . . ." He waves his hand as if searching for a word, huffing out a breath when he decides on, "Me."

"What's wrong with you? You're tall and pretty—" Noah looks

stunned by this. "When you're not scowling, that is. Or, actually, sometimes when you are? It's kind of growing on me. Plus, you're built like a brick shithouse. I don't really see any downsides for me."

"Gee, thanks."

"Also, you're the first alpha I've met. Like, ever. At those odds, I'll be in my fifties before I meet another one. I could be postmenopausal by then. Would I even enjoy it?"

"So this is an alpha thing?"

"I would be lying if I said that it's not a little bit of an alpha thing," I tell him truthfully. "But also, scowling aside, you're the most normal person I've dated all year, fake or not. I'm going to get carpal tunnel if I don't give my poor hands a break."

Noah's eyes go wide. "That's very . . . forthcoming."

I reason that it's not a good idea to make a coming joke right now. It'll probably spook him.

"Come on. We're obviously compatible. I mean, you begrudgingly think my jokes are funny, and I've come to find your perpetual grumpiness kind of cute. It's like someone dropped a sex gift basket in our laps. It would be rude not to open it."

"I don't know if I take more issue with 'sex gift basket' or you calling me cute."

"I said your *grumpiness* was cute. Kind of." I can tell he's still wavering. "I mean, aren't you curious? Don't you want to see what all the fuss is about?"

"I . . ." He still looks unsure. Like there's a chance this might all be a trap. "I don't want to take advantage of you."

"Oh, spare me," I laugh. "I promise you, Noah. I'm not reading anything into this. You can come up to my apartment and have sex with me and nothing will change. Scout's honor."

"And you're . . . sure you want to?"

"Okay. This is starting to make me seem borderline desperate, so I'm just gonna ask one more time if you want to come up for a drink, and if you say no, we'll forget this ever happened. But if you say *yes* . . . No more worrying about my delicate sensibilities. I'm a grown-ass woman, Noah, and I know what I want."

The change in Noah is subtle, so much that one might miss it, but there is less tension in his shoulders now, less uncertainty in his eyes. I take it as a good sign.

"So, Noah," I start again carefully as I give him a sweet smile. "Do you want to come up for a drink?"

———

HE'S STILL ACTING like he might bolt at any second. Like he's arguing with himself in his head about all the reasons why he shouldn't be here. He's sitting stiffly on my couch like one of those bronzed park bench statues—frowning at my carpet in a way that lets me know he is completely in his own head right now.

I study him from the kitchen counter as I pour him a glass of wine, letting myself drink him in. He really is . . . something. Now that I'm actually assessing. I'm honestly not sure how I haven't given him proper notice before all this, regardless of his formerly sour attitude. Which, I really have begun to realize, is just a weird part of his charm. His dark hair has started to curl at his temples, a product of his fingers running through it nervously one too many times, and his full mouth is pressed almost into a pout-like shape with how hard he's thinking. When I gather up our glasses to join him on the couch, I take note of the width of his forearms, completely visible with the rolled-up sleeves of his button-down. Just looking at them sparks memories of being wrapped up in them only a few hours ago, which has me pressing my thighs together.

Take the bull by the horns, Mack.

I hand him a glass, and he looks almost surprised to see it, then he notices me settling on the other side of the couch. "So, you really meant a drink?"

"It feels like you could use it. You look like you're about to jump out of my window." I chuckle as I take a sip from my glass. "If I didn't know nerves were to blame, I might be offended."

He looks confused, his hand stilling just before his glass touches his lips. "Offended?"

"Well . . ." I swirl the dark red liquid of the rioja as I avert my eyes, peering into my wineglass. "I've never had to talk someone into sleeping with me before. Not exactly great for my ego."

"It's not—" He makes a disgruntled sound, taking a sudden swig from his glass and swallowing it forcefully before shaking his head. "It's not because I don't want to."

I turn more to my side to face him, leaning on my elbow as I let it rest against the back of the couch. "Could have fooled me."

"I think we both know by the state you left me in on that deck that I very much want to," he says more quietly. He takes another swig, for courage, maybe. "I worry."

I frown. "Worry?"

"I know you're a grown woman, I know that, but . . . neither of us fully understands the implications of what we're doing here. We haven't ever experienced . . . something like this."

My mouth makes an O shape. "So, you've never . . . ?"

"No." He shakes his head. "I've never met anyone like you."

I let that knowledge settle, considering all the things that come with it as I take a larger sip from my glass this time. Everything he's saying makes sense, and there is a part of me that wonders if I *am* being reckless. No one's ever accused me of being overly careful in my life, that's for sure, but still . . . I can't bring myself to change my mind. Not after the all-over pleasure I'd felt just from *kissing* him. A girl can only withstand so much, really.

"Your apartment is nice," Noah says in what I suspect is an attempt to break the silence. "Cozy."

"You mean it's small," I laugh.

He glances around my studio, his eyes moving from the kitchen behind the couch to the bed that sits on a platform to our left. "No, no, I just meant . . ."

"It's fine," I assure him. "I've never liked big houses." I frown into my glass then. "Too much space."

"What's wrong with space?"

A familiar melancholy settles in the back of my mind, a brief glimpse of my dad's face leaving our house for the last time flashing through my thoughts. I quickly shake it away as I take another swallow of wine. "Just feels lonely, I guess."

"Oh."

More silence. Noah isn't looking at me, eyes transfixed on my carpet again as he holds his glass against his chest like some sort of tiny security blanket. My glass is nearly empty now, I realize, and the warmth the wine leaves in my belly is giving me that same courage Noah might have been chasing.

"So, if you've never been with an omega," I try carefully, watching his jaw tense, "does that mean you've never knotted anyone?"

His knuckles go white against the wineglass in his hand, and for a moment I think he could almost break it in his grip. It's subtle, the change in him, but with that one word I can sense the slight increase of his breathing, the ragged quality of it. It makes my heart pound a little faster, sets off a tingling between my legs.

And his *scent.*

It might as well be a wax melt, with the way it's filling the room.

"No," he says quietly, almost hoarsely. "I haven't."

I finish my glass with one quick tilt—reaching to set it on my coffee table as I slowly scoot closer to him. I can feel the warmth of him when my body presses to his side, feel the slight trembling in his skin when my fingers graze over his forearm. It makes me feel strangely powerful, knowing I can make this big alpha shake like this. I pluck his glass away to set it by mine, bringing my hand to his chest to tease at a button there, my mouth inches from his jaw.

"Would you like to?"

This close I can see the subtle flecks of green hidden in the clear blue of his irises, the discovery short-lived with the way his pupils continue to dilate to a point where his eyes almost appear black. His heart is pounding so hard I can feel it against my fingers, and at this point, its cadence more than matches mine.

I like the way that his breath catches when I lean into him, the way his hand settles at my waist as if by instinct (and well, I guess it is, if I took the time to really think about it) when I situate myself so that my knees press on either side of his hips, straddling his lap. Already I can feel the press of a hard *something* against my core when I settle there, and I find I like this too.

"Mackenzie," he says roughly, his voice seeming to have dropped an octave. "Are you sure that you want to—?"

I catch the rest of his sentence at my lips, kissing him gently as his continued attempts to be chivalrous fade into a soft groan. He really does talk too much, for someone whose preferred form of communication I'd previously thought was scowling. On any other day, I might celebrate a man being so decent—but it's been at least a year since I've been past second base, and right now I am wanting Noah to be entirely *indecent*.

There's a bit of a bite of his nails as they press into the softness of my hips, a slight sting that I can feel even through the material of my dress. His lips part immediately when I urge them to with my tongue, and the taste of him when I deepen the kiss might be more dizzying than an entire bottle of the forgotten wine on my kitchen counter.

I don't mean to rock into him; my body seems to have some sort of unconscious need to be closer, but the feel of his cock slotted against me, rigid and hot, seems to undo him. I feel his fingers in my hair, winding around the length of it to fist it tight so that he can pull me in, and then there is the shape of one large hand on my ass that grips me in a way that is anything but decent.

Yes, I think. *This is what I want.*

I'm not sure if he actually recognizes that I'm undoing the buttons of his shirt; I guess I would have trouble being overly aware of my surroundings, too, if I was kissing someone senseless like he is—but when my fingers slide across bare chest and press higher over his shoulders, I feel him shudder against me, a pained sound in his throat.

"Bed," he grinds out, his mouth hardly breaking from mine.

Not much of a question, but the meaning is all too clear. "Yes."

"Condom," he grunts. "I don't—"

"IUD," I urge breathlessly. "And hell, you might know my gyno. She works on the second floor. So as long as you're negative, we can—"

I yelp with surprise when he lifts me from the couch in one smooth motion, hands gripping the backs of my thighs as he takes me to bed.

I guess that answers that.

My back hits the mattress when he practically throws me into the middle of it—the earlier hesitancy Noah had shown nowhere to be found as he crawls up and over me lightning fast as if he can't stand to be away from my mouth, his lips finding mine greedily.

"You smell"—I feel his breath huff against my cheek—"fucking *incredible*."

I'd like to tell him he smells pretty good, too, but his tongue at my throat makes me forget the desire altogether.

"You taste even better," he growls against my pulse, his voice sounding unlike him.

His hips roll into me, and I can feel his cock straining in his jeans where it rubs against my thigh. There is a mess between my legs already, my body seeming to know more about Noah's alpha than I do, if the slick there is any indication. I can't actually remember any time before this when I've ever been as wet as I am now. Then again, it's hard to remember much outside of the way Noah is continuing to suck at my pulse.

"Noah," I gasp, tilting up my hips in a silent plea. "Will it hurt?"

"I won't hurt you," he says in a more soothing tone, a whisper on my skin. "Not you." His teeth nip at my shoulder, and I can feel his fingers tucking under my dress to slide over my thigh. "Because you're a good omega, aren't you?" My breath catches when I feel him pressing against my underwear, teasing the wet slit beneath them. "You can take it, can't you?"

I feel a shiver pass through me, his crooning words speaking to some part of me that feels almost tight with disuse. Like I've never actually touched it before. I feel some sensation like a stretch inside me, like waking up from a very long nap—an all-over pleasure from his praise that I've never felt.

And maybe that's biology, too, most likely is, actually . . . but I'm too far gone now to care.

"I can," I promise. "I can take it."

I whimper in protest when he pulls away from me—pushing up on his hands to look down at me with glazed eyes. I notice they're a dark, stormy blue now that is nothing like their usual clear color, and Noah's lips are parted as shallow breath escapes between them.

"I don't—" His jaw clenches. "I don't feel like myself." His eyes rake down the front of me with something that only can be described as *hunger*. "Maybe we shouldn't—"

Something inside begins to whine, a steady chant of *no no no* in the back of my head as panic seeps into me at the idea of losing whatever he's about to give me. Suddenly, the idea of Noah not touching me feels almost *painful*.

"Don't stop," I manage, tugging at his shirt with too much force until I hear the last remaining buttons tear away. "Please?"

There's a rumble in his chest when my hand finds the front of his jeans, palming him through the denim. "Mackenzie," he warns, "I'm having a hard time being gentle with you. I don't—" He groans as I squeeze him through his pants. "I don't know what's wrong with me. The way you *smell* right now. It's driving me insane."

I lean up on my elbows, turning up my face until I can flick my tongue against his throat, where I know he's sensitive, where his scent is strong. "Then be rough," I purr. "You can be rough with me." The word is on my tongue, one I've never used before but that somehow feels *exactly* right at this moment. I reach to pop open the button on his jeans, pulling at the denim until I can reach inside to feel the shape of him through the cotton beneath. "I *want* you, Alpha."

"*Fuck.*"

His mouth is on my skin—lips and teeth tasting every inch he can reach as his hands tug at the hem of my dress. I'm not sure it will survive the night, with the way he's wrenching it up my body, but I can't find it in me to care when I feel the heat of his wide palms on my bare skin. I lift my arms so he can tear the dress off, and he tosses it somewhere on the floor before sitting up and wrenching off his own shirt to add it to the pile.

Every inch of Noah seems to have been carved or manufactured, my eyes greedily drinking in every ridge and line of him as the urge to touch and taste threatens to consume me. I notice him working on his zipper next, and I curl my body to bat his hands away so I can do it myself. Even through his underwear the shape of him is daunting—the fabric stretched and straining as the thick length of him presses against it. My hands still at his thighs, fingers curled into the waistband of his jeans as I'm momentarily struck with just how *much* he is.

He's always been larger than life, even when I barely knew him, but looking at him like this—with his impossibly wide shoulders and his too-thick arms and his cock that looks like it might be a health hazard—now I'm finding it hard to believe that he was able to hide his alpha status for so long. Everything about him *screams* it.

I tug his jeans a little farther down his thighs. "Did you know we learned alpha anatomy in med school?"

"Mm." His lips press together as he watches me shuck down his pants. "I did."

I let my nails scrape lightly up his thick thighs when his jeans become trapped at his knees, which are pressed against the mattress, allowing me to feel him shiver. "Did you learn about me?"

"I—" His lashes flutter as my fingers tease at the waistband of his boxer briefs. "I—we did."

"So, we both know how this works. Technically."

"Mackenzie," he huffs as I peel the fabric away, the flushed head of his cock slipping out and glistening at the tip. "I can smell you. Jesus, Mackenzie, you're so *wet*."

His voice is further away now, my attention solely on the heat of him in my hand as I pull him free from his underwear. There's a little curiosity and a *lot* of want when I see what all the fuss is about—the velvety skin of his cock sliding under my hand as I stroke down the length of him to meet the slightly thicker skin at the base. It's only a hint, only a slight premonition of what it could be, I think, but even like this, seeing his knot sets off a fresh trickling of slick between my legs as if my body has a mind of its own. Like it *knows* what Noah can give me.

And I want it, I'm realizing more than anything else.

I want everything.

I meet his eyes when I lean in, peeking up at him through my lashes when I let the tip of my tongue flick over the head of his cock, and the answering rush of air that escapes him, like he can barely stand to keep still—it's enough to make anyone feel a little hedonistic. I swirl my tongue there, the taste of him somehow *better* than the all-encompassing scent of him that has somehow grown sweeter, more irresistible, and all I can think about as he looks at me like he can't decide what to do with me for the want of needing all of me at once is: *This was definitely worth all the fuss.*

My teasing is short-lived, his thick fingers grazing my jaw to tangle in my hair so that he can tilt my head back and pull me up into his kiss as he comes crashing down to meet me. I can't for the life of me say how he gets my bra off—I actually think it might be in two pieces now, not that I'm complaining—but by the time I'm naked beneath him, I realize that somehow he is nothing but heat and hard muscle against me, not a stitch left between us as he settles over my body.

His hips rut against me like he can't help it, his teeth and tongue still tasting at my mouth and lower at my throat and back again. I feel his breath in my ear when his big body forces my legs to spread wider, his voice low and gravelly when his cock slides against the core of me.

"Tell me again," he urges, one hand at my jaw as the other pins my hip to the bed, to restrain me or him, I can't say. "Tell me you want this."

"Please," I hear myself crying, my voice nothing like it's ever been. I'm practically *begging*. Have I ever begged before? Why don't I *mind*? "I want this. So can you just—*ah*."

Even with the steady stream of slick I might be embarrassed about at any other time—it's a stretch. I close my eyes so that I can focus on the delicious friction of it, so I can feel every inch of him as he slowly presses inside me. I gasp when I feel the slightly thicker base slip through, leaving all of him rooted deep as we both struggle to catch our breath just from this.

Even with the bad dates and the busy year and the model trains—I am no stranger to sex. I'm a modern woman who is perfectly fine seeking out what her body craves with whoever she chooses, but *this*—I don't think it's ever been like this. It's not just the pleasure of it, because there is a lot of that, but it's also the strange sensation of Noah *fitting*. In more ways than just this. It's the odd feeling of being filled for maybe the first time.

And if that's all from hormones, then they are some *strong* fucking hormones.

"Mackenzie, I—" His head buries against my throat as his hips flex minutely. "I could fucking come like this. *Fuck*, it feels good inside you."

"You can move," I tell him breathlessly. "Can you move? I want to—*oh*."

The first slide takes my breath away, my toes curling as he draws back, only to push inside once more. Again I feel the ever-so-slight resistance that comes from his knot, and I am torn between worry about what it will be like when it swells and utter impatience to have just that. I *want* to feel full of him, more than anything I've ever wanted, for reasons I can't even begin to comprehend. My knees press at his hips, shifting so that I can take more.

"Mackenzie," he half whines. "I don't think—*fucking hell*. I am not going to last. It's too good. Tell me what to do. Tell me how to make you feel good."

I want to tell him that I already feel pretty damn amazing, but I can't seem to remember how to make words right now. I pull his face down to mine to kiss him instead, enjoying the feeling of his tongue tangling with mine as he thrusts inside me just a little harder. He catches my groan against his tongue as I wrap my legs fully around his waist—urging him to keep going. He holds on to my waist with one hand as he pumps inside me, each stroke making his knot swell just a little more, making it that much tighter as he forces it back inside again and again.

And my body . . . my body seems to know exactly what to do. That thickness touches me in places I didn't know existed, stroking some part of me that leaves me a mewling mess beneath him.

"You can come," I tell him. "I want you to."

"But—I need to—"

"Just come," I urge. "I want your knot. Wanna feel it. *Please*, Noah."

God, I don't think I've ever wanted anything more.

"I'm—" His forehead rests on mine as his lips brush aimlessly against my mouth. "I can't—I'm going to—"

Someone shouts, and I honestly can't say if it's him or me, but my eyes squeeze shut as stars explode in my vision when I feel his body tense, feel his cock twitch deep inside me right as his knot begins to swell and *swell*. It expands until I think it can't possibly be thicker, locking him inside me as he shudders through his orgasm. I can't exactly say what I just felt, but it was . . . definitely something.

"You didn't come," he pants, sounding frustrated.

I kiss his cheek. "Honestly, it still felt incredible."

"You're going to come," he growls, already moving to a more upright position as he holds me by the waist.

The movement tugs at his knot that is rooted inside, drawing a gasp from me. I have to reach above me to grab for the pillows, needing anything in my hands to steady myself as he lifts my ass to pull me flush against him as my legs fall on either side of him. He's biting his lip with concentration as sweat beads at his forehead, and I can tell that every time he moves—it's just as torturous for him as it is for me.

His thumb slides across my swollen clit as sparks dance over my skin—my head falling back and my lips parting as he rolls the sensitive bundle beneath his fingers.

"*Noah.*"

"You're going to come for me," he tells me again. "You're going to come on my knot. I *need* you to, Mackenzie."

I nod dazedly as my teeth press into my lower lip, hearing needy sounds in the air that I suspect are coming from me. His touch paired with the fullness inside me is almost too much to take, my skin feeling like a live wire as he circles the slick-drenched bud of my clit again and again and *again*. I can already feel a pressure building deep in my belly, the muscles there tightening and forcing my insides to clamp down even harder on what is an already incredibly tight space.

Every swipe of his fingers has me clenching around his knot, and each occurrence has Noah hissing through his teeth. I'm aware distantly that he's just watching me come undone beneath him, but considering everything that's happened tonight, I can't find it in me to be embarrassed. I hear his quiet little urges and his rasped praise in the air around us—murmured utterances of *so good* and *look at you* and *that's it* ringing in my ears even as he says them quietly.

"Keep touching me," I beg. "Just like that. *Right there.*"

"You're getting tighter," he grinds out. "I'm going to fucking come. *Again.*"

"Don't stop," I breathe. "Just keep—*fuck.*"

Every muscle in my body draws up tight like a bowstring right before I dissolve into a trembling mess, my thighs quivering and my insides trembling even more as a wordless cry escapes me. Even after, I can feel the slow circling of Noah's thumb on my too-sensitive clit, and I only open my eyes when I feel his hand leave me, watching as he brings that same digit to his mouth to clean it with his tongue. Watching his eyes nearly roll back as he does it.

I open my arms in quiet invitation, and it takes no convincing for Noah to fall into me, pulling me against his chest as my thigh settles over his, feeling boneless and sated even as his knot still pulses dully inside me. Neither of us speaks at first, the sound of our breath mingling in the air as we both attempt to catch it. His eyes are on me when I finally peer up at him—holding that same wild look that had crept into them when he'd kissed me on my couch and every moment after.

"That was . . ." I clear my throat. "Something."

"Something," he echoes dazedly. "Yeah."

The mood feels heavy now that it's all over, and since I am literally stuck with Noah for the unseeable future, I try to lighten it. "See? Sex addenda are great."

"Right," he says, still looking out of sorts. "And we're . . . okay?"

Oh. That's what he's worried about. I laugh softly, turning up my face to kiss his cheek.

"Don't worry," I assure him. "I won't be asking you to bite me anytime soon."

"Okay," he says evenly, his brow still furrowed. Maybe he's not convinced I won't mate him against his will. "Right."

I laugh at the thought, nuzzling his chest and smiling at the absurdity of it. I mean, it was just sex, after all. "Go to sleep, Dr. Taylor," I tease. "You have a morning shift tomorrow."

I feel a barely-there kiss at my hair paired with his quiet agreement, and I close my eyes as fatigue seeps in, lulled by the satisfied quality of my limbs and the pleasant throbbing of his knot still inside me, the fullness eliciting a faint pleasurable sensation, even now.

I smile again as I yawn, thinking once more how silly it is that so many people might lose their minds after getting a taste of something like this. Sure, it was mind-blowing, but turning your whole world upside down for a great lay? Utterly ridiculous.

I feel his knot pulse slightly, sending a shiver down my spine as I squeeze my eyes shut, focusing instead on the steady *thump* of Noah's heart against my ear as I will myself to sleep, to not let things get weird.

Still, I think absently as I start to drift. *A girl could definitely get used to this.*

10

Noah

IT TAKES ME a moment upon waking to remember where I am.

The sheets are brighter than mine—soft, lavender linens beneath a plush, plum comforter. I don't immediately open my eyes; the events of last night and every moment of what Mackenzie and I have done plays in full HD behind my eyelids, and every worry and cause for hesitation that I'd thrown out the window when she'd kissed me comes rushing back with the clarity that morning brings. Despite the admittedly incredible night I had, I can't help but worry about how complicated things will be now.

I open my eyes slowly, warily, reaching to my left until my hands meet cold sheets. I blink up at the ceiling in surprise for a moment before lifting my head to find the bed empty. I sit up slowly to glance around Mackenzie's tiny studio, seeing no trace of her in the living room or the kitchen and realizing I'm alone.

What the hell?

Swinging my legs over the side of the bed, my feet hit the wood floor briefly as I bend to snatch up my pants and fish out my forgotten phone from the pocket. I still have an hour until my shift starts, which is plenty of time, really, but it's unlike me to sleep in this much. Honestly, I can't think of a single time in my life when I slept as well as I did last night, and I can't pretend that my restful night isn't one hundred percent because of the brazen omega whose mouth I can still taste and whose body I can almost feel still pressed against me.

My entire adult life I have given little thought to the more explicit bits of my biological makeup—I mean, it's hard to miss the idea of knotting when it can only be done with some near-mythical counterpart. One I have near zero chances of meeting, anyway. I assumed it was all just some hormonal nonsense that was made to sound much better than it actually was, probably.

That is . . . until Mackenzie Carter fell into my lap. Literally. Fuck. I can *still* feel her when I close my eyes, still hear the soft sounds she'd made when I'd buried myself inside her. I can honestly say that there is *nothing* in my life that can compare to it.

And I think it's exactly that fact that has me so concerned.

There's no chance that we can carry on our simple agreement after a night like that. It seems impossible to me that we could spend time together ever again without feeling some urge to succumb to our baser selves now that we've both had a taste for it, and won't that make everything we're trying to accomplish that much harder? I can barely even *think* right now without flashes of a soft, naked Mackenzie panting beneath me, her scent haunting me even now.

Surely she must be in a similar predicament. That has to be why she's made herself scarce before I could even wake up. She must be out of her mind worrying that I'll get caught up in some primal alpha ridiculousness, that I'll start stalking her in hallways asking her to take my last name or something. Christ. She's probably going to call the whole thing off. She's going to delete my number and pretend we never met. She's going to—

"Morning," the omega in question calls brightly from the other side of her bedroom, stepping out of a door I hadn't noticed before with a towel wrapped around her hair. "Thought you were going to sleep all day. I was wondering how many heart attacks you would cause and then have to fix when you showed up late for the first time ever."

"I—" I can feel my mouth opening and closing like a goldfish. "Morning." I'm distracted all over again by the sight of her in nothing but a bra and her scrub pants, her skin pink and fresh from a shower and her smile bright as she closes the distance from what I assume is her bathroom to plop down on the other side of the bed. "Did you . . . sleep okay?"

"Like a log," she laughs. "You're kind of cushiony under all the muscle. What about you? I was surprised you're not a snorer. I had you pegged as one."

I can feel myself gaping a little still, her completely normal attitude taking me by surprise. Hadn't I been worried about everything going to shit only a minute ago? But here she is, acting like nothing even happened.

"I slept fine," I tell her, watching her as she casually undoes the towel from her head and begins to comb through the wet strands that fall tantalizingly over her breasts, which I can almost still feel against my hands and tongue. "Very good, actually."

"Told you so." She stops what she's doing to crawl over the bed, pushing up to press her mouth to mine. "Sex addenda are great."

I don't know what surprises me more, her casual demeanor, or the way that I melt into her kiss even after all my worrying only moments ago. Her fingers slide across my jaw to hold me close, a smile at her lips when she breaks away to linger near my mouth.

"Yes," I murmur. "Great."

She gives me another quick peck before pulling away entirely. "You'd better get in the shower. I think someone really will pass out from shock if you're late."

She saunters from the bed to grab her top from where it's draped over a nearby chair by the window, pulling it on unceremoniously before giving me a wink.

"At least you won't have to scent me anytime soon," she teases.

I watch her disappear into the bathroom again before a hair-dryer sounds only seconds later, feeling exponentially more confused than I had when I woke up. It seems that I had been worried for nothing.

And why is that even more concerning?

~

MY CONFUSION ENDS up coloring the rest of my day, as I find myself out of sorts from the moment Mackenzie and I part ways at her apartment. I've tried my best to go about business as usual, but besides the confounded state of my brain in regard to Mackenzie and what we did and what it means—there is also the all-too-vivid memory of the actual *act* that is doing its best to ensure I can't focus today.

Because in every quiet moment there is the echo of Mackenzie's gasps, her soft moans, and in each instance that I find myself alone there is the expression on her face when I pushed inside her waiting to throw off my day, the way she'd felt around me threatening to make me hard all over again in the most inappropriate of circumstances.

It's almost unfair, how easy she seems to be handling it. Especially since it was *me* who'd made such a fuss about complicating things to begin with.

I'm packing these tangled thoughts away for what must be the dozenth time since I got into work this morning, forcing myself not to scan the halls *again* for a familiar figure, knowing that she has no reason to visit this floor in the first place.

I focus instead on my clipboard, which contains the chart of the pre-op consult I'm going to meet, frowning when I notice it's one of Dennis's patients. I'm not exactly pleased to have another reason for him to come visit my office. Still. I guess that's just the job.

The door is already ajar when I locate the correct room number, and I give it a light knock before stepping inside and pasting on my best attempt at a smile.

"Hi. Mrs. Pereira?"

The small woman gives me a nervous smile, peeking at me from over the red frames of her glasses. "That's me."

"Perfect." I tuck the chart under my arm and extend a hand to shake hers. "So, we have some blockage going on, is that right?"

She nods, pulling her shawl tighter as her lips purse. "That's what they tell me."

I pull the clipboard back out, flipping through her notes. "It says your EKG came back abnormal." I go for reassurance. "Nothing too out of the ordinary. I can definitely get you fixed up."

She adjusts her glasses, looking me up and down. "You don't look any older than my son."

"Ah." My smile is tighter now. This part I'm used to, mostly. "I get that a lot. I promise, I've done this a thousand times. You have nothing to worry about."

"What exactly are we looking to do here?"

"Well," I start, "we're going to take you to do a heart cath and inject a dye to take a look at what's going on. Almost like an X-ray, but for your vessels. It will give me a better idea of the severity of the blockage so I can assess if we need to place some stents to help with the blood flow to your heart."

"I'll be knocked out for this, won't I?"

"Of course," I assure her. "You won't feel a thing. If the blockage is severe enough, we'll place stents to open the vessels back up so we can flush it out and get the blood flowing normally again. Just think of it like a mechanic doing an oil change."

She laughs at that. "That sounds a little less nerve-racking."

"You're going to be fine," I promise. "You're in good hands."

"That's what they tell me," she says again.

I check her notes again. "So, if you have any questions, I'd be happy to answer them. For today, I'm going to send you to the lab first for some blood tests, and pending those we'll schedule an angiogram—that's a scan that's going to give us a better look at the blockage—and then when that's all done we can go ahead and schedule your—"

I hear a light knock behind me, interrupting my spiel, and I try not to show my irritation when I turn to see who's decided to barge in.

Dennis's gray hair appears around the doorframe, his sanguine smile only worsening my impatience.

"Hey, there, Mrs. P," he calls sweetly as he steps into the room. "I happened to be passing by and thought I'd check on you."

Mrs. Pereira looks brighter than she did a moment ago. "Dr. Martin! It's good to see you."

"I hope Dr. Taylor is treating you well," Dennis says with a teasing edge to his voice that grates my nerves. "He can be a bit of a grouch sometimes."

"Oh no, no," she laughs. "He's treating me just fine."

"We were just discussing scheduling, Dr. Martin," I tell him flatly. "So . . ."

"Always straight to business, this one," Dennis laughs, clapping me on the shoulder. For some reason I feel like breaking his hand. "He doesn't like to chitchat like us old folks."

"I couldn't believe how young he is," Mrs. Pereira admits. "When you told me I'd be seeing the head of the department, I imagined someone our age!"

"Well." Dennis shrugs, shoving his hands in the pockets of his white coat. "We try not to hold his years against him. He does just fine for a young pup."

I have to grind my teeth to keep from saying something I'll regret. Our mutual patient might not realize Dennis is being condescending, but I sure as hell do. It's something I'm more than used to—but for some reason, I'm finding it a lot harder to let it roll off my back today.

"Dr. Martin," I say tightly, gesturing toward the door. "I actually had a question for you, do you mind?"

"Of course, of course," Dennis says with that same infuriating grin. "It was good to see you, Mrs. Pereira. Don't let Dr. Taylor here give you a hard time."

Mrs. Pereira laughs. "He'll do all right."

I'm already stepping into the hall to leave them behind me, feeling my blood pulsing in my ears. I clench my fists at my sides while I wait for Dennis to join me, making sure he's closed the door behind him before I address him.

Dennis looks innocent when he steps outside, leaning against the wall by the door. "What's up, Noah?"

"What the hell are you trying to pull in there?"

He cocks his head, feigning confusion. "What do you mean?"

"Don't give me that shit," I huff. "Some people might not be able to see through your slimy condescension, but I do."

"Wow. Someone's in a mood today." He looks at me like I'm being ridiculous. "I was just saying hi to a patient. No need to get all worked up."

"Just keep your fake nice to yourself," I warn him. "I've had about as much as I can take."

To my surprise, Dennis smiles. It's almost . . . gleeful. Like I've just given him good news. It makes me absolutely livid.

"I guess this is that famous temper we hear about." His smile widens, and he stuffs his hands back into his pockets, pushing off the wall as he looks me up and down. "Guess you really are an alpha after all, huh?"

He leaves me stunned and fuming, torn between wanting to throw a chair or a punch—I can't decide. It takes me a good minute to collect myself, unable to really calm myself back down until his footsteps have faded away, and when I'm alone again I can't help but wonder what the hell is wrong with me.

I don't do this. I don't let dumb fucks like Dennis get under my skin like this. And despite the stories about making nurses cry, I can't remember a time when I've ever berated a coworker openly like I just did. It seems that with every passing day sans suppressants—I am becoming less and less like myself. It has me wondering if this charade I'm clinging to so tightly is worth the insanity it's driving me to.

Guess you really are an alpha after all, huh?

I push Dennis's snide voice from my mind, taking a deep breath to collect myself as I remember I still have a job to do. This mess is something I can handle later, I think.

Hopefully.

THE ENCOUNTER WITH Dennis follows me for the next few hours while I see two more consults, and even now at lunchtime, there's a sense of unease on my skin that feels almost like an itch I can't reach. Granted, Dennis and I have never been and most likely will never be anything remotely close to friends, but at least until today I've been able to successfully remain professional with him despite all his thinly veiled barbs. Everything about the confrontation has me slightly worried that at this rate, I am going to get myself fired for the exact sort of behavior I am trying to prove isn't actually something to worry about.

I'm telling myself that it's a perfectly normal thing, me going down to her floor. We're supposed to be mates, after all, right? Surely it can only bolster our facade, me checking in on her. Not that any of these justifications offer any enlightenment as to what reason I will give *Mackenzie* in regard to me coming down to the ER floor—a place I've visited more in the last two weeks than I have in two months. I have no good reason to be here, but with each passing hour since this morning, I find myself plagued with an increasingly pressing urge just to *see* her. Something I've been trying to justify in my head as a polite check-in on her state of being after everything that happened last night.

I've noticed at least three nurses and two physicians turning their heads to watch me pass as I move through the hallways down here, each of them staring at the side of my head like I'm some sort of alien visitor they can't make heads or tails of. It's making me wonder if there was actually something to all that "Boogeyman of Denver General" ridiculousness everyone has been talking about.

I've been wandering around for five minutes after stepping off the elevator, but I finally hear a familiar laugh down the hall and around the corner, and just the sound of it has some tension in my shoulders unwinding, which I hadn't even fully realized had been there until this very moment. I notice my step quickening as my body seems to attempt to close the space between us more quickly, as if my body has a mind of its own, and it is only seconds later that I see a soft, sandy ponytail tilted back with her laughter as she reaches to push at someone's shoulder, almost like she's just been told a joke.

I also notice that the shoulder is very male.

This does strange things to me as well, for entirely different reasons.

I stop walking almost twenty feet from her, watching her continue to chat with a good-looking shifter who is only a few inches shorter than I am. His scent makes my skin prickle, mostly because of its vicinity to Mackenzie, and his handsome face with its charming dimple only makes his smile seem all the more bright. But what's worse is that even from here, I pick up on the soft way he's looking at my mate.

My *fake* mate, I mentally correct.

The distinction does nothing for the sticky heat I feel suddenly dripping into my chest.

Mackenzie notices me after another second, her laughter dying as confusion bleeds into her features. "Noah?"

"I . . ." My eyes dart from the man next to her, who looks less happy than he did a second ago, back again to Mackenzie, who is still looking at me with an obvious curiosity as to what I'm doing down here. "I just came to see how your day was going."

"My day," she echoes in a faraway voice. I can almost feel myself melting into the floor, but she recovers quickly, flashing me a smile.

"It's been okay. Kind of a slow morning, actually. Haven't seen a single broken bone."

"That's surprising," I note. "Given that it's ski season."

"That's what I said," she laughs. She seems to remember there's another person here then, giving the man beside her an apologetic look. "Sorry. Noah, this is Liam. He works with me in the ER."

Liam offers me his hand, but I notice his smile doesn't meet his eyes. "I've heard a lot about you, Dr. Taylor," he says politely.

"Noah is fine," I correct. His smile is starting to bother me, for reasons I can't pin down. "Sorry. Mackenzie has never mentioned you."

My tone must come off tighter than I intended, because Mackenzie's nose wrinkles just as Liam's expression falters slightly.

"I didn't?" Mackenzie's laugh is off, coming across slightly awkward. "My bad. We're usually too busy talking about open chest cavities and what to have for dinner."

"It's no big deal," Liam assures us. "Mackenzie is usually too busy to look up half the time. Never met a more focused physician."

"She is amazing," I say matter-of-factly, my eyes moving down her face as she blinks with surprise. "I'm lucky to have her."

"Of course," Liam laughs with only a slight hint of uneasiness. He reaches to gently squeeze Mackenzie's shoulder, and that same sticky sensation threatens to fill up my entire chest. "I was just telling Mackenzie that I was going to throw the entire ER a pizza party if we can make it to the end of the week without setting another broken bone."

"And I said that is absolutely not going to happen," she laughs.

"It's very doubtful," I muse flatly. I notice his hand is still on her shoulder, and despite my best judgment my body seems to move on its own, pulling her against me gently so that I can hug her to my side, effectively ensuring Liam's hand slips away from her. "I suppose that's why it's so fortunate that Mackenzie is so capable."

There's an awkward sort of silence then, and it isn't until Liam clears his throat that I realize we're just standing in a circle and that I haven't given a good reason for being down here.

"Anyway," I say in my best attempt at a casual tone, looking down at her. "I just finished with my appointments for the morning and wondered if you wanted to grab lunch."

"Oh." Her eyes widen a little, genuine surprise covering her face. "Oh! Well . . ." Her eyes flick to Liam for a moment before finding mine again apologetically. "I just thought you said that you'd . . . you know. That you'd be busy most of the day. So I told Parker I'd grab lunch with him."

"Oh." I nod more emphatically than necessary. "Of course. I probably should have texted first."

"No, it's fine!" She reaches to touch my arm, and even this gentle press of her fingers through my sleeve seems to ease the odd feeling inside. "You can totally come with us. If you want?"

"No, no," I insist. "That's okay. Honestly, now that I think about it, I need to sign off on some charts, anyway. I should probably get a jump on that. I'll just . . . see you later."

"Okay," she says, still touching my arm. "I'll see you at home?"

It's a lie, and I know that, so why does it make me feel better that she's said it?

I think it takes her by surprise, when I close the distance between us, and the closeness pulls her even further from Liam as I lean to pull her mouth to mine. I know it sure as hell takes *me* by surprise, given that I don't think I even made a conscious decision to kiss her. It just sort of happens.

It's quick, almost chaste, even, but still I linger a second longer than I need to, reveling in the tiny victory that is Mackenzie immediately yielding to my kiss. I hear Liam make an awkward sound under his breath beside us, and something in me half purrs with contentment at having made it fully known that Mackenzie is entirely off-limits.

Even in my head that sounds insane.

I pull away from her, doing my best to look like I'm not a mess of conflict and uncertainty, echoing: *See you at home* against her mouth before I step away from her and make for the opposite end of the hall. There's nothing appropriate about what just occurred, and I know if I allow myself to dissect all that I just did, I will be even more concerned than I already am.

I don't slow my pace until I'm safely back on my own floor and locked inside my office—sinking into my desk chair and sighing as I ponder the mess that the morning has been. Maybe I'm coming unraveled.

My phone vibrates in my pocket about the time I'm considering banging my head on the desk, and I fish it out quickly to notice Mackenzie's name flashing across the screen.

> **MACKENZIE:** Did something happen? You
> seemed kind of weird.

If she only knew the half of it.

> **ME:** Just some shit with Dennis. Figured it
> would be good to be seen together.

> **MACKENZIE:** Oh. Good call. Nice touch with
> the kiss. I think you gave Liam a heart

attack. Everyone on my floor is pretty sure
you're a serial killer in your spare time.

I take a few seconds more than I need to as I contemplate how to answer that, chewing on the inside of my lip as I try to reason out myself why in the hell I kissed her. I heave out a sigh as I resignedly tap out a lie.

ME: Just playing the part.

I drop my phone on the desk without waiting for her reply, finally giving in to that urge to let my head hit the wood as I groan into it. Of all the tumultuous emotions I have experienced today, none of them can compare to the frightening realization that I might be in over my head here.

I really don't think it's a good idea, I'd told her. *It could make things very complicated,* I'd said. And I'd meant it, at the time. I truly had.

I just never imagined that it might potentially be *me* making things complicated.

11

Mackenzie

"SO, YOU WERE just . . . stuck?"

Parker's expression is equal parts horrified and intrigued—his brow furrowed in thought as he leans across the table in the hospital cafeteria.

"Basically," I confirm. "Honestly, I assumed that part had been mostly exaggerated in the biology textbooks, but it's pretty much exactly how it sounds."

Parker's face screws up like I've just told him that I spontaneously lay eggs. "And what the hell did you do during that time? Play checkers?"

"No." I laugh. "We just went to sleep afterward. I'll say this for Noah, he really knows how to wear a girl out."

"How could you possibly go to sleep like that?"

"You know, it's weirdly comforting? Like that best kind of after-workout sleep."

"So he gets his rocks off, and then it just . . . swells up like a balloon."

"That's one way to put it, I guess." I smile around a bite of my flatbread. "Had me feeling like a bottle of wine." Parker cocks an eyebrow in question, and I grin mischievously. "Corked," I clarify.

He makes a sound of disgust. "You're heinous."

"That's what they tell me," I laugh.

He shakes his head as he turns his attention to his lunch, stabbing his salad with gusto. "I still can't believe you had sex with *Noah fucking Taylor*."

"At least I've given validity to your constant abuse of his name."

"Hilarious." I frown as I turn my neck, and Parker cocks his eyebrow at me. "What?"

I shake my head. "Just a little stiff. Maybe I slept wrong."

"That's what I've been trying to say," Parker scoffs.

I grin, rolling my shoulders to shake out the weird tightness I've been feeling this morning. "Oh no. *That* part was absolutely right."

He rolls his eyes, pointing his fork at me. "Have you even thought about how weird this is going to make things?"

I make a face as I chew. "Why would it be weird?"

"You went to school two times longer than I did," he huffs. "You're supposed to be smart."

"Wow, thanks."

"I'm just saying. You already had a weird web of lies going on with this guy, and now on top of that, you've thrown sex into the mix. And with an alpha! What happened to you being worried he'd stake some wolfy claim on you?"

"I think maybe I overinflated the issue in my head," I tell him with a shrug. "Noah seems fine."

"Uh-huh." Parker hmphs. "I'm sure the newly unsuppressed alpha is just peachy after knotting his first omega."

"Can you keep your voice down? You might as well stand up on the table and start shouting about Noah's dick."

A body dropping into the chair beside me gives me a start, and I tense until I spot a grinning Priya settling at our table. "Oh, are we talking about Noah's dick?"

She leans in excitedly as she sets her tray on the table, tucking her dark tresses behind her ear and looking like we have a present she wants to open.

"No," I assert quickly, shooting Parker a look to let him know this is all his fault. "We weren't."

"Oh, come *on*," Priya whines. "You can't rob me of the good stuff. I've already missed out on a forever's worth of stories."

"We were just saying how silly all the gossip is," I offer nonchalantly, keeping my attention on my food. "I've heard all kinds of nonsense this week."

Priya nudges me conspiratorially. "About Noah's dick?"

Honestly, I can't say that's a lie. I've definitely walked into a couple of rooms to whispers about the possible mechanics of my fake mate's equipment. But then again, I guess now I can confirm the curiosity is more than valid.

"Among other things," I mutter.

"Well, *I* heard that you got a visit down in the ER today from your hubby," Priya practically sings.

Parker pauses midbite. "Wait, what?"

"It's not a big deal," I say flippantly.

"Not what I heard," Priya tuts. "Jessica from Radiology told me that you guys were making out in the hallway."

"Seriously," I huff. "Who the fuck is Jessica from Radiology, and why is she always reporting on me?"

"It's not just her," Priya tells me. "They were buzzing about it all the way up in Anesthesiology. My tech mentioned it after an epidural."

"It's barely been an hour," I grumble. "People need better things to do than gossip about Noah and me."

"Okay," Parker chimes in. "But why exactly didn't you start with this when you sat down? Making out with Noah in the hall is pretty noteworthy."

"We didn't *make* out," I say with a shake of my head. "He just kissed me."

"And you don't think that's weird?"

Priya cocks her head. "Why would that be weird? They're mated, right?"

"Right," I say through slightly gritted teeth, narrowing my eyes at Parker. "There's nothing weird about that."

Parker matches my expression as he stabs at his salad and shoves a bite into his mouth, chewing thoughtfully as he shrugs. "I just meant he didn't ever kiss you in the hallway *before*."

I know what he means, even if Priya doesn't—but I can't exactly tell Parker that Noah was simply playing his part when Priya is sitting right next to us.

"He's probably just happy he doesn't have to pretend anymore," Priya ventures. "Must be nice to have an alpha who can't keep his hands off you for a whole day."

I make a face, quickly masking it as Parker meets my eyes with one cocked *this is what I'm saying* brow. I roll my eyes, looking away from him. It's not like the kiss meant anything. He was only doing it for—

"And poor Liam," Priya tuts. "He must be so crushed to find out you're mated."

My nose wrinkles. "Wait, what does Liam have to do with anything?"

"Jessica said he looked like a kicked puppy when he was telling her about the kiss."

"Wait," I cut in. "Liam told Jessica from Radiology? Why?"

"Mackenzie," Priya says with a shake of her head. "You gotta know that dude has been half in love with you for like six months."

"What?" I snort in disbelief. "No he hasn't."

"Actually, I'm pretty sure that's true," Parker adds. "I've seen the guy laugh at your jokes."

I frown. "What does that have to do with anything?"

"They're pretty terrible jokes," Parker says matter-of-factly.

"Oh, fuck off," I scoff.

"I can't believe you didn't know this," Priya says. "Like, I'm pretty sure everyone from floors two to six knows about it. At least."

I consider this, scanning back through my interactions with Liam and trying to find any validity to what they're claiming. I mean, sure, I would consider us good friends, but I can't think of anything to suggest he's been quietly pining after me. I cringe, thinking about how awkward that kiss must have been for him. It had been so out of the blue, after all, given that Noah had practically dragged me away from Liam to reach me and right into his—

I pause with my hand suspended halfway between the table and my mouth, the straw in my drink dangling uselessly only inches from my mouth. Is it possible that Noah kissed me *because* Liam had been there? I mean, he'd seemed a little weird from the moment he happened upon the pair of us, but at the time I had just assumed he'd had a bad run-in and was annoyed he couldn't give me the lowdown on it.

But that's silly. Noah doesn't have any reason to start getting all jealous and territorial. Especially not after one night of admittedly mind-blowing sex. Unless . . . Surely all of those stories about alpha behavior are bullshit, right? There's no way that Noah would do a one-eighty after *one* night.

I shake my head, taking an aggressive slurp from my straw as Parker and Priya's chatter fades back in from where I'd stopped listening.

"I think it's really cute," Priya is saying.

I look up at her. "What is?"

"Noah going all soft now that everyone knows you're mated."

The more juvenile part of my subconscious snorts; after last night, I'm pretty sure there isn't anything *soft* about Noah.

"I think it's weird," Parker grumbles.

Priya rolls her eyes. "You're just jealous. You need a cute boy and a massage, dude."

"I *have* a cute boy," Parker says smugly.

Priya's eyebrows shoot up. "Oh my God, you guys have been holding out so much good gossip. Who is it? How cute are we talking?"

"Do you remember the instructor from that time you went with us to hot yoga?"

"Yeah," Priya grimaces. "I will not be doing the sweaty yoga ever again, thank you very much. Instructor was definitely yummy though. Wait." Her mouth drops open. "*No.* He's gay?"

"Mhm." Parker grins. "My massages are well taken care of for the foreseeable future."

Priya hmphs. "You guys suck. My last date took me to a *drive-in* porn movie. In 3D! We sat there for forty-five minutes watching stuff splatter against the big screen."

"Wait," I say. "Why do I want to try that?"

Parker snorts. "You would."

"Trust me," Priya scoffs. "Count yourselves lucky to be off the market."

Parker and I share another look, and I know that if Priya wasn't sitting here with us, he'd probably be ranting at me again about the irrationality of my actions lately, but my mind is already delving back down into the spiral that is: Why *did* Noah kiss me earlier? Had it really been him simply adding another layer to our ruse, or had it been sparked by something else?

I don't know what confuses me more: Noah's possible reasons or the fact that I hadn't even thought twice about it until now.

"I've got to run," Priya tells us, throwing the wrapper for her sandwich onto her tray along with her napkin. "I've got an intubation in a half hour." She points at us both, giving us a stern look. "I expect more hot goss when I see you two again. I'm now officially living vicariously through you."

To his credit, Parker waits until she's out of sight to start in on me. "He *kissed* you?"

"Don't even start."

"That didn't strike you as odd?"

"I told you. He was just playing the part."

Although, I'm even second-guessing that now. Not that Parker needs to know that.

"I'm just worried about you," he says with a sigh. "I don't want you catching feelings for some guy who's going to jet off to Albuquerque in a few weeks and leave you high and dry."

I shake my head, making an indignant sound. "That's not going to happen."

"Famous last words," he mutters.

I roll my eyes, grateful when Parker becomes focused on his phone seconds later since it gives me a moment alone with my thoughts. I can see why my friend would be concerned, given that supposedly Noah and I being together is supposed to be some grand, destined thing—but outside of a spectacular night of sex, there's absolutely nothing that has changed about our original arrangement. Kiss or no kiss. Reading too much into this is just going to give me an unnecessary headache. Best just to pack it away.

I pop the last bite of my flatbread in my mouth, staring at a blank spot on the cafeteria wall as an indeterminable number of seconds tick by. I reach to rub my neck as that same tightness sets off again, a prickling following after that I ignore as my mind wanders.

But why *did* he kiss me?

I HAVEN'T HEARD from Noah since the hallway incident earlier, and honestly, I've been a little hesitant to text him again. I'm blaming all of the muddled thoughts I've been wading through since viewing his actions from earlier in a different light. Still, I know I can't avoid him forever, and I probably should clarify that we're okay.

The hall where his office is located is decidedly empty this late in the afternoon, and part of me worries that I might have missed him. He would have at least let me know he was leaving, surely. Then again, why would he? Despite my assurances that nothing about our relationship—or rather, our fake relationship—would change after one night . . . For some reason little things like this are a bit blurry to me.

My skin feels a little clammy, like I'm about to break out in a sweat, and I chide myself quietly for being so worked up about something so small. Surely it's fine that I'm coming to see him. There's nothing weird about that.

I knock lightly at his office door, hearing his quiet answer only a second after. I turn the knob to crack the door and peek around it, finding Noah bent over his desk and glaring at his laptop.

"Hey," I greet tentatively. "You busy?"

His expression changes when he looks up at me, his frown turning up to more of a neutral shape and the wrinkle at his brow softening.

"Hey. I'm not busy."

I grin, nodding toward the screen that seems to be currently offending him as I step inside of his office and close the door behind me. "Could have fooled me."

"Documenting some procedure notes. I let myself get behind."

I make a face. "Yikes."

"Yeah. I'll be working late, but I should be able to get caught up tonight, at least."

"There goes our romantic dinner," I tease.

His eyebrows shoot up. "Did you want to get dinner?"

Oh, Jesus. I forgot who I'm talking to. I make a mental note not to make any more dumb jokes that insinuate there's something romantic between us.

"No, no. Sorry, I was just being funny."

"Oh."

Now he looks mildly disappointed. What the hell?

Things feel awkward all of a sudden, and I can't wrestle down why. Or rather, I can, I'm just not sure if I should address the fact that he was inside me less than twenty-four hours ago or if we should just keep that sort of talk behind closed doors. I suppose it depends on whether or not I want to do it again. More importantly . . . if he does.

Jesus, I feel flushed just thinking about this. What happened to not letting things get complicated?

"So our little hallway incident apparently sparked some new gossip."

"Oh." He looks down at his desk. "Sorry about that."

"No, that's what we want, right?"

"Right. Of course."

I shuffle my weight from one foot to the other, telling myself that I should probably leave it alone but still feeling a little addled by all the questions I've rustled up in my head. I clear my throat as I go for casual, turning to make it seem as if I'm very interested in Noah's diploma hanging on the wall.

"Are you okay?"

I hear his chair creak as he most likely turns it in my direction. "What do you mean?"

"I don't know." I shrug nonchalantly. "You just seemed like something was bothering you earlier."

"Ah. Well." I hear him blow out a rush of air. "Had a run-in with Dennis."

"The bitter bitch again?"

I catch Noah's same barely-there grin when I turn my head just enough to look at him from the corner of my eye. "Yes."

"What did he say?"

"He's apparently decided to be less overt with his distaste for me. Evidently, now he's comfortable making dick remarks in front of mutual patients."

I turn to face him, my mouth falling open. "He didn't."

"I doubt the patient picked up on what was going on, but I sure as hell did."

"Do you want me to kick his ass?"

Noah makes a face. "What?"

"I'm just saying. I feel like I could pull an 'enraged mate' card and get away with it."

His smile widens then, and my stomach does something funny, like a swooping motion.

"It's fine," he assures me. "I can handle him."

"I was just surprised that you came down to my floor again."

"I . . ." He sighs, scratching the back of his neck. "I guess I can't lie and say I haven't been a little off today."

"Off?"

He gestures between us. "About you and me. I guess I expected . . ." He breathes in just to blow it out. "I guess I needed to make sure we were okay."

"I told you," I remind him. "I'm not going to freak out on you. This can be whatever we want it to be."

"I know," he says. "I know you did. I just . . . wanted to be sure."

So, was his entire reason for coming down to see me *really* only because he was worried I was off somewhere pining for him? What was that kiss about then? It makes my head hurt thinking about it, but I can't bring myself to say anything.

"I hope I didn't cause any problems with your friend," Noah adds, pulling me from my thoughts.

My brow furrows. "My friend?"

"Liam," he clarifies.

"Oh." I'm searching his face for any signs of jealousy or alpha nonsense—but his expression remains frustratingly blank. "No, no. He's really just a friend."

Or at least, that's what I thought before today.

"Okay," Noah says evenly. "I was afraid I had overstepped with . . . you know."

Ah. So he *had* been second-guessing it.

"You mean making out in the hallway?"

He flinches. "More or less."

"You were just playing the part," I say, mirroring what he texted me earlier.

"Right," he answers immediately.

"It's not like you were being jealous or something," I laugh, passing it off as a joke even though part of me is perking up for his answer. "Right?"

It takes him a second to answer, but only a second. "Of course not."

I consider it, reasoning that regardless of *his* reasons—I definitely didn't *hate* him kissing me in the hallway.

"I think maybe we're both probably walking on eggshells," I admit. "I can tell you're still worrying about last night changing things, but I think we got through it fine. I mean, you're not mauling my male coworkers, and I'm not begging you to bite me, so all in all, I'd say it was a successful experiment."

"I guess that's . . . true."

"And we both enjoyed it . . . right?"

I don't miss the way his throat bobs with a swallow, nor do I miss the way his jaw tenses as if remembering. "I did."

Okay. So we can work with this. Maybe it wouldn't be so awkward if we laid out some ground rules to begin with.

"You know," I start, moving away from where I'm standing to circle his desk, "there's nothing that says we can't help each other and also, you know, *help* each other."

Noah looks up at me as I approach. "How do you mean?"

"I don't think it will be the end of the world if we get a little enjoyment out of this relationship—even if it is fake."

"Enjoyment?"

"I just mean . . . we don't have to think so much about our little addendum."

"We don't," he parrots, eyes on my mouth.

I press my hands on either side of his desk chair. "We both know what this is, and there's no risk since we aren't looking for anything to come out of it."

"Right," he murmurs. "Since I'm leaving."

For some reason the reminder of the expiration date of our little arrangement gives me pause, but only for like a second. I remind myself that's the best part of the whole thing.

"Exactly," I tell him. I curl my body to bring my mouth inches from his, reaching to cup his jaw. "So let's enjoy it until then. No more worrying about how I'm doing, okay?"

"If that's what you want," he breathes.

I close the distance, letting my lips brush against his in a lazy kiss that makes his scent bloom around me, making my knees wobble. I have to press my legs together when I pull away, and Noah's expression says he'd like to do a lot more than just this. It's a very different look for the normally taciturn Dr. Taylor.

It's weirdly arousing, being the only person to know this side of him.

"It is," I assure him. I give him another quick kiss for good measure before I pull away. "If you weren't working tonight, I'd say that you could show me your place."

The implication is clear, and thankfully, Noah looks much less wary than he did the last time I propositioned him.

"You want to see my place?"

I have to bite back a smile, my earlier uncertainty currently being washed away by anticipation. "For research purposes, of course.

I need to be able to tell people with confidence that you don't *actually* sleep upside down in a cave."

He doesn't laugh, but I think it's because he's looking at me now like he wants to pull me into his lap. Should I tell him I would probably let him?

"I could . . ." His throat bobs. "I could do this tomorrow."

I *do* crawl into his lap then, my lips curving against his. "Noah Taylor? Procrastinating? *Now* I've seen it all."

Turns out Noah's mouth is an effective method of shutting me up.

Who knew.

12

Noah

WE BARELY MAKE it inside my front door.

I think maybe it had been the promise of what was to come when we got to my place; maybe that's why she'd smelled so much sweeter on the drive over. Almost like she was anticipating it. Almost like she was *excited* for it.

It's been a very long time since anyone has been excited to be with me.

My white coat is on top of hers in a pile, her back against the wall as my hands explore every inch of her they can reach. I'm learning that something about Mackenzie makes me impatient, and impatience is not something I'm used to experiencing. I don't think I've felt restless in a long time, but Mackenzie makes me feel damn near unhinged.

"I like your place," she says breathlessly.

I lift my head from her throat, her eyes as glazed as mine must be. "This is just the entryway."

"Shut up and keep kissing me," she huffs.

I thought I might have imagined it, might have made it seem in my head somehow more than it was—how sweet she tastes. Her honeysuckle scent is just that against my tongue, like chasing that one bead of sweetness from the flower and left wanting more with each little drop.

I feel her fingers in my hair, her nails scratching lightly at my scalp as she turns her head to allow my lips better access to her throat. "Did you"—she shivers as my teeth scrape across the trail my tongue has made—"really want me to show you my place?"

"After." She sighs.

I feel my heart thumping in my chest, my lips pressing under her jaw. "After?"

"Bedroom is fine for now," she clarifies.

She squeals when my hands curl under her thighs to lift her up and against me, her legs wrapping around me as if by instinct as her mouth finds mine. I would like to say that my hands curving on her ass are for her benefit, that I'm simply holding her tighter while I walk to my bedroom—but that would be almost entirely untrue.

Not that Mackenzie seems to mind.

Jesus Christ, I can *smell* how aroused she is. It's something I could never get used to. What it does to me.

I want to be gentler with her this time, to be able to focus more on her sounds and taste and her body. But even as I'm laying her across my bed, one that has always been large but feels so much *larger* with her small frame sprawled across it—already I can feel that same strange sensation of being lost to something taking over. Will it always be like this?

Not always, something whispers in the back of my head. *Only temporarily.*

I push those thoughts far away as I crawl over her.

It takes me by surprise, as it has many times since we made this arrangement, just how *stunning* Mackenzie is. For what must be the hundredth time since she agreed to this insanity, I wonder why in the hell she would even *need* this fake relationship. How in the actual fuck has someone with half a brain not snatched her up?

And how is it *me* that ended up being the one who she came to for help?

"You just gonna stare at me or are you going to take my clothes off?" Her fingers tease my tie that hangs between us, her lips tilted in a smile as she winds it around her fist. "I know it's just scrubs. But use your imag—"

"I don't have to imagine anything," I murmur, sliding my hand under her scrub top. "You're fucking beautiful."

I bend to press my lips to her stomach, the gentle slope of her belly quivering under my mouth as I push her scrub top higher. This close, the sweet fragrance of her slick is stronger, more potent, making the blood rush in my ears. I peek up at her as my mouth trips over her hip bone, finding her lips trapped between her teeth and her lids heavy with anticipation as I hook a finger into the waistband of her scrub bottoms.

"Last night I . . ." I have to close my eyes as her scent makes my head spin. "I didn't—I want to—"

"You can do anything you want, Noah," Mackenzie says huskily. "Just touch me."

I don't need to be told twice.

Her skin is soft—*so fucking soft*—and I find myself kissing every inch that I can reach as I roll her scrubs down her thighs and over her legs to toss them aside. The lime green of her underwear is darker between her legs, a glistening shine on the insides of her thighs as her slick threatens to drive me insane.

I hear her breath hitch when I duck to press my tongue there, licking a wide stripe against her thigh and shuddering as the flavor of her explodes across my tongue. It's a tempting thought to remain like this, to keep tasting her skin just as I am—but I want more. I'm as careful as my trembling fingers will allow, peeling her underwear off her, and she lifts her hips eagerly to assist me until there is nothing but her scent and her skin and the slick wet between her legs that makes my cock ache.

"Fuck, Mackenzie," I rasp. "Look at you."

It's still a little frightening, the urges that roil inside me to make my emotions murky and my senses turbid when I'm with her like this. It's almost like there is another person inside me trying to claw its way out and touch more of her, taste more, just . . . *more*.

I hear her breath catch when I nudge my shoulders between her thighs to settle there, my fingers curling around each one to hold her close as the aroma of her slick only worsens the feral urges that I'm doing my best to bridle down. My breath is ragged, and I can feel my eyes roll back as I breathe her in, barely able to contain myself as I lean in to let my nose nuzzle against the patch of dark blond curls as I tentatively tease my tongue through her wet center.

"*Ah*," she gasps. "Noah, that's—"

I do it again, with less hesitance this time. My tongue passes through her folds as the taste of her makes me dizzy. The front of my slacks is stiff and uncomfortable, and I flex my hips against the bed for some relief as I swirl my tongue around the little bundle of nerves at her apex. I like the sounds she makes, like the way her fingers card through my hair to tug—all of it only spurring me on, only making me want more.

I grip her thighs tighter as her heels dig into my shoulders, focusing my attention on the swollen bud of her clit even as her slick wets my chin. I close my eyes as I let the soft sounds of her hitched breath heat my blood, teasing her with the back-and-forth swipe of my tongue before I wrap my lips around the most sensitive part of her to suck. She cries out in a quiet, almost wordless way—as if it's trapped in her throat. Her hands falling to my shoulders and the scratching of her nails against my shirt say more than enough though.

"R-right—right there," she chokes out. "Can you—a little harder—*ah*."

I hum against her core, pulling at the taut bud of her clit as her back begins to bend, her hips jerking as if trying to escape of their own accord. I grip her thighs tighter, sucking at her messily as she softly gasps my name. Her skin under my hands is almost as hot as the softer flesh between her legs, so warm that it almost feels like she might melt against my tongue.

With every pull of my lips there is another trickle of her slick, each little bit only worsening those urges to bury myself inside her and keep her knotted until morning. There is a distant thought that wonders if these urges will just keep getting worse the more I touch her, but there is a more present one that says it absolutely doesn't care as long as I *can* keep touching her.

"You taste"—I lick one hot stripe up her center—"as good as you feel." I wrap my lips around her clit for one long pull that makes a wet sound when I release it. "I want to know what you taste like when you come."

She lets out a strained laugh. "Well, if you keep doing that, it won't be a prob—*fuck*."

She lifts her hips to press deeper into my mouth when I focus all my attention on her clit, unwrapping one hand from her thigh and bringing it between us to tease a finger at her entrance. I hear her whimper when I press it inside, stroking her inner wall and pressing against it to rub deep circles there as my tongue makes a mess of her.

Her fingers go from tapping at my shoulder to tugging at my shirt and back again—a chorus of whined *yes*es and *mhm*s ringing out into the quiet of my bedroom. Her thighs press harder against my ears as they begin to shake, and her back bows from the bed as her fingers drop to the comforter to twist in the fabric.

She's panting my name when I feel her tip over the edge, and there is a satisfying gush of slick that I lap up even as it makes a mess. I can feel it on my lips and chin and even trickling down my neck, and still it's like I can't get enough. I want to do *this* almost as much as I want to be inside her again. I only pull away from her when I feel her hand snake between us to grab for my tie, urging me up from between her legs as I look at her in a daze.

There's a dreamy sort of smile on her mouth as she winds the silk of my tie around her fist, giving it another gentle tug. "Get up here."

I come like a puppy being called, with just as much eagerness—crawling over her until I'm hovering with my hands braced on either side of her. My breath is still ragged and I still feel a little wild, but her fingers reach to brush along my cheek, her thumb sliding across my lower lip; I can't say why it's so calming.

"Your first consult isn't until nine," she says calmly.

I nod. "That's right."

"And I'm on mid-shift," she goes on.

Another nod. "I know."

Her mouth tilts on one side as I feel her hand sliding over the front of my slacks to give my straining cock a squeeze. Her hands feel just as hot as the rest of her. "How much sleep do you need?"

Before I kiss her, I think to myself that I might be in real trouble.

EXPECTEDLY, I DON'T get very much sleep, but even with the workload that I'm facing for the day, I can't find it in me to be at all put out by it.

I left Mackenzie in my bed this morning, and something about knowing she was sleeping naked and tangled in my sheets as I drove to work had been satisfying in a way I never could have anticipated. Jesus, I even left her a spare *key* so she could lock up. Everything about it feels like the kind of complications I had told her we needed to avoid.

So why am I sitting at my desk, hiding my smile behind my hand?

I check my watch and note that I need to meet my consult in less than thirty minutes, willing myself to get a handle on my own feelings before then. I reach across my desk for the patient's chart so I can have a last-minute review, barely getting my fingers underneath it before I feel my phone start to vibrate on the other side of my desk.

It's embarrassing, how quickly I snatch it up, even *more* embarrassing how a flicker of disappointment passes through me when I notice it isn't Mackenzie calling. I really need to get a grip.

Who *is* calling, however, is effectively sobering.

"Hello, Mother."

I hear her click her tongue. "Don't you 'Mother' me. Why haven't you called?"

"I've been busy," I say evenly, my earlier giddiness dissipating. "You know how things are here."

"Apparently," she says in that tone that I know means I'm about to get scolded. "They're even so busy that you couldn't find time to tell your mother you're *mated*?"

Shit.

Mary Anne Taylor is a lot of things, but most of all, the woman is resourceful. I should have known better than to think I could keep this from her until it blew over.

"Listen. About that—"

"And I had to hear it from *Regina*, of all people. That horrible woman from my crochet club. Apparently, she heard it from her daughter Jessica."

That name vaguely rings a bell, although I can't pin down from where.

"Look, it isn't what you think."

"How can it not be what I think? How could you get mated without telling us? You didn't even tell us you were *dating* anyone. Your poor mother didn't get to meet her daughter-in-law before you went and—"

"I'm not actually mated," I sigh.

"—could be the mother of my future grandchildren, and I've never even—Wait. What?"

"I'm *not* mated," I repeat more firmly.

"Then why is the entire hospital apparently buzzing about you and some woman you've been secretly seeing?"

I scrub a hand down my face. "It's complicated."

"You think you got all those brains from your father?" She snorts. "Try me."

"Fuck," I groan.

"Language."

"It's the board," I say defeatedly. "They found out."

She immediately discerns my meaning. "Oh no. How? You've been so careful."

"An 'anonymous tip,' apparently. It's utter bullshit."

"*Language*," she stresses. "Were you reprimanded?"

"Well . . ."

"My goodness," she huffs. "After all that work you've done. And the Albuquerque job is on the line! Is that going to be affected now that you—"

"I didn't get any formal sort of reprimand," I tell her. "I didn't get anything more than a slap on the wrist, really." I hesitate a moment, knowing that I'm about to open a can of worms. "It was all thanks to Mackenzie."

"Mackenzie?"

"The, ah, mate you heard about."

"But you said you weren't actually mated."

"I'm not."

"But there's a woman named Mackenzie."

"There is."

"And you're not mated?"

"No."

"But people think you are."

"Correct."

My mother is quiet for a moment, and I feel a little like a boy again, waiting for her to yell at me for breaking her favorite vase.

"Tell me everything," she says calmly.

My mother listens quietly as I recount everything that's happened in the last couple of weeks—only cutting in to ask clarifying questions as she lets me explain how Mackenzie and I got wrapped up in our arrangement and how it benefits us both. I pointedly leave out our recent *sex addendum*, as Mackenzie calls it; that's a level I haven't even really figured out myself yet, after all.

"So, you're pretending to be mated to this woman."

"Or dating her, where her grandmother is concerned."

"Oh boy."

"I know what you're going to say," I sigh.

She makes a disgruntled sound. "No, you don't. Despite that fancy doctor brain of yours—you don't know *everything*."

"Fine," I grumble. "Then say whatever it is you're going to say."

"What is she like?"

This takes me by surprise. It's definitely not what I expected my mother to follow up with. "You mean, Mackenzie?"

"No, I mean Regina at the crochet club," she scoffs. "Of *course* I mean Mackenzie."

"What does that have to do with anything?"

"I'm curious what sort of woman throws herself into such an intricate ruse to help out my son. Especially since she apparently barely knew him before all this."

"I don't know." I frown down at my desk, thinking. "She's . . . funny? And competent. Everyone here seems to love her. I mean, I'm not really sure why she even agreed to this in the first place. She's very pretty, after all. I find it incredibly hard to believe that she needs help in the dating department. I guess I should just be grateful that she—What are you giggling about?"

"Oh, honey," she laughs. "How much do you like this woman?"

"What?" I make a face. "It's not like that. We're helping each other."

In and out of the bedroom, apparently, I think guiltily.

"I've known you for thirty-six years, son," she says. "And I've *never* heard you talk about a woman the way you are now."

"You *asked* what she was like," I mutter.

"Oh, this is wonderful," she practically cackles. "Maybe this will make you think twice about packing up and moving to another state."

"It's not *like* that," I continue to protest.

"Sure, sure," she chuckles. "Does your fake relationship entail her meeting your parents?"

"Absolutely not."

"It would probably be good for your charade if the two of you—"

"*Absolutely not*," I stress.

"Fine, fine." She goes quiet for a second as I pinch the bridge of my nose. "I just worry about you," she admits. "You're always so closed off, Noah."

"I am not—"

"Yes, you are," she argues. "You've been so worried about keeping that part of yourself hidden that you never let yourself get close to anyone. Hell, you barely talk to us about your problems anymore!"

"Language," I say sarcastically.

"Oh, shut up," she huffs. "All I'm saying is . . . it sounds like Mackenzie might be a special lady. After all, it takes a pretty exceptional person to turn her entire life upside down to help a stranger."

"I told you, this also benefits—"

"Yeah, yeah, I heard you," she says, cutting me off. "I'm just saying. There's one person who clearly stands to gain more from this arrangement than the other, and one person is *clearly* putting more on the line for the sake of the other."

"Mom, you're losing me here."

"Oh, for heaven's sake," she scoffs. "*You* stand to gain more, and *she* is putting more on the line. All I'm saying is . . . maybe that's something worth looking into."

"You just want this to go a certain way."

"Well, you aren't getting any younger, son."

"Wow. Thanks, Mom."

"It's not a crime to want *grandchildren*, Noah."

Maybe my mother and Mackenzie's grandmother aren't so different. Mackenzie would probably think this conversation is hilarious. Not that I can ever tell her about it.

"Okay, Mom. I really have to go. I have a consult coming up."

"Just don't dismiss this like you do everything else," she scolds. "You can't just shut everyone out for your whole life. You'll end up missing out on something . . . special."

"Yeah. Okay. Will do."

"And don't you ever lie to me again. I don't care how big you are, I'll whoop your—"

"Okay. Love you, Mom. Call you later."

I end the call before she can go off on a rant, dropping my phone on the desk and resting my head in my hands. My mother would lose her shit if I were to tell her I'm *sleeping* with my "special woman" and that I'm slowly losing my mind because of it. I haven't even worked out the specifics of that myself yet.

My phone buzzes again, a text this time, thankfully, and I assume my mother is following up with some last bit of advice, so I'm surprised (and secretly excited) when I see Mackenzie's name. I swipe open her text thread and nearly drop my phone—a picture of Mackenzie's bare legs in my bathtub with a caption underneath.

> **MACKENZIE:** I want to take this tub home
> with me.

I'm grinning before I can stop myself, feeling a visceral urge to pack up everything, cancel my appointments, and go back to my place to join her—but even in my head that sounds ridiculous. Not to mention dangerous.

I tap out a quick reply, one that reveals none of the heat currently rushing through my blood or the sudden stiffness in my slacks, and I take a deep breath, blowing it out as I set my phone back down. The problem is, I think, that I *want* to drop everything and go be with her. That the urge to do so gets stronger and stronger with every instance that I'm with her. Everything about this predicament screams *danger*, and I can't bring myself to do a single thing about it.

Don't make things complicated.

I really am in trouble.

13

Mackenzie

IT IS MUCH harder than it should be to leave Noah's Jacuzzi tub. It's big enough to be used as a small swimming pool, which makes sense, given that Noah's legs are of the Olympic swimmer variety. I'm toweling off my hair when I step out of his bathroom around lunchtime, wondering again if it's weird that I stayed behind at his place while he went into work. It had seemed like a lovely idea in the early hours of the morning when I'd been tangled in his sheets and blissed out from a full night of orgasms—but now that I'm a little coherent, I've been questioning if it's crossing some sort of line. Though to be fair, the lines of this agreement have never been very clear. And as much as I hate to admit it . . . the sex definitely doesn't help matters.

Although . . . one might argue that sex with Noah is worth it.

I sigh as I fall back against Noah's gigantic bed, trying to distract myself from thoughts of my quiet fake mate. His bedroom is exactly like I expected it to be (his entire house, really, for what I've seen of it). Save for the furniture and his very wide, very *roomy* bed—there wasn't much to explore in Noah's room after he'd left this morning. There's a moderately sized flat screen resting atop his chest of drawers, and above his bed, one lone painting of soft colors that remind me of quiet water and breezy trees. It's a surprising burst of color in his otherwise dreary-looking bedroom, and had I been able to notice anything other than Noah's mouth and hands and body last night—I might have commented on it while he'd still been here.

I throw an arm over my face as my skin tingles with the memory of the night before. Noah's hands on my skin and his voice in my ear have been right there waiting every time I let my thoughts stray this morning—something that seems like it might get worse every time we're together. Every tiny reminder has me pressing my thighs together as everything south of my navel begins to pulse with arousal.

It's not enough for Noah to be the most capable person at work; no, of *course* he would be an absolutely wonderful lay. I'm starting to wish I could pick out a flaw just so I didn't feel inadequate. A slight curve to his dick or an unsightly mole on his ass or something. A fruitless wish, since I can confirm that he has a perfect dick and an even more perfect ass. I don't see myself finding any flaws in the foreseeable future.

Not to mention the way having sex with Noah feels a lot more . . . intimate than it should. I'm not an expert at the whole friends with benefits thing—in fact, I'd say I'm still at apprentice level at best—but I have to assume that most hookup buddies don't look at you like you're some kind of goddess and whisper sweet things in your ear while they give you mind-blowing orgasms.

I don't have to imagine anything.

I press my lips together as my stomach flutters with the memory of his low voice, sounding entirely sincere when he'd looked at me last night.

You're fucking beautiful.

I sit up with a sigh. The room is too warm. Feeling flushed seems like it might be becoming my base state, if the last couple of days have been any indication.

"Damn it," I grumble to the air.

I think it's probably a smart move to grab my (hopefully) dry scrubs from Noah's dryer and start getting ready for work—and I have every intention of doing that. At least, until I get two steps from the bed, and my foot hits Noah's dress shirt he'd shucked off last night. I pick it up with only a little hesitation, biting at my lip as I test its weight.

I picked it up with mostly innocent intentions, running my fingers over one sleeve and caressing the fabric that feels too fine, too pretty for me. I can imagine that same material wrapped around his bicep, curling my fingers there to hold on as he pulls me closer, as his mouth descends to—

I shake away the thought, startled. I don't *pine* for anyone, and yet here I am waxing poetic in my head about a fucking shirt. What the hell is wrong with me today? Even as I scold myself, I can smell the material still in my hands, tempting me. It smells like detergent and the clinging bit of Noah's scent—something fresh and masculine that makes me want more. It isn't even a conscious thing when I press the fabric against my nostrils and breathe in deep. It's become somehow thicker since we first agreed to all this, even the faded bit clinging to his shirt from yesterday is enough to make my eyes roll back.

I feel a prickling sensation in my skin, like it's being stretched too tight—the tingling feeling becoming almost uncomfortable as the throbbing between my legs worsens. How can I be horny again after spending most of the night losing sleep with Noah? What's worse—despite having just spent an hour soaking in Noah's too-large tub, I can feel a bit of slick trickling out to wet my thighs. Almost like my body is hoping he'll pop out of the closet and come take care of us.

You said you wouldn't get all dickmatized, I remind myself. *Remember, this is all temporary.*

The thought sobers me a little but does nothing for the throbbing between my legs.

I push my fingers inside one sleeve to feel the soft material against my skin, tempted briefly to put it on, to feel its weight on my shoulders like an embrace.

Too tempted, as it turns out.

I drop my towel as I push my arms into both long sleeves, my body almost *sighing* with relief when I am fully enveloped in the scent of him. I can't explain it, can't even begin to make sense of it—but being wrapped up in something of *Noah's* seems to soothe that odd sensation in my skin. Almost like it's calming me.

It's probably a bad idea (not to mention uncouth) to touch myself in Noah's bed while he's away, but I reason that it's *his* fault that I'm so worked up only an hour before my shift starts, so that assuages my guilt a little. It makes it a lot easier to crawl back into his bed wearing nothing but his shirt.

Like this, the smell of him is more overwhelming, giving me the illusion of pressing my nose to his chest, his throat, maybe. I close my eyes as I imagine thick arms wrapped around me; an innocent fantasy, really, but the effect it has on me less so. I press my thighs together as I imagine his weight settling over me, as I imagine that same scent of him surrounding me as he pushes me into this big, big bed of his—and it's easy, wrapped in his shirt, to remember how he *covers* me. He's so *big*, after all.

My throat is dry now, and there's an obvious slickness between my legs forcing me to spread them a little just to ease the sensation. A mistake, I realize, given that I've somehow become wet enough just from *imagining* him touching me for it to make the inner creases sticky.

My heart rate picks up a dozen beats or so as I again press my nose against the soft fabric of his shirt to breathe him in—and my fingers *just* graze below my navel from beneath the ends of his sleeves. There's a heavy throbbing between my legs now, some strange ball of heat in my belly that threatens to spread into my limbs.

I bite at my lower lip as I attempt to swallow, but there's a lump there now that makes it difficult. I rub my wrist against my belly until the sleeve bunches enough to allow my fingers to delve between slick folds, gasping when they slide across the rapidly swelling bud of my clit.

I hiss between my teeth when I apply a slight pressure, an immediate *zing* of pleasure that melds with the odd relief Noah's scent brings to nearly steal my breath. My body rolls until my face presses to his comforter, lying on my side with my nose buried against my shoulder. I keep my eyes shut tight, breathing in deep so that I can pretend he's here, that *he's* touching me.

I roll my fingers against my clit without any pretense, without any type of teasing or buildup—having only the singular mission of slaking the heavy thirst that seems to have control of my senses at the moment. I imagine hands that are larger, a body so much *wider*—letting the fantasy fuel me until I can practically *hear* that deep, deep voice of his murmuring praises in my ear. I hear impossible encouragement of how *good* I am for him, things I've never considered outside of porn, things I might have even called *laughable* before this—but I'm not laughing at the thought of being *good* for Noah. I'm not laughing one fucking bit.

My breath is little more than desperate panting now, my wrist aching, but I'm *so close*. I can hear myself beginning to whimper, working my hand as quickly as I'm able, drawing out that friction until blood rushes in my ears. I'm so close. So fucking *close*, and I—

The trill of my cell phone nearly causes me to jump out of my own skin.

It startles me so severely that I physically *jolt*—scrabbling to my back and withdrawing my hand from between my legs so fast that my slick fingers curl into the edge of his sleeves to smear my fluids there, making me grimace. My phone continues to ring nearby on the bedside table, and I blink up at Noah's ceiling in a daze as I try to reconcile it with what I was just doing. It occurs to me that it could be work, and I know that despite the *terrible* position I'm in, I have to answer it.

I manage to scramble to the other side of the bed and grab for the phone, trying to shake back the long sleeves of Noah's shirt. My eyes widen for only a moment in surprise before I accept the call in a fit of panic because—

"Mackenzie." His voice comes through the phone, as low and tempting as I was just imagining.

My clit throbs as if in recognition, still demanding that I finish. "Hey, Noah."

"Everything okay? You sound out of breath."

"Y-yes," I say too quickly. "I was . . . drying my hair."

"Drying your hair?"

"Yes," I try again, keeping my voice as even as I'm able. "There's a lot of it."

There's a terrifying moment where I think he'll press me on the matter, but he blessedly moves on from the subject. "Oh. Well. I was calling to see if you wanted to eat together in the cafeteria on your lunch break," he asks innocently. "It could appear weird that we never do."

I might laugh if I wasn't still so horribly turned on. Here I am abusing myself in his bed, and he's worried about appearances. It only cements how utterly ridiculous I'm being right now.

"That's a good idea," I say airily, closing my eyes as his voice keys me up despite the innocuous words coming out of his mouth. "Sure."

"We don't have to if you don't want to," he offers contritely, almost like he's afraid the question is annoying me. "It might be a stupid idea."

"No, no," I argue. "It's a good idea."

God, how am I still this turned on from such an innocent conversation? Just his voice is somehow both worsening and relieving the feverish quality of my skin.

He laughs a little, a low, pleasant sound that trickles down through me to settle right at the still-throbbing bundle of my clit. "I figure the least I can do is make sure you get lunch since I didn't feed you last night."

Mayday. Mayday. Don't think about last night right now.

"I wasn't really worried about food last night," I manage tightly.

"Neither was I," he murmurs.

There's a torturous stretch of silence where the prickling in my skin gets worse with every second.

"Okay . . ." My heart continues to pound as I listen to the sound of his breathing, spanning only a moment. "I guess I'll see you later?"

"You're . . . okay. Right? You sound off."

I close my eyes. Surely I can't tell him that I sniffed his shirt and suddenly lost my mind. He'll be sending me packing if he thinks I'm over here developing some sort of unhealthy attachment to his discarded clothes.

"I'm fine," I lie. "Just a little tired."

"All right," he says. "If you're sure. I'll just see you when you get here, then."

I let him go before I completely ruin everything, dropping my phone to the mattress and staring up at the ceiling as I try to come to terms with what I almost did. It's beyond the realm of what I thought I was capable of, what just happened. I've never done *anything* like that.

But then again, there are a lot of things I hadn't considered until this . . . agreement.

I don't touch myself again, even as my body *screams* that I finish—mostly because I am appalled at myself for getting so worked up over something as simple as the *scent* of Noah. That stretched sensation is still in my skin, and that pulsing is still heavy between my thighs, and even as I stumble to the dryer on shaky legs, sneaking Noah's shirt into his laundry—there is still something that feels . . . off. Even if I can't for the life of me imagine what that something is.

I don't have to imagine anything, the memory of Noah's voice whispers. *You're fucking beautiful.*

A shiver passes through me. This is going to be a long day.

—⁓—

"YOU DON'T LOOK so good."

I purse my lips, cutting my eyes to my right at a discerning-looking Parker. "Thanks."

"I just mean, you look sick or something."

"I'm fine," I toss back. "Just worry about the computer."

"Pretty sure they deleted the program icon from the desktop again," he grouses.

I shrug, looking over the chart in my hand. "Well, I've listened to three different nurses bitching about it, so just fix whatever it is so I don't have to hear about it anymore."

Parker stops working on the buggy terminal behind the nurses' station, eyeing me strangely. "Someone's in a mood. Are you sure you aren't sick?"

I screw my eyes shut, trying to block out the slight pounding in my head. It's true that I have felt off since this morning, but what I'd thought was a bad case of being dick drunk had turned into more and more of a puny feeling with every passing hour. Maybe I *am* getting sick.

"I don't know," I sigh. "My head is killing me."

"It's probably your conscience trying to knock some sense into you about your recent sexcapades," Parker quips.

"Not today," I huff. "Not unless you're offering a big fat ibuprofen."

"When did it start?"

I pinch the bridge of my nose. "It seems to be getting worse since this morning," I tell him truthfully. "Ever since I left Noah's."

Parker scoffs. "You're staying over now?"

"It just made sense," I tell him wearily. "Since I was there so late."

"I know you think I'm being a dick—"

"A valid opinion," I cut in.

"—*but* I'm worried about you, Mack. That's all. I thought it was a bad idea when you got wrapped up in this whole fake-mate non-sense, but I don't think you're considering the possible fallout of all this."

"Keep your voice down," I hiss, looking around to find us still alone. "You're making too big of a deal about it, I promise. It's a damned headache. Not an existential crisis."

"I know, but you've always been so careful about how close you get to people, and now you're diving into this pretend relationship headfirst without a second thought. I know you want to help Noah, but I worry you'll end up getting hurt."

"I said, keep your voice dow—"

"Hey," a lilting voice calls from the counter behind us. "Do you have a list of Mr. Wheeler's medication?"

I turn, immediately feeling my spine stiffen as I notice the last person I want within earshot of this conversation. Dennis Martin is smiling at me from the other side of the counter, his expression seemingly devoid of any indications that he might have heard what Parker and I were talking about.

"Oh," Dennis says with innocent surprise. "I didn't see you there, Dr. Carter. I mean, Mack." He chuckles to himself. "Right?"

"Right," I say woodenly. "Mack is fine."

"I thought you were a nurse," he says with another quiet laugh. "Any idea where they've all gone?"

"Staff meeting," I tell him. "Parker was just looking at a wonky terminal while they were gone. They should be back soon, though, if you need something."

"No, no," he says casually. "I can come back. It isn't urgent." He braces his elbow on the counter, leaning against it. "How is Noah?"

I feel myself bristle. "Noah is . . . fine."

"Good, good," Dennis answers cheerfully. "He's seemed a little off lately, hasn't he? I worry, you know."

I bet you do.

"Just stress, I think," I tell him, trying not to let the panic in my belly show on my face. "He's been very busy."

"Oh, well, that's good to hear," Dennis offers, that same unreadable smile at his mouth. "I know all that fuss with the board must have been such a hassle."

I keep my expression even, refusing to tear my eyes from his for fear of seeming guilty. "Fortunately, it was just a misunderstanding."

"Right," he says, his smile tilting up further.

He stays like that for a second too long, finally drumming his fingers against the countertop as he pushes away from it.

"Anyway," he tells us in that same cheery tone, "I guess I'll come back in a bit. Hope you guys get this situation sorted."

He points to the terminal Parker has been gaping at him from behind for the last few minutes, and I give Dennis a tight nod. "Sure thing."

"Tell Noah I said hi," he calls over his shoulder as he starts off down the hall.

I don't answer, Parker and I keeping quiet until Dennis's footsteps have faded away down the hall. How in the hell had we not heard him coming up to begin with? I blow out a heavy breath when it's clear he's gone, bending to brace my hands on my knees. My headache is exponentially worse than it had been before Dennis's interruption.

Parker makes a choked sound beside me. "Do you think he heard anything?"

"I . . ." I consider this for a long moment, finally shaking my head. "I don't think so. He would have been way more smug, from what I know about him. I think that was just his normal bullshit."

"I'm going to have a heart attack before all this is over."

"I'll prescribe you some Klonopin."

"That feels unethical." He must notice the way I'm shaking then. "Hey, are you okay? I really don't think he heard anything."

I shake my head, which feels foggy all of a sudden. "I don't know."

On top of my headache there is now that same strange tightness in my skin, similar to this morning but entirely worse with the still-pounding rhythm of my heart after the nerve-racking encounter with Dennis. I feel dizzy and weak, and my knees are trembling as if I might collapse at any given second.

What is wrong with me?

I feel myself stumbling before my ass even hits the ground, my head beginning to spin and my tongue seeming too thick. I sense Parker's hand against my forehead, hear his muttered curse when he pulls it away.

"Jesus, Mack. You're burning up. You are definitely not okay." I hear him shouting for help, and I wince at the loudness of his voice, shutting my eyes in hopes that it will ease the pain in my head. "Hey! We need some help over here!"

There are footsteps that sound far away even when I can sense another body nearing, and I try to blink my eyes to discern who's joined us, only to learn my vision is now blurry. There's a cramping that's starting up deep in my belly, a fire in my lungs that worsens with every breath.

But the worst of it doesn't come until I hear Parker's voice again—hear him asking someone I can't see what on earth is wrong with me.

And just as I feel a growing wetness between my legs I hear a tight voice mutter back:

"She's going into heat."

More than the panic, I notice the deep disappointment when I realize the voice doesn't belong to Noah.

14

Noah

WHEN IT HITS me, it's like a lightning strike.

I scent her the moment I step off the elevator onto her floor, and everything that comes after is hazy, like I'm watching it happen from outside my body. Coming to find her so that we can have lunch is a faraway thought, drowned in the all-encompassing sensation of being struck with Mackenzie's scent that is practically dripping from the fucking walls. Even without being able to see her, it is immediately clear to me what's happened. I can't say why, or even how, but my body *knows* that she needs me. It becomes the driving force that seems to keep me moving.

The hairs on the back of my neck stand up, my heart rate rising and my blood rushing in my ears as my feet start to carry me down the hall in search of her. I can feel them pad one after the other as I move as if being pulled by a string, a hypnotic chanting in my head of *omega omega omega* that seeps into every facet of my being. I can't begin to know what's happening, or why my body is responding the way it is, but right now I am little more than a blind need to *get to her.*

There's a small crowd around the nurses' station, and even

though I can't see her, I *know* Mackenzie is here even before I begin to push through the small gathering of people. I can hear a male voice that sounds tight and strained, one that is asking another person if they can hear him, if they're okay.

But it is only when I can see her—see her small body curled in on itself with flushed skin and damp hair clinging to her temples—that I really start to lose it.

Because someone is touching her. Another wolf who looks up at me with a hardness to his eyes that I can somehow sense is bordering on challenge, and with the way red flashes in my vision, it takes me a second longer than it should to recognize Mackenzie's nurse friend from yesterday hovering near her panting form, looking at me like he wishes I were anywhere else.

Mine. Omega. Mine.

I grind my teeth together and clench my fists, a brief urge to tear him away from her, one that is hard to ignore, but somehow I manage to keep it contained. "I need everyone to back away from my mate now, please," I ask as evenly as I can. Even to my own ears it sounds rough. It takes every shred of my control to keep from tearing the others from her physically. "I've got her."

Liam's fingers linger at her arm for almost longer than my frazzled senses can stand, but when I take another step to close the distance between us, I notice his hand curling from her forearm and pulling away before he slowly moves to stand.

"She's going into heat," he says in a hard tone.

My nostrils flare, the evidence of this practically burrowing itself into my brain. "Yes. Which is why I am taking her home. But I need everyone to give us some space."

Mine. Omega. Mine.

"Why would you let her leave home this morning?"

My jaw clenches so hard it might crack my teeth if I keep it up. His scent is agitated, and sampling it mixed in with Mackenzie's is making my stomach turn. Scenting her with *anyone* else feels completely wrong. Especially now. "She wasn't showing signs this morning."

And it's true, she hadn't—but that knowledge doesn't stop me from wanting to kick my own ass for possibly being even a little at fault. For letting *anyone* else see her like this. The more primal part of my brain is actively berating me because *I* should be the only one to see her like this, it roars.

"Well she sure as hell is now," Liam grinds out. "She's burning up. She needs—"

"I know exactly what she needs," I hiss. "Thank you."

I ignore him then, moving to Mackenzie's side and pushing down the territorial rumbling in my chest when I notice her friend—Parker, I think she said his name was—is still touching her. The fact that I can tell he is human and therefore can't possibly scent her like this is the only thing keeping me in check. It's the only thing keeping me from ripping his hand from her body.

Parker frowns at me, still clutching Mackenzie's shoulders. "She collapsed. She was complaining of a headache, and then she started looking pale, and she just . . ." He looks down at her with concern. "She really is burning up."

I nod absently, not bothering to look at him. I can't tear my eyes from Mackenzie now. "I've got her," I murmur. "I'm going to take her home."

Parker's hand pushes between us just as I reach for her, his expression hard and showing not even an ounce of fear at getting between an alpha and an omega approaching her heat. Actually, he almost looks like he might attempt to kick my ass if I keep going.

The shred of sanity I'm clinging to reminds me it would be bad to make an enemy of Mackenzie's best friend.

"We both know why I don't think that's a good idea," Parker says, low enough for only me to hear. "I don't know if I should just let you—"

"Noah?"

Mackenzie surprises us both when she pushes up from the floor, tearing herself out of Parker's grip and winding her arms around my neck and pulling herself closer so she can nuzzle at the front of my shirt. I can feel her inhale, hear her soft sigh after.

"Noah," she breathes again, almost like a coo. Like she's *relieved*.

I bring my arms around her. "I'm here."

"Hurts," she groans quietly.

"I know," I soothe. "I've got you."

She pulls her head back to blink at me, turning her neck slightly to take in the small crowd. "Can we go? I don't . . ." Her fingers clutch at my shirt tighter. "Take me home."

"Of course." She doesn't protest in the slightest when I pull her into my arms before standing, holding her against my chest to cradle her there. "I'll take you home." I look at Parker then, noticing he still looks more than wary of me. I step closer, lowering my voice. "I would never do anything she doesn't want, but right now, my scent can at the very least keep her calm. Let me take care of her. If all she wants is to be near me, then that's as far as it will go. You have my word on that. All right?"

He still looks unsure when I pull away, looking from me to Mackenzie and back again, finally nodding reluctantly. "I'm going to fucking hold you to that, Taylor."

I'm already turning away from him before he's even finished speaking, pushing through the crowd with Mackenzie in my arms even as she burrows closer against me, her face tucking into the crook of my neck as her breath puffs against my skin.

"Don't let go," she murmurs, sounding pained and tired.

I don't know if she hears me answer—*Never*—since she dozes off then, but it's probably for the best, given that I have no idea why I even said it.

~

I'VE BEEN WATCHING her sleep for more than an hour.

On any other occasion, I might worry that I was being a total creep, and there's still a high possibility that I could be—but I don't think I can physically take my eyes off her.

She'd woken only for a moment when I laid her in my bed after I had gotten her back to my place, only long enough to bury herself in my sheets and wildly pull the blankets around her. Almost like she's nesting. Every so often she makes a tiny, pained sound in her sleep, and each one tugs at something inside of me that I don't recognize. Each one pokes at that barely checked mania that seems to seep out of me whenever I'm near her. And those feelings are a thousand times worse now, with her scent filling my bedroom and most likely permeating the walls to the point that it might never fade. I can't even find it in me to mind, honestly.

Admittedly, this isn't the first time I've experienced this. I'm seasoned enough that I've helped more than one shifter woman I've dated through her heat in the last decade or so—but I have *never* felt something as blinding as what I'm feeling sitting only a foot from the tiny omega in my bed whose scent threatens to drive me insane. What I'm feeling now seems bigger, more consuming, even. What I'm feeling now makes it hard to keep still. Almost like every fiber of my being is protesting that it isn't wrapped up in her.

And if it's this bad now, how much worse will it be when she fully goes into heat? I know this is just a taste of what's to come, and that idea both delights and terrifies. Will I be able to keep my control when she loses hers?

I wonder if there had been some sort of sign I should have picked up on, if there had been any subtle tells that I might have sussed out this morning before leaving her alone. In all my experiences with someone's heat, it has been something very scheduled, something that comes about almost like clockwork. It's always been a building of recognizable symptoms that allowed for someone to *plan*—but I have never seen anyone go into heat this suddenly, and definitely not this fiercely.

It's enough to make me wonder about all sorts of things, but mostly I find myself concentrating solely on the rise and fall of her chest, the soft sounds she makes in sleep, and the enticing fragrance of her, which washes over me in waves.

I don't know how long I wait before I catch her lashes fluttering, sitting up straighter when I notice her stirring, her hands slowly pushing her into a more upright position as she blinks around the room in a daze. She notices me sitting at the end of the bed then, her brow furrowing as she seemingly tries to rectify my presence there with what she's feeling—or at least that's what I would guess.

I keep perfectly still, wrestling with the urge to touch her, even slightly. "How are you feeling?"

"Tired," she croaks. "Hot." She wrinkles her nose down at her rumpled scrubs. "I'm all sweaty."

I cannot tell her that I've been fantasizing about licking the sweat from her body for the last hour or so. Definitely not.

"Did you . . . expect this?"

Her eyes find mine only to widen, looking taken aback. "What?

No! I had no idea. I've never . . ." Her eyes drift closed as she makes a quiet sound, one that feels like it touches me all over. "Definitely never had one come all of a sudden like this."

"How off schedule?"

"A month? Maybe? It's barely been six weeks, and they usually come like clockwork. I promise, I wouldn't have ever kept this from you."

"I know you wouldn't," I assure her. We both know how irresponsible it might be to dive into something like this without any sort of caution; surely she is as aware as I am of how many mating bonds occur like this, only for those same couples to be undergoing painful procedures later on to break the bond when they realize they're no good for each other. "But it doesn't make sense," I tell her truthfully. "I've never heard of a heat coming so off schedule."

She shakes her head. "Neither have I."

"There weren't any signs?"

"None that seemed super obvious," she says. "I've been a little flushed since yesterday, but I thought that was just because you—" She blushes, and as much as I'd like to beg her to finish that sentence, I keep quiet, letting her talk. "I didn't think anything of it. I had a horrible headache earlier, too, but even that's weird. It's never been that bad before a heat." She looks at me intently. "Have you ever heard of anything like this?"

I shake my head. "Never."

"What do you think it means?"

"I think . . . it might be one of those consequences I mentioned that we couldn't have possibly known when we . . . added our little addendum."

She averts her gaze, sounding almost disappointed. "Consequences?"

"That doesn't mean I regret the addendum," I tell her immediately, needing her to know. "But it does mean I have no idea what we should do."

She looks more placated now. "I know."

"Does it still hurt? Your head?"

"Not as bad. Not since—" She blushes again. "It got better when you got there. I think your scent is helping."

"That part, at least, makes sense," I muse.

We're both still, both looking at each other from across my bed with what is likely the same question on our tongues. Even if neither of us seems to be able to come out and ask it.

"You'll need to shift," I say. "It'll start to hurt if you don't."

"I know," she sighs. "Usually, I book a stay at the heat retreat at the edge of town, but there's no way they'll be able to work me in on such short notice."

I have to physically restrain myself from prodding about how she took care of this in the past, who she took care of it *with*—focusing instead on what's happening right now. I know if I let my mind wander too much in that direction it will be hard to keep as calm as I'm attempting to be for her sake.

"I know a place," I tell her. "It's not far. Maybe two hours. We could go there. If you want."

Her eyes look rounder, brighter, like she's curious. "We?"

"That is—" I clear my throat, looking away from her. "I didn't mean to imply that—I just meant—Fuck." I run my hands through my hair. "I don't know what the protocol is here. I could still make arrangements for you to go alone, if that's what you want."

"And that . . . You could do that?"

It's almost agony, imagining sending her away from me the way she is right now, but I remember my promise to Parker, and I remember that I am *not* a fucking animal despite what I am, and I nod heavily. "If that's what you want. I will do anything you want me to, Mackenzie."

She looks down at the sheets that are rumpled around her waist, her finger teasing the edge of one as her teeth imprint slightly against her bottom lip. I watch this intently, battling urges to nibble at that same lip myself before I use my mouth elsewhere. Does she have to smell so goddamn *good*?

"And if . . ." I can hear her swallow, see the way she shifts her body minutely. My eyes track every little movement. "And if I wanted you to come with me?"

Yes. Omega. Mine.

I grit my teeth against the loud growling somewhere deep in my subconscious, willing it to be quiet. "Do you?"

She holds my gaze, her bright, amber eyes much darker now— a raw, deep honey that I could easily get lost in. "I want you to come with me."

"You want . . ." My fingernails bite into my skin through the material of my slacks, and I let the slight sting ground me. "You want my help."

It takes her at least ten seconds to answer, "Yes. We . . . we said we could help each other, didn't we?"

And even as she says it there is a growing part of me that knows it's becoming dangerous, that the lines of our agreement are blurring astronomically—at least for me. It's for that reason alone that I should send her to my cousin's cabin outside of town, that I should put as much distance as I can between us so I don't risk tumbling headfirst into the disaster that will surely result from me sharing such an intimate experience with this woman who is invading my thoughts more and more each day.

But I don't do any of those things, because the idea of touching her right now feels more important than water. Than air, even.

"Yes. We did."

"And you know a place?"

I nod. "My cousin owns a small ski lodge in Pleasant Hill. Just under a two-hour drive, give or take," I tell her again. "I'm sure he would be willing to let us . . . borrow it. For a few days."

My body is almost screaming at the idea of being alone with Mackenzie for a string of days when she smells as incredible as she does right now. All the things I'm thinking of *doing* to her. She might run away screaming if she could read my thoughts.

"What about work?"

I blink. I hadn't thought of this yet. I frown into my lap, considering all the options before the most obvious one hits me. "I have heat leave."

"You do?"

I look up to meet her eyes. "*We* do," I correct. "You are my mate, after all."

"Mate," she echoes, and the heated way she looks at me . . . I wish I could capture it somehow. So that I could take it out and look at it whenever I want. "As far as they know."

Reality is a fickle bitch, and the reminder of the falsity of everything between us holds an odd sting. I don't have the mental capacity to explore why right now, too distracted by her soft blush and her softer mouth. I can't really consider anything outside of getting Mackenzie into a bed where I can taste and touch her to my heart's content for the foreseeable future.

"Right," I manage.

She bites her lip again, and I have to send down a silent plea that my cock calm down, knowing she needs me to be stronger than that right now. That I will have arrangements to make shortly.

"Okay," she says easily.

"Okay?" I might be an idiot for questioning her, but I have to be certain. "And you're sure you want me to . . . help?"

She considers this for a moment with her eyes still studying my face, finally rustling away from her little nest of covers and crawling slowly across the bed to bring herself nearer to me. She doesn't touch me, keeping her hands pressed firmly to the mattress—but I can feel her warm breath against my mouth moments before she brushes her lips over mine, and it takes everything I have not to take her right here, even knowing that we would most likely destroy my house when her need to shift sets in.

Right now it almost feels like that possibility could be worth it.

"I'm sure," she murmurs. "Make the call." Another kiss that is slight but threatens to make me crazy just the same. "Hurry, Noah."

I don't think I've ever moved faster.

15

Mackenzie

THE DRIVE TO Noah's cousin's place borders on torture. With every mile the fever in my skin seems to worsen, a burn building deep down inside that threatens to consume me. There are moments during the two-hour trip where I notice Noah's fingers gripping the steering wheel too tightly, others where his hand reaches out to touch me almost unconsciously, only for him to jerk it away at the last second. It's like he's afraid if he touches me, he won't stop. There is a part of me that is delighted by the idea of this, but there is another that isn't so sure how to feel about it.

It's true that it was *my* idea for Noah to come with me, to help me through this strange heat that neither of us saw coming—but in the brief moments of clarity (however few), I can't help but be wary of it all. Because the way I've been feeling since Noah found me back at the hospital, the way every part of me seems to *need* him . . . It's a feeling I've never experienced before.

It feels too heavy, too much like all the things I've spent my adult life avoiding, and yet in the face of the all-consuming heat that is building in my head and my skin and deep, deep down in my belly—I can't seem to fight it. I can't seem to even *want* to, and shouldn't that have me second-guessing this entire thing?

The snowfall is thicker the closer we get to Pleasant Hill, coming down in large flakes against the window to add to the lush blanket of powder white that coats the ground and the trees outside the car. Noah says very little during the entire trip, and outside of soft panting and low groans, I'm not exactly the picture of conversation either. The need to shift is more prominent now, that tightness in my skin worsening to the point that it feels like it might tear at any given second. It's nothing I haven't experienced before; a shifter in heat means being more of their animal self, after all, but I can't remember it ever feeling so dire before. Everything about this time feels different and almost completely new.

It has me thinking about those consequences Noah was so worried about. When I'm able to form rational thought, that is. Half the time it feels like I'm living in a foggy state of delirium that makes it hard to remember where I am.

"It's just past these trees," Noah says at some point. "Are you okay?"

I think I nod. "Still hurts."

I *do* feel his hand then, light as a feather as it brushes my temple. It's amazing how this small touch can make me feel so much better. "You're still burning up," I hear him murmur. "I should have taken care of you before we left."

Taken care of you.

It makes me shiver thinking about it, because I know that *taking care of me* means touching me, filling me, giving my body all the things it's begging for right now.

I blink with heavy lids when I get a peek of a dark structure standing stark against the white snow as we emerge through a coppice of thick, snow-covered pines, lifting my head with difficulty to peer at the lodge that is only slightly larger than a cabin and in no better shape. The wood is worn, the railing broken in a few places, and a few shingles look precarious on the roof, as if they might fall off at any moment.

"Hunter really needs to do some upkeep," Noah grumbles. He cuts his eyes at me. "Sorry, it's been a while since I've been here."

I shake my head. "It's fine."

The front door of the lodge opens when we pull up out front to reveal a large man who rivals Noah's height but is somehow impossibly broader—his dark hair a similar color but wild and curly as it juts out of his dark gray beanie. His features resemble Noah's in a lot of ways; his mouth is just as full even hidden behind his dark scruff, and he wears the same expression Noah is so fond of, one that seems mildly irritated.

"Is that your cousin?"

Noah is tense when my eyes land on him, his mouth pulled down in a frown and his eyes hard. His throat bobs with a swallow as he turns his head to look at me, his eyes dark and wary. "Stay here," he says, less of a request and more of a command. "Don't get out of the car."

"Okay?"

He looks back at his cousin, who gives us a brief wave from the porch, huffing out a breath. "Hunter is also an alpha." His voice sounds tighter. "I don't want—" He shakes his head. "I don't want him scenting you like this."

"I'm sure he wouldn't do any—"

"You have no idea what you smell like right now, Mackenzie,"

Noah growls. "It's taken every ounce of willpower I have this entire trip not to pull over this car and knot you in the backseat."

A quiet gasp escapes me, and hearing it makes Noah blink, his expression changing to one of mild surprise.

"I'm sorry," he says in a rush. "I . . ." He turns back to the front, closing his eyes as his fingers squeeze the steering wheel roughly. "Please stay here."

Oh.

There's a pulsing between my legs, and I feel a little trickle of slick seep out into my underwear. Noah's nostrils flare, and it does something strange to me, knowing he *knows*. That he can smell how much I want him right now.

"I'll stay," I tell him softly.

He nods rigidly. "Thank you."

I watch him as he climbs out of the car, pulling his coat tight as he stomps across the snow to meet his cousin on the porch. Noah still looks slightly flustered as they talk, and there is a moment when Hunter turns his head to look at me through the windshield, and the hard set of his eyes makes me shiver.

The genes in this family, I swear.

Noah looks anything but happy with Hunter's curiosity, everything about his posture screaming that he's uncomfortable with someone else being so close to me right now. Especially someone like Hunter.

And why does that feel so satisfying? It makes me feel warm in a way that has nothing to do with my heat, the warmth resonating solely in my chest like a heated stone that's taken up residence there. It's true that Noah's behavior during all this has been fairly possessive and unlike him, but I've been telling myself it's just a byproduct of his hormones reacting to mine. It's nothing more than his alpha instincts kicking in and even going into overdrive since they've never really been used before. Because it can't be anything more than that . . . can it?

I'm still pondering this as Hunter hands Noah a set of keys before slapping him on the shoulder, watching as Hunter's mouth tilts in a lopsided grin before he sets off down the stairs toward an old, dark green Bronco parked on the side of the lodge. Noah watches him drive off, that same tense expression on his face, with that same hard line of his mouth. Even as agitated as he looks, watching him makes me feel more flushed, if that's even possible, my breath turning shallow as that tightness in my skin worsens. My entire body is screaming at me to go to him, seeming to know that Noah can give us exactly what we want. In this moment, knowing that we're alone, nothing seems as important as the broad, agitated-looking doctor coming down the lodge steps after me.

I don't move as he closes the distance between the lodge and the passenger door, waiting until he opens the door and leans down to look at me to release the breath I'm holding. "You can come now."

Fuck.

I shiver all over. It's not what he means, the way my brain is interpreting it, but it doesn't stop me from needing to press my legs together. Noah reaches out with his hand in silent waiting, and it feels cool on my fevered skin when I place mine inside it. His thumb strokes my palm in a slow back and forth, and then he's pulling me from the car and helping me stand on unsteady legs as I fall against him. Even in the cool air it feels warm between us, and Noah's hand at my lower back is downright hot through my clothes.

"Let's get you inside," he hums. "It's just you and me now."

The giddiness this makes me feel has to be dangerous, given what we are, but knowing that does nothing to stop me from feeling it. Not a damn thing.

~

I'M WATCHING HIM set up some sort of emergency heat station on the wooden dresser in the bedroom he helped me to; it seems like Noah thought about this a lot more than I did, if the water bottles, easily accessible snacks, and towels are any indication. I can see how he's stressing over it—like he might be afraid that he's missed something—his hand over his mouth and his brow furrowed as he most likely mentally checks off anything else we might need. I could almost laugh; only *Noah* could be so calculating during a time like this.

My stomach clenches as I consider how much he's thought about me, about taking *care* of me, but that confusion is something I can't handle right now.

"Is there really no one else here?"

Noah turns to regard me. "Hunter went down to stay with his aunt, Jeannie. Since business isn't what it used to be . . ." His eyes are heated now. "It's just us."

"Wow," I answer with a choked laugh. "A whole ski lodge for a sexcation. How romantic."

Noah doesn't laugh. "How are you feeling?"

"Okay at the moment," I tell him honestly. "The headache isn't as bad, and I don't feel like my skin is catching on fire, mostly."

"Your scent is still"—he rolls his lips together—"very thick."

I can't help it; in this moment of clarity I find myself curious. "Is it really hard to stand?"

"It isn't . . . easy," Noah says. "Actually, it's fucking hard."

And why does that make me even more giddy? Do I *like* the fact that Noah is admitting to going a little insane over me? It definitely feels more like the "complicated" way of things. Then again, it feels like everything about Noah and me has been complicated lately. The more I assess it, the more it sort of scares the shit out of me. I can't let myself read too much into this, knowing that he'll be gone within a month or more. It's exactly the sort of scenario I wanted to avoid when I agreed to this. The same scenario that felt *impossible* when I agreed to this. I don't get giddy over men I've known for so little time. Hell, I don't get giddy over men, period, really.

So why does the way Noah looks at me make me feel so warm? Is it my heat? Or something else?

"It's hard being around you too," I half whisper. "You smell really good."

His hands clench at his sides. "Do I."

"You've always smelled good," I answer truthfully, the words falling out of my mouth almost beyond my control. "It's calming. Like being in the snow, but . . . it's warm too."

"Warm," he echoes, eyes caressing my face.

I nod. "Or at least . . . it makes me feel warm."

"Really," he says softly. There's another clench of his fists, and then a step, and I feel the breath in my lungs get hung up like it's forgotten how to work itself out of my body. "Do you know what your scent does to me?"

He takes another step, and the distance between us is so short now, with the way I'm teetering on the edge of the bed, leaning forward to try and lessen it even further. "No."

"It makes me feel like I have no control," he breathes, feet bumping against mine as he curls his body to brace his hands on either side of my waist. "And I'm very good at keeping my control."

I swallow thickly. "What else?"

"What else . . ." He leans in, his nose brushing against my throat to breathe me in as I shudder. "Now that I know what you taste like, what you *feel* like—your scent makes me remember everything." I feel a barely-there press of his lips against the scent gland at the base of my throat, and if I weren't already sitting, my knees would most likely be buckling. "The sounds you make when I'm inside you." His tongue flicks against that same place, and I gasp softly. "The way you taste when you come on my tongue." I have to close my eyes; I'm not sure I could have ever imagined Noah talking to me like this, but I can't say I dislike it. "How fucking soft you are when you're spread out on my bed, wrapped around my knot."

"Noah," I whimper, feeling that heat building all over again, obliterating the little calm I'd been experiencing.

"Do you want that, Mackenzie?" His teeth graze my skin, and I have to grasp his shirt just to keep me grounded. "Do you want my knot?"

I squirm under him, all reason whooshing out the window and into the snow. "Noah, I—"

"I can smell how wet you are," he growls. "I always can. Do you know how crazy it makes me, knowing that's for me? That *I* made you that way?"

He's right; my underwear is practically soaked through, and every inch of my skin feels stretched to the point of burning. In fact, *I* feel like I'm burning. Burning from the inside out.

I let a hand wander, fingertips grazing his shirt as they trail down to the bit of skin bared at the hem. When I cup him lower I can *feel* how much he wants to give me what he's offering, his cock straining against his jeans and feeling hot even through the fabric. I know what it will feel like now, how it'll stretch me to points of pleasure that could almost be pain they're so intense—and I *do* want it. Right now there's nothing I want more.

"Fuck," Noah hisses as I squeeze him through his jeans. "You make me crazy, Mackenzie."

"I kind of feel a little crazy too," I whisper.

I draw a sharp breath then as a cramp tears through me, a burst of heat like a current of electricity coursing under my skin to make me feel like I'm on fire. I make a pained sound as Noah pulls away from me, his eyes looking dark with arousal but his brow wrinkled in concern as he presses a hand to my cheek.

"You need—" His breath is ragged, making it obvious that I'm not the only one affected here. "You need to shift," he says, almost disappointedly. "Soon."

I can feel his disappointment as a mirror to my own, because I don't exactly want to give in to the basic instincts of my biology right now, not if it doesn't involve Noah fucking me in this bed until the burn subsides.

But I know he's right.

"Can you—" I swallow, but my throat feels dry. "Can you come with me?"

Noah tilts up my chin, his thumb swiping along my lower lip slowly before it slips past my teeth to press against my tongue. I can't help but lick the pad, rewarded with a rumbling sound from deep in Noah's chest, his mouth parting with a stuttered breath.

"I'm not going anywhere," he says. "As long as we're . . ." His jaw clenches, and there's that same wildness in his eyes that I can only glimpse in moments like this. I know he is feeling not like himself right now, can scent on him the way he's affected by what's happening to me, but strangely, instead of being scared, there is an unfamiliar thrill coursing through me. "As long as we're here . . . you're mine, Mackenzie."

Rational me is still worried this is all hormonal nonsense.

Irrational me doesn't fucking care.

16

Noah

IT'S BEEN A long time since I've shifted, and the fresh snow against my paws is a welcome sensation as I run through it, following Mackenzie's trail. I had only caught a glimpse of her before she bounded off into the tree line after shedding her clothes, just a flash of sand-colored fur before she'd disappeared into the woods. It's clear that with her impending heat she is more in tune with her instincts than I am, especially given how long it's been since I've used them.

The suppressants really do stave off the urge to shift, just like I'd told Mackenzie weeks ago, but running like this makes me wonder why I hadn't chosen to do so sooner, anyway. Like this, the worries of work and my personal life seem further away, leaving only the scent of Mackenzie in the air and the strong desire to get closer to her.

I catch sight of her in a clearing, the sun filtering through the trees and casting a spray of sunlight against her fur, and I notice she's just standing there on all fours, waiting for me. She's smaller than me, but no less strong, I think. Her amber eyes are sharp, and her ears are turned up attentively as she watches me approach—her head low to the ground as if she is ready to flee at any given moment. What is she doing?

I yip at her, wondering if there is a chance she doesn't recognize me in her primal state, and she snorts against the snow, snapping her jaws in answer. She turns in place to kick up a bit of a flurry as she watches me near, and just as I move to spring myself closer, she bounds off again as fast as her paws will carry her through the trees, leaving me puzzled. She gets another thirty yards away, only to stop and turn back and look at me again, giving that same guarded pose that is starting to feel somewhat like a challenge.

She's toying with me.

Even in this form I can almost see her teasing grin, can almost hear her sweet voice calling out some taunt solely to try and get under my skin so that she can laugh at my reaction. My fur bristles with the anticipation of her game, kicking up a bit of snow and throwing back my head to make a warning sound, letting her know I'm up to play. Her answering huff of air and the toss of her head seem unfazed, and I paw at the snow, lowering my head while I ready to pounce.

It feels like a different time; what we're doing seems reminiscent of an age where our kind lived in woods like these, where we hunted our food and claimed our mates in a similar dance to this one. And with my hindbrain running the show right now, that thought is a satisfying one.

I don't move until she takes off again, giving her a moment's head start before I fully put my paws to the ground and chase after her. I run until my muscles burn, the slight sting oddly enjoyable. I watch her lithe body wind between the trees as if she were born in these woods, making sure that catching her is no easy feat. It doesn't deter me in the slightest; in fact, the difficulty of it all only makes me want to catch her more. Only makes this game we're playing more pleasurable.

I let my human thoughts slip away to give way to the more basic part of me, letting my alpha move my body as if I *am* hunting Mackenzie. As if she is prey that I want to taste—and in a sense, I suppose she is. Because even shifted I can scent how every moment pushes her deeper into her heat, and out here among the snow she smells positively *ripe* for the taking. I know when I get her back to the lodge she will be warm and wet and wanting, and just thinking about the way she will feel on my knot makes me actually *howl* with anticipation.

The sound makes Mackenzie pause further up, and I skid in the snow only a dozen or so paces from her as I catch my breath. I can see in her eyes a glimpse of that need they held earlier, see a spark of the human part of her practically begging me to come take her. I hear a rustling behind us that makes me turn with a growl, tearing my eyes from Mackenzie to warn whatever intruder might be stalking us, only to find a bird taking flight up into the trees. I snort in irritation as I turn back, noticing Mackenzie is nowhere to be found as a flicker of panic pulses inside me.

My alpha has me pacing as I turn this way and that trying to catch sight of her, feeling a growing dread at having lost her, even though logically I know she must be somewhere close. I turn in place and yip worriedly, still able to scent her but unable to see her.

Where the fuck did she go?

It might be because I am so panicked that I don't hear her approach; maybe it's the blood rushing in my ears that hides her steps as she nears from behind, meaning that I don't know she's on me until she's actually *on* me. Her body collides with mine as we roll, the force of it so much so that it knocks us both back into human form, leaving our naked bodies tangled in the snow.

Her skin is flushed pink, no doubt still too warm from being in her other form, and her soft blond hair is wild around her face, just as wild as the look in her eyes as she gazes down at me. Her thighs straddle my waist to keep me pinned to the ground, and I can immediately tell that I was right, that she's dripping wet for me, if the slick against my navel is any indication.

"Got you," she practically purrs, her breasts heaving in the chilled air.

I run my hands over her thighs, watching her shiver with my touch. She's burning up now, no longer close but surely fully in heat, but I know the air will still make her sick if left unchecked. "You'll get cold like this."

"Mm." She leans, her nipples brushing my chest as my breath catches, her lips hovering against mine as they curve with a smile. "Then you should probably keep me warm."

I'm half-ready to take her right here in the snow, but given that she flings herself from me only to shift again—I don't get the chance. I follow suit moments later, and I notice now that when she runs, she is running the way we came, back toward the lodge. She pauses only for a moment at the top of the hill, tossing her head the way we came in a silent invitation, as if challenging me to come get her.

And that's exactly what I intend to do.

～

IN ALL OF my adult life, I have never felt desperation like this.

Even when I have her safely tucked away in the bedroom we've chosen, I feel urges to tie her down so that she can't escape. Every cell in my body begs for her, dizzied by her scent and drunk on her taste as my tongue tangles with hers. Her body is hot against me, my hips rutting unconsciously against her as the head of my cock slides across her stomach to leave a sticky trail. Strangely, I have a distant desire to mark all of her like this, so that no one else would ever dare touch her.

She moves backward until her legs hit the bed, and it's so easy to lift her small frame, to throw her up to the middle of the mattress so that I can crawl over her. My mouth never leaves her body, not for a second, my tongue and teeth tasting every inch of her I can reach as she squirms beneath me.

"Burns," she hisses as my tongue laves at the swell of her breast. "Hurts, Noah."

"Shh," I soothe, swirling my tongue around her nipple as my fingers brush a line down her stomach. "I'm going to make it better."

It's a mess between her legs, her slick streaming from her to coat her thighs and the blankets and my hand as I tease my fingers through the wet crease of her. She groans when I push two inside, and they slip in easily, making a lewd sound that rings in my ears with every slow in and out.

She rolls her hips against my hand as her fingers tangle in my hair, and I moan against her nipple when she tugs, her nails scratching my scalp in a silent urging that I hurry. If I felt unlike myself in the times that I've touched her before this—right now I feel like another person altogether. Gone is my rationality and my worries about what might come after this, and in their place there is just the raw need for her, to give her everything she's asking me for.

I wrap my hands around her waist, flipping her to her stomach without warning, and she makes some surprised sound when she goes, wriggling in my grip.

"Noah, what are you—"

"Lift your hips," I urge, tugging at her waist. "I want to see you."

Her legs are trembling, so much so that I have to help her lift her ass in the air to bare the hottest part of her, my blood thrumming at the sight of her slick trickling down her thighs as if taunting me to lap it up.

I think it catches her by surprise when I do just that, pressing my tongue to the back of her thigh and cleaning the thin, clear line of her slick with my tongue until I can nuzzle between her legs. She makes some garbled sound against the mattress as I lick through her folds, dipping my tongue inside her only to draw it out and pat at the swollen bundle of her clit, which is practically throbbing now.

I can taste it on her, her heat; like honey and liquid sex and all of it enough to ensure that I am out of my mind for her. I eat at her hungrily, my lips and tongue working through the soft flesh of her as my hand curls under her belly to find her clit and roll it under my fingertips. She pushes back against my face in surprise when I begin to tease her clit, and I hold her there, lapping at her like a starving animal as I work her sensitive bud with my fingers.

"N-Noah," she gasps, her lower half shaking. "Noah, I—*ah*. I—"

"Alpha," I practically growl against her, applying more pressure against her clit with my fingers. "I want you to call me Alpha."

I don't sound like me, I don't *feel* like me—but the normally calm, composed Noah seems to have taken a back seat, unable to even fight the raw instincts that are driving me now. That Noah stands no chance against the warm, pliant omega who's begging for his touch.

I let my tongue slip inside her again, enjoying the sharp cry it draws from her.

"Alpha."

The word makes my blood sing, makes parts of me I never

knew about twist and howl with delight. I can feel her trembling all over now, hear her toes popping and her breath catching, and I know she's close. I can smell it on her. Can *feel* it on my tongue. I close my eyes as I slide my tongue through this part of her, never relenting, unable to do so until I can feel her coming apart against my mouth.

And when she does, there is no relief for me, as I thought there might be. When she dissolves into a shaking mess that is mewling my name as her slick gushes against my mouth—that howling inside only worsens, only cries out for more.

I'm not gentle, not like I'd prefer to be, when I push up to my knees. My hands at her hips are too rough as I pull her back against me, my palm too heavy as I hold her ass in place just so I can rub the heated length of my cock against the slick center of her. She doesn't give me any indication that she minds, seeming to *welcome* it instead—but there is a flash of clarity in the cloud of her heat then, one that has me going very still even though I'm only seconds from burying myself inside her.

"I need you to be sure," I grind out, my alpha growling in protest at having stopped. "I need you to be sure you want me to do this. If I knot you now . . ." I suck in a ragged breath. "I don't know if I'll be able to stop."

I feel Mackenzie's slim fingers reaching to touch my knuckles, rubbing a soothing circle as her face turns against the mattress to look back at me. "*Please*, Alpha," she whispers hoarsely. "Please give me your knot."

I hiss a curse when she pushes against my cock, waving her hips tantalizingly to accentuate her point. I smooth my hand over her lower back as I dip my hips to notch at her entrance, holding my breath as I watch the swollen head slip inside to disappear inch by inch. It's mesmerizing, watching her stretch around me—her body tight and warm and wet and taking me inside like she was *made* for me. I make a choked sound when the only slightly swollen base of my knot disappears to leave me rooted fully inside, knowing that soon it will swell, that she'll take everything I can give her and more.

And it's that thought that forces me to move.

I can see *everything* like this—unable to tear my eyes away from the sight of her body opening up for me again and again, and I can hear words that I've never spoken fall from my mouth, like they were waiting for her.

"Look at you," I rumble. "Look at how good you take my cock."

"*Yes*," she whines. "Just like that."

I slap my hips against her, slamming inside a little more roughly. "Is this what you need? Did you need your alpha's knot?"

Not her alpha, some small voice whispers from far away. *Not hers.*

I completely ignore the voice.

"Say it," I growl. "Say you need your alpha's knot."

"I—*fuck*." Her face buries in the blankets as she makes an unintelligible sound. "I need—*please*—I need your knot, Alpha."

"Good girl," I hum, smoothing a hand down her spine.

Her hair looks darker dripping with sweat, clinging to her skin at her temples and shoulders. Her mouth is parted and swollen and red when she turns her face to press her cheek to the mattress, and when her eyes flutter open, when they find mine—the amber irises almost seem to *glow* with how bright they look.

"I'm going to make it feel better," I grit out, the slap of my skin against hers ringing in the air. "I'm going to knot this pretty little body until you can't take it anymore."

"Mm. *Yes*," she pants, her fingers curling into the blankets to fist the material. "What I want."

"So fucking beautiful," I manage through clenched teeth. My lashes flutter as the pressure in my cock swells to unbearable levels. I can feel my knot already beginning to thicken, making it more and more difficult to push inside her with every thrust. "You're perfect, Mackenzie. You know that? So goddamn perfect."

"Noah, I—"

She cries out when I hit deep, the head of my cock sliding against the most sensitive place inside of her as she trembles around me. I can feel how close she is in the ragged pants of her breath and the shaking quality of her limbs, and I can just wind my arm around her middle, my fingers slipping between her legs to tease the still-sensitive bundle of nerves there.

"*Fuck*," she hisses.

I roll quick circles against her clit, feeling her clench around me with every swipe of my fingers as her voice comes out in a garbled mess of my name and *Alpha* and *please* and all sorts of filthy utterings. There is so much of her slick between us that the sound of my skin colliding with hers is wet and sloppy, and I can feel my stomach clenching as the pressure in my cock reaches the tipping point, barely able to hold on as I wait to feel her let go.

I barely make it, letting go only seconds after I feel her coming apart around me, practically roaring with relief as I push as deep inside her as I can and curl my body around hers as the sweet pleasure of release washes over me. The sensation of her body accepting my knot is indescribable, like every good thing I've ever felt all rolled into one as I lock inside her, ensuring that she can't be anywhere but right here with me.

Even after, when the howling of my hindbrain calms ever so slightly, when it gives way to some semblance of rationality—I still can't find it in me to feel worried about this. With all my talk of consequences and being careful . . . Right now I can only focus on how *good* she feels. How *right*. She snuggles against me afterward like she was made to, her body fitting with mine as if by design. I wrap my arms around her tightly as I nuzzle her hair, my chest rising and falling heavily against her back.

When I hear her breathing even out, telling me that she's slipped into a peaceful sleep—I press a kiss to her hair, pulling her impossibly closer, like I'm afraid that she might not be there when I wake up if I don't. I close my eyes and try to will myself to rest, too, knowing that this is only the beginning and that there will be more of this frenzy to come—but in my head there is a buzzing of something that wants to make itself known, something that I've been doing my best to ignore, I think.

Because with Mackenzie in my arms like this . . . I'm realizing that I don't want to let her go.

17

Mackenzie

THE LAST FEW days have been a blur of sweat and sensation—and today is no different. In the haze of my heat, everything feels far away and also impossibly close, my senses in overdrive and my body in a constant state of burning pleasure and pain.

And Noah has been there for every second of it.

I can't remember a time when it's been like this, when I've seemed to *need* someone like I've needed Noah—and with every passing hour where I give more of myself to him, an anxiety grows on my hindbrain like a parasite, fueling my actions, making me needy. I cling to him in sleep and while awake, and every second that he isn't inside me feels like torture. Which, to be fair, hasn't been very often.

My eyes are shut tight so I can focus on what I'm feeling—my thighs spread over his lap as I ride him, his fingers digging into my hips to help rock me against his cock. My body is just as lined with sweat as his, and the entire room at this point is a cloud of our scents morphing together to make something new, something intoxicating.

I gasp when his thumb finds my clit to tease, still sensitive from the orgasm he gave me only a few minutes ago. I have to brace my hands on his shoulders as my head lolls forward, trying to keep up the rhythm of my hips as he bounces me on his cock.

"Look at you," he hums, slipping his thumb between my folds, where a gush of my slick escapes. "You're making such a mess."

"I'm—*oh*. I'm sorry, I—"

He leans up from the pillows to leave kisses at my jaw. "Don't apologize," he murmurs. "I like it."

He's been like this ever since we came here; he uses words and gives praises that are filthier than I've ever heard from him, and apparently the more primal parts of me fucking love it. His voice whispering dirty things in this sequestered room just for us makes me shiver, almost as much as his touch.

"I'm so close," I groan.

His thumb continues to rub circles against my clit, his other hand curving against my ass to squeeze as he starts to meet my thrusts. "Can you take me again?"

His knot.

I'm practically addicted to it now. As good as it was before, now—when my entire brain seems to be functioning solely on instinct—his knot might as well be a cocktail of everything good I've ever had. The sensation of him filling me until it feels like he has no room left, like I might *burst* with it—it's a pleasure that goes beyond just sexual and makes a home deep down in my bones as if my body is *finally* getting what it's always wanted. What it's *needed*.

Is this what it means to be what we are?

And because there is no room for embarrassment in my current state, I don't hesitate to curl into him when I feel the urge, to press my tongue to the hot, throbbing gland at his throat that tastes purely of Noah. I suck at his pulse until he's groaning, until his cock starts to swell like he might tip over the edge without me.

"I want it, Alpha," I whisper hoarsely, nipping at his sensitive skin lightly. "I want you."

My head spins as I start to rock my hips to match his pace, every undulation letting his cock slide against the most sensitive places inside me and setting off a shower of sparks in my belly. There is a delicious pressure that builds with every roll of his hips, and I know when it finally gives it will bring that sweet euphoria that comes with getting exactly what my body needs.

My thighs press tight against his hips as it becomes almost unbearable, so close to the edge that I can practically *taste* it, and when it finally comes, when *I* do—it's an all-over relief, an unwinding in my entire body as if every part of me had been coiled tight.

I've long since learned that I like how Noah lets go, how his eyes close and his mouth sputters loud curses and his arms hold me tight—all of it satisfying parts of me I hadn't known existed. His knot swells just like it had a dozen times before this, and it's still as mind-blowing as it had been the first time. Maybe even more so now. I can't really be sure.

I collapse against him after, my limbs heavy and my body spent, content to listen to the heavy thudding of his heart as we both catch our breath. I can feel his finger trailing back and forth along my ribs, making me shiver, his knot pulsing pleasantly inside me as he holds me to him.

I feel more aware this time, my mind less muddled in the afterglow of what we've just done, and I can tell we don't have much longer of this frenzied little getaway.

"I think it's starting to wear off," I mumble into his chest.

He doesn't say anything about it, really, but I can feel him tense against me, and then there is a soft kiss at my hair as he quietly urges me to rest.

I don't know what he's thinking, have no idea whether or not these days together have been just an itch we've both been scratching or if there is some part of him that's feeling conflicted, just as I'm finding myself to be.

And what's worse is that . . . it's just now hitting me how afraid I am to know the answer.

THE NEXT TIME I wake it's to the feeling of a cool, wet cloth against my collarbone, the chilled fabric like heaven against my fevered skin. I smile softly as my eyes flutter open, catching Noah as he pulls the cloth away, looking at me with concern.

"You were sweating," he says. "I didn't want you to get sick."

That same warm weight settles in my chest, and I bite back a larger grin as I wearily push myself up, wincing. "Jesus, I'm sore."

"I'm sorry," Noah offers guiltily. "Is it awful?"

I shake my head. "No. It's a good sore."

I can tell this pleases him, even if he tries to hide it. "Good," he murmurs.

"How long was I out?"

He checks his phone on the nearby nightstand. "Six hours or so. Give or take. You slept for a while this time."

"Ah, well." I shrug. "That's . . . good, right?"

"It probably means your heat is close to passing," he notes, sounding almost . . . disappointed?

Could I be imagining that?

I try for something light. "I'm sure you're going crazy not being able to work," I tease.

Noah doesn't miss a beat when he answers, holding my gaze with a sincerity that makes my lips part in surprise. "I don't want to be anywhere else."

"Oh," I say quietly, unsure of what else to add to it.

Those warm feelings are shifting into my chest like burning embers, the heavy heat like a fire waiting to be stoked. I had been the one to assure Noah that we could be together like this without complicating things—that this little addendum to our arrangement would be nothing more than the two of us fulfilling each other's desires without any strings attached. I had *believed* it when I said the words.

So why do I feel so unsure now?

"I'm really glad you came with me," I start again, hardly any louder than a whisper. I can't quite seem to find my voice right now. "I'm glad it was you."

Noah doesn't say anything immediately, and when I peek up at him, I notice him studying me, his eyes moving across my face and his lips pressed tightly together, like he's trying to find the correct words. There's a flicker of anxiety in my belly at what he might be trying to say; is he going to tell me that this thing between us is getting too difficult? That we should end it? Do I not *want* him to say those things? My feelings are so mixed up, even *more* so with the murky aftermath of my dwindling heat, and I can't seem to pin down one singular emotion to focus on.

"Me too," he finally settles on, and I am unable to discern a single thing from those two words.

I watch as Noah pushes away from the bed, moving to his feet and stepping across the carpet to the dresser on the other side of the room. He's slipped into his boxer briefs—which leave little to the imagination when it comes to his sculpted ass that might almost make me envious—but mostly I find my eyes tracing the hard lines of muscle in his back, pink lines scattered here and there from what I assume are my fingernails. It makes me blush looking at them, and that heat spreads down into my chest and lower as it dredges up memories of everything we've done these last few days.

He grabs a water bottle from the dresser, bringing it back as he takes his place at the side of the bed again and, with a concerned expression, reaches out to hand over the bottle. "You need this," he urges. "You barely ate any breakfast this morning and I've been having to practically force you to drink something."

"Okay, Mom," I laugh, taking the bottle. I unscrew the cap and take a heavy swig, gulping down a good bit of the bottle before replacing the cap and holding it up for him to see. "Happy?"

"Yes," he deadpans. "The last thing we need is for you to get dehydrated."

This makes me laugh harder. "Wow, that would be a great one to explain. Noah Taylor fucked all the nutrients right out of me."

"I . . . probably could have been a little better about taking care of you."

"What?" I frown, scooting away from the headboard, bringing the sheet with me and keeping it wrapped around my chest (which seems almost silly, given everything Noah has seen). "Noah. Seriously. My heats weren't a picnic before this, but this one . . ." I make a face. "It would have been a real bitch without you. Like, completely miserable. You did great taking care of me."

I see a bit of the tension in his face soften then as he nods lightly. I can tell he's been worried about this, and that he needed reassurance. With everything I've seen of him in the last few days, I can undoubtedly assume that it's an alpha thing. Especially if the strange urges to please him I've felt while we've been here are any indication.

"Good," he answers warmly. "I'm glad."

I'm realizing that this is the longest conversation we've had in days, and that it is just more proof that my heat is waning. Knowing this for certain makes me uneasy, because those unsure feelings are pushing their way back into my brain, wheedling their way into my subconscious to make me wonder about all sorts of unnecessary things. Things like: *What will we be after this?* and *Do I even want to be something?*

I realize that through this entire train of thought I'm staring at him, just as I'm noticing that he's staring back at me in the same way. I wish I knew what he was thinking, wish I could read him just enough to help me figure out my own muddled thoughts, but all I can see in Noah's face is the clear blue of his eyes, the strong line of his jaw, the plush curve of his lips—all the things that make it hard to look away from him. When I met him they were simply nice things to look at, but now just a glance is enough to give me butterflies. When the fuck did that even happen?

"Mackenzie," he says suddenly, making me jump a little.

I meet his gaze, finding a warmth in his eyes now that makes the butterflies worse. I can tell he wants to say something, can practically see it stuck to the tip of his tongue, and for some reason I am *desperate* to know what it is. Whether it's the hormones or this place or just Noah himself—my entire being seems *hinged* on whatever he is about to say.

So it's surprising when he says nothing, but only for a moment, since he leans in instead to brush his lips with mine. That frenzy that has always come after his kiss seems less now, and in its place is a slow, molten burn that starts just below my navel and spreads deeper until it's pulsing between my legs. It seems impossible that I could still get aroused after the amount of times we've been together just *today*—and yet his fingertips at my skin are like sparks of electricity, and his mouth on mine is sweet like wine, making me just as dizzy.

I feel his finger hooking into the sheet over me to ease it away, his palm covering my breast after and squeezing gently. He catches my gasp against his tongue when his thumb teases my nipple, and I unconsciously arch into his hand to chase after more of his touch.

"You're so soft," he rasps against my mouth. "So beautiful."

My head falls back when his mouth wanders, reveling in the sensation of it on my throat, my collarbone, lower to capture my nipple. His tongue swirls there before he sucks it deeper into his mouth, and the sensation zings straight down to my core, making me want more.

"Noah," I breathe.

His hand skims over my belly, his fingers curling between my legs to slip inside me. I'm embarrassingly wet even from just this, and the sound of his fingers sliding in and out of me is lewd and loud and yet all I can worry about is how to get *more*. He's taking his time now, the frenetic pace I've become used to long gone as Noah seems to be intent on taking his time.

He pumps his fingers inside slowly, only to withdraw at the same tortuous pace, just to repeat it all over again, all the while teasing and nibbling at my nipple until my skin tingles all over. I can't decide if I want him to keep doing this, keep teasing me at this pace that seems designed to drive me crazy, or if I want to beg him to get on with it, to give me more than just his hand.

His body covers mine as he touches me, his wide shoulders the perfect place for my hands as I keep him close against me. He licks at the swell under my breast, pressing his teeth there afterward, and my back bows as I let out a soft cry, feeling like I'm on fire in ways that have nothing to do with my heat.

So it's almost painful when he stops, when all of it ends suddenly as he lifts his head to look at me with glazed eyes, and I'm panting my protest as I lean up to meet his gaze.

"Go on a date with me," he says in a rush.

I blink, still keyed up and frustrated that he isn't still touching me. "What?"

"A real date," he says.

"A real . . ." I rear back, trying to comprehend what he's asking. "But . . . complicated. You didn't want to make things complicated."

"But it is," he says firmly, never tearing his eyes from mine. "It's complicated. At least for me."

And all that worry and all that uncertainty come crashing back down, every reason I've had for keeping him at arm's length rearing their ugly heads to make themselves known. I don't believe in this fate shit; in fact, I outright reject it—it drove my dad insane and left me alone, after all, and so I have every reason to calmly reject him, to cut my losses and realize that this good thing we've had has run its course.

But my heart is still fluttering, and that heavy, hot stone is still rolling around in my chest, impossible to ignore, and I'm realizing all at once that I might be more afraid of walking away like none of this matters than I am of risking something to see if it *does* matter.

"A real date," I echo dazedly. "What about Albuquerque?"

"We'll figure it out," he answers immediately, without a shred of doubt. He says it like he will do everything he can to make it work, even if he has no idea how to. "Just say *yes*."

"Noah, are you sure you want to—"

"I want to," he cuts in. "I don't think I ever even stood a chance of touching you and then just walking away."

I can't pretend this doesn't rustle up those same butterflies in my stomach that might be building their own permanent residence, and despite all the wariness and all the reasons why I should say no . . . I feel my lips quirking in a smile, having to lean in and press my mouth to his just to keep it from spreading that smile to embarrassing levels.

"Okay," I mutter against his mouth. "A real date."

Noah doesn't hide his smile in the slightest, his lips curving widely only a moment before they cover mine with a deep kiss. I melt into it as his tongue slides across my lower lip, opening for him as he crawls up the bed a little further to cover me completely. His hands are less patient now, sliding down my ribs to my hips as he squeezes me there, pressing a knee between my legs to part them even as I'm tugging at his boxer briefs to get them down.

His cock bobs free to slide across my stomach, and his groan falls against my tongue when I fist him, squeezing gently before pumping him all the way down to the base.

"Wrap your legs around me," he says thickly.

I don't hesitate, locking my ankles behind his waist and gasping when I feel the thick head of his cock notching at my entrance, holding my breath after as he slowly pushes inside to fill me up. I close my eyes to try and focus on the sensation of my body stretching around the hard length of him, and just as I do Noah snaps his hips forward, filling me to the brim as my breath catches.

"Open your eyes," he urges. "I want to see exactly how you look when you're taking me."

It's a struggle, keeping my gaze level with his as he starts to move—the last shreds of my heat making the room spin a little as I cling to my rationality. Noah braces his hand near my head as he leans on one forearm, rolling his hips again and again as he builds a steady rhythm. I'm too sensitive from all the times before this, already feeling that hot pressure swelling deep inside with every slide of his cock inside me. That warmth in my chest is blooming outward—filling every part of me until I'm nothing but heat, the pinnacle of it all deep, deep inside where that looming pressure threatens to give way like a dam poised to break.

"Noah," I gasp, gripping his shoulders and undoubtedly adding more marks. "Noah, I—"

"That's it," he huffs. "Come for me, Mackenzie. Need you to come for me again."

My lashes flutter as he growls for me to keep my eyes open, and even with them opened wide, my vision blurs with my impending orgasm, my body drawn up tight like a bowstring, ready to be let loose.

I feel it in my toes first, when it happens, feel it rushing up my legs and into my thighs and deeper like a humming current—exploding in an array of sparks as I start to tremble with it. Noah grunts through it as he dips inside with more difficulty now, and the thickness there only heightens my pleasure, his knot touching me in the best of ways as it locks inside until he can no longer move. I can feel Noah shuddering under my hands, his skin twitching everywhere I touch him like he's oversensitized, and I rub slow circles on his shoulders as my body melts into a Jell-O-like quality, warm and soft and satisfied beyond measure.

We lie like that for a while in the quiet, the wind blowing gently outside the window and the sounds of our breath mingling in the air. He's still inside me when he lifts his head some time after, his lids heavy and his blue eyes darker, stormier.

"You'll need to shift again," he manages roughly, still sounding a little out of breath. "Otherwise, you might be uncomfortable."

I kiss his cheek. "There's time in the morning. Before we go back."

"Back," he parrots. He turns his face to let his cheek rest against my breast. "How out of character would it be for me to say I don't want to go back to work?"

"Terribly out of character," I deadpan. "I would have to assume you've contracted some brain disorder and have started speaking exclusively in gibberish."

His lips curl, his eyes peeking up at me. "Maybe I have."

"Doubtful," I chuckle. "Although, it would make you wanting to go on a date with me make a lot more sense."

He nips at my breast, and I yelp. "If that's plausible," he chuffs. "Then you might be the one with the brain disorder. Maybe I should get you a referral to the neurology floor."

I can't help but grin as I take in his dark hair falling into his eyes, making him look younger than he is—moving on to the soft curve of his mouth and further still to the broad width of his shoulders, which still feel somehow larger than life. He really is kind of beautiful, for a boogeyman. The annoyed expression he would surely make is almost worth telling him so.

I shake my head, still chuckling quietly. "Hardly."

"We should probably get some *actual* sleep," he says with a bit of a yawn. "Especially if I'm going to have to chase you down again in the morning."

"I'm definitely looking forward to making you eat my dust again," I tease.

He snorts, winding his arms around me as he snuggles closer. "I let you win," he mumbles.

"Sure you did," I laugh. "Then tomorrow, I'll make sure you never catch me."

"Oh, I will catch you," he says, sounding amused.

I roll my eyes. "You think so?"

"I do," he hums, his eyes drifting closed. "I'm not letting you get away from me, Mackenzie."

My pulse quickens as my mouth parts in surprise, but Noah is already drifting off, slipping into a satisfied sleep as if he hasn't thrown me for a loop at least a dozen times since we got here. I'm deciding I *like* the weird heat that comes from the more intimate things that have been happening between us, and even if it's still a little terrifying . . . I think maybe it could be worth it, if I give it a chance.

I bend my neck to press a kiss to Noah's forehead, falling back against the pillows after as fatigue seeps in. "Maybe I'm not letting you get away from me either," I say to the air.

18

Noah

WHAT ARE WE *going to do when we get back to work, Noah?*

I am doing everything humanly possible to focus on work, but it is decidedly . . . difficult. It's only been forty-eight hours since Mackenzie and I left the lodge, and I've had to endure a scathing text from Hunter *and* his aunt Jeannie about the state we left the bedroom in. It was well worth the bill they're going to send me for cleaning, I think. More than, even.

Mackenzie had seemed so unsure when we piled up in my car to head back here, everything about her demeanor speaking of an uneasiness about what would happen when we got home. I hadn't been able to find the exact words to explain it to her then, how after only a few weeks with her I'm considering turning all my plans upside down—too afraid to scare her off. But still she'd melted into my kiss, and she'd said again that she would go on an *actual* date with me when we got another night off, and I think that's a start, at the very least.

I spoke to the board director at the hospital in Albuquerque this morning, and it's funny. Before all of this, I couldn't wait to get out of here. The idea of packing up and moving to another state for a fresh start with more open minds had been *exciting*—and now it only makes me unsure. Logically, I know the fact that I'm so unsure now of what I want to do is one thousand percent to do with Mackenzie and this strange thing blossoming between us, just as I recognize that hesitating for these reasons could end up being a massive mistake. So why am I dragging my feet, suddenly asking the director to give me some time to consider his offer?

Maybe I really am losing my mind.

I shake my head as I give my attention to my laptop, clicking over to my email client to find a message from the enigma herself. My smile is immediate, my entire body perking up at the idea of speaking to her even in this small way, and I think to myself fleetingly that I really could be losing it.

> I have had two people ask me this morning if you took me to a cave for the last few days. I hope your morning is going a little less annoyingly.

I grin as I tap out a reply.

> So, I'm assuming it wasn't a good idea to hint we took a spelunking trip on the side?

I can imagine the way she'll roll her eyes when she reads it, can practically hear her laugh, which makes my chest feel tight.

Seriously. *Am* I losing it?

I'm distracted from my musing by a knock at my door, sitting up in my chair as the doorknob turns and the door creaks open to yield a familiar head of sandy blond hair peeking around it.

"Hey," she calls, and that one word is enough to make my heart pick up its pace.

"Hey," I answer, watching her step inside with a brown paper sack. "I was just emailing you back."

"Probably writing me poetry, right? Just make sure you give me a really stellar analogy for my eyes. None of that 'bright pennies' bullshit."

My lips curl as I shake my head. "Duly noted."

"I brought you lunch," she tells me, sitting the sack on my desk.

My eyebrows shoot up in surprise. "Really?"

"It's not a big deal," she says almost defensively. "I just know how you get when you're busy, and you have that heart cath later." She shrugs. "I figure after robbing the entire hospital of you for three days I can make sure you aren't getting shaky fingers from low blood sugar."

It's a small thing, but it makes me happy that she thought of me, a feeling of thrill stemming from the simple brown paper sack that's now sitting on my desk. "Thank you."

"It's only a sandwich," she says flippantly. "Just plain old turkey. Don't get too excited."

I chuckle as I reach for the bag. "I will make sure not to read too much into the sandwich."

"Good," she says with a grin. "I don't want you to get any preconceived notions before we go on that date."

I pause from opening the sack. "Preconceived notions?"

"Yeah," she says seriously. "Like, that you can get away with just a sandwich or something."

My eyebrow quirks. "Oh?"

"I'm an expensive date, Noah," she tells me pointedly. "I'm a five-star kind of gal."

"Your favorite food is soup," I remind her.

She waves me off. "Yes, but I'll be ordering the *fanciest* soup," she assures me. "Gold flakes in the broth, maybe."

"Right," I chuff. "Of course."

She plops down on the edge of my desk. "So how has your day been?"

"My day?"

"Your day," she echoes. "Have *you* been listening to whispers going quiet every time you walk into a room?"

"I've been here, mostly," I tell her truthfully. "I had a lot of procedure notes to document. Playing catch-up."

She winces. "Sorry about that."

"Don't be." I reach across my desk to place my hand over hers. "Seriously."

There's a flush of color at her cheeks when she smiles softly, but she turns her face shortly after so I can't see. "It does feel weird," she notes. "Coming back. It felt like we were gone way longer than we were."

"I know what you mean," I murmur.

I don't tell her that I didn't want to leave, knowing it might be too much, too fast. The last thing I need is to spook her when I've just gotten her to agree to considering a real shot at this.

When I open the bag, I notice there is only one sandwich. "Are you not eating with me?"

She shakes her head. "I have to get back. We're pretty short-staffed today."

"Well, I appreciate you taking the time to bring me a mediocre sandwich with no meaning attached to it," I tell her flatly.

Mackenzie barks out a laugh. "Oh my God, sarcasm? I need to write about this in my diary. No one will ever believe it."

"You're a bad influence."

She hops off my desk and circles around it, leaning down with her hand braced against my knee. My lips part in anticipation only a moment before hers touch mine, and I close my eyes as I relish the weight of her kiss, the softness of it still enough to make me want a hell of a lot more than just this.

"You'll get over it," she teases when she breaks away.

I swallow. "I have a feeling you might be right."

She steps away like she hasn't just made the idea of working that much harder—blowing me another kiss when she stops at the door to my office. "I'll text you when I get off."

"All right."

I have to sit very still in my office chair after she's gone, reminding my body that it can't get worked up right now, no matter how much it would like to. I can't believe that something as simple as a kiss—hardly even a kiss, really—could have my heart racing and my slacks tenting, but my body seems to have shifted into a state of constant neediness where Mackenzie is involved. It's both heaven and hell.

I'm just starting to resign myself to finishing my notes a few minutes later when my phone starts vibrating across my desk, perking up instantly like an overzealous Chihuahua at the possibility of it being Mackenzie, as unlikely as that situation is. I'm not disappointed per se when I realize it's my mother instead, but my zeal from a moment earlier dissipates slightly, and I chide myself for being so ridiculous.

"Hello?"

"When are you bringing this girl to dinner?"

"Hello to you, too, Mother."

"Noah Taylor. I will come over there and put you across my knee. I don't care how big you are."

I close my eyes, leaning back in my desk chair. "I don't think I will be bringing her to dinner anytime soon. It's still very . . . new."

"Not so new that you're sneaking away from work to Hunter and Jeannie's lodge, apparently."

I frown. "It really is ridiculous that you know so much about my personal life, considering how little I share with you."

"I know," she snorts. "Imagine. Your poor mother begging for scraps about your life from Regina like some sort of stalker. Do you know how many times I've had to sit through that woman's recollection of the time she met Roseanne Barr at a bar twenty years ago? She thinks it's *so* clever that she met Roseanne *Barr* at a *bar*. And here I am, having to sit through this time and time again, pretending that I find it funny just so I can hope to gain any kind of insider info on my son, since he won't ever—"

"Okay, Mom. I get it. You're very mistreated."

She hmphs. "I'm glad we've established this. Now tell me why I can't meet my future daughter-in-law."

"Well, you referring to her as your future daughter-in-law is a pretty big tick against you."

"What? I mean, you're already spending her heats with her, surely that means you'll be—"

"We are not going to discuss Mackenzie's heats."

"Fine, fine. I just want to meet the woman my son is all gaga over."

I want to argue with her assumption that I'm *gaga* over Mackenzie, but even in my head it feels like a feeble effort.

"Well, for one, I just got her to agree to go on an actual date with me," I sigh. "Subjecting her to my parents feels like something that will scare her off."

"You make us sound like a form of torture."

A chuckle escapes me. "Can you guarantee that you won't ask her if she wants kids at some point during the dinner?"

"Well, I could certainly try," Mom mutters unconvincingly.

"I think you and Mackenzie's grandmother would get along well," I say, grinning.

"I wonder if Mackenzie's grandmother has to pull information from her granddaughter like pulling teeth."

"Just . . . let me figure out what this even is between us, okay? Provided that she doesn't realize that she's entirely out of my league, I'm sure I can arrange the two of you meeting . . . at some point."

"Oh, shut up. You're a catch. When you're not being a surly hermit."

"Your confidence in me is reassuring."

"Have you heard anything on the Albuquerque job?"

I press my lips together in a frown. I *have* heard from them— but it's something I haven't mentioned to anyone, Mackenzie included. Mostly because I'm so unsure as to what I want to do about the opportunity. It's most likely imprudent to be reconsidering my entire future based on the possibility of *one date*, but since I've already established that my mother's assessment of me being *gaga* for Mackenzie isn't entirely unfounded . . .

"I had an email from them when I got back from Pleasant Hill," I admit. "I . . . asked for more time."

"Are you still considering the job?"

"I . . ." My fingers drum along my desk absently as my frown deepens. "I should be, shouldn't I? Not considering an opportunity like this just because I met someone would be ludicrous."

I don't say it like a question, realizing I'm talking to myself more than my mother.

"Someone and *the one* are two very different things," my mother offers.

My voice comes out softer, like I'm afraid to say anything in relation to the possibility. "There's no way I can know that. Not after so little time."

"Honey, I've known you your entire life, and I can confidently say that the fact that you're even struggling with this is a good indication that you at least have an idea."

She's right. I know she is. Pre-Mackenzie me wouldn't think twice about climbing the ladder career-wise, no matter what it meant for my personal life. It's all I've ever been concerned with. But then again . . . I've never had anything else to *be* concerned with.

"I just worry she'll . . . change her mind about all of this."

About me, I don't say.

My mother doesn't answer right away, but I can practically hear her thinking from the other end of the line. Eventually, she sighs into the receiver. "That's the funny thing about love, Noah. It's terrifying, and there are no guarantees. We don't fall in love because it's a sure thing. We fall in love because our hearts don't speak the same language as our brains. Your heart doesn't have that little voice that worries about what-ifs. It sees something good and it goes all in. Sometimes you just have to listen to your heart more than your head."

My thoughts trip over the word *love*, because that also feels like some sort of foreign concept that couldn't possibly relate to whatever it is Mackenzie and I are doing. It's too soon. It has to be. At least . . . that's what my head is telling me. I wonder if my mother is right when she says I should be listening to something else instead.

I shake my head, collecting myself.

"I just need a little time to sort through everything," I settle on

resolutely. "We haven't even been on an actual date. It's entirely possible that giving this a real go will make Mackenzie see that she has
better options out there than, as you put it, a surly hermit."

"Don't do that," my mother chides. "Don't hide behind your
insecurities. I know alphas are supposed to be tough and imper-
vious to everything, but we both know you've kept that part of yourself so carefully hidden all of these years because you're afraid
someone will see the real you and not like what they see. You're
afraid to let people in."

"It's just easier," I admit.

"Yeah, well," my mother says. "Love sure as hell isn't easy either."

I chuff a laugh through my nostrils. "Language."

"I'm your mother," she tuts. "Do as I say, not as I do."

"Right."

"Just try not to get too in your head about this," she urges. "I
have a good feeling this Mackenzie of yours might surprise you."

I don't tell her that Mackenzie surprises me every day.

"Sure," I answer, my lips tilting up at the corners. "I'll try."

"And bring her to meet us soon, damn it."

"Lang—"

"Yeah, yeah." Her tone is softer when she adds, "I love you. Even
if you're a surly hermit."

My grin spreads. "Love you too."

I hang up the phone, tossing it aside as I open my laptop to
search for somewhere to take Mackenzie. I have every intention of
finding her the fanciest damn soup she's ever had.

19

Mackenzie

"WHAT ABOUT THIS one?"

Parker looks up from my bed, where he's scrolling through Tik-Tok, wrinkling his nose at the dress his boyfriend, Vaughn, holds against me. "I don't like the color."

"You bought me this for my birthday," I remark dryly.

"Did I?" His brow knits. "There's no doubt in my mind that my mother must have picked that out for me. You know I have no eye for this shit. Hence"—he gestures in the general direction of his boyfriend—"I brought backup."

I huff as I push Vaughn aside to go back to my closet. "I thought you were supposed to be good at this."

"Not all queer people have good taste," Parker snorts. "Don't put me in a box. We can't all be Tan France."

"Oh, he's got *great* style," Vaughn says. "I should get you on that show."

"I'm not straight," Parker answers. "Clearly."

"Babe, if it gets you out of Levi's, I'm willing to be flexible," his boyfriend laughs.

Parker rolls his eyes, muttering something under his breath as Vaughn winks in my direction. He reaches past me then to grab something from the back of my closet. "Oh, this one is nice."

"I haven't worn that since college," I say with a frown. I take the black number from him, giving the plunging neckline a once-over. "I don't even know if I own a bra that would work with this."

Vaughn waggles his eyebrows. "You could always just go without."

"And let her nipples say hello to everyone they pass?" Parker looks at us incredulously. "It's snowing outside."

"Please don't talk about my nipples," I toss his way before pulling my shirt over my head.

Parker makes a disgruntled sound. "Just because I'm not interested in your goods doesn't mean I need to see them all the time."

"You've seen me naked a million times," I laugh. "I assume you view my body as one does abstract art or something."

Parker cocks an eyebrow. "Did you just refer to your body as art?"

"She's not wrong," Vaughn says as he zips me up.

I shoot Parker a smug grin. "At least one of you has taste."

"Don't encourage her," Parker says, clucking his tongue. "She'll become more insufferable than she already is."

"You love me," I say as I blow him a kiss.

Vaughn pushes me out of the closet so I can look myself over in the mirror.

"Oh, I think this is the one," he says appreciatively as I turn this way and that. "And I really can't see your nipples with that fabric."

"Tragedy," Parker mutters. "Dr. Alpha will be so disappointed."

"I'll let him see them after," I deadpan. "Don't worry."

Parker makes a face. "Gross."

The dress really *does* look good, admittedly. The snug, black fabric clings to my hips in a flattering way and the low neckline paired with the soft curls Vaughn coaxed into my hair give me a really sexy vibe. It's a far cry from scrubs and white coats, that's for sure.

I bite my lower lip. "You think he'll like it?"

"You let the guy cart you off to a sex cabin for days on end, and you're worried how he'll like your dress?"

I shoot a glare over my shoulder at Parker. "This is different."

"You're going to marry Dr. Alpha, aren't you?"

My stomach flutters dangerously, and I turn away so that neither of them can see the way my cheeks flush. "It's not like that. We're just going on a date."

"Mhm," Parker says, sounding unconvinced. "Only you could hook up with the biggest asshole we've ever met and turn him into a house husband."

"Maybe her vagina is magical," Vaughn muses.

Now *I'm* making a face. "No talking about my vagina either."

I give myself another once-over, pressing my hands to my stomach to try and calm the nerves still fluttering around inside. I've been on a lot of dates this year alone, but I can't remember the last time I've been so . . . anxious about one. I can't even pin down all my feelings on the matter; I think I'm equal parts excited and nervous as hell. Which really is silly, considering all Noah and I have done, but something about tonight feels more real than anything else that's happened between us.

I don't think I ever even stood a chance of touching you and then just walking away.

I have to bite my lip just to keep from smiling at the memory.

Parker's voice brings me back to the present. "What time is he picking you up?"

"He's supposed to be here at six."

"You're cutting it kind of close, aren't you?"

"Relax," I tell him. "No one is ever on time anym—"

The sound of my doorbell makes me jolt. There's no good reason for me to panic, but I look back at Parker with wide eyes, my gaze flicking from him to Vaughn as I duck to scoop up my shoes. "You guys need to hide."

"What? Why?"

"I don't want him to know I needed *help* to get ready for a date!" I slip one shoe on, hopping a little. "I'm trying for 'put together' here."

"Clearly, you're doing a great job," Parker chuckles.

Vaughn tugs him up from my bed. "Come on, babe. We can hide."

Parker looks around my small studio apartment.

"Where do you propose we do that?"

Vaughn gestures to the open door on the other side of my bed. "The bathroom?"

"If you think we're just going to shove ourselves into her bathroom—"

Vaughn tugs his arm again. "Be good, and I'll make it up to you later."

I watch my best friend's face flush pink, from his cheeks to his ears all the way up to his hairline. "Fine," he mumbles. "We'll let ourselves out."

"No sex in my bed," I chide with a laugh.

"Ugh," Parker groans. "We're not going to—"

The doorbell rings again, and I shoo them away as Vaughn pulls Parker into my bathroom. I pat my hair as I take one last look in the mirror hanging off the back of my closet, smoothing my hands down my dress after and telling myself that I have nothing to be nervous about. This is just a normal date, and Noah has already seen *all* of me.

Doesn't mean my hand isn't shaking a little when I reach for my doorknob seconds later.

I don't know what's more overwhelming, the sight of Noah or the scent of him. His suppressants have been a thing of the past for a while now, and the full blast of his fresh, clean aroma is dizzying in the best way. It rouses memories of his hands on me and his body covering me, and I have to swallow around a growing lump in my throat as I take in his dark jeans and his soft, black sweater that looks suspiciously like cashmere.

"Well." I flash him a smile as I look between us, noticing how similarly dressed we are. "Clearly, one of us is going to have to change."

Noah's eyes traveling down the length of my body feels like an actual weight, feeling every slow inch as if he's sliding his finger along my skin. "I hope it's not going to be you," he says quietly.

A little shiver passes through me, and I hear a soft sound from behind me that sounds a lot like a snort. I grab my coat quickly, stepping out into the hall and closing the door behind me to join Noah. "You look too good in that sweater for it to be you, so I guess we're going to be *that* couple."

My heart rate kicks up when I realize what I've said; it's definitely too soon to be calling us an actual *couple* or anything, and just saying the words makes that lump in my throat swell a little larger.

Noah seems completely unfazed, though, reaching to thread his fingers through mine before he brings my hand to his mouth to press a kiss against my knuckles.

"I don't mind," he says in that same quiet tone.

He tugs me along like we didn't just have an honest-to-God *moment*—and I trail behind him, trying to remember what words are.

I'm afraid that if Noah doesn't do something annoying—like mention model trains on this date—I might be in real trouble of not minding myself.

———

"YOU'RE REALLY NOT going to tell me where we're going?"

It's a mild night, for Denver; the temperature is just warm enough that Noah and I are able to walk the sidewalks downtown without shivering in our coats. He's still holding my hand, something that is definitely new for us, but since I haven't made any sort of move to extricate my fingers, I have to assume that I like it.

"You'll see in a second," Noah chuckles.

"I think now would be a good time to tell you I don't like surprises," I grumble.

"Even a good surprise?"

"That's the thing, how does anyone ever know? Someone says, 'Oh, it's a surprise,' and we're just supposed to take them at face value that they're going to, I don't know, throw us a surprise party instead of stealing our kidney."

Noah's eyebrow arches even as his lips twitch. "I *do* have ready access to the tools, I suppose."

"Wow. You're just going to admit it, huh? This whole thing was all an elaborate setup to get a kidney," I tsk. "There's probably no

Albuquerque job. Just some bad guys you got mixed up with in the black market who—"

We come to a halt after rounding a corner, and nestled under a covered pavilion lined with well-manicured shrubbery are several rows of small food trucks, lined up in a square shape with tables put out in the center of everything.

I quirk a brow at Noah, who's still smiling softly. "Remember when I said I wasn't a cheap date?"

"I think you'll make an exception," he says confidently.

"What is this?"

"Local food-vendor market. They do this every other weekend. All the cuisines are different, but there's usually a theme for what menus they offer."

"A theme?"

"Mhm." I feel his thumb trace across the back of my hand, and I think to myself that I might let him feed me out of the dumpster if he keeps doing that. "Can you guess what tonight's theme is?"

I'm still distracted by the slow back and forth of his thumb. "Um . . . Taco Tuesday?"

"It's Friday," he laughs.

"Just spill. I told you, surprises are bleh."

Noah tugs my hand again, and I fall into step beside him as he casually tells me, "It's soup night."

"You're fucking joking."

Noah barks out a laugh, and the sound of it makes my chest feel funny. It might be the first time I've ever heard him laugh like that. "I am not."

"Oh my God." I might actually be bouncing up and down. "I'm getting one of everything. Can I get one of everything? Do they have mini sizes? I want to try it all."

Noah looks incredibly pleased with himself, and let's face it, he should be, pulling my hand to his mouth again to brush his lips across the back in a move that is quickly becoming addictive. "You can get whatever you want."

"All right," I warn, trying not to sound as breathless as his innocent kiss makes me feel. "Don't say I didn't warn you."

Noah just continues to smile, never letting go of my hand.

THERE ARE ELEVEN little cups of soup at our table. Eleven. I should probably be embarrassed by that, but I just can't find it in myself to feel anything other than giddy excitement. There's miso, pho, taco, and even some gazpacho I'd been chomping at the bit over—and Noah seems content to let me try each one, taking my overexaggerated moans and delighted sounds in stride as he nurses his own bowl of minestrone and sneaks the occasional bite of something I force him to try.

"I had no idea this was a thing," I say eventually, after he recounts a difficult stent he put in the day before. "How did I not know this was a thing?"

"It's fairly new," Noah tells me, licking his spoon clean in a move that makes me feel too warm. I blame the outdoor heaters they have set up under the pavilion. "They only started doing it a couple of months ago."

"Careful," I tease. "That sounds dangerously like fate."

Noah smiles as he scoops up another bite. "And we know how you feel about that."

"Hey, just because it doesn't exist doesn't mean I don't enjoy a good coincidence."

"So, you . . . like this?" I look up to catch the nervous flicker in

Noah's gaze, watching him eye me warily as if he's unsure. "I know you said you weren't a cheap date, but this just felt like something—"

I reach across our little table to cover his hand with mine—partly to reassure him and partly because I am quickly becoming addicted to the weight of it—giving him what I hope is a reassuring grin.

"I love it," I tell him earnestly.

Noah's shoulders look visibly less tense after hearing this. "Good. I would hate to end up as one of your regaling horror stories."

"Hey, you've gone an entire hour without once mentioning the gym or crypto—so I'd say you're already leagues above any of the other dates I've been on this year."

"Good," he says again. "I wanted . . ." He peers down into his bowl, looking a little embarrassed. "I wanted it to be perfect."

That heavy thing in my chest that's taken up residence ever since our time at the cabin throbs as if to make sure I haven't forgotten about it, and I take a second to appreciate just how *beautiful* Noah is—something I never thought I'd be thinking when it came to the Boogeyman of Denver General. But he is, I decide. And not only on the outside. It scares the hell out of me, but it also makes me feel warm in a way I never have before.

"It is," I tell him. "It's perfect."

His smile is slow and shy, and on someone his size, it should look ridiculous. Instead, it makes my stomach flutter. I have to break eye contact before my heart beats out of my chest, focusing on the French onion I'm currently working on to distract myself.

"Does any of this feel weird to you?"

Noah cocks his head slightly. "How do you mean?"

"It's just . . ." I stir my spoon aimlessly, still not looking at him. "I mean, with the whole arrangement we made, and then after all the things we've done . . ." I do look up then when the scent of him suddenly thickens, and I can see a flash in his gaze that tells me that at this very second he's thinking about *all* of the things we've done. It makes me press my thighs together a little tighter under the table. "I just worry that this is all going to blow up in our faces."

Noah doesn't answer for a moment, looking thoughtful. Then he clears his throat. "I suppose in some ways, it is weird."

"Oh." I feel myself deflate a little. "Right."

"But," he adds quickly, letting his fingers slide against my open palm until his middle finger can trace barely-there circles on my wrist. "I'm finding I like a little weird."

My lips curl in a grin. "Yeah?"

"Mackenzie, I—" He looks mildly embarrassed again, but he manages to hold my gaze. "I'm finding there isn't much I *don't* like where you're involved."

That hot, weighted thing inside me might as well be ballooning to fill up all the nooks and crannies of my chest now, and it feels dangerous, allowing myself to bask in it, to take even a moment to revel in the sensation. Maybe it is dangerous, but it doesn't stop me from doing it, anyway.

"Same," I say lamely. "I mean—you too."

His smile really should be illegal, I think idly. I'm almost grateful that he only seems to bring it out when he's around me; if everyone else knew how good he looks when he smiles, I might have some healthy competition gunning for me.

Wow, Mack, you might as well be writing his name in your notebook with little hearts.

"I was thinking," Noah says, breaking through my pathetic thoughts. "We're both off this weekend."

My pulse picks up. "Yeah?"

"It's just . . . last weekend." He clears his throat. "We didn't have a lot of time to just . . . be, I guess."

Images flash through my mind, ones of me begging and him thoroughly giving. I press my thighs a little tighter against each other. "We didn't."

"I was just thinking . . . If you wanted, that is. No pressure if you don't, but I was considering how much closer my place is to downtown, and I thought that if you didn't have plans—which you might, and that's completely okay—but if you didn't, I thought—"

A giant of a man who looks like he does and smells like he does should not be this *adorable* when he's floundering. "Spit it out, Noah."

"You could spend the weekend at my place," he says in a rush. "If you wanted. Just to . . . spend some more time together. See what's here."

"It almost sounds like you're trying to lock me in your bedroom and have your way with me," I tease.

His eyes darken slightly, his throat bobbing with a swallow. "Among other things," he tells me slowly, looking half-surprised that he's said the words. "But . . . I just wanted to spend more time with you."

My chest might actually burst with the way it continues to swell. I have to bring my bowl to my mouth and sip down the last bits of my soup just to hide the giddy grin on my face, collecting myself for a moment before setting it back on the table and lifting one shoulder in a shrug.

"I'm game if you are," I tell him, showing much less excitement than I'm feeling in some last-ditch effort to play it cool.

Noah looks relieved, his lips rolling as he wets them and drawing my eye to the movement. At this moment, I can almost imagine myself chucking every last bit of the soup still waiting for me to try in the nearby garbage can just so I can get out of here faster and back to Noah's bedroom.

I realize then that I might be in real trouble.

20

Noah

"DR. TAYLOR?"

I blink, noticing the woman in scrubs looking at me expectantly. "Hm?"

"You okay?" She quirks an eyebrow at me. "You've been kind of . . . smiling at the coffee maker for like a full minute. It's sort of creepy, to be honest."

"Sorry." My eyes flick to her name tag. "Jessica." I frown, her name sounding familiar but I can't place from where. "Can I help you?"

Jessica smirks. "Been hunting you down for almost an hour. You still haven't signed off on Mr. Guzman's chart."

"Oh." *Shit.* That's unlike me to make them wait so long. "Sorry, I was . . . distracted."

"Mhm." The nurse crosses her arms, looking less annoyed and more . . . smug. "I'll bet you are."

"Pardon?"

She waves me off. "If you could just get those signed off for me, I promise I won't come hunt you down in the doctors' lounge again."

"Right, right." I straighten the collar of my white coat in a flustered gesture. "I'll do that right now."

Jessica is still smirking when she turns away, tossing her hand up over her shoulder in a wave. "Congrats on your mating, by the way!"

That was . . . odd. I shake my head, trying to pull myself together. It's not the first time since last weekend that I've lost myself in the memories of Mackenzie in my space for an entire weekend. Her scent is in my sheets and my kitchen and all over my couch— and in the time since she's gone back to sleeping at her place, I find myself missing her presence in my home more and more. Which makes no sense, given that we've only been on one *official* date.

I think the staff thinks I might be on the verge of some sort of psychotic break; I've walked into a room more than once to ceased conversations and wide-eyed stares—not to mention how hysterical Mackenzie finds the matter of the hospital being abuzz with "Dr. Taylor smiling for the first time ever." Which can't be true, I would think. Surely I've smiled before I met Mackenzie. Surely.

I abandon the task of getting coffee, shuffling out of the lounge and back to my office so I can sign off on that chart before Jessica the RN comes looking for me again. When it's done, I consider texting Mackenzie, wondering if twice in one morning before she's had time to reply would come off as annoying. I check my emails instead, trying to distract myself from anything that might make me seem more obsessed than I already seem.

There's a response to my dodgy reply to Albuquerque asking for more time to consider, reminding me that they need an answer from me as soon as possible. I ignore it, telling myself a few more days won't hurt. I can discuss it with Mackenzie soon, I think. Now that we're—

I frown, leaning back in my chair. It occurs to me that we haven't exactly . . . defined what we are. I would like to think that we are more than just pretend now, but given my lack of experience in the matters of dating—I can't be entirely sure. Maybe that's something we should talk about as well. Even if the thought of doing so ties my stomachs into knots, because what if she thinks it's too soon? What if she isn't interested in entertaining the idea of a real relationship with me after only one date and a handful of intimate encounters?

It's a question that's been plaguing me since the night I took her out.

I blow out a breath as I sink down further in my chair, closing my eyes and wondering how I've allowed myself to fall into such a predicament. Attachments have never been my thing, and Mackenzie is the *last* person I ever would have pictured myself with—so why is it that everything about her has me on a constant edge, counting the seconds until I can hear her voice again, enjoy her scent again, *touch* her again. It's all I can think about anymore. A steady beat pulsing through my brain of *Mackenzie Mackenzie Mackenzie*.

"Dr. Taylor to room 807. Dr. Taylor to room 807."

I sit up, my brow knitting together. The eighth floor is currently undergoing construction, which means they're barely using it at the moment. What could they possibly need me for up there?

I push up from my desk with a sigh, thinking that it will at least distract me from texting Mackenzie again. The elevator is blessedly empty, and I ride it up to the eighth floor with mild curiosity as I wonder what could have happened, hoping that someone on the reno team didn't have an accident. Then again, if something did occur, I would have to assume they would bring them down to my floor, not the other way around.

I step off the elevator to more empty space, noting the scattered equipment and tools but the distinct lack of workers. Half the hall lights are off; the overheads seem to be missing several bulbs, giving the entire floor a creepy sort of feel. I wonder idly if I'm being pranked somehow, which irritates me. I huff as I pick up my pace to room 807, preparing to give someone a piece of my mind if they're wasting my time as some sort of joke at my expense. I know I'm not flush with friends in this place, but really, this is just—

"Mackenzie?"

I grip the handle and cock my head, lingering in the doorway I've just opened as I take her in. She's lounging in one of the medical chairs, one arm resting above her against the headrest and the other twirling one of her scrub pant strings.

"Hello, Doctor," she says slyly, her mouth turning up at the corners as she flashes me a smile. "I was waiting for you."

I'm still very confused. "Mackenzie, what are you—"

"They told me you come highly recommended," she barrels on, cocking an eyebrow at me expectantly. "And I'm feeling *so* bad."

I can feel myself frowning as I try to make sense of what's happening here, but then her scent teases under my nostrils, warm and thick and *aroused*.

Oh.

Oh.

I swallow, shutting the door behind me and locking it. I've never done anything remotely as reckless as what she seems to have planned. The old me would have scolded her for even suggesting it, but right now . . . Right now, all I can think about is the look in her eyes as they roam over me. Like she's been thinking about me as much as I've been thinking about her. Like she *wants* me. It's still a novel thing for me, being wanted by someone like her.

"Hello . . . Ms. Carter. What brings you in today?"

Her smile brightens, looking pleased with herself. "I have this . . . ache that won't go away."

This is so ridiculous, like something out of a bad porn movie, and yet I can already feel my cock stiffening in my dress pants.

I take a step closer, fisting my hands at my sides to keep from outright pouncing on her, something that is extremely difficult with the way her scent blooms in the air, making my blood heat. "What sort of ache?"

"Mm. That's the weird thing. I can't seem to pinpoint it. I was hoping you could help me find it."

Dear God, this woman is going to be the absolute death of me.

"I would—" I clear my throat, my tongue feeling almost too thick. "I would need to touch you to make a proper diagnosis. Would that be okay?"

"Of course, Doctor," she practically purrs. "You're the expert."

I close the distance between us, my fingers teasing over her ankle bone lightly as I let them slide higher underneath the pant leg of her scrubs. "How does this feel?"

"Fine," she says, only slightly breathless. "Nothing hurts there."

I reach tentatively with my other hand to let my fingertips graze the sliver of skin exposed between her waistband and the hem of her scrub top, circling her belly button gently. "What about here?"

"Maybe a little," she breathes, her lashes fluttering. "I think you're getting warmer."

I press a knee on the chair to half cover her, leaning in until my nose can skirt the length of her throat so that I can breathe her in deep. Just the scent of her is enough to make my mouth water. "And here?"

"That's . . ." I hear her gasp when my lips touch her pulse. "That doesn't hurt at all."

"It doesn't?"

She shakes her head lightly. "It actually feels good there."

"I see." I flick my tongue against her skin, reveling in the way she shivers. Knowing that *I* made her do that. "I'll have to keep looking."

"Please, Doctor, make me feel better."

I smile against her throat, unable to keep from breaking character. "You know someone could come up here, don't you?"

"This is a hospital, Doctor," she says coyly. "There are people everywhere. I didn't think this would be a . . . long exam."

"Are you telling me to hurry up?"

"I just want to make sure I get the full treatment before your next appointment."

A breathy laugh escapes me. "I'll make sure that you do."

I push her scrub top higher to expose her stomach, watching it rise and fall with each heaving breath. I can't even decide what I want to do with her—whether I want her on my tongue or my cock or even just my hands. I only know I want to hear her make those sweet noises she makes when she falls apart.

"I'm going to suggest something a little . . . unorthodox."

She bites her bottom lip. "Oh?"

"I'm going to need you to turn over for me, Ms. Carter."

"Turn over?"

"That's right. I want you to get on your knees for me. Put your hands on the headrest."

I watch her pupils dilate, her scent growing thicker, and I can *smell* the way she grows slick with the suggestion. "I can do that."

I help ease her up on her knees, holding her steady as she turns, and when she arches her back to grab hold of the headrest, the perfect curve of her ass pushed out like an offering, I almost lose all my control.

She turns to look at me over her shoulder, the tip of her tongue flashing to wet her bottom lip. "Like this?"

"That's perfect," I rasp, my hands sliding over her hips. "So good."

And she is. So good. She's the gift-wrapped wet dream I never even knew I needed. My hands actually *shake* with the knowledge that I get to touch her. That she *wants* me to.

The chair is low enough that I can straddle the seat of it, even if my stance feels too wide, but if I raise a knee to let it rest by one of hers, I can almost comfortably curl my body into hers. I smooth my hands down either side of her hips, bending until I can press soft kisses along her throat. She presses back against me when my thumbs tuck into the waistband of her scrub bottoms, making a needy little sound that has my cock growing impossibly harder.

I swipe my tongue along the fevered gland nestled in the bend of her shoulder, nipping it with my teeth as I tug down her clothes. "You seem a little feverish, Ms. Carter."

"Do I?"

"Mm." My palm glides over hips and down, fingers teasing where her scrubs are scrunched above her knees and quietly urging her to adjust so I can ease them off her. When she's naked from the waist down, I continue my lazy exploration, gliding my fingers over the inside of her thigh until it reaches the hottest part of her. "Especially here." She sucks in a breath when I press my thumb against her entrance, already slick for me. "Does it hurt here?"

"So bad," she gasps.

I press deeper, teasing her with my thumb. "Maybe I can help with that."

"Can you?"

Her fucking *scent*. It makes my eyes roll back with how thick it is, and somewhere in the clearer parts of my lust-addled mind, I know there is no way no one will realize how I've touched her if she walks out of here smelling like this. The thought should have me wary, but all it does it make me burn hotter. I realize I *want* them to know I've touched her. I want everyone in the goddamn hospital to know that she's *mine*.

I go still, trying to get a handle on my racing thoughts. My breath huffs against her skin, and as if she senses my momentary episode, I feel her hand reach behind her until her fingers push into my hair. "You okay?"

Am I?

The thought is still there—some primal urge to mark her, *claim* her—to ensure that there is never a doubt that she belongs to me, and that I belong to her.

And in this moment . . . it's terrifying thinking that I might be alone in that feeling.

"I just . . . Are you sure this is a good idea?"

She turns her face to let her lips graze my jaw, and my eyes drift closed as I relish the sensation. "I've been thinking about you being inside me all day. Do you really want to wait until we're not on opposite shifts again to touch me?"

She has a point. She'll be on the night shift for another five days while I work the opposite—meaning that there will only be a small window where our schedules overlap and I can see her at work. The thought of not being inside her for five days feels like absolute *torture*.

"No," I admit roughly. "I don't."

"Stop worrying, Dr. Taylor," she says soothingly, her nails scratching lightly at my scalp as she presses back against me. "Just don't knot me, and we're golden."

"Fuck," I groan. Just the word *knot* on her lips is enough to make my cock ache. I push my thumb deeper inside her, enjoying the little mewl that escapes her. "You want my cock? Right here?"

"Fuck, yes," she sighs, wiggling against me. "Come on, Doctor. Gimme a shot."

A different kind of groan escapes me. "You're ridiculous."

"You love it," she laughs.

I might love you.

It punches through me, threatening to swallow me as if the ground has opened beneath me, but I shake it away. It's too soon—both the feeling and the time to even remotely begin to entertain the possibility of sharing it—so I focus instead on the way her skin tastes. I home in on the feel of her hot and wet in my hands, practically begging for me to fill her. It's the distraction I need to keep the other worrying thoughts at bay.

I watch her skin pebble with goose bumps as the stark sound of my zipper sliding down fills the space, rubbing my palm over my heated length through my underwear to seek some momentary bout of relief. Relief I know I won't find until I'm buried inside her. Nothing else can ever compare to her. Mackenzie Carter has unknowingly ruined me, and I'm not even upset about it.

It takes a moment for me to get rid of my pants and coat—I know that making a mess of either will be a dead giveaway to what we've done here—but I'm rewarded with a quiet, breathy moan falling out of her when I finally let my cock slide along the crease of her ass. My pre-cum smears against her skin, marking her just like

I wanted. A less civilized part of my brain hopes that it dries there. That any other shifter she meets today will smell it on her.

It takes some situating to notch against her; Mackenzie slides down a little further while I dip my hips, and I'm still wholly aware that this is the most reckless thing I've ever done, but I can't bring myself to care in the slightest when the slick heat of her envelops me. I close my eyes as I push inside, focusing only on the sensation of her around me, of the easy glide as her body opens up for me, like it was made for me. Like she was made just for me. Part of me wonders if maybe she was. I can't decide if that's my brain or my instincts pondering the idea.

Like this, I can see the way she stretches to take me; I can see myself disappear as I sink further and further inside. I grab her hips to pull her back in a sudden move that forces me all the way inside, and the startled yelp she makes morphs into a low moan that I can feel under my skin.

"You're so good," I half slur, feeling that increasingly familiar fog that comes from being deep inside her while surrounded by her scent that drives me mad. "So good for me." I pull out slowly just to roll back inside. "Always take my cock so well."

"Noah," she whimpers, reaching behind to scrape her nails against my thigh in a silent plea.

I know what she wants; she wants me to stop teasing her, to take what she's offering, but I've never been quite myself with Mackenzie. Not like this. *This* Noah enjoys her begging. *This* Noah wants to take her apart and put her back together.

"You want more?" I curve my body so that my teeth can nibble at her earlobe. "You called me here, Mackenzie. I want to hear you tell me what you wanted when you did. Tell me how much you wanted my cock."

"Needed it," she gasps. "Needed you."

"You needed me to fuck you? Here? You needed my cock so badly that you couldn't wait for it?"

"*Noah . . .*"

I keep rocking in and out of her at a steady pace that I know will offer neither of us any relief, but I'm too far gone to stop. Whatever it is inside me that Mackenzie triggers . . . it's running the show right now.

"Say it, Mackenzie," I rasp against her ear. "Tell me you want my cum."

"*Fuck.* I want it."

"What do you want? I need to hear it."

"I want—*ah.* I want your cum. *Please*, Noah."

"Good girl," I coo, sliding my hand down her spine as I pull back, some rutting thing inside me preening at her submission. "You sound so pretty when you beg."

I pull out once more, still that same slow pace that is driving us both insane, lingering at her entrance for only a second before I snap my hips to plunge back inside as she cries out.

"That's it," I say on an exhale, my breath catching when I do it all over again. "I'm going to fill up this perfect pussy until you're overflowing. And you're going to take it, aren't you?"

"Yes," she whimpers, her body rocking with the force of my increasing thrusts.

I grip her hips with both hands, my nails biting into her skin as I start to move inside her in a way that feels frantic. "Yes, *what?*"

"*Yes*, Alpha," she whines. "Fuck, Noah, I'm—"

"Touch yourself. I want to feel you come with me inside you. I want to feel the way you come apart."

I can feel it, when her slim fingers graze the base of my cock as it slides inside her over and over. I can feel the rhythm she makes as she swipes at her clit since I can't reach. A strange part of me is jealous of her *hand* for being the one to touch her.

"I wish I could knot you," I grit out. "I want to feel you wrapped around my knot. Wanna feel you full of me."

Her only answer is a choked sound, but I can feel the flutter of her inner walls around me as each thrust becomes just a little harder, her body tightening impossibly further as I grit my teeth in ecstasy. How can it be so *good* every time? How can each time seem *better* than the last?

"Noah, I'm—*oh fuck, Alpha*, I'm—"

It's messy when she comes, always so *messy*—but I love every wet slap of skin, every slick glide of her thighs against mine as I fuck her harder, *faster*—a pressure building deep, deep inside until it threatens to consume me. My lips part, and my breath heaves from my chest, and everything is hot, so fucking *hot*, until I—

"Fuck."

It takes every bit of restraint not to knot her deep, to keep the thick base of my cock flush against her opening instead of letting it swell inside, and the cool air of the exam room feels downright arctic against my heated skin. I grit my teeth so hard they might chip as I fill her with pulse after pulse of my orgasm, shivering through it almost as hard as she is.

And even when it's over, when my cock goes still and her body collapses against the chair—the thumping of blood in my ears doesn't quiet. She winces when I pull out of her suddenly, and then a startled sound fills the air when I push my fingers through the mess I've made of her, collecting everything I can and pushing it back inside to hold it there, since my knot can't. I keep her full of my fingers for an insurmountable amount of time, catching my breath as I leave soft kisses on her skin, waiting for my body to calm.

"Dr. Taylor to X-ray room 204. Dr. Taylor to X-ray room 204."

Mackenzie's laugh is breathless but loud, her body shaking against mine even as I press one last kiss to her hip before straightening. I'm loath to pull my fingers from her, a twinge of leftover instinct practically growling in my chest, wanting me to keep her full of me.

"Someone's in high demand today," Mackenzie teases as she turns to slump down in the chair.

My eyes rake over her—her hand draped haphazardly over her belly button, tracing idle circles on her skin like she's still out of it—having to fight the urge to take her again. "Today might mark the most popular I've ever been."

"Mm." She catches me off guard when she yanks on my tie, nearly sending me off-balance since I've only got one leg back in my pants. She lets her lips brush mine, the action entirely too soft and sweet for what we just did. "I should page you more often."

I chuff out a laugh. "Much more of this, and they'll have to find an interventional cardiologist for *me*."

"Wow, that was either the sweetest or the cheesiest thing you've ever said to me."

"You're a bad influence," I mumble, righting my pants and buttoning them.

Her grin is blinding, threatening to steal the air from my lungs. "I think you like it."

No, I love it. I love you.

I have to clench my jaw to keep the words in my throat so they don't escape into the air. It's like now that the seed has been planted . . . I'm desperate to let it grow.

"Maybe a little," I say instead, bending to kiss her again as I hand her her pants. I tuck my face against her throat after, inhaling from her. "You're going to smell like me for days."

"You don't sound very upset about it."

Another long pull of her scent. "I'm not." I straighten, frowning back at the still-locked door. "Should we be worried about hallway cameras? Are they still functioning on this floor? It might be strange if we're both on camera heading to a floor no one is using, right?"

"There's the Noah Taylor we all know and love," Mackenzie laughs, hopping off the table and grabbing for a paper towel dispenser on the wall to clean up.

I remind myself that she doesn't mean it as literally as I'd like her to. What is *wrong* with me?

"I might have . . . bribed the IT guy to shut them off for an hour," she goes on sheepishly, throwing the napkin away and busying herself with getting dressed.

My eyebrows raise. "That could be considered a gross misuse of resources, Ms. Carter."

"Probably." She practically skips to close the distance between us, pushing up on her toes to press her mouth to mine. "Are you going to tell on me?"

My eyelids drift closed as she deepens the kiss, and my arm circles her waist to hold her closer against me. "Doubtful," I say as seriously as I can manage. "Like I said, you're a bad influence."

She grins. "Stick with me, Doc. I'll teach you all sorts of fun things."

She leaves another peck at my lips, sauntering past me like she didn't just turn my entire fucking world on its head. She pulls open the door and tosses me a look over her shoulder. "You owe me another date, but until then, feel free to page me."

I watch her go with my tongue glued to the roof of my mouth, wondering how in the hell I'm going to get through the rest of my shift with her slick on my fingers and the feel of her still humming under my skin. Or how I'm going to make it through the next five days while we're on opposite shifts without losing my mind.

But more important . . . how in the hell am I going to tell her that I love her?

21

Mackenzie

"THANKS FOR COMING down," I tell Priya. "I saw this once in residency, but it wasn't this bad."

Priya waves me off with her free hand while the respiratory therapist finishes inflating the balloon on the patient she's just finished intubating. "Don't even. These can be tricky. I've been doing this for years, and I'm still afraid I'm going to chip someone's teeth with the laryngoscope."

The patient she's working on was admitted with severe pneumonia that progressed to levels that made it difficult for them to breathe—not uncommon during this time of year, but still hard to see. They're sleeping now after the sedatives and paralytics given to them before Priya started intubating, the entire process marking the end of what turned out to be a very long night.

While she lets the RT finish up, Priya pulls off her gloves, tossing them into the waste bin while I let the nurse know to monitor the patient and call me if there are any changes. "Six can't get here fast enough," she says with a slight yawn.

"You're telling me. It should be illegal to work when the sun isn't out."

She stretches as she checks her watch. "Only an hour left."

"Thank God," I grunt.

She flashes me a sly grin. "Must be nice that you get to go home to your grumpy bedmate, at least."

"Hardly," I snort. "He's been on day shift."

"Ah," Priya sighs dramatically, pressing a hand to her heart. "They were like two ships passing in the night."

I roll my eyes as she follows me toward the doctors' lounge. A cup of coffee is exactly what I need to drag through this last hour. "Shut up."

"Seriously, it's gotta be hell to be mated to another doctor," Priya says. "Do you guys, like, have to schedule your sex?"

I feel my cheeks heat in a blush, thinking back to only a few short days ago when Noah and I had very *unscheduled* sex in this very building. I clear my throat, trying to look nonchalant. "It's not *that* bad."

"Man, I still can't picture the two of you having sex."

"Maybe you should just . . . not then."

She grins. "Are you kidding? My friend is mated to the equivalent of a hot hospital cryptid. Like, there are *legends* about Noah, Mack."

"They're all—"

"—*grossly overexaggerated*," she finishes with a snicker. "Yes, you've told me. You're even starting to sound like him."

That makes me smile. Maybe he's rubbing off on me. Well, in ways other than the literal sense. Which he most definitely is. The thought only makes me blush again.

"What's he like at home?"

I tap my chin thoughtfully before I grab an empty paper cup near the Keurig. "Do you remember when we used to have conversations that *didn't* revolve around Noah? Those were the good old days."

"No one asked you to mate Noah fucking Taylor in secret and withhold all the juicy details for an entire year," she says, clucking her tongue.

"He's just . . ." I imagine Noah in his own space—his wool socks he's so fond of and his cotton sleep pants he's partial to—feeling a smile tug at my lips. "He's just like any other guy, really."

"That's very hard to believe," she scoffs.

It's funny. I used to think the same thing.

Priya sighs again. "I'm just jealous. You really are living the dream? You bagged a sexy alpha who makes bank *and* understands our schedule. Who cares if he frowns during sex?"

"He doesn't *actually* frown during sex," I laugh.

"Shh." She closes her eyes. "Just let me picture it the way I want."

I shake my head. "You're horrible."

"You love me," she says, blowing a kiss.

The door to the lounge reopens while I'm loading a K-Cup into the machine, the next sentence hanging on my tongue getting lost in the air when I notice Dennis striding in. I haven't seen him since the day I went into heat, and his smarmy grin as he enters the room seems to get more and more intolerable every time we run into each other.

Priya makes a face. "I'd better head back up to my floor. Need to finish a few things before I take off."

I look from her to my cup that is still catching the stream of coffee, leaving me trapped here, giving her a look that I hope says: *Don't you dare leave me with this creep.*

Her answering look responds something along the lines of: *Sorry, it's every woman for herself.*

Ugh. I can't even blame her. She gives me a little wave as she retreats, and I try to look busy with the Keurig, hoping that Dennis can read the room.

He can't, apparently.

"Mack," he says in a way he probably thinks is friendly, but it comes off more oily than he intends. "How are you? I haven't seen you since your . . . incident."

How is it even possible that I never ran into this guy before I met Noah, and now he seems to be everywhere?

"I'm fine," I say curtly, keeping my attention on my cup. "Just a case of a mixed-up calendar."

"Never heard of that happening," he says in a curious tone. "Especially for mated pairs. Those things are supposed to be pretty predictable, aren't they?"

I turn my head enough so that he can see the hard set of my gaze. "No offense, but this isn't really something I want to discuss with a near-stranger."

"Of course, of course." He raises his hands palms out in an apologetic gesture. "Just concerned, that's all."

"I appreciate it," I answer flatly, "but I'm fine."

"Good to hear," he says with another slimy grin. It really is creepy, the more you look at it. He smiles the way I imagine a Venus flytrap would when it sees a fly. He shoves his hands in his pockets, leaning against the opposite wall, seeming to have no intention of leaving. "It must be nerve-racking to think of him leaving."

I turn again with a cocked brow. "Excuse me?"

"Oh, I just meant . . . Well. You know the rumor mill. There's all the talk of Noah transferring to Albuquerque. I have friends over there. Bunch of gossips."

"I see," I answer measuredly.

I turn back to my cup, pulling it from underneath the Keurig spout and moving to the canisters where we keep the cream and sugar.

"He's still considering," I finally say, as carefully as I can. "We're . . . still talking about it."

Which is entirely untrue since I have absolutely no say in the matter. The knowledge of that is hitting me full force at this moment, and it leaves me with a strange feeling. One that's . . . unsettling. With a wrinkled brow I stir my coffee, forgetting for a second or so that Dennis is even here until he speaks again.

"Ah, well. I know we'd certainly miss our resident genius. Plus, I can imagine it would be hard for you if he took the job."

But I don't know that. It's possible—probable—that he will.

Why does my chest feel so tight?

I hide my tumultuous emotions with a slow sip from my cup, my eyes focused on the warm liquid as I manage a half shrug. "I'm sure Noah will come to the best decision."

"He always does," Dennis replies with that smile that is starting to make my skin crawl.

"Right." I tip my mug in his direction, needing to get out of this room. "Anyway. Better get back to it. Have some things to finish up before I go home."

"Of course, of course," Dennis says with a wave. "Good to see you again, Mack."

I nod, because I can't possibly return the sentiment, escaping the lounge with my cup in hand as I release a measured breath. I really, *really* don't like that guy. I can see why Noah doesn't either.

Thoughts of Noah tug at something inside, Dennis's talk of the possibility of Noah moving and the reminder that it's been a possibility since this . . . thing we're doing started—it causes a twinge in my chest that doesn't go away even when I rub my hand there. If my mood weren't suddenly so dour, I'd be texting Noah making a joke about needing a consultation. As it is, I walk in the direction of the nurses' station with slow steps, my thoughts scattered, bouncing around in my head with nowhere to settle.

I can imagine it would be hard for you if he took the job.

It's funny, until Dennis said it . . . it never occurred to me that it would be.

～

"THIS SHOW IS completely inaccurate."

I grin at Noah from my side of my small couch, fighting the urge to laugh at his disgusted expression aimed toward my television.

"It's not supposed to be accurate," I tell him. "It's supposed to be dramatic."

He makes an indignant sound, folding his arms across his chest and spreading his legs out further in front of him in a move that shouldn't be as sexy as it is. My couch isn't the largest piece of furniture out there, but with Noah on it, it looks downright small.

It's been days since my run-in with Dennis, and I haven't been able to make myself bring any of it up to Noah. It's our first shared day off since the weekend I stayed over, and I'm not exactly dying to ruin it with talks about his least favorite person at the hospital or my growing insecurities about what we are and what his possible new job might mean for . . . whatever this is. It doesn't sound like a fun conversation in my head, and I can't imagine it being any better spoken out loud.

And besides, I've realized these last few days that the possibility of bringing it up only for Noah to brush it off would be far more painful than it has any right to be. Because what if he gets freaked out that I'm even worrying about it? This entire thing between us was built on a lie, and just because he asked me on *one* real date doesn't mean he's ready to propose or anything.

Not that I *want* him to.

Jesus. My brain is a mess.

"Did you see that?" Noah points at the screen, his brow knitted together. "He just touched his arm after scrubbing up for surgery. That's a contamination hazard!"

"I'm sure they were really worried about medical accuracy when writing Derek Shepherd's character," I laugh.

"And that woman is wearing earrings in an OR," he grumbles. "Seriously, who wrote this shit?"

"You know, I'm starting to wonder why I thought it would be a good idea to watch this with you."

He catches my eye, a sheepish half smile curving on one side of his lip. "Sorry."

"Nah. You're cute when you're grumpy."

He frowns. "I'm not cute."

"I think so." I scoot across the inches of couch that separate us, leaning into him to brush my lips across his cheek. "Adorable, really."

He turns his face just enough to let my mouth catch at the corner of his. "Mhm."

"We can watch something else."

"It's fine," he murmurs. "I'll try not to be too critical."

"The day you stop being critical is the day I start worrying about your health," I tease.

"My mother says something similar," he huffs. "Often."

"Oh? Your mom isn't as . . . rigid as you are?"

I waggle my brows on the last word, and he rolls his eyes. "My mother doesn't know the meaning of the word." He eyes me speculatively. "She's much more like you, if I'm being honest."

"Like me?"

"You know . . ." He waves his hand in a circular motion, smiling. "Personable. Outgoing. *Fun*."

"I think you're lots of fun," I tell him, trailing my fingers across the T-shirt stretched over his chest.

He snorts. "You're probably the only one."

"They just don't get to see the sparkling personality you hide under all those frowns."

"Right." He chuffs out a quiet laugh. "My mother would adore you."

For some reason his casual statement makes my pulse quicken. "You think?"

"Oh, definitely. She's been badgering me to bring you to dinner for weeks."

My heart is thundering now, and I can't say why. "She has?"

He seems to realize what he's said then, his eyes widening and his lips parting. "I . . . I mean . . . Don't worry. I told her it wasn't a good idea."

"Oh." My heart rate feels almost like it comes to a dead halt. Why am I so disappointed? "Right."

"I just mean . . ." He looks flustered, like he doesn't quite know what to say. "I only meant that I wouldn't want to put you on the spot or ask you to do something you didn't agree to when we started all of this."

Something you didn't agree to.

It's like a gut punch, those five words, and I do my best not to let it show. Nothing he's saying is untrue, or even unwarranted; logically, I know that just because we are wading into new territory, it doesn't negate how we started out—but the lines that seem to be blurring are so muddled that I can't figure out what's what anymore. It leaves me feeling uncertain. Something I hate feeling.

I school my features, waving my hand in front of my face and doing my best to look unbothered. "It's fine. You're totally right. It would probably be weird."

"Right . . ." His expression is hard to read, but for a second I can almost imagine a flash of disappointment in his eyes, but that doesn't make sense. It's gone as quickly as it comes. "Exactly. Especially since we're in such . . . uncharted territory right now."

"It's fine, Noah," I tell him with as much assurance as I can muster while my stomach is tying itself up. "Better not to rock the boat before we figure things out between us."

He looks at me like there's something he would like to say, but isn't sure how to voice it. His lips are pressed into a firm line, and there's a wrinkle between his brows that is deeper than usual, and I can't decide if he's worried that he's offended me, or if he's worried that I'm hoping for things that I shouldn't be. The latter alternative is something I have a feeling would gut me even further.

Seriously, what is *wrong* with me lately?

"Sure," he says finally, reaching with his hand to cover my own, still resting against his chest. "Not until we figure things out."

And maybe part of me hopes that he'll broach that conversation, the one where we *figure things out*, but either Noah is hoping the same, or he's just not ready to have it. His thumb slides back and forth over my knuckles, and then he leans to press a kiss to my forehead, clearing his throat before returning his attention to the show.

"Oh, for God's sake. He's not even wearing eye protection! What about blood splatter?"

Despite my roiling emotions, I can't help the tiny chuckle that escapes me. "They wouldn't be able to see into McDreamy's eyes if he wore goggles in surgery."

"Honestly," Noah mutters grumpily.

He's still holding my hand, the warm weight of it offering some comfort in face of the errant thoughts flitting through my head. I can't remember a time when I've ever been in a situation where I wanted to talk to a man about what we "might be," and honestly, with the anxiety it's giving me, I'm not sure I'd ever wish for it if given the choice. Everything about Noah and me was supposed to be a casual thing that we both benefited from, and as it's slowly morphed into something decidedly *less* casual—I find myself stuck in limbo without any direction.

This romance bullshit is for the birds.

I snuggle closer into Noah's side as if the heat of his body will somehow quiet the loud war raging in my head, and his arm immediately circling my shoulders weirdly only makes things worse. Apparently, against my will I now analyze everything Noah does, my brain forcing me to search for the hidden meanings that might not be there.

It's fine, I tell myself. *Stop worrying about things that might not even matter. Just enjoy where you are now.*

I take a slow, surreptitious breath just to let it out, hoping that emptying my lungs will somehow empty my head. Not that it works. I close my eyes as I listen to Noah continue to pick apart *Grey's*

Anatomy, hardly even hearing what he's saying as I allow the low timbre of his voice to wash over me, basking in his heady, warm scent that calls to my blood and centers me in a way that nothing else ever has.

It's funny, when I asked Noah to be my fake boyfriend . . . I never imagined a possibility where I might wish for it to be real.

22

Noah

I APPRECIATE THE opportunity for employment at your hospital, but as my circumstances have changed, I feel it best to remain at my current position at this time. I hope that in the future should things put me in a position to be reconsidered, you will keep me in mind.

I've been staring at the drafted email to the HR department for the hospital in Albuquerque for the last hour—typing and erasing and editing things over and over and never being satisfied. I still worry that it's crazy to even consider sending it; I haven't been able to find the courage yet to even broach the subject with Mackenzie, and after putting my foot in my mouth a few days ago at her place when the subject of dinner with my mother came up . . . it makes me wonder even more if I'm doing the right thing.

It's unlike me, doing things on a whim. But then again, can I really call it a whim? It's not like I haven't been agonizing over this very thing for weeks, at best. And now that I have the added revelation of realizing the depths of my feelings for someone who is supposed to be my *pretend* mate—continuing to ignore this looming fork in the road has become harder and harder to keep doing. As ill-advised as it may seem, I know deep down that unless Mackenzie tells me herself that she no longer wants to participate in this . . . new territory we're exploring, there is no possible way I will be able to physically part from her.

Mackenzie Carter is in my skin now. She lives in my blood. Without ever intending for it to happen . . . my pretend mate became the very *real* woman I'd like to spend the rest of my life with.

And maybe it's too soon to think that way. Perhaps someone more sensible than me might theorize that it is simply biology and our DNA that draws me to her—but it doesn't change the fact that every cell in my body seems to have modified itself to complement hers. Almost as if the organ in my chest no longer cares about its basic functions of moving blood through my body and oxygen to my brain—no, apparently now it just beats for her.

I make a self-deprecating sound as I run my fingers through my hair, wondering when in the hell I got so emotional. A short time ago, I would have laughed at someone for saying the things going through my head right now, or at the very least looked at them like they'd grown a second head. And yet . . . I don't feel any sort of cringing embarrassment at my own thoughts. If anything, coming to terms with my feelings has only filled the lonely spaces inside me I hadn't realized existed, leaving behind a warm fullness that somehow makes it harder to breathe and yet makes breathing *easier*. With that in mind, I return my attention to the email in front of me, telling myself that I will draft this, save it, and then the very next time I see her tell Mackenzie everything going through my head.

Well, maybe I will save a certain four-letter word for a later date, given that there's a good chance she might run screaming if I voice it out loud after only a few short weeks. Still, I can tell her that I want something real. I can hope beyond hope that she might want the same. The conversation with my mother last week flits through my mind, and I try to cling to her advice.

Try not to get too in your head about this. I have a good feeling this Mackenzie of yours might surprise you.

I really, really hope that she does.

I can't say how much time passes with me still agonizing over one email when a knock sounds at my door, and given that Mackenzie has already gone home for the day, I barely glance at the door when I bid whoever is on the other side to come in. I can't say that anyone *other* than Mackenzie would be a welcome presence in my office, if I'm being honest, but there's a particularly special wave of distaste that washes over me when I see it's the *last* person I want to see right now, or ever, for that matter.

"Noah," Dennis greets me with a pleasantness that feels entirely fake. "I was hoping you had a minute."

I frown instantly. "I'm actually kind of busy right now, Dr. Martin."

"Oh? Well, I do hate to bother you." He practically pouts as he shuts the door behind him anyway, his face saying otherwise. "But it *is* very important, so . . ."

I sigh, pinching the bridge of my nose as I turn my chair away from my desk. It's probably better to just let him have whatever moment he's trying to have here so he will go away that much faster. I just have to be sure not to let him get to me like the last time we ran into each other.

"Okay," I say resignedly. "What is so important?"

"It's actually pretty embarrassing," he says, looking uncomfortable but in a way that, again, doesn't feel real. "I really hate bringing it up at all, you know . . ."

I feel myself getting irritated despite my resolve. "Then just spit it out so I can get back to work."

"Right," Dennis says as a slow, unsettling smile creeps across his face. "Well. You see . . . I've had a dilemma for a while now, and I don't really know how I should handle it."

My jaw ticks. "What sort of dilemma?"

"Well . . ." I can see it a moment before it happens, the way his features shift into utter glee, like he's been planning this moment for longer than I could possibly know. "I was wondering what I should do about you and Dr. Carter lying to the hospital board about your pretend relationship."

I feel my blood run cold. My mouth parts as I struggle to make words, my brain feeling scrambled. "What?"

"You heard me," he says, his earlier pleasantness gone and in its place nothing but thinly veiled contempt. "You lied to the board. You and Dr. Carter aren't mated at all. Which means you purposely lied about your designation *and* your unmated status to keep your job. Don't know how you roped poor Dr. Carter into all this, but I guess it doesn't matter, now that she's complicit."

"Dennis," I say dazedly. "There's been a misunderstanding, we—"

"I don't think there's been a misunderstanding at all," he chuckles. "But by all means, keep lying. It will only make it that much worse for you when I go to the board and turn the both of you in."

The both of you.

"You're wrong," I say more forcefully, trying to keep my expression even. "Mackenzie and I—"

"Are liars," he laughs. "Yes, I know. Listen, there's no use in denying it, I heard your little pretend mate talking to her friend before you carted her out of the hospital for what I'm sure was a great time."

Heat floods my chest, and I clench my fists to keep from reaching for him. "I think maybe you misheard."

"I didn't mishear anything," he says. "It was pretty clear from their conversation. Now, you can come clean and we can move on to what comes next, or you can keep lying, and I can walk out of your office and go straight to the board." He clicks his tongue. "I imagine that will be a big surprise for Dr. Carter."

My heart is pounding so loudly that it's possible Dennis can hear it, panic clawing in my chest. I realize immediately that I am a thousand times more worried about the idea of Mackenzie's career being affected by this than mine, and because of that his threat cuts deeper, making me tense. I sense there's little reason to keep up the charade; it's obvious Dennis has sunk his claws deep into this discovery. I have no idea what sort of scenario resulted in Dennis overhearing Mackenzie, and I'm not even sure it really matters. All that matters is that I save her from any repercussions, if I can.

"There's no need for all that," I try, my instincts going into overdrive to protect her. "She isn't the one who you dislike so much."

"That's true," Dennis says thoughtfully. "It would be a shame to damage her career like that just because you dragged her into your lies."

"I never lied," I argue.

Dennis laughs outright. "I think the board would see it differently." He clicks his tongue. "Submitting a false disclosure form to avoid a reprimand over your application omission? How would that look with your cushy new job in Albuquerque?"

"How . . ." He's managed to knock me on my ass twice in five minutes. "How do you know about that?"

"I don't think that matters, does it?" He shrugs. "What matters is what you do next."

My mind is frantically sifting from one scenario to another, trying to find a solution for this, but every different way I look at it all leads to the same place. I know that no matter what I do Dennis will make sure this ruins both myself *and* Mackenzie for good measure; I always knew he hated me and wanted my job, I just never knew he would stoop to such levels to get it.

Actually, as surprised as I am by what's happening, I definitely don't find Dennis stooping so low all that surprising.

"What do you want, Dennis?"

He crosses his arms. "You know what I want."

"If you knew I was leaving anyway, why not just wait until I'm gone to take the job? Why threaten me?"

"Because you're thinking about not taking the job. Isn't that right?"

I try to keep my expression blank, but I can feel my eyes narrow. "What makes you say that?"

"You're not the only one with friends in high places, Noah. You've been dodging them for weeks. Pussyfooting around on giving them a straight answer. I think we both know why that is."

"Do we?"

"Of course we do." His Cheshire cat smile nearly reaches his eyes. "Because you actually started fucking Dr. Carter."

My blood rushes in my ears, and I shift in my chair, my body starting to move without my say-so.

He holds out a hand to stop me. "We all heard about her going into heat downstairs and then you carrying her out and disappearing with her for three days. I mean, she's gorgeous, don't get me wrong, but it seems idiotic for someone of your intelligence to do something as stupid as sticking around just because you're finally getting some ass."

"You might want to be careful about what you say," I warn. "Or I won't be able to be as civil about this."

"Right, right. Big scary alpha. That will look even better for you, won't it? Mauling a fellow employee because you couldn't hold your temper? By all means." Dennis snorts, looking down at me. "You've waltzed around this hospital for years acting like you own the damned place. You think just because Dr. Ackard treated you like a little prince and recommended you as his replacement that you're some sort of genius. I've been here three times as long as you, and that job *should* have been mine."

"It isn't my fault that Paul thought I was better qualified."

"He only thought that because of the way you kept your head up his ass for so long. You charmed him right into this job, didn't you? Took everything that should have been mine." His glee is gone, looking disgusted now. "And now you think you can turn your nose up at an even *better* opportunity that you most likely don't deserve so you can hang around for steady sex? No. You need to know how it feels when things don't go your way."

I take a deep breath, trying to calm the roaring in my head. "I'll quit," I tell him. "I'll take the job. We don't have to involve Mackenzie at all. You can have whatever you want."

And I would think that this would be the end of it, but Dennis looks unconvinced, clicking his tongue. "Yeah, see—That's not going to cut it, I think."

"What more can I possibly do?"

"Well, you see . . . I've met your 'mate,' as you know. She's smart. Too smart. Something tells me she isn't the type who would take this lying down. I think we both know she would have a lot to say about you just up and quitting on my say-so." He looks annoyed when he adds, "She's very protective of you, for whatever reason."

My heart flutters with something other than rage for the briefest of moments.

"I don't have to tell her the specifics," I urge, still trying to save this.

Dennis makes a face. "Yeah . . . I can't really leave that much up to chance. Blackmailing isn't exactly a good look for me."

"Then what the fuck do you *want*, Dennis?"

He smiles again, that same awful smile that says he's getting every terrible thing he's ever wanted, and I would give anything to be able to tear it right off his face right now.

"You're going to have to end things with Dr. Carter."

I feel the air leave my lungs. "Pardon?"

"I think it's the only way to be sure that nothing goes awry."

"Absolutely not," I scoff. "I won't."

"Aw," Dennis coos maddeningly. "That's so sweet." He throws up his hands. "By all means. Don't. I'm sure she'll be fine when the board finds out she lied on a disclosure form. Eventually. She's, what, a year out of her residency? Your career might bounce back after a scandal like that, I mean, you *are* a genius, after all. I wonder if Mackenzie would be so lucky?"

Hearing Dennis say her name makes me want to break something, and I grip the arms of my chair to keep me grounded, just to ensure I don't fly out of it and wrap my hands around his throat.

"She doesn't deserve that," I say through gritted teeth.

"I have no doubt. Which is why you'll do the right thing and end things. Free and clear."

"There's no way that she will just accept me ending things out of the blue. She's too smart for that."

Dennis throws up his arms in another shrug, still looking

pleased with himself. "I guess you're just going to have to be *very* convincing then. Aren't you."

"I could tell the board about the blackmail," I say as a last-ditch effort. "Mutually assured destruction is at play here."

"Hardly," he snorts. "You think they'll care more that I found out about your little scheme and *urged* you to come clean more than they'll care about your lies? You and I both know you don't have a leg to stand on."

I'm vibrating with rage and frustration and even fear at the idea of what he's asking me to do, knowing he's put me in an impossible position. Dennis senses my struggle, and possibly even my murderous intent—stepping backward toward the door with his hands outstretched.

"Just think it over," he says. "I'll give you tonight to decide."

"If you hurt Mackenzie," I warn, "I will rip you apart."

Dennis flashes me one last smug grin as he opens my door, raising his shoulder in a nonchalant gesture. "That all depends on you, now, doesn't it?" He gives me a pointed look. "I'll expect an answer by tomorrow, Dr. Taylor."

I count to ten in my head as he closes the door, trying to keep myself from chasing after him. Even without ever having felt violent urges like I'm feeling at the moment, I know if I touched him right now it would end with me in prison and him in his own blood. Every cell in my body is concerned only with protecting Mackenzie, the idea of her being in jeopardy sending my senses into overdrive.

I know that Dennis is right, that Mackenzie would certainly have a *lot* to say about his threats and would most likely kick his ass herself and throw her entire career away for my benefit, because that's the kind of person she is—just as I know that's something I can't allow. Dennis's taunts about her career being so new are one

hundred percent valid; there is a good chance she *wouldn't* ever re-
cover from something like this. All her years of school, all her hard
work . . . just gone. All because of me.

I don't know how much time passes before I'm able to sink
down into my chair, my rage ebbing and giving way to bone-deep
defeat that makes my body feel heavy. It's unfair that I've just
opened myself up to another person, especially a person as special
as Mackenzie, only to be told I have to give her up. And what's
more—that I have to break her heart in the process.

It's a bitter reminder of all the reasons why I worked so hard to
keep people at arm's length for the entirety of my life leading up to
the last few weeks—having wanted to avoid complications like this.
I think I had actually deluded myself into thinking that I could
have it all, that things would work out for the better, and I could
have someone see me, actually *see* me, and keep them. I'm realizing
now that it was nothing more than a fantasy. That I reached too
high and now I'm paying the consequences. Strangely, I don't care
about any of the dangers that are looming over my head, not concerned in the slightest about what might happen to me.

Because all of it pales in comparison to the woman I'm being
asked to give up.

23

Mackenzie

"DOES IT LOOK straight?"

I hold the curtain rod as still as I'm able, my arms starting to burn as I wait for Gran's approval.

"Mm," I hear behind me. "Maybe a little more to the left."

I groan, moving an inch on the step stool. "I'm buying you a level for Christmas."

"You're doing a fine job," she assures me.

I roll my eyes, knowing she can't see me do it. "Here?"

"Oh, that's perfect," she informs me. "Do you need the screws?"

I shake my head, pulling the pencil from my ear and marking on the wall where the rod holders will go. I step down from the stool after, dropping the rod gently against the pile of Gran's new curtains on the floor.

"You're gonna have to give me a minute," I tell her, rolling my shoulder. "You had me holding that curtain rod for half an hour practically."

Gran clicks her tongue. "You're still young. You're fine."

"Still," I grumble.

"Well, get your gripey little butt in the kitchen, and I'll make you some coffee."

"That sounds more like it."

I leave the project that she tricked me into taking over at the sliding glass door—following her into the kitchen and plopping down at one of the padded stools at her kitchen island. She busies herself with the coffeepot, warming what's left from the morning, pulling down two mugs from her cabinet.

I take the spare moment to check my phone, frowning when I notice that Noah still hasn't replied to my text from this morning. I know he has work today, and that it's not a big deal that he would be too busy to respond—so why do I keep checking like some twitterpated teenager? His text from last night had been pretty sparse too; he'd said something about being tired from a long day and told me he was going to bed, and that's completely normal, *expected* even—it's just me who's being weird.

If I'm honest with myself, I've been weird for days. Weeks, even. Since we left the lodge and started doing things that felt very much *not* pretend. Between the date and spending the weekend together and cuddling on couches and the constantly growing desire to see him, to talk to him . . . everything feels unclear. I can't seem to decide if what we're doing is something we should *keep* doing. Not because I don't want to—on the contrary, because I want it *too* much. I've been happy to hide in the bubble that was a limited agreement that would end the moment Noah left the hospital, but now in the face of that, after everything . . . Well. I'm definitely experiencing several of those *complications* that Noah had been so worried about.

"You're going to stare a hole in the screen if you keep up like that," I hear Gran say from across the counter.

I turn up my head abruptly. "What?"

"What's got you so absorbed in your phone?"

"Oh." I frown again, shaking my head. "Nothing. Just checking my texts."

"Looking for something from Noah?"

I notice Gran's expression is smug, and I roll my eyes. "You are way too invested in this."

"Is it so bad to want my granddaughter to be happy?"

"I *am* happy," I stress. "Meeting Noah hasn't had any effect on that."

The coffeepot beeps, signaling it's done, and Gran purses her lips as she gives her attention back to it. "Tell that to your phone," she tuts. "Haven't ever seen you so glued to it before."

I could dodge the question, and that's probably what I *should* do—but Gran already thinks that this whole thing is real. Maybe it wouldn't be a big deal to get some advice.

"Is it weird when someone suddenly stops texting you as much?"

Gran turns to hand me a mug, setting it in front of me. "What do you mean?"

"I just . . ." I blow out a breath. "It's not a big *deal* or anything, but Noah usually texts me back pretty quickly. Like, annoyingly quick, even, but . . . I don't know. He's been sort of radio silent for the last couple of days."

"Did you two get into a fight?"

"No?" I think back to the last time I saw him. Sure, the whole debacle with him mentioning dinner with his mother and me having a whole-ass moment about it was uncomfortable, but I'd been pretty sure it was only me who had felt that. Noah had seemed oblivious to my inner turmoil. "He said he was tired last night. Maybe he just had a bad day and I'm reading too much into it."

When I look up again, Gran is beaming, and I sense I've said too much.

"Don't," I say before she can start.

She shrugs, still smiling. "I'm just saying—it seems like you really like Noah."

"Well, I . . ." I'm not sure how to navigate this conversation, knowing that Gran thinks this whole thing is *real*, and I struggle to find the right words. "I mean . . . he's a nice guy. We get along really well."

Gran takes a slow sip from her mug, thoughtfully eyeing me over the rim. She makes a satisfied sound when she swallows her coffee, staring at me for a long few seconds as she considers.

Eventually, it makes me squirm. She only gives me this look when she is about to scold me. "What?"

"I'm just wondering how much longer I have to pretend that I don't know you've been trying to pull one over on me."

My mouth falls open in surprise. "Wha—What do you mean?"

"Mackenzie," Gran says, not looking upset but instead almost amused. "Have you forgotten that I raised you through the teen years? I might as well have a PhD in reading your lying face."

I feel at a loss; there's no way I could have prepared myself to be cornered by five-foot-three Moira Carter. In fact, I had been so certain that we were getting away with it, the possibility of telling her the truth hadn't even crossed my mind.

"How long have you known?"

"Since you brought him over," she says matter-of-factly.

I feel myself reeling. "How could you tell?"

"Honey," she laughs. "The man didn't even know you were an omega. His eyes got as big as saucers when I mentioned it."

"I . . . Shit. Why have you let us go on like we have?"

Gran chuckles. "Because I could tell you liked each other. Even if you didn't know it yet."

"You could?"

"The both of you were sneaking glances every other second like you couldn't help it. Seemed like the two of you were so deep in your lie you couldn't even make out the truth of it."

I consider that. Sure, at that point there had been attraction between us; I practically begged him up to my apartment that night, after all, but I can't imagine that there had been anything deeper than that so early on in our ruse, right?

"I don't know," I sigh. "It's still probably way too early to read much into it. We've been on *one* real date."

"Well, you *did* spend your heat together."

I almost spit up the sip of coffee I've just taken. "How in the hell do you know that?"

"Oh, Parker told me," she says casually.

I close my eyes, pressing my lips together. "I'm going to kill him."

"Oh, hush. He was worried about you. You were so off schedule!"

I rub my temples, having a hard time looking at her now that I know she's aware I spent a three-day sexcation with Noah only a couple of weeks ago. "It was . . . definitely a surprise."

"It just means you're compatible," Gran says.

I do look at her then. "What do you mean?"

"When two shifters have a high compatibility, it can throw off your heat cycle. The pheromones just affect you a little more." She scoffs. "Honestly, Mackenzie. You're a doctor. You should know this."

"I don't exactly have shifter compatibility very high on my list of priorities," I deadpan.

"Well, if you gave anyone a chance," she chides. "You find something wrong with every person you go on a date with."

"They weren't exactly great dates," I grumble.

"Oh, you just wanted something to be wrong with them."

"Model train fanatics, Gran!"

"Mackenzie Carter. You can pitch those silly excuses to me all you want, but I'm not buying it." She sets her mug down on the counter, looking at me sternly. "We both know you're always looking for things to be wrong with someone, because finding something *right* with them would mean opening yourself up to something that you can't control."

"That's not true," I mumble, looking down at my lap.

"Like hell it isn't," she huffs. "You've done it since you were a kid. Honestly, if Parker hadn't come along, you probably would have been content to just stay in your room when you weren't at school."

"Listen, to be fair, you have set me up on some *really* bad dates."

"Have I? Or have you just been looking for reasons to not give anyone a second date?"

"Gran, seriously, there have been some—"

"Mackenzie," she says, her tone softer now. "I get it. There have been some stinkers. But you're twenty-nine, and you've never been in a relationship that lasted more than a few months at a time. There's always some flaw or some habit that gets in the way. He snores too much, he watches too much football, he picks his teeth after dinner—"

"Oh, come on, that one is disgusting."

"I'm *just* saying," she stresses. "You always find a reason to end things before they can even start."

I feel an emotion welling in my chest that seems too heavy, too raw—one that I've spent a good portion of my life suppressing. I rub my arm idly as I avert my gaze, knowing that this, too, is something I can't lie to her about. Not this. She knows me too well.

"It's not like I mean to," I say quietly. "It's not exactly fun being permanently single."

"I'm not saying that I blame you," she says, reaching across the counter to cover my hand with hers. "You had to deal with a lot of hard things as a kid. Things that were way too much for someone as young as you were. Your dad . . ." She shakes her head, looking away from me. "He lost a big part of himself when he lost your mom. He couldn't handle it. I love my son, but he wasn't the man he should have been. He should have stepped up for you, no matter how much he was hurting." She looks at me again, her eyes fixed on mine. "But that doesn't have to be *your* life. Just because your dad left you hurting doesn't mean everyone will." Her eyes start to water, the wrinkles around her mouth deepening as she frowns. "Maybe I should have said all of this to you sooner. Maybe it's partly my fault."

"No," I protest, my voice thick. "Gran. You guys are perfect. You always have been. I just . . . I guess I've just been afraid." I feel a single tear roll down my cheek, and Gran squeezes my hand. "I wasn't enough for Dad. I couldn't make him stick around. How in the hell can I expect to be enough for anyone else?"

"Oh, honey." Gran releases my hand, toddling around the counter to wrap her thin arms around my body. "You are amazing. You're beautiful and smart and funny—Well, sometimes."

A watery laugh escapes me, and I snuggle further into her embrace. "I get my sense of humor from you."

"Yeah, well, you sure as hell don't get it from your grandfather."

We both laugh, and she pulls away to look at me, reaching to cup my face in her hand.

"You are enough," she tells me, her eyes full of emotion. "And then some. Anyone you choose would find themselves damn lucky."

I choke out a sound that is a mix of a sob and a broken laugh, reaching to wipe the tears from my eyes that feel both painful and somehow good. Cathartic, even. I've spent so long pretending none of this bothers me . . . it feels like a weight has been lifted off now that I can finally admit it always did.

Gran pats my cheek. "Even if that someone isn't Noah, there's someone out there who will be worth letting in. I just hope you let yourself find them."

"Gran," I say thickly. "I . . . think I like Noah. Like, really."

"Can't say I blame you." She whistles as she pulls back. "That man is . . . Wow."

"*Gran*," I laugh, wiping away the last few errant tears from my eyes.

"I'm just saying," she chuckles.

I bite back a grin. "He is . . . definitely something."

"I'm sure he's just busy. Don't get too worked up about it. Just remember that you are amazing. Anyone would be lucky to have you."

"Okay, now you're embarrassing me," I groan.

"It's my job," she retorts. "Now finish your coffee before it gets cold."

I'm still sniffling a little when I turn back toward the counter, Gran going back to the pot to top off her own cup. I only notice my phone all lit up when I reach to bring my mug closer, pausing what I'm doing and leaning over the screen to catch Noah's name. There's an undeniable surge of excitement that courses through me when I pull my phone closer, wondering when in the last month I got to the point where just seeing his *name* made me giddy.

I swipe open the text, his reply short but butterfly-inducing nonetheless because—

> **NOAH:** Could we meet up after I get off?
> Maybe at that cafe we went to last time?

I'm grinning like an idiot as I read his invitation, realizing I'm happy just from the possibility of seeing him again. Maybe I've gone crazy.

I just hope you let yourself find them.

I smile, thinking that Gran might be on to something as I tap out a response.

> **ME:** Can't wait.

~

THE CAFÉ ISN'T as busy as the last time we were here, but there are still a handful of couples and college students hanging around the trendy little tables when I step inside. Outside, the snow's started to come down, and I dust it off my shoes, starting to pull off my coat as I look around in search of him. He's sitting at the same booth we had our first pretend date in, and realizing this makes me smile as I wave at him. I don't waste any time going to join him, sliding into the other side of the booth and laying my coat on the seat beside me as I give him my attention.

Noah definitely *looks* tired; there are dark circles under his eyes as if he's had little sleep, and there's a frown etched on his mouth that feels somehow grumpier than the one he'd been so fond of when we first struck up our deal.

"Wow, someone had a rough day," I tease. "Were you yelling at nurses again?"

"I told you," he says wearily, "that was—"

"*Grossly overexaggerated*," I laugh. "Yeah. I know. But really, you look tired as hell."

"I feel it," he says quietly. "It's been . . . a long day."

"I'm sorry." I reach across the table to trace a finger across his knuckle, lowering my voice. "I know a few good ways to relieve stress, if you're interested."

"Mackenzie . . ."

I'm just starting to notice that there's something underneath all of the fatigue; his blue eyes look duller, and his hair looks messy, like he's been running his fingers through it. He's chewing on the edge of his lip like he's worried about something, and it's amazing to me that I'm not only able to pick up on these things, but apparently my first instinct is to soothe him. Honestly, I'm having a hard time not switching to the other side of the booth and wrapping my arms around him. I'm not even sure if his mood is to blame for that or if it's just a constant desire that I have now.

"What's wrong?" I squeeze his hand, my thumb stroking back and forth. "Did something happen?" He looks at our hands, his mouth turning down and his brow furrowing. His eyes dart around like he's struggling to find the words, and there's a flare of worry that flashes inside me. "Noah. Tell me. Is it Dennis? Is he bothering you again? Or is it the board? You can tell me. We'll figure it out."

When he finally looks up at me, he seems . . . sad. Regretful, maybe. I can't say why, but something about the way he looks at me is uneasy. Almost like I've seen it before. I'm trying to place where, but it isn't coming to me.

"Mackenzie," he tries again. "I need you to know beforehand that this is not an easy decision for me. I never wanted to hurt you."

My hand slips from his, too surprised to even adequately process what he's said. Why is he still *looking* at me like that?

"Noah, what are you . . ."

But I can see it now. His expression. I can *really* see it. It's the same one that a father wears when they tell a little girl that they can't stay with her anymore. It's the same one you never really forget.

"Mackenzie," Noah says carefully, his voice tight. "I think we should end our arrangement."

24

Noah

I KNEW THAT everything about this was going to hurt, but seeing the realization on Mackenzie's face—the dissipation of her smile, the surprise in her eyes that quickly turns to pain, the way her mouth parts like she can't comprehend what I'm saying—experiencing it all proves enough to actually *gut* me. I can almost feel the knife twisting in my belly.

And I can't let it show.

She pulls her hands from the table to tuck them in her lap, looking away from me as her brow furrows. "What do you mean?"

"I just don't think it's going to work," I say flatly, everything inside me screaming to reach out and touch her, to take away the hurt forming in her eyes.

She laughs, but it's humorless. "You don't think it's going to work."

"I heard from Albuquerque, and they want me to start right away."

"Do they," she says hollowly, and I feel the knife twist deeper.

"It's just that it's going to be a lot more responsibility than I originally thought. Between the move and the workload . . . I don't know if it's the right time to try juggling a long-distance relationship."

She laughs again, a brittle sound that makes my chest hurt, finally looking at me with teary eyes. "You don't know if it's the right time."

"Listen, it's not anything that you did, it's—"

"Please don't give me the 'It's not you, it's me' speech," she says angrily. "Don't you dare, Noah."

I feel my resolve wavering, the pain and anger in her face breaking me down. She's trying to hide it from me, the way my words are cutting her, but I can see it in the rigid set of her shoulders, the way her jaw juts forward and her teeth worry at her lower lip like she's trying to keep them from quivering. It's something I've never seen before on Mackenzie, sadness, and I feel every ounce of it like it's my own, like it's a wound that I'm actively poking at. I know that after this it's one that might never heal.

I have to remind myself that I'm saving her from a lot more hurt than this, knowing that she would never forgive me if I ruined her career. I can still hear Dennis's smug voice ringing in my ears.

I guess you're just going to have to be very convincing then. Aren't you.

I take a deep, agonizing breath.

"Mackenzie . . . This was always supposed to be temporary."

"Oh, fuck you," she hisses. "You and I both know we moved past temporary out at that lodge. You asked me on a fucking date. Why did you ask me on a fucking date, Noah? And all the other shit lately? What was all of that, huh?"

I'm struck for a moment, seeing the exact second that I'm losing her playing out all over her face. I don't think I could have ever anticipated it would hurt this much. Or maybe I did, and I just didn't want to acknowledge it. I think that before this moment I had somehow convinced myself that it *would* be something that we could both move on from; it feels like such a short time has passed since she first approached me in that tiny break room at the hospital, so how could something cultivated over such a brief amount of time have a lasting impact?

Love sure as hell isn't easy.

"I'm sorry," I say. It's all I *can* say, really, because it's the strongest thing I'm feeling. "I honestly am, Mackenzie. I never wanted to hurt you."

"Yeah, well," she huffs. "Good. Because I'm not." Even through her tearstained eyes, I can see the way she tries to lock down her emotions. The way she's desperately trying not to let it show how much this is wounding her. It only makes me want to soothe her more. "Like you said. This was always supposed to be temporary."

She looks right into my eyes then, and part of me is begging her to see the truth there, begging her to *fight* me on this. Surely she has to know how I truly feel. I know I didn't imagine these last few weeks and all the little things that have been growing between us. I didn't imagine the way this arrangement has started to shift into anything but casual. I want her to see through the lie. I want her to *fight* me. Just a little.

She makes a frustrated sound, slapping her hands on the table. "Did you ask me here just so I wouldn't make a scene? Really? You had to choose the first place we ever went to? What, being an ass-hole wasn't enough, you had to make it fucking personal?"

God, even like this, she's beautiful. Even when she's hating me. My hands itch to touch her, to take away every ounce of pain I've caused and tell her this isn't what I want at all, and I have to keep them clenched tight beside me just to keep from doing so. It feels impossible to imagine never touching her again, *torturous*—but torture is exactly what I have to look forward to. There's no coming back from this.

I keep reminding myself that I'm doing this for her. Even if it hurts like hell.

"I really am sorry," I offer quietly, not knowing what else to say. What else is there to say?

"You're sorry," she echoes dryly. "Perfect. That means a lot."

"Mackenzie, I—"

She grabs her coat, gathering it up hastily as she starts to slide out of the booth. "Just save it, Noah. Seriously. I get it." She shoves her arms through the sleeves of her coat, untrapping her hair from the collar. The motion brings about a wave of her scent, and it's less bright, almost bitter. It's painful, knowing I'm to blame. "You didn't want a scene, right? So let's just cut this short." She chuffs out another spiteful laugh. "We had a good time, right? We enjoyed our little addendum? No harm, no foul, really."

"No, Mackenzie, that's not what I—"

She pulls her coat tight, casting me one last hard expression, and I know it'll be the last of her I'll ever see. "Congrats on the new job, Dr. Taylor."

I watch her walk away from me, seeing the way she wipes at her eyes while everything I am fights my decision to keep still. Part of me wonders if there had been another choice, if somehow we could have figured things out—but the more rational part of me knows that Dennis wouldn't have stopped until he ruined my life *and* Mackenzie's for good measure.

So I say nothing, and I do nothing, feeling all the happiness I've gained in the last few weeks ebb out of me slowly, leaving me empty and hollow, most likely never to be seen again. Mackenzie doesn't look back as she storms out of the café, and for a long time after she's gone, I remain frozen at the table, letting it sink in that she's gone. That she'll never come back, and that I'll always be a bad memory for her.

It's almost funny how badly I had wanted to avoid complications like this. How I found them, anyway. How I'd do anything to get them back.

A bitter laugh bubbles out of me. *Complicated.*

Turns out there's nothing more complicated than love.

~

THE HOSPITAL IN Albuquerque is ecstatic to hear that I'm accepting the position—and two months ago, I would have been too. Instead of celebrating, I'm hiding away in my house, trying not to think about all the places inside it that Mackenzie's been.

My bedroom is unbearable; her scent still clings to my sheets, offering both relief and pain, and after three days, I gave up trying to sleep in there, resigned to the couch until she fades or I move. Whichever comes first. There isn't a moment that passes that I don't want to call her and apologize, to explain everything and beg her to forgive me, but every time I pick up the phone with that intention, I remember how easy it would be for Dennis to destroy her career. How it would be entirely my fault if he was to do so. Ultimately, being with me isn't worth being robbed of everything she's worked so hard for, and I know that.

Which is why I've spent every moment I'm not working this past week wallowing in my armchair with a drink in my hand. It helps, but only a little.

I think that what I hadn't considered before forcing Mackenzie to walk away from me was just how much she's left a mark on me, how much I would feel it when she was gone. I reason that there had been no time to consider it, since I spent the first few weeks of our arrangement refusing to acknowledge that I'd been fighting a losing battle from the start—because I was, I now realize. From the moment Mackenzie asked me for a stupid selfie . . . I never stood a chance. She's just too good, too *perfect*, and there was never any possibility that I wouldn't completely fall for her.

It's almost laughable that I would only fully realize it after there's no chance to tell her.

Tonight is no different; I'm two drinks in while staring at the fire and feeling sorry for myself, but unlike every other night between the café and now—I can hear my cell phone trilling on the side table by my chair, the irritating ring grating my nerves. I pick it up with every intention of silencing it, since there's no chance it will be the one person I want to talk to, but the name on the screen makes me pause, and I wrestle with the decision to ignore or pick up for at least twenty seconds before I sigh and answer the call.

"Oh, good," Paul says. "You're alive."

"Barely," I mumble pathetically.

"I've been trying to call you all week," he grouses.

I take a swig from my glass, relishing the burn of the whiskey as it slides down my throat. "I hadn't noticed. Been busy."

"I heard that you put in your resignation."

"Yep."

"So you took the Albuquerque job?"

"Looks like it."

"You don't sound very excited about it."

I laugh dryly. "I don't, do I."

"Have you ended your arrangement with Dr. Carter then?"

I wince. "Why do you ask?"

"Just guessing that might be why you sound like you're in such a sour mood."

"She has nothing to do with it," I mutter bitterly.

"So that's a yes, then," he sighs.

"Yes, I ended it," I answer. "A week ago."

"Again, you don't sound very excited about it."

I take another drink, a longer one this time. I hiss between my teeth at the burn. "Yeah, well. It is what it is."

"Oh, horseshit," he scoffs. "Why end things if you were going to be this miserable about it?"

I hesitate, wondering if it's a bad idea to tell him the truth. Now that Mackenzie is gone . . . I'm definitely short in the area of friends. I wonder if talking about it will help, or if it will make things more intolerable.

"I didn't have a choice," I settle for.

"There's always a choice, Noah. In all things."

"Not this time."

"Tell me what happened," he urges. "You can talk to me."

Emotion wells in my throat, making my tongue feel too thick. I haven't said her name out loud since I pushed her away; just thinking it is painful enough. Still, maybe it would make me feel less crazy to hear that I made the right choice. I think I *need* to hear it, just so I can start to try and pick up the pieces.

"It's Dennis," I sigh. "He found out about us."

"That little weasel," Paul snorts. "I assume he was ecstatic to gain that kind of leverage."

"Well, he threatened Mackenzie's job," I manage tightly, her name on my tongue stinging just as much as I thought it would. "Mine as well, obviously."

"That's ridiculous. You should report him for harassment."

"What good will that do? He knows what I am, and he knows that we lied. I don't know if Mackenzie's career can survive something like this, and I'm not willing to risk it."

"Don't you think she deserves to make that decision for herself?"

This gives me pause. The only thing worse than the thought of jeopardizing Mackenzie's future with my lie is the guilt of lying to her. I know without a doubt that Mackenzie would do exactly as Dennis said she would, that she'd fight tooth and nail to try and have it all—just like I know that there is a high possibility it would go the exact same way. She would lose her job, and maybe at first she wouldn't blame me, but eventually . . . It's inevitable. It would be only a matter of time before she realized that I am definitely not worth throwing away her future for. I don't have anything to offer someone as bright as Mackenzie. I'm not sure I ever did.

"It's already done," I answer quietly, closing my eyes as I lean back into my chair. I'd really like to down another drink and pass out on my couch right now, since the bed is out of the question. "I can't take it back now."

"So you're just going to pack up and move? Leave it just like that?"

"That was always the plan," I say with increasing irritation. "It wasn't so long ago that you *wanted* that for me."

"Well, that was before I thought there might be a shot at *real* life for you. Not just one that involves long workdays and nights spent at home. Alone."

"There was never any suggestion that anything would even come from any of this. Mackenzie and I agreed from the beginning that it was a temporary thing. She *wanted* it that way, Paul."

"And can you honestly say that's what she still wants?"

"I . . ."

I stare at the flicker of orange and red behind the grate in my woodstove, frowning. The memory of Mackenzie's face when I'd callously told her that I was ending our arrangement bleeds into my thoughts, just as gutting now as it was then. Even as desperately as she wanted to keep it from me, it had been more than clear that I was tearing her to shreds with my feigned indifference. Knowing that there's a chance she'd begun to feel something deeper for me as I have for her makes my chest ache, because with all I know about her, that in itself feels like a miracle.

And I tore it all to shreds.

"It's probably for the best." I'm nodding slowly to myself, as if this might somehow convince me. "She's too good for me, anyway."

"I'm sure you're right," Paul says. "The man who loves her is obviously the worst possible choice."

I tense, gripping my phone tighter. "I never said I loved her."

"Son," Paul laughs. "You didn't have to. No one feels this shitty about someone unless they love them."

The suffocating emotions that I've been working so hard to suppress fill my head and my chest and everywhere else—my body feeling heavy and weary. Honestly, I'd just like to sleep for a while and forget.

"I'm going to have to let you go," I tell Paul softly. "I have packing to do."

Paul sighs, sounding weary himself. "For what it's worth . . . I'm sorry, Noah. Truly."

"Yeah," I mumble. "So am I."

I hang up without saying good-bye, immediately downing what's left in my glass and shutting my eyes tight to focus only on the burn as it goes down. If I could go back—I would have never touched her. I would have never let myself know how soft she is, how warm . . . Maybe I would even go back to the beginning and tell her that it was a ridiculous idea, this plan of ours. I would face the board and take my punishment and that would be the end of it.

Except . . . I wouldn't know what her laugh sounds like. I wouldn't be able to recall the way her nose wrinkles when she's thinking. The sweet softness of her scent that haunts me, even now. I wouldn't *know* her, and I feel like that would be an even greater tragedy than losing her, to never know her at all.

I don't remember getting to my feet, but I feel my body carrying me down the hall toward my bedroom before I even realize where I'm going. It only takes seconds to fall into my bed, to press my nose to the sheets and breathe in deep. It's still there, almost as strong as the day she left it, and scenting her feels almost like touching her, like she's brushing back my hair or sighing in my ear. It makes everything better. It makes everything *worse*. It makes the reality even more crushing, because I know I will never touch her again.

I roll away from my bed as fast as I can, pushing away from the mattress like it's burned me and cursing myself for coming in here again when I promised myself I wouldn't. I stomp toward the bedroom door, only to pause just inside it, turning back to glance at the sheets as memories of having her there beneath me taunt me in vivid recollection, making that suffocating feeling inside almost unbearable.

I close the door behind me, making myself another promise not to come back even while knowing I'll probably break it. Again.

Time for another drink.

25

Mackenzie

"THAT'S IT. WE'RE getting drinks tonight."

I blink, remembering where I am, noticing Parker grimacing at me mindlessly stirring my soup. "What?"

"I actually *cannot* sit here and watch you space out like a depressed zombie for another day."

"I'm not depressed," I lie, frowning down into my soup as I stir more aggressively.

Parker rolls his eyes. "You've been giving me 'Anne Hathaway in *Les Misérables*' vibes for the past week, Mackenzie."

"I don't understand that reference," I mumble.

"Well, I can't help it if you refuse to culture yourself."

"Gee, thanks."

"I'm serious. You're making *me* depressed. I'm worried about you."

My brow knits. "I'm seriously fine."

If *seriously fine* means crying myself to sleep like some downtrodden heroine in a romantic comedy after being viciously dumped counts as fine, that is. But Parker doesn't need to know about that.

"Whatever. You don't have to cry on my shoulder or anything, but you can admit that you're hurting."

"What's there to hurt about? It was a fake relationship."

"Most people don't take heat leave with their fake relationship," he accuses. "And they don't call me crying from outside a café because their fake relationship broke things off."

"I wasn't . . . crying."

He rolls his eyes again. "Right. Sure. Regardless—We are getting drinks tonight."

"I don't really feel like going out," I protest feebly.

"Well, I don't really feel like watching you wither away in front of me because of that asshole."

It's strange; my first instinct is to defend Noah, even now. To tell Parker that he's not an asshole, he's just delivering all the things that we expected from the beginning. Why is that? Maybe it's because I had (quite literally) just opened myself up to something more, to trying out something *real*—only to have my entire heart stomped on in an old booth of a café I used to really enjoy. Which is a double whammy, because now I don't think I'll ever be able to go back.

"I'm sure it's just some hormonal bullshit," I offer. "It'll pass."

"Mackenzie," Parker sighs. "You can feed that shit to someone else, because I *know* you. I saw you with him that day when you were going into heat. I don't know what the fuck happened between you two when I wasn't looking, but something changed. And it's *okay* to admit that you're hurting."

I say nothing, setting my spoon on the cafeteria table before running my fingers through my hair, which I didn't bother washing today. Come to think of it, I'm not really sure when I last washed it.

"Just come out with me," Parker urges. "We can forget about men for a night."

"That's easy for you to say," I grumble. "*Your* relationship is going just fine."

"And I will be happy to make up several shortcomings to bitch about over cosmos."

My lip twitches despite it all. "Fine. Whatever. We'll go for drinks."

"Perfect," Parker says happily. He checks his phone. "I have to go back. I'll meet you when you get off?"

"Yeah, yeah."

He leaves me sitting at the table alone, and my soup remains woefully untouched, my appetite nonexistent. Is this what it feels like to be heartbroken? I've successfully avoided the feeling romantic-wise for almost the entirety of my adult life, and now that I'm experiencing it firsthand, I would be happy to give it back.

I've gone over that day at the café again and again in my mind, trying to pick it apart and find sense in the way that Noah had been so eager to pursue something more with me days before ending things entirely. By all accounts it makes absolutely no sense, but the aloof expression on his face as he'd told me it was over, that it wasn't the right *time* for him and me . . . it left little room for doubt.

And what's more confusing is how deep it stings, how much the hurt of it lingers like a wound that won't heal. I had been so confident that I could keep things casual, that I could explore his body while keeping a tight hold on my heart—so why does it *hurt* so much?

Deep down, I know the answer. Of course I do. I think I've known it since the first time he touched me, but I've been so desperate to keep him at arm's length that I'd somehow managed to push Noah directly into my blind spot. I held him where I couldn't see the way he was carving a place for himself inside my heart.

And now I'm experiencing the fallout, all alone.

I'm not letting you get away from me, Mackenzie.

I have to shut my eyes tight to hold back tears, refusing to let anyone at work see me give in to that weakness. I grab my bowl and my spoon and the rest of my trash and carry it to the can to throw it away, a bitter emotion I'm becoming accustomed to trickling into my chest as Noah's empty words play over and over in my head.

I'm not letting you get away from me, Mackenzie.

I laugh under my breath as I head for the elevators. Turns out . . . he pushed me away himself.

IT'S COLD OUTSIDE the entrance of the hospital where I'm waiting for Parker after my shift, the evening lights turning on and the sky darkening above as the temperature drops. I rub my hands together and breathe on them as I lean against the wall outside the door, eyeing the large bushes a few yards away.

It feels a lot like that first morning I met Noah here after we entered our arrangement, and there is a small, pathetic part of me that imagines that he might walk out of the doors at any moment. Which I know is out of the question; I haven't seen him since that day at the café. He made sure of that when he put in his resignation the very next day.

Even knowing that, I startle as the automatic doors creak open beside me, jumping a little when someone steps out who is neither Noah nor Parker, but just as familiar.

"Mack?"

I haven't really spent any time with Liam since the day that Noah kissed me in the hallway; things felt awkward after Priya informed me that Liam might have feelings for me. I still don't know if there's any truth to that, and with everything that's happened since . . . I haven't had the emotional capacity to even consider dealing with the possibility.

"Hey," I greet. "Did you just get off?"

He nods. "Just now. You?"

"Little while ago. I'm waiting for Parker."

"Oh." He looks at his feet, shuffling his weight from one foot to the other. "I haven't seen you lately."

"Oh, yeah, well . . ." I avert my eyes. "I've been busy."

"I also heard Dr. Taylor put in his resignation."

This makes me wince, and I will my expression to stay neutral. "Right. He got a great offer over in Albuquerque. Couldn't afford to pass it up."

"And are you . . . moving with him?"

I force a smile, waving him off. "No, no. Nothing like that. At least not right now. We're going to do the whole long-distance thing until we work out the details."

Look at me. Still lying, even now. Still keeping up with the ruse for Noah's benefit. Even when there's no reason to anymore.

"Oh. I thought . . ." Liam reaches to rub at the back of his neck. "You've just seemed really down lately. I thought something might have happened."

I suck in a breath. "Have I?"

"I notice these things," he says quietly.

His eyes meet mine, and there's a melancholy there that is unlike him. His normally warm brown eyes are duller, his mouth that is so quick to smile is etched into a deep frown. "Right," I say, unsure of what else I can. "Well . . . things have been complicated."

Complicated.

I could almost laugh out loud at the irony of it.

"Is it about Noah?"

I clench my jaw, turning to look ahead so that I don't have to face him. "Why would you think that?"

"I'm sorry, Mackenzie. I don't want to be an asshole . . . but something has been weird about the whole thing. I just . . . I can't picture it. And now he's leaving you here? How could someone abandon their mate like that?"

Again there is that manic urge to laugh, because it had been *incredibly* easy for Noah to up and leave me, considering I was never his mate to begin with.

"He isn't . . ." My voice sounds too thick. "He isn't exactly . . ."

"Mack," Liam says gently, reaching out a hand to touch my shoulder. "I know I should have said something sooner, but I . . . I care about you. More than just as a coworker. And I—" He makes a frustrated sound. "I would never make you look like you do now. Fucking miserable."

I look at him then, *really* look at him, and in another life, Liam would be the perfect partner. He's kind and considerate and perfectly wonderful—but the awful truth of why I can't be with him in the way that he wants is made glaringly obvious by the first thought that pops into my head, even if it makes no sense.

He's not Noah.

"I'm sorry," I say quietly, looking down at my feet. "I can't."

It's not exactly a real answer, but I think he discerns my meaning all the same, if the way he draws back his hand is any indication. I hear him breathe deep, just to let it out, and when I peek over at him I catch him nodding.

"Right," he says softly. "Right. Of course. Sorry, I . . . I shouldn't have said anything."

"No, I appreciate it, I—" I huff. "That's a terrible thing to say.

I'm sorry. Listen, Liam, you are . . . *amazing*, and anyone would be lucky to have you, but I—"

"Love Noah," he finishes, sounding wistful. "I get it. You can't fight love."

I stare back at him dazedly, trying to process this.

Love?

As much as I've been wallowing, as much as the loss of Noah has wounded me—I haven't once considered that it could be so terrible because I *love* him. That's impossible . . . isn't it? There hasn't been enough time for love. It's just . . . *impossible*.

"I . . ."

Liam shakes his head. "It's fine. You don't have to explain anything to me. I think I needed to tell you. Just so I can say I did all I could."

"I don't want to lose your friendship," I blurt out, still reeling from what he said and trying to make sense of it in my brain. "You're still important to me."

"You won't," he says with a small smile. "I'll put on some sappy movies and have a good cry and be right as rain eventually."

I smile in spite of everything. "That easy to get over me?"

"No," Liam says in that same wistful tone. "No, I doubt it will be."

My mouth gapes slightly. I'm not sure what to say to that. I wish I would have just kept my mouth shut.

"I'll see you later, Mackenzie," he says, saving me from having to answer. I think it might be the first time he's said my full name since the day we met.

I nod solemnly. "See you."

I watch him walk out into the parking lot, never looking back. I wonder if things will ever return to normal between us, and all I can do is hope that with time, Liam will meet someone who deserves him. Who can give him all the things he's looking for.

I don't move until the sliding doors open again, Parker stepping out of the building sometime later and fussing over his scarf.

"Oh, hey," he says when he catches sight of me. "Sorry, there was a server issue. I got held up."

I shake my head. "It's fine."

"You ready for that drink?"

I huff out a laugh from my nostrils as I think about all that just happened, all that's happened for the last few *months*, really—shaking my head.

You can't fight love.

I push away from the wall. "Yeah. I really am."

~

"YOU KNOW, THE alcohol was supposed to make the moping *better*," Parker grumbles from beside me at the bar.

I down the rest of my glass, rolling my eyes. "This was your idea."

"Because I thought that intoxicating you would make you more pleasant to be around."

"Wow," I snort. "You're a real pal."

"Someone has to make you take care of yourself," he grouses.

I drop my head to the polished wood of the bar, pressing my cheek against it as I sigh. The slight spinning in my head *does* make the ache in my chest less noticeable, admittedly, but it doesn't get rid of it completely.

"I just don't get it," I mumble.

Parker leans down toward my pitiful form. "You're going to have to speak up. I can't hear you over this shitty music."

"Hey." I peer up at him with narrowed eyes. "We don't slander Miley Cyrus in this house."

"Is that who it is?" He looks at the speakers with a grimace. "I liked her better on the wrecking ball."

"I'm sorry that not everyone can be Taylor Swift."

"Um, she was artist of the year *and* artist of the decade," Parker says defensively. "*No one* can be Tay."

"Tay," I snort.

"Now what did you say?"

"I said I don't *get* it," I half shout.

"Get what?"

"He asked me on a date," I groan. "A *real* date. Why did he do that if he was just going to dump me?"

"Can we call it dumping when it was contractual?" I glare at him, and he raises his hands in apology. "Okay, okay. He dumped you. He's a bastard."

"He's not a bastard," I whine.

"I'm getting mixed signals about how I am supposed to support you here."

I blow out a breath. "I just . . . I had *just* decided to try letting somebody in, you know? I had this huge talk with Gran and there was some crying and shit, and I was feeling like the whole universe was aligning or something and then *bam*." I slam my hand on the bar for emphasis. "Dumped."

"Well, clearly, Noah has a broken brain. Obviously that's why he did what he did."

"Yeah, maybe," I answer pitifully.

"Tell me how to cheer you up," Parker urges, sounding concerned. "I actually hate seeing you like this, honestly. It's like watching a puppy cry or something."

"I wish I knew." I sigh.

"Want to hear about some questionable internet usage from your fellow Denver General staff?"

I perk up. "Are you even allowed to tell me that?"

"Probably not, but if you start crying I might actually stop functioning."

This makes me smile. "I thought gay men were supposed to be good at this sort of thing?"

"How many times have I told you not to put me in a box?" he huffs. "I can be emotionally incapable if I want to be. Now, do you want to hear or not?"

"Well, obviously," I scoff.

"So, there's a podiatrist on the seventh floor who is . . . way too into his job."

I lift my head, furrowing my brow. "What do you mean?"

"Feet pictures, Mack. *Feet* pictures."

"Ew." I grimace. "Oh my God. Not that bald guy who's always haunting Radiology?"

"Maybe he likes them inside *and* out."

"That's disgusting. But I like it. Tell me another."

"Someone uses one of the terminals in the nurses' station to watch porn every Thursday night."

"No."

"Yep. I've been trying to catch them for weeks. My money is on Kevin the creepy janitor."

"Oh, he wouldn't—" I remember the way he'd seemed so pleased to have found Noah and me practically making out in a closet, and I reconsider. "You know, maybe."

Of course, now I'm thinking about Noah and me in a closet.

Which means I'm thinking about Noah. Which means I'm depressed again.

I drop my forehead to the bar top. "I really liked him, Parker. I thought it was just dumb alpha stuff, but I think I really *liked* him. I thought he liked me too."

"Honestly," Parker sighs. "So did I. You should have seen him that day when you were going into heat. He was like . . . almost predatory. I actually thought he might rip my arm off for touching you when he found us together."

"So *why* did he drop me right after? Was he just after sex this whole time?"

Parker frowns. "That doesn't really fit to me. I mean, you guys did it a *lot*, right?"

"Basically," I groan. "Maybe it was an omega thing? He heard what I was and was biding his time until I went into heat?"

"Do you really think that's it?"

I think back—remembering the careful way he'd held me in the moments where I wasn't in a fever dream–like state. I remember his soft words and his softer touch, practically still able to feel his fingers brushing lightly against my skin.

I'm not letting you get away from me, Mackenzie.

"No," I answer quietly. "That doesn't feel right."

"Not to mention all the coupley shit you told me you've been doing with him the last couple of weeks. Maybe it really was just as he said," Parker offers. "Maybe he just couldn't handle the stress of it all. The guy was already a workaholic. Now he's going to be chief of staff? Maybe he was afraid he couldn't keep up with it all. You know how men are. They think they're being noble when half the time, they're just being stupid."

"Maybe," I sigh.

I can feel my eyes welling with tears, and it's harder to fight them off with the alcohol in my system. I feel Parker's hand at my back, rubbing a soothing circle, and I reach over my shoulder to pat his hand, grateful that he's here.

"Want to hear more internet gossip?"

I nod feebly. "Please."

"Let me think . . ." He looks up at the ceiling. "There's the time I had to block Tinder from the server because some male nurse was posting dick pics from his work laptop."

"Just . . . why?"

"Maybe he got a wider view from the laptop camera?"

"Wow, he must have had a *huge*—"

"No comment," Parker says quickly, reaching for his drink. "But yes."

A laugh bubbles out of me. "Tell me something else."

"Hmm. Oh!" He snaps his fingers. "This isn't really juicy, but it is kind of sad, almost. There's this cardiologist in No—" He catches my wince. "Well, there's this cardiologist who must be super jealous of a certain . . . other cardiologist."

My mouth turns down. "What do you mean?"

"I had to update his computer recently, and his search history was nothing but alpha shit. I mean, this guy has been researching them for *months*. I'm assuming it's a wishful thinking sort of scenario."

Even through the haze of my three drinks, there's a weight on my mind, something about what Parker's saying poking at a memory that feels important. I lift up, my head feeling too heavy and instantly making me regret it, staring at the wall behind the bar intently as I try to think.

"He isn't . . ." I shake my head. "Is his name Dennis Martin?"

"Hey, I don't know if I should be giving you their *names*—"

"Parker." I close my eyes and swallow, trying to collect my thoughts even as they continue to slip away from me. "Parker, did you say that he'd been researching alphas for months?"

"At least," Parker snorts. "His entire search history was full of it."

"What . . ." I keep my eyes closed, thinking. "What exactly was he searching?"

"Um, I don't know . . . Alpha traits, alpha horror stories, alpha regulations in the workforce . . ."

I have to really focus, something that doesn't come easily to me right now, but I take a deep breath to try anyway—some memory floating at the edge of my mind just begging to be remembered. It's . . . it's only been a little more than a month. Since someone turned Noah in. If Dennis truly was jealous of Noah . . . why would he have been searching about alphas for *months*? I think back even harder, desperately reaching for whatever it is that my brain wants me to remember, feeling like my fingertips are *just there*, brushing along the edge of it.

And then it hits me.

That day. The day I had gone into heat. The conversation that Parker and I had been having, the one that I had convinced myself Dennis couldn't have overheard. How could I have forgotten about it?

I snort under my breath. I know the answer to that. Three days of sex like Noah and I had is enough to make you forget a lot of things. I think back to the way Parker and I had practically been yelling, how Dennis had popped up just after, only seconds between what we'd said and his presence, and *could* he have overheard?

If Dennis . . . if Dennis is the one who turned Noah in . . . If he wanted Noah's job *that* badly—what would he do if he found out that Noah's and my relationship was fake?

I blink, and then I gasp, warring with the possibility of hope and the fear of learning it's all for naught. I stare blankly at the wall as I consider what to do, if I should do anything at *all*, because what if I'm wrong? What if the thing between Noah and me had really just run its course, and he doesn't feel anything for me?

What if Noah actually had just wanted out?

I think that deep down, there's really only one choice for me, no matter what the outcome.

"Parker," I say, coming to a decision.

He pauses with his drink halfway to his mouth. "Hm?"

"How hard would it be to remote-access someone's computer?"

He frowns, not catching on. "Not hard? Why would you—"

I'm already slipping off my stool, slapping my cheeks to help collect myself before grabbing for my coat. "Come on," I tell him. "We're leaving."

Parker looks dumbfounded, watching me shove my arms through my coat sleeves and start toward the door. "Where are we going?"

"Back to the hospital," I toss over my shoulder.

"Are you sticking me with the tab? *Hey!*"

I'm sure he'll be griping about that for a while, but I can't stop.

Not until I know for sure.

26

Noah

"—AND ANOTHER THING," my mother is saying. "I am so tired of hearing about your life from *Regina*, of all people. It's *embarrassing*, Noah. If it weren't for that daughter of hers being as gossipy as her mother, I wouldn't know anything! I can't believe you didn't tell me you put in your resignation. Were you just going to hop over to New Mexico without even saying good-bye?"

Given the way that my mother has been grilling me for the last ten minutes, I decide it's probably a bad idea to tell her that, yes, that's likely what I was going to do. Mostly to avoid a conversation like this *while* I'm still nursing my Mackenzie-related wounds.

"It all happened very fast," I tell her, trying to placate her a little. "It's been a bit of a whirlwind."

"You still could have made time to pick up the phone," she tuts. "We could have thrown you a going-away party."

Definitely not in the mood for a party right now.

"It's fine, Mom. Really. You can come visit when I'm settled."

"You're damn right, I will," she snorts.

"Language," I remind her, earning myself another curse.

"And what about Mackenzie? What happened to trying for more?"

I wonder if there will ever be a time when thinking about her doesn't make my chest hurt. I pause from folding my shirts, taking a deep breath. "It didn't work out."

"'It didn't work out,'" she echoes blandly. "That sounds like a crock of shit to me."

I shut my eyes, sighing. "It wasn't a real relationship, Mom."

Will I have to have this conversation with everyone in my life?

I'm suddenly very grateful that my personal circle is very small.

"Don't give me that," Mom says with accusation in her tone. "We both know there was more to it than that."

"Yeah, well." I throw the shirt I was folding onto the couch, using more force than I need to. "That's how it goes sometimes."

"You can talk to me, you know," she says more gently. "You're never too old to lean on your mother."

"I'm fine," I lie. "I just have a lot to do before the move."

"Was the hospital sorry to take your resignation?"

"They did offer me a significant raise to stay, but I think this will be a better opportunity."

Another lie. There is no better opportunity for me that doesn't include Mackenzie.

"I just hate that you're moving so far away. You're going to be all on your own."

"I'm used to it," I mumble.

"Well, you *shouldn't* be," she sighs. "I worry about you so much, son. You're nearing forty, and you still have no one to come home to. I don't want you to work yourself into an early, lonely grave."

My mother can't possibly know how much this conversation is

making everything I'm feeling a hundred times worse, and I'm struggling to keep my emotions in check. If she finds out how badly I'm doing right now, I'll never hear the end of it.

"Really, Mom. I'm fine with the way things are. I like my life."

Fucking liar, I think miserably. *You only thought you did.*

"Well. I'm just saying, you could—"

A knock at my door means that I miss the rest of what she's saying, stepping back to peer down the hallway warily. There isn't a single person who comes to mind who would be coming to visit me, save for maybe Paul—but even that seems unlikely.

"—someday you're going to look back and wish that you—"

"Just one second, Mom," I mutter into the phone.

I don't think she actually hears me, because I can still hear her ranting even when I hold the phone away from my ear and start down the hall. There's another knock as I approach, one that is more insistent than the first, and I glance at the clock on the wall to notice it's nearly ten o'clock, so even a package delivery doesn't make sense. Not that I was expecting one. I reach for the handle just as a third knock sounds, one that's practically a fist beating at the wood, pulling open the door and nearly dropping my phone entirely when I see who's standing there.

It takes me several seconds to remember how to form words, but then: "Mackenzie?"

Her hair is wild, almost like she's been running, and she appears out of breath, her eyes bright but hard under her knitted brow. I notice she's still in her scrubs, which makes no sense, given that she got off hours ago. Which I know. Because I still know her schedule. Like a pathetic weirdo. She looks almost angry, pointing a finger at me.

"You're a fucking *liar*, Noah Taylor."

I rear back, thrown for a loop. I don't know what I expected her to say, but that was *definitely* not it. "Excuse me?"

"You heard me. I can't believe you would—" She notices the phone in my hand. "Are you on the phone with someone?"

"Shit." I remember my mother, who is *still* lecturing me, oblivious to the fact that I haven't been listening. I put the phone back to my ear, cutting her off. "Mom, I'm going to have to call you back."

"I'm not falling for that! You and I both know you won't—"

"Talk soon," I say, still addled.

I put my phone in my pocket slowly after I hang up, still reeling from the angry woman standing on my porch. "Did you want to come in to yell at me?"

"Oh." She looks less irate for a moment. "Yes. Sorry."

She walks right past me without sparing me a second glance, and I shut the door slowly behind her, wondering if I've finally lost it. Maybe this entire thing is a hallucination. When I find her in the middle of my living room—her arms are crossed as she regards me irritably, tapping her foot.

"How could you lie to me?"

"Mackenzie, I . . ." I'm torn between utter confusion and elation that she's *here*. That she's within reach, for however brief a time. *Fuck.* Her scent is thick with her anger, and I have to resist the urge to close my eyes and inhale deeply, knowing that would most likely worsen her mood. "I'm sorry, I don't follow."

"Dennis threatened you. Didn't he."

My mouth falls open, and I lose every reason why my lie was so important as I'm left stunned. "How did you . . . ?"

"I *knew* it." She claps her hands together, looking like she's just solved a very complicated puzzle. "That little fucker. He turned you in to the board, and then when he heard Parker and me talking the other day, he must have put two and two together, and then he—" She looks almost contrite. "I'd completely forgotten, it was the day that I went into heat, and I was feeling so awful, and he walked up while Parker was laying into me for letting myself get too close to you, and I just . . . forgot."

"Wait. Parker thought you were getting too close to me?"

She scoffs. "That's your takeaway?"

"I'm sorry, I . . . I am very confused right now."

"About which part, Noah?" She takes a step, poking a finger into my chest. All I can think about is how happy I am that she's touching me again. "About the fact that you lied to me? How you broke my damned heart because you didn't trust me enough to tell me that Dennis was threatening you?"

I blink, still reeling. "I broke your heart?"

"Do you want me to beat you up? Is that it? I don't care how big you are, I swear I will—"

"How did you find out?"

"Parker. He told me Dennis has been researching alpha shit for months. I put two and two together, and I knew something had to be up. When we broke into his computer, we found pictures he'd taken on his phone of the results of one of your physicals, which you'd left on your desk. I guess that's how he found out."

"You *broke* into his computer?"

She throws up her hands. "Why are you focusing on all the wrong things?"

"So *Dennis* turned me in?"

"I mean, are you surprised? That weasel has been gunning for your job for forever, right? It's not that much of a stretch that he'd be the most likely candidate to sabotage you like that."

"I can't believe it," I breathe. "I knew he hated me, but I never thought he'd go snooping through my office like that."

"What he did was a *crime*, Noah. We can get him on a HIPAA violation at the very least. Then there's the blackmailing. We can nail that shithead to the wall."

"We?"

She pauses, looking unsure for the first time since she came here. "Unless you . . ." She wrinkles her nose. "Unless you weren't lying at the café?"

"Mackenzie, I . . . I really hurt you."

"You're damned right you did. Here I am, finally thinking I can try out this whole relationship thing, and you come along with your stupid 'I don't know if it's the right time for us' bullshit, and if I didn't think you were doing that because of some nonsense alpha idea of protecting me, then I wouldn't even be here." She juts out her chin, staring me down. "*Is* that why you did what you did, Noah?"

I could keep up with the lie, even now. There is still a part of me that thinks eventually she would have realized I wasn't enough, that there are better options for her out there, and maybe a good person would give her that opportunity. Maybe a better person would usher her out the door to make sure nothing bad ever touched her.

But maybe I'm not a better person.

"He threatened your job," I tell her slowly. "He was going to turn you in for lying to the board."

"That absolute fuckhead," Mackenzie hisses. "I'm going to give him a testicular torsion when I see him again."

"You're not . . . mad at me?"

"Oh, I'm mad at you," she assures me angrily. "You should have told me the truth. We could have figured out a solution together. You should have *trusted* me, Noah."

"I should have," I echo dumbly, knowing she's right. "I'm sorry."

"I'm not some damsel in distress who needs you to save me. This was *my* career on the line, too, and I deserved a choice here. You took that away from me when you went all alpha male."

"I know. I know that, but I—"

"This is exactly what I wanted to avoid when you found out what I was. I have never wanted or needed someone to protect me, do you understand? I can do that myself. What I want is someone who is there for me. Even when times are tough." She blinks, looking surprised. "Fuck. I didn't even know I *wanted* that until you."

"Mackenzie, I . . ." I run my fingers through my hair anxiously. "You're right. You're absolutely right, okay? I never wanted to hurt you, you have to believe me on that. It's just I . . ." I huff out a breath, struggling for the words. "I've never cared about someone like I care about you."

She blinks in surprise, whatever angry thing that had been on the tip of her tongue falling away. "What?"

"I don't know when it happened, and I know we wanted to avoid it, but somewhere in the middle of all this fake mate nonsense, I started to have *real* feelings for you. And that terrified me. Not only because your career was suddenly put in jeopardy, but because I knew that one day you would figure out that you deserved a hell of a lot better than me."

"Better than you," she parrots slowly.

I nod, looking down at my feet. "I'm older than you, and I'm not very fun, and I'm learning that I'm entirely too possessive, and . . .

Look at you." I gesture to all of her. "You're funny, and bright, and everyone loves you. I mean, they call me the damned Boogeyman of Denver General, for fuck's sake."

"Noah—" she starts, but I can't seem to stop talking now.

"The last thing I *ever* wanted to do was hurt you, but I knew you would dive in headfirst to fight this thing, and I couldn't risk you throwing everything away. Not for me. Because you might not regret it today, or tomorrow, but one day . . . you'd resent me for it. And I would deserve it. It felt like that future would be a lot more painful for you than ending things here. I thought . . ." I breathe in deep, blowing it out as I finally lift my head to meet her eyes. "I thought it would be easier for you to just forget me before I had the chance to hurt you even more."

She doesn't say anything for a long time, the seconds ticking by as we both just stare at each other. I can't fathom what she might have to say to all that, but I'm preparing myself for the worst.

She shakes her head. "You're right."

I feel defeat weighing down on my shoulders. "I know," I say dejectedly. "I understand if you—"

"I *would* have dived in headfirst to fight this," she interrupts, and I forget what I was about to say. "Not just for me, but for *you* too."

I feel stunned all over again. "What?"

"Noah," she sighs, pinching the bridge of her nose. "You're not as bad as you want people to believe. You're a good doctor, and a good person, and you make me laugh . . . even if you don't mean to. You're not a boogeyman of anything. You're just a big stupid genius with good intentions and bad execution."

"I am?"

"Yeah," she says wearily. "Yeah, that's what I'm starting to realize."

"I really thought I was doing the best thing for you," I offer feebly.

She nods. "But you understand why it wasn't now. Right?"

"Yes," I answer softly. "I think I do."

"You said you cared about me," she says with an unreadable expression.

I suck in a breath. "I do."

"Why?"

"Because . . ." I falter, not because I don't know the answer, but because I am having trouble finding the right words. "Because when I'm with you . . . I don't feel like I'm just going through the motions in life. When I'm with you . . . I feel like I'm actually *living*."

Her lip trembles, but that's the only thing she gives me before she clears her throat. She nods her head slowly, and then she takes me completely by surprise when her lips curl ever so slightly. "That was dangerously close to poetry, Noah Taylor."

I perk up, feeling hope spark in my chest. It's an unfamiliar feeling. "It was pretty terrible."

She taps her foot idly, still studying me. "You really did hurt me."

"I know," I tell her, feeling that pang of guilt tear through me. "I'm so sorry, Mackenzie."

She's not smiling anymore, her nose wrinkled in thought and her eyes moving over my face. I count ten seconds, and then twenty more—each one agonizing as I wait for her to either give me another chance or walk out of my life for good. I know for certain which option I deserve, in any case.

"Yeah, well," she says finally, huffing out a breath and pressing her fists to her hips. "You're definitely going to make it up to me."

That tiny flame of hope is back, threatening to climb higher. "I am?"

"Obviously," she snorts. "You're going to be groveling for a very long time, Dr. Taylor."

I can't help it. My lips twitch. "A very long time?"

"Years, maybe," she says in that same grumbling tone. "I'm talking about soup on demand. Chain orgasms. More of that terrible poetry. I haven't decided."

"I can manage that," I say, feeling a blinding, happy feeling swelling inside. "I can grovel for the rest of my life."

This makes her suck in a breath, her expression softening a fraction as she bites her lip. "I'm going to be a pain," she tells me.

"It's fine," I assure her, taking a small, careful step to close the distance between us. "I'm an expert at being insufferable."

"And I'm going to get scared sometimes," she barrels on.

"I can be there to make sure it doesn't last," I promise, closing the gap another inch.

Her fists slide from her hips to let her arms hang at her sides, her eyes fixed on mine. "And you can't ever leave."

"I never wanted to in the first place," I say, my fingers reaching to curl gently around her arms. "I never want to leave you ever again."

"And if you ever—"

I can't wait another second, my mouth crashing against hers as I pull her into me. She melts into it like she's been waiting for it as desperately as I have, her fingers gripping my shirt as she tries to pull me closer. My lips move against hers roughly as my tongue dips inside her mouth, my hands sliding over her arms and her shoulders and up her neck until my fingers tangle in her hair.

"I'm sorry," I breathe between kisses. "I'm so sorry."

"Groveling," she gasps. "Lots of groveling."

I smile against her mouth as my hands slide down her spine. "I don't have any soup, but . . . I can probably start on that list."

"Well, if you think you have t—*ah*."

I pull her up into my arms as my mouth covers hers again, practically sprinting down the opposite hall toward my bedroom, afraid that if I waste another second she might disappear. That I'll wake up and this will all be a dream. Her hands are under my shirt, tearing at the fabric so hard in her attempt to get it off me that she almost rips it.

I drop her on the bed and finish the task for her, tossing my shirt somewhere on the floor before pushing up hers to press kisses to her ribs. She smells so good, so fucking *sweet*—all of it so much more intoxicating at this moment after thinking that I would never experience it again. I shove at her bra roughly so I can mouth at the soft underside of her breast, nipping gently with my teeth as she squirms in my hands.

I'm pulling her scrub top off her arms, tossing it over my shoulder as I bring my attention back to the swell of her breasts spilling from the top of her bra. The taste of her skin is as honeyed as her scent, and I think if given the chance I could spend hours tasting every inch of her, if she let me. I only pull away when she reaches between us to flick at a little plastic piece between her breasts, grinning at what is surely an awestruck expression on my face when the cups fall aside to bare everything to me.

"Front clasp," she chuckles.

I duck my head to twirl her nipple with my tongue, murmuring into her skin, "Fucking genius."

"*Noah*," she gasps when I suck her into my mouth.

Her fingers curl over my shoulders, her nails biting into my skin, and I relish the slight sting, a reminder that she's here. That she's *really* here.

I start to move down her body, mouthing at her skin the entire way, until my teeth scrape at the swell of her stomach while my fingers hook into the elastic of her scrub bottoms. I roll them down her thighs with her underwear not far behind, immediately curling my hand around her so I can kiss at the softness of her thighs, which are smooth and warm against my tongue.

"Noah," Mackenzie says impatiently. "It's been almost two weeks, don't you want to just—"

She yelps when I nip at her thigh. "It *has* been almost two weeks. And you did say that chain orgasms were part of the groveling process."

She shivers when I drag my tongue over her skin, bringing it closer to the heated core of her, which is already wet for me. I'm rewarded with an airy sound of pleasure when I lick a hot stripe between her legs.

"Oh."

To think I might have never been able to taste her like this again. I close my eyes, humming as I do it again more slowly. She squirms just enough that I have to curl my hands over the tops of her thighs to hold her still, using my tongue to catch the bit of her slick that escapes her. I know that she'll feel as good as she tastes, the memory of her warmth wrapped around my cock enough to make me ache for it.

But first things first.

I tease her, trailing the tip of my tongue around her clit but not quite touching—hearing her make frustrated sounds as she pushes her fingers through my hair to tug softly. I tap her taut little button before covering it completely, using my tongue to roll it in a slow circle before wrapping my lips around it to suck.

The effect is immediate; she pushes her hips upward mindlessly and her fingers tug at my hair harder than before—and when I pull a little more roughly, suctioning her to make her whimper, I can feel her thighs pressing at my hands like she's trying to shut her legs to escape the sensation. Like it's too much for her.

"Noah," she gasps. "*Noah*. Don't st—*fuck*."

I'm not teasing her now; it *has* been almost two weeks, after all, and what might seem like a short span of time feels like forever when I haven't been able to touch her. I release her thighs just so I can slide one hand underneath her, lifting her to bare more of her to my mouth. I use the other hand to curl two fingers inside her, pressing against the sensitive spot that I know I'll be touching with my cock shortly after this. I can almost *feel* the way she'll fit around me when my knot swells.

I pump my fingers in and out of her messily as I suck deeper at her clit, her thighs pressed against my ears so tight that it is almost uncomfortable, but that sure as hell isn't going to stop me. She starts to tremble when she's close, her hands clawing anywhere they can reach, be it the sheets or the pillows or my shoulders and back again, and when she finally lets go, shaking against my tongue as she makes a breathless sound of contentment—it's almost enough to make *me* come right along with her. Almost.

She's already tugging at my shoulders even before she's fully come down from it, my fingers still moving inside her to prolong her pleasure as my mouth collides with hers. I know she has to be able to taste herself on my tongue, and I can't say why that warms me further, but it does. I can feel her hands insistently shoving at the sweatpants I'm still wearing, to try and roll them off me, and it takes only seconds for me to take over the task, to kick them away so that there is nothing but our skin and her warmth and the hot ache of my cock as it slots against her.

"Never thought I'd have this again," I rasp against her mouth.

She tilts her hips so that I slide over her wet folds. "Hurry, Noah."

She wraps her arms around my neck as my arm curls beneath her, holding her tight as I press against her entrance to slowly slip inside. I watch her expression as I give her inch after inch, enjoying the slight part of her mouth, the hooded quality of her lids, the way she's looking at me like I'm giving her everything she needs.

She kisses me when I'm fully inside her, her tongue tangling with mine and her teeth nibbling at my lower lip, nodding softly as if wordlessly telling me to move. Not that I need any motivation. Her nipples are hard against my chest as I move into her, tickling my skin as I savor the wet slide of my cock as it fills her. I press my hand near her head on the mattress to brace myself, making sure to keep my hold around her waist so that I can hold her close as I roll my hips into hers.

I can feel that urgency building inside; there's a steady thrumming of *mine mine mine* pulsing under my skin that comes from a place I'm just beginning to understand. One that only *she* can touch. It makes me feel wilder, more desperate—it makes me feel like I'll never get enough of her.

"*Fuck*," I grind out. "I never want to stop doing this."

Mackenzie laughs breathlessly, pulling me down so she can kiss my jaw. "That's tempting."

"I could keep you here," I hum, letting my head loll so I can scrape my teeth over her shoulder. "Keep you full of my knot forever."

Her breath catches when my lips brush the warm, throbbing gland at the base of her throat, flicking my tongue against it. "*Noah.*"

I have nonsensical urges to press my teeth here, to mark her for the rest of her days so that everyone will always know that she belongs to me, that I belong to her—but a small, nagging part of my brain that is still clinging to a scrap of sanity knows it isn't time for that. Not yet. I kiss her there once more for good measure, hard enough to leave a mark, at the very least.

Someday.

"Can you come for me like this?" I push deeper, deep enough to have her moaning in my ear, and that only makes me feel *wilder.* "You're so *wet.*" My lips skirt down her jawline, my breath washing against the skin there. "Is that for me?"

"Y-yes, Noah—*ah*—Keep doing that."

"This?" I snap my hips, grunting when I feel my cock starting to swell as hot pressure begins to build. "This what you want?"

"*Yes.* I'm—I'm so—"

"Come with me," I breathe. "I want to feel you come on my knot. Can you do that?"

"Oh. *Oh.*"

Her teeth sink into my shoulder, her cries muffled against my skin as she falls apart, and I grit my teeth when my knot starts to swell, stretching her to what feels like impossible measures until I can no longer move inside her. We're both breathless after, my body trembling as I gush deep inside to fill her, and her hands smoothing across my shoulders feel like a searing heat in the aftermath of it all.

I can't believe there was a moment where I almost chose to live without this, without *her*—everything about my intentions before tonight feeling utterly stupid now. Her eyes are glazed and her smile is languid when I pull up to look at her, and my lips curl to match hers as she reaches to push damp hair away from my forehead.

"As far as groveling goes," she says after a ragged breath. "It's a start."

"I'm prepared to spend an *incredibly* long time making it up to you," I tell her seriously. "Multiple times a day, if I have to."

She chuffs out a laugh. "Wow. Talk about sacrifice."

"Sometimes they're worth being made."

She's still smiling as she kisses me, and when I fall down to meet her, there is a slight tug at my knot that makes me wince, my breath catching.

"You'd better never do that again," she says suddenly, and when I pull my head back, I can see worry in her eyes. "Don't ever lie to me like that."

That guilt surges through me again for having put it there. "Never." My hand slides up her spine to cradle her head, ensuring she can look nowhere but my eyes and hoping she sees the sincerity there. "I'm not leaving you, Mackenzie. Never again. I was an idiot to think I could in the first place." My forehead rests against hers. "I know you don't believe in fate, but . . ." My lips press gently at the corner of her mouth, whispering, "I think I might."

"I might be"—I hear her swallow—"coming around to the idea."

I raise up, grinning. "Yeah?"

"Maybe," she amends. "Just a little."

"I can live with that."

She looks serious again. "We're going to the board tomorrow."

"We are?"

"Yes. We're going to make sure that son of a bitch doesn't get away with any of this. I want him to fry, Noah."

"Look at you," I chuckle, combing my fingers through her hair.

"Here I thought I was protecting you, but you're the one protecting me."

"Someone's got to," she deadpans. "I mean, you're so fragile, after all."

My lips twitch. "Am I."

"Face it, Dr. Taylor," she teases. "You need me to look after you."

I'm not laughing now, my smile barely there and my eyes studying every inch of her face. "Yeah," I tell her quietly. "Yeah, I think I do."

Tomorrow will be a nightmare, and there's no way of knowing what it will hold—but right now . . . right now, there is nothing but Mackenzie's warmth and her soft sounds and her softer body that fits perfectly against mine. All of it makes one thing glaringly obvious, something that I should have figured out a lot sooner.

I am *never* letting this woman get away from me again.

27

Mackenzie

"SO, YOU'RE SAYING . . . you are *not* mated?"

Noah and I share a glance, and he nods at me with encouragement.

"No," I answer, holding the gaze of the elderly board member. "We aren't."

Another man pipes up from across the table. "So you lied on the disclosure forms?"

"You didn't exactly give me a lot of options," Noah says irritably.

"Now, Dr. Taylor," a graying woman cuts in. "There was never any talk of any disciplinary measures in regard to your designation, I need to make that clear. This facade was entirely unnecessary. And unethical, I feel."

"No," I retaliate angrily. "What's unethical is the atmosphere of this facility. We all know the unsaid repercussions for someone like Noah. Never mind the fact that he's the most qualified physician who any of you have ever employed, probably."

"Now, Dr. Carter, that isn't—"

"If you're so tolerant, why ask for one's designation at all during the hiring process?" I cross my arms. "How does that affect a person's skill set?"

The first elder board member clicks his tongue. "Now, see here, it's the responsibility of this board to ensure the safety of our staff, even if that means asking uncomfortable questions."

"And has Noah ever once given this hospital any indication that he was dangerous in any way? Hasn't he performed his duties with exemplary expertise?"

A few of the board members share a look. "That's . . . true," the older woman says. "Dr. Taylor has never given us any indication that he was in need of supervision."

"Because he's a damned good doctor," I seethe.

"Mackenzie," Noah warns gently, reaching for my hand.

I glance at him with my chest full of indignation, and he squeezes my hand, offering me a smile before he turns to the board. "The blame for omitting my status when I was hired falls entirely on me. As does the idea of presenting Dr. Carter as my mate to protect my job."

"Noah, don't—"

He cuts me another warning glance before continuing. "But nevertheless, I have fulfilled all the requirements of my position ten times over during my time here, and if given the opportunity, I would like to continue."

"Well," one man says, "you did already put in your resignation . . ."

"About that," Noah answers. "I've been informed that the person who reported me to the board was a fellow cardiologist, and I've since learned that he obtained this information by riffling through my office and violating my HIPAA rights by going through my personal medical records. Since then, Dr. Martin has threatened me, blackmailed me with not only my job, but Dr. Carter's, and I think both of these instances warrant a lawsuit, should I choose to pursue it."

"Not to mention the discrimination suit we're going after if you choose to permanently let Noah go just because of what he is," I say.

The board members all share a glance, looking nervous. "Now, let's not get ahead of ourselves. We haven't officially decided on any punishments here. Maybe we all just take a breather, huh?"

"I don't think I'll feel comfortable returning with Dr. Martin so willing to break the law just to take my position," Noah says. "Had he not interfered, there would never have been any issues to begin with." Noah looks the head of the board right in the eye. "Besides, since you never *officially* took a stance against alphas during your hiring procedures, there aren't *officially* grounds to let me go over it, are there?"

"But your resignation—"

"I believe I was offered a significant pay increase should I choose to stay," Noah says cheerfully. "I haven't given my official answer on that, have I? I'd like to accept the terms."

All four board members look shocked, their mouths hanging open as they realize we've backed them into a corner.

"We'd also like to officially disclose our relationship," I add.

The woman looks confused. "But you said—"

"Oh, we aren't mated," I assure her.

Noah clears his throat. "Not yet."

My mouth falls open as I look at him, a giddy sensation bubbling in my chest. His eyes are warm, too warm for the situation, and I have to bite back a grin as I return my attention to the board. "And we would also like to officially call for Dr. Martin's termination. That is, if you want to avoid us taking legal measures for the multiple offenses he's committed."

The oldest board member leans into the woman sitting next to him, both of them looking nervous as they whisper rapidly to each other before turning to repeat the same song and dance with the other members seated around the table. As they deliberate quietly, Noah doesn't let go of my hand, keeping a tight hold on it to remind me that he's here—that no matter what happens, we're in this together.

It's a new feeling for me, but one I find I don't dislike.

"Dr. Taylor," the old board member finally calls, sounding weary. "In light of these new findings, I think it's safe to say that you can resume work starting next week. We would like to officially apologize for making you feel as if you would be unwelcome on our staff because of your designation. It is not in this board's interest to dally in exclusion of any kind. Especially not with someone as gifted as yourself."

I feel myself beaming, victory surging through me. "And Dr. Martin?"

"Right," the older woman says. She gestures for the secretary taking minutes at the end of the table. "Patricia, could you please page Dr. Martin? It seems we have a lot to discuss."

"We'll be sure to forward an official transcription of this meeting for both of your records upon completion," a middle-aged, balding member says. "And again, our deepest apologies."

"No apologies necessary," Noah tells them, sounding sincere. He looks down at me. "It ended up being worth it."

Noah Taylor? Being cheesy? Next thing I know, the sky will start falling.

He pulls me out of the boardroom after we say our good-byes, neither of us saying anything further until we're down the hall and far out of earshot. I squeal when he suddenly turns and lifts me from the ground, pulling me up and against his body before covering my mouth with his for a searing kiss. He holds me there for far longer than is appropriate, given where we are, but I can't find it in me to care, just enjoying the warmth of his arms and his kiss and everything else.

I fall back down to the floor slowly, my body sliding against his until my toes touch the linoleum before my feet fall flat. He's beaming at me like I'm some sort of present, and I find it infectious, my mouth mirroring the motion.

"I can't believe we pulled that off," I laugh.

Noah shrugs. "You mention lawsuits to these people, and they'll just about piss their pants."

"Probably should have been our *first* course of action," I say with faux irritation.

Noah chuckles. "Turns out I'm not as smart as I thought."

"That's okay," I deadpan. "I'll be sure to teach you a thing or two."

"Perfect," he says with a grin.

We don't hear the footsteps over our own chatter, so it's a mild surprise when we hear his grating voice.

"Well, if it isn't the lovebirds," Dennis calls. "Funny seeing you here. You decided that your job wasn't worth it, after all?"

I feel Noah tense beside me, but I press a hand to his chest, smiling at Dennis sweetly. "Actually, we just had a long talk with the board about something a lot worse than lying on a relationship disclosure form. Didn't we, Noah?"

"That's right." Noah nods stiffly. "Turns out, they're much more interested in things like extortion and HIPAA violations." He clicks his tongue. "Doesn't look too good for the hospital when one of their staff is messing around with things like that."

The color draining from Dennis's face is beyond satisfying, and it's clear by his expression that he hadn't considered this possibility in the slightest. He *really* thought he'd won, that he'd pulled a fast one on us, and that in itself makes me want to kick him between the legs. I decide the complete ruining of his career will be much better.

"Have fun in there," I coo.

"You fucking *bitch*," Dennis growls as he takes a step toward me.

He doesn't even make it a foot before Noah has him pinned against the wall with his forearm pressed to Dennis's chest, Noah looking murderous as he speaks slowly and carefully.

"Dr. Martin," Noah says, a simmering rage in his tone. "If you ever touch her, I will show you *exactly* what that famous alpha temper looks like and rip both of your arms off to ensure it never happens again. Do you understand?"

I notice Dennis swallow thickly, his face white as a sheet. He looks older like this, frailer. Still, I don't feel the least bit sorry for him. He is a complete fuckhead, after all.

"I'm going to set you down now," Noah tells him. "And you're going to walk away. And you aren't even going to *look* at Mackenzie."

Dennis says nothing, his mouth opening and closing like a fish out of water.

"I said," Noah repeats darkly, "do you understand?"

Dennis's lips roll together. "Yes," he says quietly. "I understand."

"Good." Noah smiles cheerfully, his entire demeanor changing in the blink of an eye. "You have a good meeting."

Dennis turns on his heel quickly, like he's afraid that Noah might come after him, and I can't pretend it isn't incredibly hot, seeing Noah turn on the alpha switch like that. I'm all for feminism . . . but hot damn.

"That was . . . intensely satisfying," Noah says after a second, turning back to me.

"Mm." I press my hands to his shoulders. "It would have been better if you'd hit him."

Noah shakes his head, laughing under his breath. "I think the board is going to hurt him more than I ever could."

"God, I wish we could be in there to see it. Do you think he'll cry?"

"I am choosing to imagine that's how it goes down, yes."

I grin. "Still okay with giving up the Albuquerque job? It's a good opportunity, you know."

"Mackenzie . . ." He pulls me against him, his hand pressing against my spine. "You're the best opportunity I could choose."

I feel warmth flushing my cheeks down into my chest. "Wow, you're getting downright sappy, aren't you? What's next, a sonnet? You know, you could—"

Noah's mouth really *is* a very effective method of shutting me up.

I wind my arms around his neck as I sink deeper into his kiss, not caring in the slightest that we're in a very public hallway of a very public hospital, which anyone could come strolling down. We are officially *official* now—nothing fake about it. They can just keep walking. I feel his hands curve around my waist to squeeze, and my head starts to dizzy with the potency of his scent, already thinking about how I might persuade him to get out of here with me and take me back home so we can resume his "groveling."

Noah pulls away with a blissful look on his face, happier and lighter than I've ever seen him. And it's for *me*. It makes my heart pound and my head spin, and all those notions about fate and destiny are still foreign to me, still a little outside of my wheelhouse—but looking at him now . . . it makes me feel things I never thought were possible.

Noah looks down the hall. "Should we get out of here? If we keep this up, I'm going to drag you into another clos—"

"I think I love you," I blurt out, blandly, like I'm announcing the weather.

Noah looks at me like I've just told him the sky is made of cheese, blinking down at me dazedly as he processes what I've said. "You think you love me?"

I nod, feeling the words rising out of my throat before I can stop them. "I'm not totally sure, because I've never loved anybody before. Well, except for my grandparents. And Parker, obviously, but that's just as a friend. I know it's probably silly, because it hasn't been that long, but someone said something to me not long ago, and it got me thinking, and I think there's a good chance that I—"

He shuts me up with another kiss—he really is getting so good at that—and all the nerves that I'd just been experiencing melt away, my pulse thumping in my ears and under every inch of my skin as actual *joy* pumps through my blood. I relax with the pressure of his mouth, and he lets his lips linger for several seconds, as if he's savoring this moment.

And when he breaks away, he's actually *beaming*. "I love you," he tells me. "I don't care how long it's been. You're the only one I've ever wanted, and you're the only one I ever *will* want. I don't care if it's silly or crazy or whatever else—I *love* you, Mackenzie."

"Oh, okay," I answer airily, still processing everything myself. "Is it okay that I'm still only *kind of* sure that I love you? Because I don't want to—"

"I will take"—he presses another heavy kiss to my lips—"whatever you have to give. I just want you. However I can have you."

"I mean," I say quietly. "I am *pretty* sure."

He grins, lowering to let his lips brush against my cheek. "Pretty sure is good enough for me."

The happiness I'm feeling is scary, but there is also a sweetness to it, a sense of satisfaction, almost like fitting the last piece of a puzzle to see the picture as a whole. I can't say if it's fate that I'm feeling, I don't know if I'll ever believe in that—but it's something incredibly close.

We break apart when we hear more footsteps, Noah clearing his throat as a petite brunette clacks down the hallway, looking pre-occupied. She stops short when she sees us, her eyes widening and her mouth parting in surprise. "Dr Taylor? Dr. Carter?"

I cock an eyebrow. "Yes?"

"Sorry," she offers. She points to herself. "I'm Jessica. From Radiology. It's just, like, *so* awesome to see you together. You're the talk of the hospital!"

My eyes widen, realization hitting me.

This is fucking Jessica.

"Yeah, well . . ." I shuffle awkwardly, looping my arm through Noah's. "It's been . . . a whirlwind."

"Wow," Jessica laughs. "This is just great. I've totally been root-ing for you guys."

"Thanks," I tell her, willing this conversation to end. "Anyway . . ."

"You'll have to excuse us," Noah says, saving me. "We've got somewhere to be."

"Oh, right, of course." Jessica waves us off. "You two go on." She looks positively ecstatic. "See you around!"

She waves good-bye before continuing on her way, and Noah

waits until she's out of earshot before leaning down toward me. "Why does she look so familiar?"

"Trust me," I sigh. "You don't want to know." I let my hand slide down his arm to grasp his hand as I give it a tug, but he's still got this scrunched look on his face.

"Jessica," he mutters.

I arch a brow. "Know her?"

"She congratulated me on our mating the other day."

"Apparently, we have our very own fan club."

He narrows his eyes. "Is her mother's name Regina?"

"I'm . . . not sure? Why?"

Noah mumbles something under his breath, shaking his head. "Doesn't matter." He slips his hand into mine. "How do you feel about meeting my mother?"

"Wow, one 'I love you' and you're dying for me to meet the folks."

"No," he scoffs. "This is self-preservation. My mother sniffs out gossip like a bloodhound on a trail. If she finds out from the rumor mill before I can tell her . . ."

"How romantic," I coo. "'Meet my mother, Mack, so she doesn't murder me.'"

He rolls his eyes. "Might as well get it over with, since you're going to be around for a very long time."

"Oh?" My heart squeezes. "A long time, huh?"

"Forever, if I have anything to do with it," he murmurs, leaning to brush his lips against my temple, and I have to fight not to become a puddle.

Fuck "pretty sure." I *love* this guy.

My face splits into a wide grin. I'll tell him later.

"Come on," I urge, tugging at his hand. "If we wait outside the entrance, maybe we'll get to see them escorting Dennis off the premises."

Noah chuffs out a laugh, shaking his head. "You're sort of terrifying, do you know that?"

"Maybe," I answer as I pull him along. I look back to give him a wink. "I guess I'm braver with my alpha around."

The look on his face says that I will most definitely be feeling the repercussions of that phrase later, in either his bed or mine, but that's hardly bad news. I smile as Noah follows after me, unable to stop as the gravity of all that's happened washes over me, marveling at how much of my life has changed in such a short time.

Because Noah Taylor might not be my fake mate, not anymore—but he is mine.

And that's absolutely enough.

Epilogue

Noah

"**STOP FIDGETING,**" I tell her, grabbing her hand that had just been worrying about her hair.

"What if this is a disaster?"

I can't help but chuckle. "It's going to be fine."

"It hasn't been long enough since I met your mother, and we're going to spring my gran on her? She hasn't even had enough time to make sure she approves of me yet."

"*Approves?*" I bark out a laugh. "My parents aren't aristocracy. Trust me, they're just thrilled that you exist."

"Gee, real low expectations there," she snorts.

I reach across the car to curl my fingers around hers, bringing them to my mouth to kiss her knuckles. It's been months since we disclosed to the hospital—for *real* this time—and it only took one meeting (that took place approximately three days after disclosing our relationship; truly, my mother and Mackenzie's gran were sisters in another life) for my mother to fall completely in love with Mackenzie, not that I ever had any doubts. It's impossible not to. Honestly, she probably loves her more than she does me. Which is also completely understandable.

"I have to admit I am looking forward to seeing your gran and my mother in the same room," I muse.

Mackenzie grimaces. "Is it going to be awful? What possessed us to agree to this blended family bullshit?"

"It's a special occasion," I remind her. "We might as well just get it over with. Like ripping off a Band-Aid."

"That's easy for *you* to say," she grumbles. "You're not the one in the hot seat. My gran grills me enough as it is. I bet her and your mother gang up on me. We're going to have to spend the entire night dodging baby talk."

I can't pretend the idea of it doesn't make my stomach swoop, but there's plenty of time for that later.

"Now you know how it feels," I laugh, thinking back to that harrowing night when she took me to meet her gran. Things had been very different then.

"Parker is bringing his boyfriend," she tells me. "His name is Vaughn. He's very chatty. Maybe he'll keep the old women busy."

"One can only hope," I murmur.

"I heard about today, by the way," she says with a teasing tone. "One of your patients sent you flowers?"

I feel heat rising in my cheeks. "She was just grateful that I took such good care of her."

"Should I be jealous, Dr. Taylor?"

I scoff. "She's seventy-four."

"Your skiing accident was a seventy-four-year-old woman?"

"Apparently, Mrs. Wythers and her husband decided it was time to strike skiing from their bucket list."

"Wow, I have to admire her tenacity."

"She was definitely a character. Insisted I call her Wanda and refused to let the nurses help her to the bathroom."

"Come to think of it, how did you end up with a ski accident patient?"

"Evidently, she's suffered a heart attack before, and came in with worrisome angina after a fall."

"Wow, I hope her handsome cardiologist didn't give her an arrythmia."

I roll my eyes. "She's *seventy-four*, for goodness' sake."

"Sounds like she's been around long enough to know what she's doing, sending you those flirty flowers," Mackenzie deadpans.

I groan. "Please don't put those images in my head."

"Fine, fine," she laughs. "You sure have come a long way from making nurses cry."

I roll my eyes; I haven't heard this one in months. I'd thought (hoped) she'd forgotten about it. "How many times do I have to tell you? That was—"

"—*grossly overexaggerated*," she chuckles. "Yeah, I know."

"Here we are," I point out, slowing down so I can turn into the driveway of my parents' place.

"God, I can't ever get over how huge their house is," Mackenzie marvels. "Are we sure they aren't aristocracy?"

I shake my head, shifting into park as I come to a stop behind what I recognize as Mackenzie's grandparents' car. "I'm sure."

She nods to herself, as if she's psyching herself up, and I reach to cup her jaw, stroking my thumb there. "Hey." She turns to look at me with worried eyes. "It's going to be fine," I promise. "Everyone in there loves you."

"How do you know?"

"Because *I* love you."

"Okay." She nods again, surer this time. "Okay. You're right."

"I know."

I open the car door to move around to the passenger side, pulling open her door and extending my hand to help her out. She looks stunning in a deep olive dress that makes her hair appear brighter, but all I'm thinking about is how I'd like to pull the pins out of her hair and wrap my fingers in it—but I imagine that's not what she needs right now.

She still looks focused, like she's giving herself a mental pep talk, only coming out of it when the door shuts behind her. She glances at me then with a raised eyebrow, looking distracted. "Hey, Noah . . ."

I pause with my hand at her waist. "Yeah?"

"Why *was* that nurse crying?"

My lips twitch, and I shrug lightly. "Her contact ripped. I'm told it's a very painful experience."

"Oh my God." Her mouth parts in surprise. "Really? That's it?"

"Does it shatter the illusion?"

"Of course it does. How can I continue using my 'the boogeyman belongs to me' card to get free cookies from the cafeteria?"

"Have you *actually* been doing that?"

"No," she admits. "But I sure as hell won't be able to if the truth gets out. You'd better keep it to yourself."

My mouth tilts on one side. "Yes, ma'am."

Mackenzie looks ahead at the wide front door of my parents' house, her throat bobbing with a swallow as she gives herself one last encouraging nod. "This is going to be fine."

"It is," I assure her.

"We will not let either of them intimidate us into having babies this soon."

"We won't," I answer, crossing my fingers behind my back. I

don't have to tell her I'm not as opposed to the idea as she is. "It's going to be *fine*."

"I'm always worried your mother secretly hates me because of all the fake mate stuff," she admits quietly.

"My mother might like you more than *me* because of the fake mate stuff," I snort. "She kind of thinks you're the most badass woman she's ever heard of."

"Right." She looks determined, her nose wrinkling. "Right. I *am* the most badass woman she's ever heard of."

I chuckle under my breath, leaning to kiss her temple. "You are," I encourage. "And besides . . ." My fingers drift down from her nape, the tip of my index finger circling the dark imprint of my teeth that hasn't yet begun to fade. It makes me feel a myriad of emotions every time I see it, knowing that it matches the one she gave me, that it means she'll be with me for the rest of our lives. I duck to kiss her there as she shivers. "It isn't fake anymore."

Mackenzie smiles up at me, reaching to squeeze my hand, and I wonder idly if she realizes that she holds the entirety of my being in the palm of hers.

"No," she answers quietly. "No, it isn't."

I still don't know if Mackenzie believes in fate, but one thing is for certain.

I sure as hell do.

Acknowledgments

It's odd to be writing acknowledgments for a book that I am finishing up copyedits on only a month after my first book published! The most topsy-turvy part of this entire "being an author" process has been getting used to the schedule of the whole publishing thing. I would love to tell you that after more than a year I've totally got it down, but if I were sly enough to say that, I am sure my entire team would give me bombastic side-eye (cue TikTok sound). Speaking of my team—my continued love and adoration for every single one of you hasn't dimmed in the slightest. My editor, Cindy Hwang, who is the horny cheerleader of my dreams, and whose agreement that this book needed exam-room shenanigans just confirms that she is, in fact, perfect; Jess Watterson, who I am happy to confirm is still petting my hair whenever it's warranted (which is a lot, since I am the human equivalent of a natural disaster—think tornado, full-on cows circling around, just mooing up a storm while people shout in terror), is seriously the best, and even if she ever fires me for being insufferable (which would totally be fair) I will still love her; Jessica Mangicaro (marketing) and Kristin Cipolla (publicity, and my little onion babe)—I think of Jess and Kristin as a duo, and maybe that's not true, but it won't stop me from consistently cc'ing them together (and more recently, forcing them to endure me in a group DM chat on IG). These two ladies deserve gold medals for the sheer number of all-caps emails and neurotic questions they have had to endure (sometimes the SAME questions, since I have the attention span of Doug from *Up*). I would love to tell you both that things WILL GET BETTER, but . . . I am not a liar. I will always be a tragedy of the non-Greek variety, since I am not nearly important enough. However, I am sorry for saying "raw dog" so much. The Penguin creative team, who owns my entire heart and my whole ass (yeah, I am making it weird); Monika Roe for another FANTASTIC cover (may she always be available for more); and a special thank-you to Ruby Dixon, who not only blurbed my first book but then suffered through an entire year of me badgering her to be my friend with grace and poise. (I love her books, but I love her more.) And on that note, thank you to ALL those that blurbed my book after Ruby; every single one had me rolling in bed like a cat on catnip.

The Fake Mate had many champions while being worked on, even if my oldest friend, Dan, was not one of them. (Dan, you bland, tasteless jerk, you will never know the glory of knotting!) My sweet Katie, who loves everything I do, even if it's not remotely interesting; my lovely Keri, with her less-than-superior taste in Sleep Token thirsting (iv is superior, I'm sorry) but her more than competent encouragement of my horny wolves; my pseudo-mama, Andria, for FaceTiming me to yell at me when I got mopey; and my daddy, Kristen, for pointing out after a beta read that this book DID IN FACT need horny exam-room shenanigans (the universe brought you into my life to give us this, and I am all the better for it).

Shout-out to all the amazing bookstagrammers, bloggers, journalists, readers, booktokers, and reviewers who yeeted about my first book and shared hype for my second—I won't pretend I haven't feared that people would pass on this book with it being (or as it feels to me, at least) so experimental in genre, but if you made it this far, know that I am grateful. I love these two, and I hope you did also. (I mean, come on, KNOTS.)

And to my dude of more than a decade—I'm sorry I haven't made you a househusband yet, but I'm still working on it, never fear.

Keep reading for a preview from

Overruled

"OBJECTION. LEADING THE witness."

I bite my tongue, quietly seething as I resist the urge to look back at the owner of the deep, honeyed voice calling out in a bored tone.

"Let me rephrase," I say as evenly as I can manage, keeping my attention on the man in front of me. "You said in your statement that you would often see a visitor coming to the house while Mrs. Johanson was home alone. Is that correct, Mr. Crane?"

The man nods, peeking warily at the woman in question. "That's correct."

"And during those visits, where was Mr. Johanson?"

"He was usually at work, ma'am."

"And this visitor, was it a man or a woman?"

"It was a man."

I bite back a grin. "I see. How long would this man stay?"

Mr. Crane reaches to scratch at his thinning hair, shifting in his seat. It had taken me a hell of a lot to get him on the stand; in the end it was only the promise from Mr. Johanson that he would keep his gardening job regardless of the outcome of this trial that he finally agreed.

"It varied," Mr. Crane said. "Sometimes an hour. Sometimes more."

"So it's safe to assume that Mrs. Johanson knew this man . . . well, correct?"

"Objection." I hear a sigh behind me. "Speculation."

"Rephrase," I say tightly, still refusing to look at him. "Did you ever see Mrs. Johanson and the man interacting when he would visit, Mr. Crane?"

Mr. Crane shakes his head. "No, ma'am. He always went straight inside the house."

"But it was always the same man?"

"Yes, ma'am. As far as I could tell."

"Thank you, Mr. Crane." I give my attention to Judge Hoffstein. "No further questions, Your Honor."

I try not to look at him when I return to my table, I really do—but that pull is there, the one I so desperately wish didn't plague me anytime we're in the same room together. I can feel his eyes linger on me when I'm finally able to avert my gaze, feel it like the weight of his fingers along my skin as I retake my seat.

He stands slowly, one hand reaching to fasten the button of his suit—a deft, practiced motion that makes the veins in his too-large hands flex—and I can't help the way my eyes are drawn there, remembering the warmth of them on my body hardly even a week ago. I catch a hint of a smirk when I turn my face to meet his eyes, feeling warmth creep up my neck as I clench my teeth.

Fucking Ezra Hart.

I train my eyes forward, keeping them on the nervous older man on the stand, in quiet support.

"Mr. Crane," Ezra starts. "Did you know Mrs. Johanson's visitor?"

"No, sir," Mr. Crane answers. "I was told that—"

"That's hearsay," Ezra cuts him off. "What you *heard* is irrelevant." He shoves his hands in his pockets, strolling casually to the side and flicking his gaze to mine for the briefest of moments. "I'm asking if you ever actually *met* Mrs. Johanson's visitor."

Mr. Crane's eyes dart to mine, looking unsure. "Well, no, I didn't."

"So there's no possible way for you to know the purpose of that man's visits. Correct?"

Mr. Crane is quiet for a moment, and my heart thuds in my ribs. There's no way that Ezra can possibly suggest—

"No, sir," Mr. Crane answers. "I could not."

"I see." Ezra's mouth turns up in the ghost of a smile. "Just as you couldn't know of Mrs. Johanson's recent interests in spiritual direction?"

"I . . ." Mr. Crane blinks with confusion, and I can feel the same emotion playing on Mr. Johanson's and my faces. "No? I didn't know that."

"Of course you didn't," Ezra practically coos. "It's not something she advertised. The only people who knew this were her close friends. Well, and her husband, of course." Ezra looks back at our table. "Although I very much doubt Mr. Johanson would recall this, given that he rarely took note of Mrs. Johanson's interests."

"Objection," I call. "Speculation."

"Withdrawn," Ezra says with a grin. "Mr. Crane, did you know that the man you saw coming in and out of Mrs. Johanson's house was her spiritual advisor?"

Oh, what a load of horseshit.

"Objection, Your Honor," I almost laugh. "This is irrelevant."

Ezra directs his attention to the judge. "This is completely relevant, Your Honor, I assure you."

Judge Hoffstein nods minutely. "Overruled."

"Thank you." Ezra inclines his head. "You see, Mrs. Johanson's visitor, a Mr. Jacobs, had been hired several weeks prior by Mrs. Johanson to oversee her spiritual direction. There was nothing nefarious about their encounters. If you'll be so kind as to take a look at Exhibit 13—you'll note the credentials I've provided to prove Mr. Jacobs's employment at a company offering such services."

Son of a bitch. How did we miss that?

Ezra looks smug as the judge peruses the bit of evidence in question; to an outsider he would simply look contemplative, but I've seen that look on his face too many times. In *and* out of the courtroom.

"Mrs. Johanson was simply exploring her new faith," Ezra continues. "There is no evidence to suggest that she and Mr. Jacobs were meeting under false pretenses, and she paid him for his time. Therefore, this line of questioning isn't relevant to this alimony hearing."

Ezra waits until the exhibit has been passed to the bailiff before he turns back to the witness. "Thank you for your time, Mr. Crane." He looks to the judge. "No further questions, Your Honor."

Ezra takes his seat on his side of the courtroom, a small smile on his lips, practically laughing at the way I'm shooting daggers right now. I feel Mr. Johanson lean into me, whispering, "She can't seriously pull this shit, can she?"

I want to tell him no, that cheating spouses get what they deserve—that *doesn't* include an overly fat alimony check—but I know that without any concrete evidence of infidelity, which we haven't been able to unearth no matter how hard we've looked, it's likely Mrs. Johanson will be milking her soon-to-be-ex-husband dry for years to come.

Fucking Ezra Hart.

———

I PINCH THE bridge of my nose as I wait for the elevator to open, trying to stave off the headache forming behind my eyes. It had taken weeks to find out about Mrs. Johanson's little *spiritual advisor* who came twice a week like clockwork, unbeknownst to her husband while he was at work, and it had felt like an ace in the hole. Until Ezra swooped in and plugged it right up, that is.

They call him "the heartbreak prince" in the papers; it's a stupid fucking moniker that he absolutely eats up, I'm sure. His win record is astounding, and every time I have to be in the same courtroom with him, I know I'm in for a world of bullshit. Not to say I haven't won against him, because I have—but not nearly as much as I'd like, today included.

The elevator dings, and I climb inside, grateful to find it empty as I settle against the back wall to let my head thunk against the cool metal. I close my eyes as I wait for the doors to close, only snapping them back open when I hear something nudging between them to force them back open.

"Room for one more?"

I narrow my eyes at him. "You could always take the stairs. Get a workout in."

Ezra laughs as he strolls into the elevator, leaning against the bar at the back wall as I scoot away from him. "You've never had any complaints about my body."

I glare up at him as the elevator doors slide closed, trapping us inside. He always knows exactly what to say to push my buttons, just like he knows that his stupid face and body are lethal distractions when it comes to remembering how much I dislike him. It's not the dark blond hair that always looks like someone just ran their fingers through it, not the full mouth or the piercing green eyes or the amazing bone structure that makes his face look carved—it's all of it, really. The broad shoulders that fill out his tailored suits a little too well, his long fingers that stir up wicked memories, even his stupid cologne makes you want to lean in closer to get a better whiff.

At least he only has four to five inches on me—I've always been on the taller side, and not having to crane my neck up to his six foot three from my five foot nine gives me an ounce of satisfaction. Especially in my heels.

"Yeah, well, that's just about the only good thing you have going for you," I mumble back, facing my eyes forward to watch the numbers tick by and mentally urging them to go faster.

There's a contrast between us in the reflection of the shiny metal doors—my inky black hair to his golden brown, my pale skin to his bronzed, his brawn to my lithe figure—looking at us side by side, one would never think to put us together.

Which we aren't, I mentally correct. Together. Because we aren't. Except . . .

"Really?" He inches a little closer. "I'm told I'm pretty charming."

"Are those people on your payroll?"

"I can think of a few times when *you've* found me charming, Dani."

I roll my eyes. I'm used to people calling me Dani; when you have a name like Danica, I guess it's easy to jump to the nickname— but something about the way Ezra says it always makes my stomach do something funny. I'm sure I'm not the only one Ezra amuses himself with. There's no doubt in my mind that his easy playboy act comes from vast amounts of real-life experience—yet I can't help but wonder if anyone else in what is surely a very wide net of his sexual conquests succumbs to his annoyingly effective charms quite as often (albeit begrudgingly) as I do.

"I can assure you I have never found you charming," I toss back dryly. "Maybe mildly amusing. Your dick, at least."

He clutches his hand to his chest, and I try not to notice how large it looks against his tie. "Only mildly? That isn't what you said when you were screaming my—"

The elevator doors slide open as we come to a halt, and I immediately bolt out of it, trying to put distance between Ezra and me before he notices how flushed my neck most likely is. Not that he lets me escape that easily, since I hear his footsteps, heavy and quick as he catches up to me.

"I'm free tonight, you know," he says casually.

I keep my expression blank, hoping the people milling around in the lobby don't notice how close he's walking beside me. "Good for you. Sounds like an excellent time to take up a hobby."

"Oh, but I would much rather enjoy the one I've already got."

I glance at him from the side, frowning. "What's that?"

"See, there's this certain opposing counsel who makes the most delicious noises when my fingers are—"

I spin on my heel, hissing under my breath as we come to a stop in front of the large glass doors that lead outside of the courthouse. "I told you," I grit out. "Last time was the last time."

"Right." He flashes me his white, perfect teeth—stark against the deep pink of his lips, and I have to force myself to keep my eyes on his. "But you said that the time before that." He leans in a little closer, practically looming over me as he lowers his voice. "And the time before that . . . and the time before that . . ."

"I mean it this time," I argue, trying to convince him or me, I'm not sure. "It was stupid to begin with. You're an asshole, and I was . . ." *Hard up? Horny? Out of my mind?* "It was a lapse of judgment on my part."

"Eight lapses of judgment," Ezra says with a low whistle. "I think they call that a bad habit, Dani. Maybe *you* need a hobby. You know, besides me."

I clench my fists at my sides; I know he's teasing me, but it hits a little too close to home. Especially because I *know* that constantly sleeping with Ezra—someone I barely tolerate outside of what we do behind closed doors—is the stupidest thing I've ever done. After everything with Grant . . . you'd think I would make smarter decisions when it comes to the opposite sex.

It's just sex, I soothe myself. *Just scratching an itch.*

Even if I've scratched this particular itch more times than I'd like.

I make a frustrated sound, shoving him away and pushing through the doors as I stalk off quickly. He doesn't follow me this time, but I can hear his stupid laugh even from halfway down the steps.

Fucking. Ezra. Hart.

~

I FEEL A little less out of sorts when I'm back at the firm; I'm not thrilled to tell my boss how miserably today went with the Johansons, but at least here I can put the headache of Ezra and my antagonistic . . . whatever we have . . . at the back of my mind for a little bit. I drop my case files in my office, noticing on my way out that Nate's and Vera's are empty; I guess they've already headed home for the day.

The door to Manuel's office is cracked at the other end of the hall, however, and I step toward it to update him on everything before I finish up for the day myself. I find him sitting behind his desk poring over a stack of papers, his neat, salt-and-pepper hair swept into his usual perfect style. I don't think I've ever seen Manuel Moreno with a single hair out of place, and since Chicago is known as the Windy City, that is a feat.

"Danica," he greets as I knock lightly against the open door. "Come in, come in. How did it go today?"

I purse my lips. "Not as well as I would have liked. The guy she was seeing was apparently her 'spiritual advisor.'"

The deep wrinkle that lives permanently between Manuel's brow worsens. "That's the horseshit they're spinning?"

"Well, horseshit does happen to be a specialty of Ezra's."

"I want to hate the bastard," Manuel snorts. "But he's damn good."

I refuse to even acknowledge how "good" Ezra is.

"I've got a lead on a housekeeper who quit a couple of months ago," I tell him. "I'm trying to get in touch with her. Maybe she saw something between them of a more *physical* nature."

"Great. Let me know."

I'm about to return to my desk when he stops me.

"I actually wanted to talk to you," he calls.

I turn back. "Yes?"

"We had a potential client call today. A Mrs. Vassiliev."

I frown. "Why does that sound familiar?"

"Her husband owns Vassiliev Development."

"Shit." My mouth parts in surprise. "The real estate mogul?"

"He owns half the city, practically. God knows how many others."

"They're divorcing?"

"It appears so. A friend of mine recommended us."

"That's great." I wince. "Well, not for *her*, but . . ."

"I was thinking that you should take it."

I blink back at him. "What?"

"You've been here for six years now. You mentioned last year that you were interested in a junior partner position, and with Hinata retiring . . ."

"Wait, are you saying . . . ?"

"I'm saying that Mrs. Vassiliev stands to make this firm an enormous amount of money if she comes out on top in her divorce. She claims to have all sorts of evidence of his infidelity."

"Holy shit."

"But there's a catch."

"There always is."

"She signed a prenup."

I groan. "Of course she did. How solid is her evidence?"

"I guess that's for you to find out."

"Not making this easy for me, huh?"

"High risk, high reward," he chuckles before his expression turns serious. "I think winning this case would be the perfect thing to bring to the other partners and prove you're ready to step up."

"You'd be willing to go to bat for me?"

Manuel rolls his eyes. "I've known you since you were seven. As many T-ball games as I went to with you and your parents, I have 'gone to bat' for you plenty of times in your life."

"That's corny, but I'll take it," I laugh. "I just . . . You already stuck your neck out giving me this job, and I don't want anyone to think I'm getting special treatment just because you and Dad are old friends."

"You graduated top of your class at Harvard Law. It was hardly a burden to offer you a position here. Just like it won't be when you win this case, and I show the other partners what an asset you are."

"I . . . Wow. Yes. Of course. This is . . . Wow."

"You have a meeting with Mrs. Vassiliev at the end of the week," he informs me. "She's a character, but I think you can handle her."

I nod aimlessly. "Yes. I . . . Thank you, Manny."

"Don't mention it." He waves me off. "Feel free to loop Nate and Vera in. I'm sure they'll be foaming at the mouth to be a part of it regardless."

I grin. He isn't wrong about that. This is one of the biggest cases we've had since I started. I can already hear Nate squealing. "I will."

"Don't stay up at your desk all night," he chides. "You have to sleep sometime."

I roll my eyes. "Yeah, yeah."

He gives me a dismissive gesture as he turns his attention back to his paperwork, and I leave his office with a wide smile on my face and a fluttering in my stomach. I've been waiting for this opportunity for the last year or more, and now with it so close—I can feel a bubbling excitement humming under my skin.

A buzzing in the pocket of my slacks distracts me as I walk back to my desk, and all the elated feelings simmer out into annoyance as I take note of the message.

> ASSHOLE: I'll be home all night if you
> change your mind about . . . coming.

I grimace. That was terrible, even for him. Which makes the little flicker of warmth in my gut all the more infuriating. Sleeping with Ezra Hart had been a bad idea the *first* time it happened, something I blame on temporary insanity and thinking with my vagina—and the next seven times definitely didn't help things.

If only he wasn't so *good* at it. Bastard.

I tap out a quick response, shoving down the urges that bubble up in spite of his stupid fucking text.

> **ME:** Sorry. Better things to do.

I feel smug for about three seconds before my phone pings again.

> **ASSHOLE:** I highly doubt there's better than me, but keep telling yourself that. ☺

I scowl, shoving my phone in my pocket.

Fucking Ezra Hart.

Praise for

The Nanny

'I need more books like *The Nanny*, stat. A smart, educated heroine (Yes, please!) meets a driven, career-focused single dad. Sparks fly . . . and fly, and fly. Seriously, this book is like if Ali Hazelwood and Tessa Bailey had a smutty baby. I devoured every page and was sad to see it end. This is the spice BookTok wants! Now I need Lana Ferguson to work faster, because I want to see everything she writes'

Ruby Dixon, international bestselling author of
the Ice Planet Barbarians series

'Smart, fun, sexy, and sizzling with romantic tension, *The Nanny* is a mouthwateringly delicious take on second chances, with a healthy dash of steam. I can't wait for more from Lana Ferguson!'

Sara Desai, author of *The Singles Table*

'*The Nanny* is sweet, beautifully sexy, and Aiden is the single Zaddy you want in your life. An amazing debut'

Elena Armas, *New York Times* bestselling author of
The American Roommate Experiment

'Ferguson makes the will-they-won't-they sing with complex emotional shading and a strong sense of inevitability to her protagonists' connection . . . Rosie Danan fans should snap this up'

Publishers Weekly (starred review)

Don't miss out on Lana Ferguson's steamy debut ...

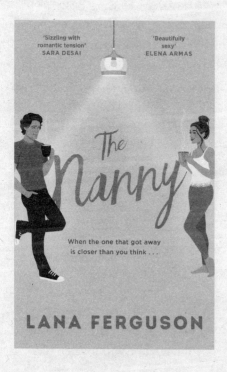

Available now from

PIATKUS

Do you love contemporary romance?

Want the chance to hear news about your favourite authors (and the chance to win free books)?

Kristen Ashley
Ashley Herring Blake
Meg Cabot
Olivia Dade
Rosie Danan
J. Daniels
Farah Heron
Talia Hibbert
Sarah Hogle
Helena Hunting
Abby Jimenez
Elle Kennedy
Christina Lauren
Alisha Rai
Sally Thorne
Lacie Waldon
Denise Williams
Meryl Wilsner
Samantha Young

Then visit the Piatkus website
www.yourswithlove.co.uk

And follow us on Facebook and Instagram
www.facebook.com/yourswithlovex | @yourswithlovex

PIATKUS